A GIRL
WITHIN
A GIRL
WITHIN
A GIRL

Praise for
A GIRL WITHIN A GIRL WITHIN A GIRL

"A captivating debut from an exciting new voice in fiction. Told with bold and beautifully layered prose, *A Girl Within a Girl Within a Girl* is a heart-wrenching and inspirational exploration of survival, resilience, and grit. Complex, compelling, and masterful, this book shines, teaches, and rewards."
 —DIANE MARIE BROWN, author of *Black Candle Women*

"A devastating and tremendous debut. This artfully constructed story delivers suspense, terror, thrilling self-salvation and life-transforming moments of human compassion. It's about all the selves we try to shed, and how we must stitch ourselves whole, humble, and powerful again. I can't remember the last time I was impacted so emotionally by a novel."
 —ANGELA MI YOUNG HUR, author of *Folklorn*

"[This] kaleidoscopic investigation of identity and its shaping forces explores what happens when you're forced to confront the past you thought you left behind. A riveting story of one woman's journey to build and protect her life, Nanda Reddy's debut will hold you in its grasp until the final page."
 —ALINA GRABOWSKI, author of *Women and Children First*

"Propulsive and gripping. Reddy's dynamic narrative seamlessly weaves a coming-of-age tale with a turbulent and suspenseful account of migration. This edge-of-your-seat read packs quite a punch."
 —MAI SENNAAR, author of *They Dream in Gold*

"An urgent and necessary novel. Set in the 1980s, Reddy's story of a young trafficking victim could just as easily have taken place today. As bighearted as it is heartbreaking, *A Girl Within a Girl Within a Girl* does not dwell in darkness. This is a story rich in empathy, riveting and redemptive."
—LEYNA KROW, author of *Fire Season*

"*A Girl Within a Girl Within a Girl* peels back its complex, powerful heroine's folds with slow precision, revealing an explosive, shocking story that ultimately transforms into an ode to love."
—NAYANTARA ROY, author of *The Magnificent Ruins*

A GIRL WITHIN A GIRL WITHIN A GIRL

A NOVEL

NANDA REDDY

ZIBBY PUBLISHING
NEW YORK

This novel contains sensitive subject matter pertaining to domestic violence, sexual assault, and substance abuse. Please read with care.

A Girl Within a Girl Within a Girl: A Novel

Copyright © 2025 by Nanda Reddy

All rights reserved. No part of this book may be used, reproduced, distributed, or transmitted in any form or by any means without the prior written permission of the publisher, except as permitted by U.S. copyright law. Published in the United States by Zibby Publishing, New York.

ZIBBY, Zibby Publishing, colophon, and associated logos are trademarks and/or registered trademarks of Zibby Media LLC.

This book is a work of fiction. Names, characters, places, historical events, and incidents are the product of the author's imagination or are used fictitiously. Any resemblance to actual persons, living or dead, events, or locales is entirely coincidental.

Library of Congress Control Number: 2024943189
Paperback ISBN: 979-8-9895325-1-3
eBook ISBN: 979-8-9895325-3-7

Book design by Neuwirth & Associates, Inc.
Cover design by Mumtaz Mustafa

www.zibbymedia.com

10 9 8 7 6 5 4 3 2 1

For my big, fat, fun-loving Guyanese family,
especially my parents and sisters.

And for the Vodur Reddy boys, all three.

> What you looking at me for?
> I didn't come to stay . . .
>
> —Maya Angelou, *I Know Why the Caged Bird Sings*

> You have shed
> a thousand skins
> to become the person
> you are today.
>
> —Nikita Gill, *A Thousand Versions of You*

MAYA

ATLANTA, GEORGIA

Some moments sear themselves onto your brain. Me standing by the kitchen sink, the dogwood flowering outside the window, this envelope in my trembling hands.

They've found me.

The air thickens and sounds recede.

The blue-and-red-striped envelope is covered in foreign stamps and bears names I haven't heard in decades. My heart hammers and buried memories stir as I turn it over. The flap is barely affixed, the glue having failed. Inside is a yellowed sheet of paper. Thin and soft, its rough edge hints at a former life in a school notebook. This is third-world paper with faint, weirdly spaced lines, a cockroachy stuck-in-a-box-for-years smell. Dated over a month ago, the letter addresses someone dead.

Dear Sunny,
 Ma pass last year, 23 May. She had the sugar, lost one eye, and infection in left foot. But cancer get she. I try to find you, but I never reach you.

Now, cancer get me. The doctor find a lump in my breast couple months ago. My daughter in New York search at a government place and find this address for you. I pray it work because I am scared the cancer is bad, and I hope to see you one more time. Plus the doctors say you should check for a gene.

Sunny, I never believe the lies about you. Even Daddy accept the truth now.

But even if you can't forgive Daddy, please come see your dying sister.

With love,
Roshini

A long-distance telephone number, a website, and an email address sit below the signature.

My eyes rove the lines again and again, but the words swim without quite sinking in and singsong creole fills my ears. *Ma pass, lump in my breast, check for a gene, dying sister.*

"Time to go, boys." Dwayne's booming voice snaps me back to myself, and I resist an insane urge to bring the paper to my face and eat it. As if that could return us to the *before* world. But this letter has cleaved time. There will only be life after.

I will have to tell him. My husband. A man who's never heard the name *Sunny*. Who's never heard of Roshini. Who believes I don't know my mother or father. Who knows me by only one name. He's on the upstairs landing-turned-play-space talking to our boys, saying, "Backpacks together, TV off, toys away," unaware the planet just tilted.

A familiar documentary continues to blare, something about white dwarves and red giants, and I picture our seven-year-old son, Nico, belly-down on the floor, glued to the screen; eleven-year-old Camden riffling through LEGO bins, his hearing aids turned off. My babies.

Gene. The word grips me and I understand. I might leave them motherless after all. Despite everything I did to protect them from that fate.

Dwayne claps and repeats his commands, and the TV goes silent. They'll be down any second, and here I am with this bomb in my hands.

I can't detonate it. Not yet. I need more time.

I stuff it in my sweatshirt pocket, blink my eyes clear, and shake the fog from my head. The kitchen island is covered with food. Cold eggs, bacon, and bagels. A colander of blueberries. Bread, lunch meat, and vegetables. Normally, I'd have plated blog-worthy breakfasts and lunches by now. *And* have cleaned up. The clutter overwhelms me.

My hands move sluggishly as the letter hijacks my mind. *Ma pass last year.* How did I not know? There must have been a jolt, some noticeable shift in the universe. Had I ignored it? To do what instead? Clean teeth and saturate myself with the minutiae of patients' lives? Decorate bulletin boards at the boys' school that I'd dismantle a month later? Organize drawers and sort LEGO blocks by color? Or could I have been laughing as she died? Learning choreography with Dwayne at our ballroom dancing class? Gossiping and curating pictures for the cooking blog I manage with Dwayne's sister and my two best friends? Best friends who don't know me.

I force a smile as the boys descend the stairs, Nico whooping on Dwayne's back, Cam skipping ahead because he's outgrown that kind of thing. My perfect family. Will I lose them? Will they lose me? Dwayne fills the room, not just with his six-foot-two football-player frame, but with his signature ebullience, which never fails to lift me. Even now, with earth-shattering words in my head, my body lightens a little when he says, "Morning, Mama."

He sets Nico on his stool with fanfare and adds, "The sky's falling." It's what he says when there's a global stock market dip, one that could send his investment clients into a tailspin. "Blue skies today" would have told me he spent the morning watching foreign markets soar after his 4:00 a.m. run, a run that always ends with him grabbing the newspapers and the mail. He'd dropped the letter onto our counter this morning, hidden amid catalogs. He doesn't realize how ominous his words are today.

The breakfast plates are a jumble of eggs, bread, and fruit. I move berries in a wobbly circle around the food—a small attempt at my usual photogenic presentation—before placing the plates on the eat-in counter.

"Mom, did you know the sun's gonna explode?" Nico asks, swiveling his stool and accidentally hitting Cam's.

Cam gives him a dirty look before shifting away, and Dwayne shouts, "Boosh" to give Nico's words a sound effect.

My heart swells at this noisy, familiar routine.

"Is that right?" I say, simultaneously signing "Good morning" to Cam. I also sign Nico's question so Cam feels included, even though he barely glances up.

"But it's not for, like, five billion years," Nico says. He stuffs berries into his mouth, seemingly unaware of his chaotic plate. He swivels before adding, "We'll be dead by then."

Dead. My eyes twitch. I don't sign that sentence. I turn and busy myself with the blender I'd washed earlier, drying it with a towel. *Ma pass last year. Dying sister. Gene. A gene!* How much longer do I have with them? A black hole opens inside me, and the blender slips. I catch it in time and set it on the counter, shaken.

Dwayne hugs me from behind and says, "Thanks for breakfast, babe." He plants a kiss on the messy bun atop my head while reaching for one of the spinach smoothies I'd made.

I nod, and my body tightens as the letter crinkles in my pocket. I never wanted to lie to him. Not when our eyes connected in that bookstore almost two decades ago, not when we got married, not when our children were born. How did I let things get so far?

I never believe the lies about you.

My heart cramps as a memory dislodges and surfaces. That last day in Miami. *Him. He* is the reason I'm in this mess. His face invades my mind, and I grip the counter to push him back from where he's risen. I force my mind toward to-do lists as I clear away food. I need fresh spices for that cheesecake—cardamom and star anise. I should dry-clean that dress before the party this weekend. And we're low on teeth-whitening kits at work. But the mental tactics that have worked for thirty years to bury my past fail me. *His* menacing face thrusts into my brain. I shut the fridge door as if shutting it on him.

Dwayne complains about work, listing clients he might have to talk off the ledge, and I force myself to focus on his words. "Some people can't see opportunity even if it's staring them right in the face," he says, laughing.

Dwayne's magic has always been an ability to sweep me into a cascade of energy that leaves no room for mulling and downward spiraling. I smile, wanting his laughter to flood me, to reset me into a wife with her baggage neatly tucked away, a woman devoid of a past and in control of her future. I want to return there, even if for just a minute. But the future unspools before me.

"Big plans for the day off?" Dwayne asks, sipping his smoothie and finally making eye contact.

I feel caught, and my mind blanks. What am I doing today? It takes me a second to remember the plans I made for my day off. "Uh, a run, and a nail appointment for the party this weekend. Then, um, cooking group with Denise and the girls. And photocopying for Cam's teacher."

His eyes narrow. "You good?"

My face twitches as I try to fix the flaw he sees. Then my hand moves of its own accord. *No. Not like this. Think it through. Do it right.* But the offending hand, disembodied, holds up the letter. A white flag to end a one-sided war—a war I've waged for far too long. *Gene. Dying sister.* It's time. Even if that madman is still hunting me, and even if Dwayne doesn't forgive me. I have to come clean. I owe it to him. To our kids. To my sister. To myself.

I hand it to him and, shaking, turn away. How do I even begin?

In the backyard, the dogwood's pink blossoms catch sunlight, looking mockingly perfect. The tree has been blissfully tripping around the sun, never needing to pretend it's anything other than a tree. While I've built a whole life on lies.

PART ONE

SUNNY

MAY 1985
CANAL NO. 1, GUYANA

1

Dolls

From the airplane above, the two schoolgirls would have been invisible. The dirt path they ambled along would have been lost in a mat of green that stretched for miles. Passengers glancing from tiny windows might have gazed at plumes of smoke dotting the landscape for sugarcane harvests, not at the moving specks by the forest's edge.

Still, twelve-year-old Sunny and fourteen-year-old Roshi jumped and waved, their pleated navy skirts flouncing up and down. The sisters had greeted planes like this their entire lives. But as she waved, Sunny felt a dim awareness of having outgrown this childish game, of going through the motions for Roshi, and she wondered if Roshi was doing the same for her.

Roshi shaded her eyes to watch the plane disappear before starting their honed routine. She mouthed, "'Merica."

Sunny nodded.

Roshi stroked the back of her left hand coquettishly and said, "White skin," the rasped words sounding like *why sin*.

Sunny smiled.

Roshi mimed eating an apple and said, "Mmm."

Sunny recalled the sweet whiff she'd inhaled when Annette, their schoolmate with family abroad, brought a fragrant, red-skinned fruit to school, rattling around in a lunch box featuring smiling bears. The floral aroma that escaped that cloud-and-bear-covered box had elevated her envy of Annette and added another dimension to her fantastic vision of America. America was a land nestled in the clouds above the planes. A land full of paper-white people who drove down fluffy roads in cars that spoke to them, who watched TV in castle-like homes smelling of apples.

Roshi took off along the rutted path, hands at ten-and-two on an imaginary steering wheel, transforming into KITT, the talking car from *Knight Rider*. The girls had been sneaking behind Small's rum shop Saturday afternoons, fighting over the biggest gap in the pub's wooden slats to watch the show on Small's new TV. Roshi likely couldn't follow the show since she couldn't hear the sound, but she'd added the car to their game.

As Sunny watched her sister run, she welcomed the distance.

Roshi glanced back, smiling mischievously, to start the exploit they'd planned with eye contact and a few gestures after school. They'd shooed their younger siblings home and lagged behind to scavenge for burnt sugarcane, something their father forbade. Sunny gripped her cross-body book bag and jogged a few steps to egg Roshi on. As expected, Roshi darted into an opening in the dense wall of leaves, toward the singed rows that flavored the air.

Sunny stopped and breathed in the sweetened, smoky air, savoring this rare moment of solitude. Bits of ash fluttered down, and she caught a delicate black curl in her palm before rubbing it away. She pictured Roshi leaping gazelle-like over stubby, burnt-out rows, her blackened rubber slippers slap-slapping her heels and her book bag whacking her hips as she made her way to the freshly harvested fields. Sunny could never catch up, but it didn't matter. She had just decided to ditch Roshi, a thing she'd never done before.

At school, Annette had invited her over to see some fancy dolls called Barbies. "You can come, but not you pagli sister," Annette had added, laughing because this meant she might never see the dolls. Pagli—idiot, touched-in-the-head, the mean girls' name for Roshi. For years, Sunny spat at anyone who made this taunt, her *pagli* sister standing placidly by her side. The word lost its sting as Roshi began holding her own, winning foot races and gaining allies. But *pagli* had stung anew when Annette said it. Sunny would have told her off if she didn't want to see the girl's American things so badly.

She took off, back toward school, leaping over ruts and dry stream beds. Thick greenery flanked the path, before giving way to wooden stilt houses. Her lungs burned and sweat dripped from her forehead, but she pushed on. She imagined Roshi already peeling sugarcane with her teeth and coating her throat with syrupy juice, feeling smug. Roshi would wait five, maybe ten minutes before looking for her. And then what? Would Roshi go home? Sunny hoped to be nearing Annette's by then, to see the things quickly, to intercept Roshi on her way home and make up something about seeing a snake. Her head throbbed with guilt. She should go back.

The dirt path opened onto an unpaved road that paralleled a deep canal, and she slowed. Bridges connected the unpaved side to a paved road opposite. Stilt houses lined both sides in either direction as far as she could see. Left led toward town, a city miles east she'd never visited. Right led to the conservancy, a dammed expanse of tea-colored water where she and her siblings flew kites, swam, or fished some weekends.

She turned toward the conservancy, sprinting past colorful houses and the school, an airy building full of windows. Heart hammering, fearing someone might stop her and ask about Roshi, she kept her head down. But the blistering sun had chased everyone indoors. She didn't pass a soul.

She slowed down again at a rickety footbridge to cross the wide canal. A brand-new bridge, strong enough to handle cars, lay twenty yards ahead. But this dilapidated bridge was the closest connection to Annette's house, and the clock ticked.

Black water shone through gaps where the planks had rotted through, and twice she leapt over large missing sections. She couldn't avoid her reflection, a silhouetted flash across the mirror of the water. She hardly ever saw her reflection without Roshi's adjacent, without thinking it made no sense that people called them twins. Sunny—moonfaced like her mother, more gold than brown—fit her nickname better than her given name, Sunita. Roshi, whose given name, Roshini, had an extra syllable she'd never hear, looked more like their father. Bronze and sharp, a stick of wood. In the past months, Sunny had shot up to meet Roshi's height, and they were probably as twin-like as they'd ever be. But wasn't it time they began doing their own things?

Facing Annette's ornate gate, she felt like an intruder. A confection of a house loomed before her. She wiped the sweat that dripped down her face and entered, her heart fluttering.

The red roof shone. Pink shutters glimmered against limegreen paint, and a blue wrap-around verandah showed off yellow rocking chairs on the second story. The house stood on white columns, too proud to be called stilts. These ornate columns were not meant for actual use, since the paved side of the canal hardly flooded. Even if it flooded, the open area under Annette's house—the bottom-house—was a concrete slab that would never turn to mud.

The yard was better than she imagined. Ginger lilies, neverdone flowers, and marigolds hedged a pebbled driveway, peppering the air. Three colorful hammocks stretched in synchrony across the bottom-house columns, leaving ample room to run around. There wasn't a chicken, goat, or speck of trash in sight.

"Where you leave Mad Buck?" Annette laughed, skipping downstairs, her best friend, Navi, at her heels. Navi lived in a similar big house nearby, painted yellow and white.

Sunny looked over her shoulder half expecting Roshi. Mad Buck—the crazy old lady who roamed the streets. That's what Annette and Navi called Roshi when they didn't call her pagli. It was true, Roshi's occasional mouthing made her look insane. Whenever Sunny noticed it, she told her to stop. But Roshi couldn't help it. That was how she read lips.

"She in the cane," Sunny said, though she tried not to think of Roshi finding herself alone, panicking.

Annette and Navi sneered. They would never sully their nice shoes in sooty muck for a few measly slurps of sugar. They had better things to do, like watch TV and play with dolls.

Sunny wanted to see the toys and get out of there. But Annette strode over to a hammock and told her to get inside. Annette and Navi began swinging her hard, and she shrieked with joy. This was her favorite game. Her crazy big brothers swung her so hard in the hammock at home that she would do full loops. She never fell out or got dizzy because she knew how to close her eyes, tuck the hammock around her body, and ride the flip. Annette and Navi pushed, laughing, and she thought, look at me, playing with rich girls.

Their laughter subsided with the hammock. When Sunny peeked out, their faces flickered with disappointment. She should have known they only wanted to send her hurtling onto the concrete to crack her skull.

Annette and Navi had asked her to eat beside them after she placed first in an exam. She took this as a pat of congratulation, but soon realized the girls were just trying to slap her down. Every time the teacher praised Sunny's work or marveled that though she was the youngest in the class, she might place in Bishops or Queens for secondary school, Annette and Navi would show off something they got from abroad, to remind her she should be envying them. She preferred footraces and rounders to idling with the rich girls. Still, she always gave up that fun whenever Annette beckoned, unsure why.

Now Annette asked, "Why Roshi attach to you like that?"

She shrugged. Everyone knew the answer, but Annette stared as if she expected an explanation.

Because Roshi was born deaf. Because though Roshi was eighteen months older, she only croaked her first word, *Ma*, right after Sunny said it. Because Roshi needed Sunny to be her ears and mouth, the crutch God sent. Because Sunny had been promoted a grade to be Roshi's translator. Because they were the first girls in a houseful of boys and could whip out rotis quickly enough for their family of eleven only if they channeled Lord Krishna, a single being with four hands. Because even if Roshi hadn't been born deaf, she probably would have been attached to Sunny. Or the other way around.

Looking into Annette's face, she realized Annette was the first person to give her permission to reject being a conjoined twin. She shrugged. "She not here now. Where you dollies?"

These famous dolls from Annette's aunty abroad. These dolls better be worth the licking she'd receive. She bet Roshi was already headed home, that it was too late to intercept her.

"Wash you foot over there," Annette said, pointing to a spigot near a coconut tree.

She removed her dirty slippers and scrubbed her feet. If Annette gave the command to be demeaning, Sunny didn't hear it that way. "Wash you foot before upstairs" was a rule at her house, too, and she saw this as a sign of their sameness.

But Annette's upstairs offered no sameness. Polished wood floors shone, highlighting fancy chairs and plastic-covered couches that screamed, "Stay off." Glossy paneled walls touched the ceiling, curving to form round rooms. And fans vented the house instead of open gaps below the roof. Against one wall, a TV and record player sat on a table. Against a second wall, a majestic glass-fronted cabinet showed off plates, vases, and boxed dolls. Her stomach sank at the luxury, then at the thought of being caught.

"Where you ma?" Sunny asked. If her family owned such treasures, her mother would never permit a child near them.

"By the neighbor," Annette said. She opened a glass door to remove three boxes containing peach-skinned, gold-haired dolls, dressed in perfect, tiny clothes. One wore a white gown and actual jewelry—a princess headed to her wedding. The second, swathed in tight, shiny blue fabric, reminded her of Roshi with its placid smile. The third wore a heart-printed dress.

She dared not reach. Of course, there would be no touching of things clearly meant for eyes only. But Annette suddenly pulled the heart-dressed doll from its box, and Sunny ignited with heat.

Annette fluffed the dress and slipped the doll's shoes on and off its pointed feet. She posed the doll to stroke its hair as it walked on stilty legs. Sunny wanted to prance on tiptoe and touch her hair, too. She'd have to show Roshi the move, add it to their American bit. Annette removed other wondrous things from the box. Heart-shaped paper, heart-shaped stickers, a pen, and a thing called a stamp. How were such things made?

"Gimme you hand," Annette said.

"Not waste it on she," Navi pouted.

Sunny reached out her right hand, and Annette pressed the stamper into her palm. A red heart appeared amid the crisscrossing lines, and she almost exploded with joy.

"Do me hand, too," Navi demanded, extending a palm.

Annette batted her away. "You skin too dark. You not guh see it."

Navi huffed and stormed off. "Me not want play with this moo-moo anyway."

Had Annette ever stamped Navi's hand, or was she the first to receive this privilege?

"How you skin so light?" Annette asked, examining Sunny's hands in her darker ones. "You always running around in the sun."

She shrugged.

Annette stamped her own left palm, and the girls connected

their heart lines to admire the marks. Sunny's light skin was a target for family teasing, but she'd long known it was also a source of envy and the one thing she had over Annette. Seeing Annette's grayed palm cupped against her own yellowed one, she reveled in Annette's naked jealousy. The heart did look better on her. It would look better on Roshi, too.

Remembering Roshi, she rose. "Me got fuh go." If she left now, could she still pretend she'd gotten waylaid by a snake?

But Annette held out the doll.

Sunny took the weightless doll in her hands, its lovely peach skin glowing, and she sat back down. She'd do anything to examine this perfect American thing. She'd grit her teeth and take every stinging lick of the cane rod across her back. Annette removed the doll's dress, which was really two pieces, to expose its white underwear with red hearts and its slick plastic body. She blushed at seeing so much skin, even doll skin, and shifted to tuck her knee-length skirt under her calves. The ceiling fan whirred, stirring a brew of hot air.

2

Lost and Found

Her heart raced. She'd sprinted home, expecting to be greeted by a whipping, Roshi's confusion, and her siblings' snickering. But her unpainted wooden house stood quiet on its stilts.

The weathered house was a gray box on spindly legs, stairs lining its right side. A small room, tucked in the far-left corner of the open bottom, also propped it up. An outdoor kitchen had been fashioned adjacent to this room, and its outer walls were lined with shelves holding kitchenwares. Opposite the shelves, the family's fireside—a mud-daubed stove—stood between stilts, next to a metal sink. Corrugated zinc, matching the roof, served as eaves over this space. A table, benches, and a hammock furnished the rest of the bottom-house.

Beyond the kitchen, in the backyard, the shower, water tank, and outhouse sat amid fruit and coconut trees. A wire-fenced pen housed a goat, asleep in the shade, and chickens, hiding from the heat.

She slipped through the wooden gate, a low rickety thing that had been left ajar. "Ma?"

Woodsmoke perfumed the air. Embers glowed in the fireside, but the fire was out. Late afternoon sun cast deep shadows across the open bottom, and bits of metal caught light. Two homemade can-and-spool toy cars glinted yellow. An enormous tipped-over pot shone. A penknife winked next to ribbons of wood on the bench, and another knife lay across half-chopped bora beans next to the fireside. This time of day, that knife should not be resting.

Her family's ghostly energy filled the space like a bright afterimage: Her eight-year-old sister, Baby, obediently chopping vegetables. Their mother kneading roti dough. Jeeve, her ten-year-old brother, thinning bamboo with the penknife for the singing kites he churned out, kites their older brothers sold in town. Pappo, her five-year-old brother, deaf like Roshi, ramming cars at imaginary obstacles. Indy, her two-year-old sister, playing house inside the pot with her doll, a ratty thing their mother had stitched together with leftover fabric.

Sunny peered into the pot, half expecting Indy. She wasn't there, nor was the doll. Wherever Indy was, she was certainly clutching that filthy thing. Sunny had a similar doll once. It had disintegrated in the mud years ago, after she'd pulled out the cloth stuffing from a hole in the doll's spine.

"Ma? Baby?"

She had tiptoed around Annette's giant, quiet house and envied it the whole way home. Now she missed the chaotic warmth that usually defined hers. She'd never been alone in the space. The fraying hammock sat too still. Long shadows spoke of jumbies, those haunting unsettled spirits, ready to leap out from dark corners. A board creaked, and she jumped. Would her family spring out from hiding places? Had Jeeve convinced everyone to play a jumbie joke on her?

Staring at the chopped onions, garlic, and peppers mounded in neat pyramids, she suddenly understood: they were all out looking for her.

She threw her bag aside and ran to the outhouse. She rammed her fingers into the perpetually wet mud behind the building—mud the crappos loved. A huge toad blinked lazily as she smeared mud across her face, uniform, and into her palms to hide the red heart stamp. On the way home, she'd considered telling the truth, or a version of it. To say Annette had called to her, that she'd told Roshi but Roshi had misunderstood, that she didn't expect to be gone so long. She'd partly looked forward to her siblings' jealousy, even as she faced punishment. She'd been invited to a fancy house, touched fancy things, moved up in life a little. But they couldn't know.

Smelling heavily of earth and worms, she returned to the fireside. She should cook so everyone could eat when they returned. But if she washed, her lie might fall apart. She stood in limbo until Indy called, "Sun-ee!"

Her mother rushed past the gate, Indy on her hips, doll in hand. Seeing Sunny, she stopped short by the clump of flag-topped poles near the overgrown cassava tree. Sunny looked up at the nine fading prayer flags, one for each kid. She prayed on her flag as her siblings traipsed in, Roshi aiming straight for her.

Red-eyed, Roshi looked her up and down. "Where you go? Me look for you."

Sunny easily deciphered the words through the croaks. Tears pooled in her eyes.

Roshi pulled her into a hug, but Sunny remained stiff, feeling undeserving.

"What happen?" their mother demanded.

"Me run from a snake and fall down and get lost." Her big lie. Hardly believable.

"Lost where?" her mother asked.

"In the cane."

Her mother sighed, put Indy down, and walked past her to the stove.

Indy ambled up to Sunny. "Dolly call for you, 'Sun-ee! Sun-ee!'" She held up her doll, whose button eyes stared creepily into Sunny's soul.

"How *you* get lost in the cane?" Jeeve laughed. "You know that cane like the back of you hand. We think somebody take you, everybody split up this way and that. But who guh want you?" Jeeve laughed again and gathered his kite supplies.

It was a stupid lie, and she felt foolish. Jeeve was right, who in their right mind would snatch her in her faded hand-me-downs and filthy slippers? She wanted a beating. She deserved a beating.

"Go bathe," her mother ordered, her back to them. "And tell Roshi come make roti."

She avoided Roshi's eyes as she mimed rolling roti dough and pointed to the stove. Roshi stayed put.

"You done playing in that cane, you hear me?" their mother continued. "Me want you home right after school with Baby and Jeeve. You supposed to help cook. No more of this cane business."

She nodded. Had her mother believed her?

Her mother turned. "What you wait for? Go."

Sunny ran to the outdoor shower and doused her muddy uniform in the soaking tub. She'd have to wear her stained one the next day, a small price to pay. Under a cold spray of water, she rid her body of mud, but she couldn't bring herself to scrub her right palm too hard.

3

Poker Face

Wet-haired, she joined Roshi at the stove. Roshi had already rolled twenty rotis into perfect circles, overlapping them on the counter.

"Finish the salt fish," her mother ordered. "And chunkay the dal."

Her mother walked Indy and Pappo to the shower as Sunny heated ghee for the dal's seasoning. She needed to cook fast. Her father and three older brothers had just arrived home from rice harvesting, fishing, or wherever they'd managed to find work that week. She could hardly keep up and only knew Raj had secured a mine job. They were busy unpacking gear, emptying lunch tiffins.

"Me hear the cane jumbie get you," Ravi, her eldest brother said, scrubbing his hands and laughing. At nineteen, he was a man about to start his own family with a girl named Mala, who lived mere houses away. But he'd already given Sunny her first niece, two years old like Indy, only deemed an accident and labeled a Dougla, the word for a half-Indian, half-Black person. This was a rare breed Sunny only ever spotted once at the conservancy; she'd longed to study the gorgeous light-skinned, curly-haired child, but she was pulled away. Their father had forbidden Ravi to continue the relationship. The girl's family had rejected Ravi, too.

"Jeeve say you turn up black as me," Mo laughed. Her fifteen-year-old brother Mo, the darkest of her siblings, often joked Sunny was related to Arthur, a Chinese descendent in their community of coolie laborers, while he might be related to Winston, an African descendant in their midst.

Everyone laughed.

She pretended to ignore them as she stirred chopped tomatoes into the golden salt fish, releasing mouthwatering steam.

Raj, her seventeen-year-old brother, said, "Well, good thing she so yellow or she wouldn't have get invited to America."

Sunny looked up in confusion just as their father admonished Raj with his given name, "Caimraj!"

Raj was the only one in their family who'd attempted secondary school. He'd dropped out to work the mines because the travel and books grew too expensive. He was the smartest, the one who did everything right. He never got scolded. What was he talking about?

"What?" Raj asked, looking innocent. "When you guh tell them?"

"Tell what?" their mother asked, returning with Indy and Pappo, wrapped in towels sewn from old sheets.

"Me tell you to stay out of that cane," their father said, thumping Sunny's head before storming off to the shower. He smelled unmistakably of rum. Raj escaped to the outhouse, and Ravi and Mo disappeared into the downstairs room.

The sting at her nape spread across her face and down her body, and Sunny wondered if her father knew she'd abandoned Roshi. Did Raj's comment have something to do with her touching Annette's American things? Her hands trembled as she chunkayed the dal with garlic and cumin-seasoned ghee.

When liquored and angry, her father could become as scary as a jumbie. But she rarely felt his wrath. He often praised her for being as smart as Raj, and she secretly thought of herself as his favorite. She knew he would never take a stiff coconut branch to her like he'd done with Ravi. The day he found out about the pregnant girl, he'd whipped Ravi, chasing him from the house. Ravi had to kneel on dry rice grains in front of the prayer flags to return home. Though he was taller and bigger than their father, Ravi fell to his knees and obeyed.

Her mother served their father first, then the rest of them piled dal, oil roti, bora, and salt fish onto thin metal plates, no one talking. It was a typical meal, one of Sunny's favorites, but her mouth stayed dry as she made her plate.

They took their usual spots. The younger kids at the table with their mother; Raj and Ravi on the stairs; Mo in a hammock; their father on the bench; she and Roshi on the stoop of the downstairs room.

Indy hummed to her doll and Pappo made car noises, but they couldn't drown out the chewing sounds.

Sunny balanced her plate on her knees, wishing their bottom-house was large like Annette's. Then she might not have to feel Roshi pressed against her or hear so much wet lip-smacking.

Roshi gripped her hand, spying the red heart. But just then, their father cleared his throat and said, "So, me run into an old friend from school—Michael."

She yanked her hand back from Roshi as the chewing noises subsided. Even Indy stopped humming.

"He in the backtrack business," their father said.

People often whispered about this "backtrack," a secret passageway to America. Sunny imagined a dark road winding through thick jungles until it magically ascended to the clouds of America.

"Deo!" Her mother, Shali, barked her father's name. "Me not want you involve with that."

"You guh let me talk, Shali, or what?" Deo retorted.

Shali looked down.

Deo spat into the dirt behind him. "He come up to me, drunk-drunk. Been so long since me see the man, me almost not recognize him. He wear this nice shirt, shine-shine shoes, but look ready to kill heself." He paused. "He push the rum in me hand, how me could say no?"

Shali harrumphed.

"That the truth," Ravi corroborated. Their father had been avoiding rum after he'd gambled away a hundred US dollars playing dominoes.

Deo continued. "He say a big project blow up cause of a labaria bite."

Sunny sat up, surprised that the story involved the deadly labaria, the snake she'd have named if pressed for details about her lie.

"Then he show me a picture, and the picture look just like Sunny."

Confused, she stared at her father, and he stared through her, smiling.

"Just like Sunny," Ravi echoed. "The mole and everything."

She resisted touching the oval bump under her left eye.

"Michael get the papers ready for this girl, Neena. She family illegal in the states, and Michael set up a visa, passport, plane ticket, everything for the girl to join them next week. Then the labaria kill she, rest she soul. And me tell Michael, that pickney look just like me daughter Sunny."

Sunny tried to grasp meaning from these words, but meaning evaded her. Did she have a twin? A dead twin?

"Michael think me lie. But me show Ravi the picture, and Ravi say, 'Who take this picture of Sunny.' Mo say the same thing."

Mo laughed. "Identical!"

Deo said, "Everything look like Sunny. The passport and everything. And Michael say, 'Well, maybe you daughter can take Neena place and go America.'"

Sunny laughed as if this were the punch line to a long joke. Jeeve and Baby chuckled, too, but everyone else stayed serious.

"Then, come to find out, me know the people who hire Michael. The lady named Lila. She from Leguan, and me use to work she daddy rice paddy. Me own daddy work for them. After she daddy die, they sell the land. But me remember the girl, short and skinny, always barefoot. You believe that?"

Shali grumbled.

"You not see, Shali? This like God reaching out he hand," Deo said. "Me not see Michael in twenty years. And he show up right in front of me with this picture, this girl who look just like Sunny, on the day of the girl funeral. And me know the girl mother. This like God shining the way to America, God blessing all of we."

"Or God sinning you," Shali spat. "God want you in jail for backtrack business? The whole thing sound like nonsense."

"You like fuh run you mouth and not listen," Deo said, putting aside his empty plate. "Michael guarantee this. Top-notch papers, already done. Everything done arrange. Me even see the plane ticket, the father-daughter passport he doctor up. He show me the thing."

Shali sneered. "So, what Sunny guh do? Act like she this dead girl? This, this Neena? And what, the girl mother not guh know? That you plan?"

"You stupid or something?" Deo shouted. "Of course the lady know she daughter dead, rest the girl soul. The girl was they only pickney, and the lady only recently get pregnant again."

"Then what Sunny guh do?"

Yes, what would Sunny do? She was stuck on her mother's words: *Act like she this dead girl?*

"Nothing set in stone. Michael say Lila does clean house and she husband work at some farm. Lila guh need help when the baby come. Sunny could work for them, nuh? Michael guh ask. Money come easy in America. Sunny can work back the passage quick, then send money home. And when she ready, Michael guh help she marry somebody for status. Then she can sponsor all of we. He say in six years time, she can put in for tourist visa."

Sunny's head throbbed with these crazy words. They would send her away? For six years? To live with a strange lady, take care of a baby, and *marry* someone?

Shali laughed. "And you believe every word that man say?"

Deo sucked his teeth. "The man do this for a living. He guarantee this. Anyway, what Sunny guh do here? She ready for secondary school, but we not got money for that. She bright. In America, she guh get an education for free. Top-notch education."

Her father smiled at her. Reflexively, Sunny smiled back, even as her panic mounted.

Her mother softened. "Nothing ever this easy, Deo. That lady grieving she daughter. Why she guh want help people she barely know."

"Look, the lady already pay over half the fee, and who want see they money get waste? She guh get something, we guh get something. It not hurt to ask. Michael guh come by tomorrow and see Sunny heself, see if she pass."

Shali shook her head. "What we guh tell people? The school? Me family?"

"Why you worry about stupidness? When last you family come by? Just tell them she live with me sister abroad."

"The sister you not talk to?"

Deo sucked his teeth again. "Look. Geeta in Barbados, last me hear, and Reggie in Trinidad. Sunny could be with any one of them. That kind of thing normal, Shali. How you think people get to America?"

Sunny's head swirled as she thought of her father's family, whom she'd never met, and her mother's family, who lived along a different canal and whom she barely knew, who hated her father. Would they even notice her gone?

Her mother's voice got low. "What Michael charging?"

Deo stared at Shali a few seconds before answering. "The people owe two thousand."

Her mother laughed savagely, and Sunny relaxed. They didn't have that kind of money.

"But he not charge *me* two thousand. The girl family already pay three thousand, but they not guh pay a dime more now they daughter dead, rest she soul. Michael say he done use up all that money for the passports, plane tickets, bribes, and so. With this labaria bite, he guh go bankrupt. So, he give me a deal. Five hundred."

"Five hundred? Every penny we save?"

"That barely cover the plane ticket, Shali. Nobody ever go backtrack for just five hundred. And Sunny guh work back a couple hundred more when she get there."

The numbers rattled in the air, refusing to sink into Sunny's mind. *Three thousand. Two thousand. Five hundred. Couple hundred more.*

Shali didn't hide her contempt. "What about the bushland, Deo? How many years we work for that money, and you want piss it away? Like you piss half at the rum shop?"

Deo kicked his plate aside and stormed the table.

Ravi and Mo stood, and Deo held a palm out to them.

"Who make that money?" Deo shouted, hitting the table with a fist. "Who?"

Shali pursed her lips.

"Me make that money! You hear? Me and them boys, we break we back every damn day for that money. And what you do all day? Just use money! Shut you mouth about who piss money. Me do what me want with that money."

A silence ensued. Indy broke it, scrambling for her dropped doll.

Sunny was sure she misunderstood. No way would her father give up the pineapple farm so she could take a plane ride to the clouds. No way would they spend every dime they had on her. Why would God bless her that way, right after she'd abandoned Roshi and lied?

Deo stepped back and gesticulated west. "That bushland not go no place. But when we guh get this chance again?"

"We guh save for the farm again, Ma," Ravi said, sitting back down. "This sound like a good chance."

"A good chance," Raj echoed. "One foot in the door."

Sunny had long stopped eating. Her hands hovered above her plate, a shred of roti limp in her fingers. Roshi grabbed her hand, roti and all, and pried it open to expose the red mark. She looked at Sunny questioningly.

Sunny pulled back her hand and snapped the palm shut. She hated when Roshi treated her body as shared property. Then, feeling bad, she offered the palm back, not bothering to explain the mark. Roshi couldn't possibly have followed the conversation. She had no idea their father just announced he might sever Sunny from her side.

Sunny teared up as the words sank in. She regretted the stupid stamp and her daydreams, fickle things never meant to come true. She'd fantasized about a life without Roshi, a life with store-bought things up in the clouds. As Roshi gripped her hand, she didn't want it anymore.

"Me not want go," she said.

Everyone looked at her.

"You not want go?" her father asked, walking toward her, his tone taunting. "You not want watch TV every day and live like rich people? Big house, you own room, flush toilet? You not want free schooling, Sunny, to better yourself? You not want bring you family to America?"

Yes, she wanted those things. But not if she had to pretend to be some dead girl. Not if she had to be sent away.

Her father said, "You guh be in America, Sunny. Everybody in they right mind want that opportunity. And this not only benefit you. This benefit the whole family."

Sunny stared beyond their fence into deepening shadows. She understood. Once her father decided, he never changed his mind. They called him Poker at the rum shop because he was a gambler, and she was being gambled off for five hundred dollars.

4

Seesaw

AT THE OUTDOOR SINK, putting toothpaste onto her toothbrush, Roshi thumped Sunny's shoulder and mouthed, "What happen?"

Certainly, Roshi felt the current that charged through their family and the tension that erected a wall between their parents. But Sunny couldn't explain something she barely understood.

She shrugged, chewed her splayed toothbrush, and spat onto the bare ground beside the shower. She slapped a mosquito on her arm, eyeing the breeding puddles nearby, feeling jumbies edge in. Huge toady eyes reflected the flickering lamplight.

The evening blackout had started before they finished cleaning up, so she hurried, putting away her toothbrush before Roshi got done. She wondered if Americans brushed their teeth outside, if they endured blackouts, if crappos and labarias lived there, too.

"What happen?" Roshi persisted as they climbed the stairs. Sunny ignored her. Ahead of them, Baby urged Indy along, holding up a jug-lamp, a kerosene-filled bottle with a burning wick. She and Roshi followed in the orange glow of the lamp's bobbing orb. Roshi carried the pitcher of drinking water, and she held the stained, yellow posey—a chamber pot that smelled faintly of urine. They alternated these jobs nightly. She usually reviled posey duty, since whoever carried it upstairs had to empty it the following morning, but she might miss this chore in America. She'd certainly miss the nightly procession.

The door at the top of the stairs opened into their living room. The jug-lamp illuminated a wooden sofa with thin cushions, a bench-like table, and her mother's sewing machine on a corner desk. Floral curtains and a string of colorful beads hung at a window. Hindu idols—Krishna, Shiva, and Ganesh—sat on a jutting shelf that served as the family's altar, decorated with dried flowers and incense. As Roshi placed the water pitcher on the table, Sunny placed the posey on the floor near the door and made a silent prayer to Lord Shiva, the protector. But she feared God had already decided.

Her sisters entered their bedroom, one of two rooms upstairs, created by partition walls that stopped short of the ceiling. Jeeve and Pappo slept on bedrolls on the living room floor, while Sunny's older brothers shared the single room downstairs.

Indy squealed and trampolined between the two narrow beds in their room, reaching for the mosquito nets that dangled like prizes above. Baby wrestled Indy onto their bed, and Roshi loosened the wads of netting, attached to ceiling rafters. Sunny hoped this game of keep-the-nets-from-Indy would distract Roshi until lights-out.

Sunny propped her abdomen across the windowsill to unlatch the shutters. Half balanced on the ledge at the height of the coconut trees, she felt as if she were flying. Milky moonlight added to the effect. She seesawed on the ledge, and a sinful thought flashed. What if she let go and fell and died like Neena? The frightening, wicked thought propelled her back in, her heart racing.

She bolted the shutters closed.

Indy slipped out of Baby's grasp and attacked the mosquito netting that Roshi had tucked under the mattress. Sunny smiled.

She'd shrouded her body in the gauzy fabric many times, pretending to be a princess, bride, or corpse. But she'd learned what Indy hadn't yet—pull hard enough, and the whole contraption would tumble from the ceiling.

"Quiet," their father boomed. His footsteps pounded the stairs.

Indy dropped and hid under the threadbare sheet, and Roshi continued her task in peace. Baby patted Indy's back and chanted the Shanti prayer, "Om Dyo Shanti."

Sunny's mother's steps swish-swished on the landing. Sometimes Shali checked on Indy, but today she swished directly to her bedroom.

The wooden bed frame creaked and drawers grated in the other room. Sunny imagined her father splayed across the bed, her mother opening the wardrobe, doing whatever mothers did at night.

Jeeve and Pappo bounded upstairs, their feet drumming out a happy patter. They slammed the door and bolted it loudly. Pappo screeched, and Jeeve giggled, clearly horsing around.

"Quiet!" their father boomed again. He cleared his throat and snuffled.

Sunny put a finger to her lips and helped Roshi tuck the mosquito netting around their mattress. She wasn't as good at tucking as Roshi, whose side stayed tight all night. Her side was always loose by morning, likely because she rubbed her foot against the silky fabric to ease into sleep. Maybe American netting would stay tucked all night, no matter how hard she rubbed.

A table scraped across the floor, and she pictured Jeeve and Pappo setting up their beds. Pappo's bedroll between the sofa and table, Jeeve's out in the open.

Their father cleared his throat and snuffled again.

Sunny normally hated this evening music, the cloying closeness of it. She hated hearing her older brothers below, rattling the ceiling as they moved about in their hammocks or makeshift wooden beds. But a lump tightened her throat as she imagined the quiet of her future, millions of miles away. A quiet perhaps quieter than Annette's house. In her own room. The thought seemed absurd.

Their father banged on the wall and shouted, "Turn out the light!"

She quelled the lamp and welcomed the darkness, which would keep Roshi from resuming her pestering.

The acrid smell of mosquito coil filled the air. Without netting, Jeeve and Pappo relied on the chemical smoke to keep the bugs at bay. Smoke rose and drifted over the partition into the girls' room. Moonlight, shining through the ventilation gaps between the walls and roof, illuminated the swirling smoke, making her think of jumbies and America.

Baby's humming faded, and deep snores rumbled from their parents' room. Shifting noises subsided in the living room, and the chatter below ebbed. Sunny rubbed her feet against the silky netting, unable to sleep.

Roshi rattled their bed indicating she, too, was awake. Deciding it was time to tell her, Sunny untucked the netting and struck a match with a soft *ptth* to light the lamp. She retrieved a half-used notebook and stubby pencil from a trove under their mattress and wrote the words, "Me go America."

Roshi touched the words, confused.

Sunny nodded and pointed to herself.

Roshi shook her head and scrunched her face in disbelief. No.

Sunny nodded.

Roshi grabbed the pencil and wrote, "How?"

Sunny shrugged, staring down at the words on the paper. Lamplight flickered, and the words appeared to dance as if she had cast a spell. Frightened, she rubbed at the words with the almost nonexistent eraser until the soft paper ripped.

Roshi nudged her shoulder. "How?"

"Me not know!" She pushed Roshi's hand away and attacked the paper, shredding it to bits before tucking the waste under the mattress.

When sleep finally arrived, Sunny dreamt of a two-headed labaria. It darted in, but instead of biting her, it slipped underneath her back. The snake grew and grew, and she rode it into a cloud world.

The next morning, her father said, "If anybody find out, we could get jail. So, nobody in this house guh tell anybody. We clear?"

She conveyed the message to Roshi, putting her finger to her lips and mouthing, "Shh." Though, who was Roshi going to tell?

"Michael guh come tonight. Hope and pray things work out. And stay out of that cane, you hear?"

Sunny's stomach somersaulted. She couldn't untangle her feelings. Most of her wanted nothing to do with this plan. But small parts of her, the part that wanted to please her father, the part that craved perfect American things, and the part that lived for Annette's jealousy, had been kindled by the prospect.

5
Light Show

Mr. Michael oozed Americana in his blue jeans and white sneakers. Large gold-rimmed sunglasses hid the man's eyes as he tilted his chin to examine Sunny, who stood in the middle of their bottom-house as instructed.

She'd showered and donned her white lace-trimmed church dress, and her skin shone with fresh coconut oil. She'd treasured the attention from her mother, who had plaited a white ribbon in her hair. Now, standing before Mr. Michael, who circled and eyed her up and down, a deep shame threatened to trigger her bladder. Her family had scattered to the periphery, giving Michael room to assess her, and they felt miles away. She curled her throbbing toes inside her too-tight patent shoes—hand-me-downs from Roshi.

"Look at me," Mr. Michael said, his town accent flavoring even this short phrase.

She focused on the man's pebbled cheeks, pockmarked by deep gouges and bumps.

He scratched at a red bump and commanded, "Smile."

She lifted the corners of her twitching lips into an awkward grimace, a face she was certain she'd never made before.

"Hmph. They look different," Mr. Michael said, twisting his head side to side.

Her stomach dropped. All day at school, her stomach had been lodged in her throat. She couldn't concentrate on pairing countries to flags. She couldn't play rounders, eat lunch, or meet Annette's eyes. All day, her heart toggled between hope and worry that Mr. Michael would nix the plans. Now, her heart juggled relief and shame. She'd let her family down and she wouldn't see America, but she'd get to stay. She pursed her lips.

"Oh. Yes. Yes. I see it now," Mr. Michael said, nodding.

What? What had he seen?

"Yes, the eyes the same," Mr. Michael continued. "The nose. That mole, for sure."

Mr. Michael walked around her, his arms crossed below the open V of his button-down shirt. Finally, he laughed and said, "Yes. This face could pass. You're lucky."

Sunny felt she might topple from the whiplash.

Mr. Michael shook Deo's hand and slapped his back as her younger siblings moved in cautiously. Roshi hugged her, believing something miraculous had happened.

"You go 'Merica?" Roshi mouthed.

She nodded.

Roshi smiled her placid smile, and Sunny envied her blissful ignorance.

The men sat at the table to hash out details as Shali headed to the stove. She and her sisters followed their mother to cook the prepped roti, but Shali stopped her. "Sunny, go up and change that dress. And watch Indy."

Sunny dashed up the stairs with her baby sister, grateful for the chance to remove her shoes and eavesdrop from above. But then, someone turned on the tape player and thumping soca music drowned out the voices below. She released the mosquito netting and changed into her housedress as Indy danced in the translucent fabric. Slanting rays of afternoon sun caught the beads hanging in the living room window, sending a kaleidoscope of sparkling colors onto the metal ceiling—every color from the large box of crayons Annette had once shown off at school. Sunny only rarely caught this light show, and it felt like a sign. Maybe everything would be okay. She jumped on the bed to dance with Indy, swinging her hips to Byron Lee's "Tiny Winey."

As the sun set, the room plunged into a blueish dusk. Roshi appeared in the doorway, silhouetted. She mimed eating and croaked, "Food ready." It seemed a wall had already formed between them.

Following Roshi downstairs, Sunny practiced words in her mind. "Me not want go. Roshi need me. Me want stay right here."

But when she reached the bottom-house, her courage dissolved. The music was too loud. The air was now seasoned with curry. Everyone was too happy.

"Aha! There's the star gal," Mr. Michael said, his voice shrill.

A bottle of rum sat between him and her father at the table. Someone must have run over to Small's shop to buy it while she was upstairs. Ravi sipped rum, too. Maybe even Raj and Mo. They laughed over a game of dominoes, just finished. Sunny was certain her mother was saving up words to unleash later. But Shali served the men plates of butterfish curry, and when Mr. Michael thanked her, she shook her head defferentially and cracked a small smile.

Deo patted the empty space beside him, indicating Sunny should sit there.

Embarrassment liquefied her insides. She'd never eaten next to grown men before. Her mother handed her a plate without making eye contact.

Her siblings filled plates and sat apart, not a single person in their usual position.

"You know you lucky, right?" Mr. Michael boomed over the music, staring at her.

She nodded. She liked his town accent. She'd have to mimic it when she played with Annette next. Annette would die of envy.

"All you have to do is walk onto a plane. And you don't know the work behind any of it. The work! And the money. And you get to live with nice people, the Das family." He leaned into her. "They broken up about their daughter, sure sure. But they want you to come. They feel it's a blessing I find you. And it sure is a blessing for your family."

She nodded, trying to feel lucky, like a blessing. Trying to feel less terrified.

"Let we celebrate. Turn up the music," Mr. Michael called, pouring another drink from the half-empty bottle.

Jeeve obliged, blasting Arrow's "Hot, Hot, Hot." It was like Diwali or Phagwa.

A drum-heavy chutney song by Sundar Popo played next, and Jeeve leapt up to dance. Egged on by laughter, he jiggled his neck and twirled his arms like people in the Bollywood films they'd spied from behind Small's shop. He rat-a-tatted his legs to the rapid tassa beat, and Pappo, Indi, and Roshi jumped up, too.

Roshi tugged at her to join, but Sunny shook her head.

"Go. Celebrate," Mr. Michael shouted. He clapped the table so hard the dominoes rattled.

As soon as she stood, the music stopped and the lights flickered off, making her jump. It was only the nightly blackout, but it felt like another sign. Time was running out. She needed to speak fast, tell her father she wouldn't go. She couldn't go. She was too scared to go.

Mr. Michael laughed shrilly. "Ho, ho. I forget you get blackout in the backcountry here."

Raj and Mo lit jug-lamps, and flickering yellow light illuminated the bottom-house. In a dim corner, Deo handed a wad of money to Mr. Michael in a handshake. The men patted each other's backs, and Mr. Michael pocketed the money in his shirt.

Her father met her eyes, and in those seconds, she pleaded, staring squarely at him. Deo's face hardened, and he pursed his lips before looking away. She was too late. She'd upset him, too. Her father was the sun their family revolved around, but you couldn't stare at the sun without getting burned.

Mr. Michael approached Sunny, smiling widely. "I didn't even hear you talk. You can talk, right?"

She nodded.

"Good. Practice your book-talk, okay? None of that creole stuff."

She'd never heard of book-talk. Did he mean his town accent?

Mr. Michael turned to Shali. "You glad this work out, right?" He patted his pocket. "It guh be worth the money, trust me, when you have somebody in America to send for you. And you guh barely miss the girl. You got a few to spare." He laughed, gesturing to the faces about him.

Sunny flushed at the idea her family was grossly large, that she was expendable. She glanced at Shali and was surprised to see a small smile planted on her mother's face.

"I will see you Saturday," Mr. Michael said, pointing at Sunny before her father and Ravi escorted him out. Two jug-lamps bobbed through the yard and were soon swallowed by darkness.

The kids had to hurry through their nightly rituals and chores with only three remaining jug-lamps. Sunny walked over to wash the dishes and asked her mother, "What's Saturday?"

"You guh meet the girl nani before you go."

The words were spoken with a finality that stung.

After washing the dishes, Sunny took one lamp and trailed the little ones upstairs. Jeeve galloped after.

Sitting on the hard sofa, she moaned to Jeeve, "Why me need to meet the nani?" She didn't want anything to do with the girl or her grandmother.

"You pagli?" Jeeve asked. "To make sure you pass. Why else?"

An ember of hope sputtered in her gut. Could things still change?

"Plus, the nani want you lay down in the girl bed and fight off she jumbie," Jeeve added.

Sunny kicked his arm playfully as he set up his bedroll.

He laughed. "Me just mad me can't go the airport."

"Why you can't go?"

Jeeve flopped on his bed. "The man say we too much people. The plane guh leave early, so you and Daddy guh stay at the Georgetown house Saturday night. Then, you guh pretend Mr. Michael you daddy and practice some new name before you get on the plane Sunday."

Why did Jeeve know so much, while she knew nothing?

"You lucky. By this time next week, you guh watch TV in America in you own bed."

Sunny felt faint. It had all been decided.

6

Long Time

That week, the electricity of the unsaid elevated the ordinary. The sky blazed bluer, birds trilled louder, and the air constantly smelled of rain. Sunny felt hysterical exhilaration.

She ran so hard in a footrace she came in second and collapsed, sucking for air as she skidded barefoot past the finish line. She told Annette, "Tomorrow," when invited to study for the upcoming Common Entrance exam, then she blatantly ignored Annette the following day. She took long detours with Roshi after school, trespassing farms and stealing fruit from trees, and their mother didn't say a thing.

She and Roshi dared each other over dilapidated bridges and into the cemetery. They crouched for an hour in a ditch full of wild buttercups, stringing the flowers together to make hair wreaths. There, they found sleep-and-wake bushes, weedy plants that wilted when touched. Boys sometimes peed on the bushes to trigger the leaves, but Sunny didn't care about that as she pressed her body against a thornless section of leaves, trying to wilt the entire plant at once. She and Roshi roared with laughter as the plant figured out the game and fought them, keeping its leaves open even as they rolled about.

It was as if she believed exaggerated play could make the impending weekend disappear. As if ignoring the passing of time was the trick to suspending it. As if pretending the brown suitcase her father got from Mr. Michael that week was only to see how many kids they could zip up inside—Indy and Pappo together, Jeeve by himself.

But Saturday arrived, and her father yelled, "Wake up," to the whole house before the cock even crowed.

"Leave that, we late," Shali barked, as Sunny made the bed. Sunny stood in her nightshirt, an oversized T-shirt from Ravi, and reached for the strip of fabric that transformed the shirt into a day dress on weekends. Roshi grimaced at this silly act of defiance, pointing to the white dress and tight shoes their mother had set out. As Sunny forced herself into the uncomfortable clothes, Roshi packed Sunny's nightshirt in the suitcase that rattled with her meager possessions, including a simple A-line dress Shali had made from an old curtain for the airplane trip.

Half an hour later, Sunny followed her family out of the gate as the sky lightened. Ravi, Mo, and Baby stayed back. Baby to watch the house and cook, the boys to fish. Ravi squeezed Sunny's shoulder in a half hug, Mo slapped her back, and Baby waved a shy goodbye. The dawn sky offered dim light, and Sunny focused on bypassing ruts, walking on her heels to reduce the pain from her shoes. She didn't look back at the house, at Ravi, Mo, and Baby, not grasping the finality of the moment.

Their procession attracted a neighbor's attention. "Wedding?" he called, waving.

"Yeah, man," her father answered. "Wedding in town."

A van waited across the canal. The driver opened the door as they crossed the bridge, and she pictured Annette watching and feeling jealous. She ignored the suitcase Raj placed in the back and the stack of kites Jeeve brought to sell. She let the wedding myth suffuse her mind.

It was her first trip to town, and she got a window seat. The canal and houses whizzed past as the driver sped along, beep-beeping generously and jerking side to side to overtake cars or avoid potholes. Sunny slid out of her shoes and sat on her feet to see better. A smile bubbled up as her favorite calypso dancehall song blared, another of Arrow's recent hits—"Long Time." Jeeve sang the call, asking when they last partied, and the rest of them shouted, "Long time." Even Roshi sang, catching on to the refrain. Sunny held Roshi's hand in the air, and they swayed. Maybe they were actually going to a fancy wedding in town, Sunny thought. That seemed less crazy than the thing she'd been told they were doing.

Lively music and changing scenery made the hour fly by, and Sunny felt a stab of disappointment when the van parked in a tangle of cars at the ferry station. The place was full of produce stalls and bustling people. The aroma of overripe fruit, fresh fish, and diesel fuel filled the air. Sunny pictured herself getting lost or trampled, but the marketplace's chaotic energy thrilled her, too.

Her family wove through vendors and hagglers to gather at the end of the dock. Shali handed each kid a breakfast of fried eggs wrapped in a roti, and they shared water from a flask, holding the container above their lips. After eating, Sunny, Roshi, and the little ones explored the boardwalk with Raj, as Jeeve hawked kites.

Sunny and her siblings examined baskets of fish, counted colorful speedboats, marveled at piles of fruit, and hovered around candy stalls. Next to a toy vendor, a toucan sat in a cage. The bird's massive orange bill weighed down its small, dark body. They crowded around it, never having seen one up close. "Leave the thing," the vendor snapped. The bird's fiery bill poked in and out of the cage's slits as they walked off, and Sunny felt bad for it, sitting there being gawked at.

They discussed what they'd buy if they had any money. Sunny wanted a frilly yellow umbrella, something she imagined rich girls in America might use, but she met her happiness threshold when Raj bought a bag of colorful hard candy to share. She and Roshi sucked the sugary rectangles, sticking their tongues out to compare their progress until the candy's tart and juicy middle exploded in their mouths. Raj noticed Sunny's heel-first walk and suggested new shoes. Their mother objected to dumping every penny into one child, but their father agreed. They couldn't send Sunny to America looking like she came from nothing. So, she padded onto the ferry in brown buckle-strapped sandals, the first new shoes she'd ever owned. She also clutched a scuffed vinyl purse, a discounted item Raj insisted she'd need to house important papers.

The ferry was headed to Leguan Island, where the dead girl's nani lived, the woman who could still save her from going to America. But Sunny buried those details in her mind, lingering in the wedding myth as long as she could.

Relishing the squishy bed of her new shoes, she raced to the ferry's upper deck with Roshi and the little ones to wave at Jeeve and Raj, who stayed behind to sell kites while they were gone. The boat pulled away and air whipped strands of hair from her plait. Her brothers grew ant-sized on the dock before disappearing back into the marketplace. Soon, her other siblings retreated below-decks to escape the sun's scorch. But Sunny stayed, mesmerized by the churning black water, glowing amber as the waves caught the sunlight. The farther they moved from shore, the bigger the world grew. The land flattened into a thin strip along the horizon, and the sky spread so wide she couldn't take it all in. Feeling small, she rushed to join her family.

7

Touch-Me-Not

The ferry approached a long wooden landing. She spotted Mr. Michael on the uncrowded dock, standing near a white building. He scratched his face and spat in the water, and her wedding bubble burst.

After they disembarked, Deo greeted Mr. Michael with "Morning, brother."

Mr. Michael was colder. "I didn't expect all the little pickney."

Sunny felt the sting of admonishment for her father.

Mr. Michael hurried them in single file along the sandy road. They bypassed deep potholes and a cow that refused to move. A few speeding cars honked as they breezed past. After some time, they left the main road for a lush side road, which led to a narrower side road and eventually to a wooden house tucked amid banana trees.

The house wasn't as spartan as theirs, but it wasn't as ornate as Annette's. Its green and yellow paint was mostly intact, and despite exposed areas of gray wood, it looked sturdy. A multitude of faded prayer flags decorated the yard.

A hunched woman sat in the dim, smoky bottom-house on a low bench. She stared at a colorful altar, featuring statues of Hindu deities, garlands of flowers, and a smoldering havan kund. White bedsheets had been spread on the ground in preparation for group prayer. Breathing in the incense-perfumed air, Sunny realized they'd be praying over the dead girl.

The lady turned her head toward them but kept her eyes down. A long curl of incense smoke slithered toward her.

Mr. Michael bowed and approached with prayer hands. "Hello, Aunty. I brought the family. The girl here."

The woman's eyes seemed focused on Mr. Michael's shoes.

"You see the girl?" Mr. Michael asked. "Come, come, Sunny. Come here."

Her family parted for her, and Sunny stepped past them despite an instinct to bolt. She stopped by a touch-me-not bush full of pink flowers by the stairs. The plant was ripe with fuzzy pods, which, when pressed, popped open to spit out black seeds.

"She pass, right?" Mr. Michael asked. He retreated toward Sunny and held a hand to her.

Sunny didn't move.

The woman turned her bleary eyes back to her havan kund and stoked the fire.

This dismissal didn't bother Mr. Michael. He said, "Come, come, everybody. Sit down."

Sunny's family ambled around her, removed their shoes, and bowed namaste.

Her father put down the suitcase he'd been carrying and said, "Aunty, me once work for you husband, rest he soul, back when you own the rice paddy."

The old woman blurted, "Me not want this. Me want nothing to do with this!"

Everyone froze except Mr. Michael, who walked forward. "Aunty. This is what your daughter want. Lila want you meet the family to verify they legitimate. Give them a chance nuh, and you guh see they good people."

Sunny fingered a fat pod on the touch-me-not bush, and it snapped to release its seeds. She kept her eyes trained on the house's stairs, its peeling paint, but she pictured the tiny black seeds bouncing about. Shali was likely watching her, probably wanting to slap her hand and tell her to behave herself. But Sunny couldn't help it. Her fingers found another pod. And another. And another. A light grassy whiff broke through the smoky air.

"Neena like fuh do that," the old woman said. "When she was a lil pickney, she would run around and mash up that bush. And me would say she turn the bush from 'touch-me-not' to 'kill-me-dead.'"

Mr. Michael and her father laughed too hard at the joke.

Sunny glanced at the woman, who wasn't laughing, whose watery eyes seemed locked on Sunny's new shoes and the mass of black seeds about them.

The woman grabbed a stack of papers beside her and shoved them at Mr. Michael. "Lila not care what me think. Here, take what you come for and go."

When Mr. Michael's hands touched the papers, the woman pulled them back, and she launched into a rant. She didn't agree with any of this. "Neena's jumbie guh haunt me for this," she said. "And me bet Lila want that cause she blame me for everything." As if the old lady had told Neena to sneak out of school to gallivant in rice paddies with her Muslim boyfriend and get bitten by a snake. As if she wanted to come home from the market to find Neena dying, the boy crying because the fools were too stupid to go to a hospital, more afraid of getting in trouble than death. They should've known better at fifteen. She blamed the boyfriend, that Muslim, nothing but trouble. And she blamed Lila for abandoning Neena. "Old lady like me can't raise girl pickney alone. No wonder she turn out wild. Wild-wild, just like she mammy." She would forsake Lila the way all her children forsook her after their father died. The one in Trinidad who ran off with an old man. Her drunkard son in Wakenaam. And now Lila, setting Neena's jumbie on her.

Sunny squeezed more seed pods as the woman spoke.

Mr. Michael pulled the documents from the woman's skeletal fingers. "Aunty, I know for a fact your grieving daughter want the best for you. She plan to send for you, too, when she get the money."

"Me want nothing with America," the old lady spat. "With Lila? So she can tell me do this and do that? Nah."

"Last night was the thirteen-night, right?" Mr. Michael said, changing the topic. "I have a friend bringing tomato choka and puri soon. Neena favorite, right?"

The thirteenth night after her death. The night the girl's jumbie should have departed. The evening for offerings. They were too late. Sunny trembled despite the heat.

"Look," Shali said, kneeling. "Let we forget this whole thing."

Deo put his hand on his wife's shoulder. "Shali!"

"Do what you want," Mr. Michael said. "But think this thing through. Lila and Premanand, they expecting Sunny tomorrow. Tomorrow! When that flight take off, the plane expect this girl on board. And Lila, she want Sunny. She need the help. The plan already in place. And you want give up this chance, the best deal of your life?"

Shali shook her head. "Me feel the jumbie."

"Money, money, money," the old lady spat at Mr. Michael. "That all you and Lila care about. You the only one benefit. Not me, and not Neena, rest she soul."

Sunny stopped shaking. Her mother and this woman would save her.

"Ho, ho," Mr. Michael laughed. "You think Neena don't want this? You out of your mind. Look, money come, and money go.

Me not worry about money. But what me know for sure is Neena jumbie orchestrate this whole thing."

Everyone stared at him, even the old lady.

"Think about how the day, the very day of Neena funeral, bless she soul, I should run into Deo. Twenty years I haven't seen this man, and then I find out he daughter is the spitting image of Neena, that he used to work your rice paddy. Find out Sunny could take Neena place, set a course for she family betterment, and give Lila the help she need. Who else make this happen but Neena jumbie? Neena, bless the girl, she lead everybody right here. And that girl jumbie not guh rest till we make this happen. That is how me see things."

Mr. Michael's words changed the tide.

Even Sunny felt buoyed by this hint at divine action. Maybe God wanted her in America. Maybe God needed her in America. She burst another pod.

The old woman turned to her. "Come, child."

Sunny glanced at her mother, who stared into clasped hands. With no other choice, she approached the old woman.

"You everything like Neena and nothing like Neena, rest she soul," the woman said, her hazy gaze washing over Sunny. "Neena never stand quiet like that."

The woman pointed to a framed, garlanded photo with shaky hands. "This Neena," she said. "The neighbor take this picture. Lila get one copy, and that all she know of she daughter. She not see this girl in six years."

Six years' time.

The girl in the photo smiled over her shoulder. Dressed in a green school uniform, she was midstride out the gate Sunny recently entered. The old woman was right. She looked like Sunny, and she didn't. The girl in the picture laughed with her eyes and stared at the camera with a defiance Sunny dreamed of owning. Her face was thinner and a wheatier shade of brown. Yet, they resembled each other. Even if Sunny rarely saw her reflection in a mirror, the only one in their house being in their parents' wardrobe, she knew this.

The woman continued. "Neena and Lila always fight like cat and dog. Neena never want leave me for America. Never want leave she boyfriend. Never want work on some farm and live with she father she fight with and barely know. Maybe you right. Maybe Neena jumbie want this." The woman stoked the fire, and it flared. She started singing a warbled bhajan, and Sunny's family slowly joined in, "Om jai jagdish . . ."

It was as if they sang to unite Sunny with Neena's ghost. Sunny wanted to cry and laugh, but her insides numbed as she stared into the fire, flames leaping out like pecking toucans' beaks.

After the prayer, Sunny hovered outside her body as if she'd been expelled from it. Mr. Michael's friend delivered the tomato choka and puri, and Shali served it on giant eddo-leaf plates plucked from the old lady's yard. Mashed red food pooled in the leaf's cupped center, and small bits of gravy beaded on the water-repellent surface like droplets of blood. Sunny had trouble bringing the food to her mouth.

The old lady climbed upstairs and returned with an armload of clothing that she stuffed inside the brown suitcase. Then she smeared a turmeric-sandalwood paste on Sunny's forehead. Resigned, Sunny felt herself bow to accept this blessing. The woman muttered a prayer as her family filed out of the gate. Sunny didn't look back.

Mr. Michael joined them on the return ferry ride and handed her father a drink. The sun blazed low. Though Sunny watched the sunset from the upper deck with everyone, she felt alone.

When they reached the dock, the market had been all packed up. Raj and Jeeve waited for them, Jeeve grinning and waving the handful of bills he'd earned. Sunny returned to herself as Jeeve told stories of bartering, and she veered with him and Roshi toward the waiting van. Her father's hand on her shoulder stopped her.

Her mother smiled a strange smile and pulled her into an embrace. She couldn't recall her mother ever holding her so close. She was just getting used to the sensation of soft flesh pressed against her when the hug ended.

"Be good, and do what the lady say," her mother said, wiping the corner of one eye before picking up Indy and turning away.

Sunny nodded to her mother's back as Raj, Jeeve, and Pappo offered awkward hugs.

"We guh see you in six years time," Raj said. "We all depending on you."

"Yeah, you guh make more money than me," Jeeve laughed. "Send me some."

When Roshi hugged her, Sunny felt the weight of reality. *Six years' time.* She'd been given more responsibility than any of her brothers, and failure wasn't an option. All of their money was riding on her. She decided then she'd do everything asked of her. She'd listen to Mr. Michael and the lady. She would do it for Roshi. For her father. For all of their dreams.

Roshi pulled back and mimed eating an apple, still playing a game. Sunny smiled, feeling ages older than her big sister.

The driver of the waiting van honked, and Sunny pulled Roshi tight. Then, Deo planted a heavy hand on her shoulder and motioned for Roshi to leave. His hand stayed on Sunny as if to keep her from following. The van took off the second Roshi entered, and it was down the street by the time Roshi joined Jeeve and Pappo in the back window to wave. Sunny lifted an arm as the van turned out of sight. She was too late, but she waved anyway, knowing Roshi was doing the same.

8

The Backtrack

Mr. Michael took Sunny and her father to a pink concrete house amid a row of pastel homes, all an arm-span away from each other. Few trees grew among them, and a web of electric wires crisscrossed the sky.

Inside, a bare bulb cast dim orange light, illuminating a narrow hall. The air felt too thick to breathe.

"I hardly use this place," Mr. Michael said, pointing Sunny and her father to a room with thin mattresses on the floor that smelled of dust and sweat. "I share with some people who go back and forth to the States."

They left her suitcase in the room and followed Mr. Michael to an indoor kitchen. The small U-shaped space featured beige counters, a white sink, a fridge, and an electric stove. She gawked at the opulence. Everything felt surreal ever since the van had driven away with Roshi.

"We got work," Mr. Michael said, pulling drinks from the fridge. He handed Sunny a cold Pepsi, an entire bottle just for her.

She took a tentative seat next to her father at a square vinyl-covered table. The soda's effervescence stung her sinuses.

"For the next twenty-four hours, your name Anita Jagroop," Mr. Michael said, looking at her. "You understand?"

She nodded, although she didn't understand.

"If anyone ask, you say, 'My name is Anita Jagroop.' Repeat that."

She did, her voice barely rising in the stuffy room.

Mr. Michael explained the convoluted scheme. He'd procured passports from legal US residents, New Yorkers named Jagroop, a father and a daughter. Neena Das's photo had replaced thirteen-year-old Anita Jagroop's photo, and tickets and visas were issued in the Jagroops' name. Before she died, Neena was to impersonate Anita to get to America. Now Sunny was pretending to be both of them. She was a girl inside a girl inside a girl.

Mr. Michael said, "Under no circumstance will you say your real name." She nodded and scrawled *Sunny* in the bottle's condensation.

"This is my father, Narine Jagroop," she was to say if asked about Mr. Michael. She recited those words and others as she pressed and released her hands on the table, marveling at the sticky vinyl and the book-talk coming from her mouth.

That night, she was unable to sleep on the bare mattress. She felt Neena's jumbie in every dark corner. The room's mesh window failed to keep out mosquitoes, so she slapped bugs and watched the mosquito coil's smoke spiral toward an orange streetlamp that burned all night. Laughing voices drifted past, and her father snored on the floor beside her. She resisted scratching, knowing her mother wouldn't want her showing up in America peppered with scabs. She practiced, *My name is Anita Jagroop*, wondering if the real Anita Jagroop knew someone else was reciting her name, or if she was dead like Neena.

As the sky lightened, sleepiness crept into her. Her eyelids had just drooped when her father hocked phlegm and shuffled about. Heavy with exhaustion, she rose and dressed in the flowered frock, rubbing the small welts on her body to ease their itch. She wove a yellow ribbon into her plait, practicing, *My father is Narine Jagroop.* When her real father squeezed her shoulder—an unexpected intimacy—she froze and her brain groped for his name.

"You know you lines?" he asked. "Because if you mess up, we guh get jail."

She nodded as his name surfaced.

"You doing a big thing for the family, you know that?" he said, pulling her to him and kissing her head.

She gasped at the surprise of this brief embrace. His stiff chest, his lips on her head. She clenched her jaw to keep from crying.

"Me get the address. We guh write this month, see that things going okay. Michael guh keep us up to date, too."

She nodded, feeling prized, feeling like a favorite.

In the car, greens and browns flashed past, dizzying her. Then, a rainstorm started, and the colors grayed. The driver parked under an eave, and she followed Mr. Michael and her father into a large building, smelling of mildew. She practiced, *I live in New York, and we are stopping over in Miami.*

As Mr. Michael handed over papers and talked with officials, her insides churned. *I am thirteen years of age.*

When her father patted her shoulder and said, "You sharp. You guh do good," she practiced, *I enjoyed my holiday here in Guyana.*

She pushed through a turnstile ahead of Mr. Michael, marveling at the shiny metal thing, hoping for a second turn before realizing she'd been separated from her father. He stood on the wrong side with his arms crossed, a sad smile on his face. She clutched her purse and practiced. *I am meeting my aunty in Miami.* She curled her toes in her new shoes as her father nodded slightly and said, "Me guh see you at the window," before walking away.

They entered a room with rows of attached seats, and she sat down next to Mr. Michael, admiring his clean white sneakers. As the room filled up, she kept her head down, examining people's shoes, feeling pride when she spotted sandals similar to hers. A while later, a lady spoke into a speaker, and everyone rose. She followed Mr. Michael into a queue leading outside.

She expected to see her father again. But she now faced an enormous expanse of wet black concrete, on which sat an enormous airplane. The airplane wasn't smooth like a bird; it was a patched-together thing. Seams and rivets covered the beast, and a metal staircase led into its belly. Because of the rain, it emanated a heavy chemical scent, and near its wheels, oily puddles bore glistening rainbows.

She looked back at the building. To her left, a rain-bleared window obscured colorful, moving blobs. Was her father there? Waving?

Mr. Michael urged her along, and she followed him toward the plane and up the stairs. Glancing between the blurry airport window and the plane's joints, she tripped and caught herself. She looked back to see if someone had grabbed her, if someone was stopping her from getting on. But no one was there.

Electric lights illuminated the plane's interior, and a neat array of plush blue seats offered themselves up. Mr. Michael pointed her to a spot next to a window. When a stewardess approached, she ducked to make herself small, worried the woman would drag them to jail.

She sat stiffly, staring at the paper-filled pocket as the stewardess told Mr. Michael in perfect book-talk that his daughter should buckle her seat belt. She flinched when Mr. Michael skimmed her lap and snapped the belt. Mr. Michael pushed up the window shade, and light blinded her. The sun had suddenly come out, and the trees beyond sparkled as if in celebration of how far she'd gotten. But her eyes focused on the wing's seams, flaps, and motor bits. How did such a machine stay afloat?

She jumped when the plane vibrated and hummed like a tractor. A voice mumbled indecipherably through an overhead speaker, and the plane began to move. Her body bounced as if she were in a van, rumbling along a road, bypassing potholes. She pulled the blind down, opened it, then shut it again. She didn't want to witness the plane falling apart. Mr. Michael leaned back and closed his eyes as the rattling plane picked up speed. She gripped her seat's armrests and recited her lines. *I stayed with my family in Berbice when I visited.*

Just then, the noises softened, her body angled back, and her stomach floated up to her throat.

She nudged the blind open and imagined her family staring up. She pressed her face to the scratched glass, hoping to find her house, but milky clouds swirled below. Certain that Roshi was somewhere waving, she tucked her shoulder into the seat crevice and waved back at the foggy nothingness.

Suddenly, Mr. Michael was shaking her awake. She jerked up, thinking they'd been caught. But he said, "We almost there. Eat your food."

Groggy, she tried to make sense of the sealed, sectioned plastic plate on the tray before her. Green leaves, a gray blob, and a pinkish thing that looked like uncurried fish. A dark, white-frosted square resembled the black Christmas cake she loved.

Mr. Michael opened a package and dumped a plastic knife, fork, and napkin on the tray. Then, he peeled the film off the plate, releasing a smell like the inside of a used lunch tiffin.

"American food," he said, pointing. "Salad, mashed potatoes, chicken breast, and chocolate cake. Hurry up."

Unsure of how to use the utensils, she lowered her mouth and nudged food inside with the fork. Everything tasted bland, except the cake, which was delicious, if overly sweet. But it was nothing like black cake. A cup of water sat on the tray without a ripple of movement even as clouds swirled past the window. She marveled that she was moving so fast while sitting still.

The stewardess cleared her tray and dumped the plastics. Sunny swallowed remorse—her family would have reused those items lovingly. She should have saved the utensils in her purse, now wedged in the space between her seat and the wall.

"You missed the snack," the stewardess said, pulling a packet of peanuts from an apron pocket, gifting it to her.

Sunny took it without meeting the woman's eyes.

The plane's drone deepened, and her ears ached from pressure. Outside, a grid of land and roads peeked up through patchy clouds. Nothing was as she expected. The ground was simply ground. Americans didn't live in the clouds.

She'd never really expected to touch America. She'd expected to be caught, perhaps hoped for it. As land hurtled toward them, her stomach levitated once more. She gripped the bag of peanuts and held her breath. Her body pitched forward, and she bounced in her seat as the airplane thudded onto the runway. Everyone clapped as if they, too, had feared the plane might fall apart. It slowed to a crawl before stopping.

Mr. Michael said, "Unbuckle. Let's go." He stood, grabbed a bag, and walked into the aisle. She followed, focusing on the ground. She only realized they'd exited the plane when they traded metal flooring for thin, gray carpet. She paused to take in the strange flooring, looking back to figure out how they'd exited the plane without descending stairs and walking outside.

"Stay close," Mr. Michael barked.

They hurried through a tunnel that emptied into a crowded hall. They climbed staircases, turned corners, and followed a crowd that joined a mob in an atrium that was remarkably clean and white, perhaps like the inside of a cloud, unscented and cold. People had sectioned themselves into lines, and Mr. Michael steered her into the longest one.

She'd never been in a grander place. Officials spoke through overhead speakers, and the soaring ceiling gobbled up their words. The scrape of suitcases, footsteps, and chatter created a low drone as she shuffled behind Mr. Michael in line, studying people. She'd expected paper-white skin, and she felt foolish seeing shades of pinks, oranges, yellows, even brown. Not a single other person wore plaits or ribbons. The children wore sneakers like Mr. Michael's. She felt a twinge of shame for her new sandals. Then a twinge of guilt.

They approached a man in a glass booth, and Mr. Michael handed over passports and papers. Sunny shifted from foot to foot, staring at the man who asked Mr. Michael questions. He was pinkish with yellow hair, much like Annette's Barbie.

He held the passport up and stared at her unsmilingly. "And who might you be, young lady?" His eyes darted between the passport and her face.

She curled her toes. *Who might you be, young lady?* His strange and beautiful words stopped her.

He raised his voice. "What's your name?"

Names flashed through her mind. Sunny. Sunita Kissoon. Neena Das. "Anita Jagroop?" She uttered the name like a question, as if asking, is this one right?

It was right. The man put the passport down and continued stamping. "Did you enjoy your trip?"

"Yes," she said. Believing she was still being tested, she added, "I live in New York and come for holiday."

The man cocked his head, and she worried she was supposed to say "came" or "went." She'd messed up. The man smiled and said, "Welcome back," returning the papers to Mr. Michael. To the line, he shouted, "Next."

She expected a reprimand from Mr. Michael, but he motioned her forward. They passed through a hall with a scuffed, peeling floor. Then, they met a terrifying chomping staircase.

Seeming to anticipate Sunny's fear, Mr. Michael guided her shoulder. When he released her, she wobbled and peed a little. She clutched the moving handrail and floated down amid a crowd that behaved as if moving stairs were normal. Her face flushed, and wetness glued her legs together. At the bottom, she stumbled off. Afraid of losing her bladder, she held her crotch, and Mr. Michael pointed to a washroom sign.

She studied people in line to figure out what to do. Inside a stall smelling of chemicals, she fumbled to lock the door. Then she climbed onto the shiny white seat, squatting on it as if in an outhouse. She spied feet in adjacent stalls and shuddered. Had others sat directly on their seats? She used wads of the free, soft toilet paper to absorb the dampness in her underwear, and she folded squares for her purse wondering how to send some home to Roshi. Roshi would be amazed.

After, she found Mr. Michael speaking on a pay phone, leaning against a wall. He balanced the receiver between his ear and shoulder as he flipped through some papers and motioned her over with his chin.

"I just have customs left," he said before hanging up.

He led her to a place where suitcases whizzed by on a clacking metal belt. Mr. Michael grabbed her suitcase, as well as a large black one she didn't recognize. For the first time, she wondered if he was joining her at Lila's, and she found herself hoping for it, to hold on to something vaguely familiar.

They stood in another line with the luggage, and Mr. Michael threw the suitcases onto a different moving belt that entered a tunnel. He handed documents to someone, and Sunny feared more questions. But the official barely glanced at the papers before waving them on.

They exited through two sets of automatic doors into a dark, loud tunnel smelling of car exhaust. Busses and cars honked. Headlights flashed. People moved every which way.

Just as she started to panic, Mr. Michael patted her head and said, "Ha, ha. Welcome to America, girl."

MAYA

ATLANTA, GEORGIA

"Who's Sunny?"

I feel Dwayne's gaze.

Outside the window, a breeze plays with the dogwood's leaves, creating dancing shadows on the grass. I'd been staring at the shadows as Dwayne read, thinking about sugarcane and Barbie dolls. Of jumbies and soca music. Of ferries, toucans, and a plane ride. But like the flickering shadows, which seem to have little to do with the tree, the memories feel separate from me.

"Who's Sunny?" Dwayne repeats, tossing the letter on the counter. "What's this about?"

He pours coffee, and the half-folded letter sits there. Just paper. Just ink. Saying things that barely affected him. *Ma pass last year. Gene. Dying sister.*

I meet his eyes and wonder if he glimpses the cracked dam inside me, the swirling memories that cramp my gut, memories I haven't visited in so long. I pull out the envelope and place it next to the letter. I could say, *I'm Sunny. Roshini is my sister. Maybe Vernon can help her and test me for the gene.* But these words collect in my throat, and rightly so. They're the wrong ones after a lifetime of lies,

lies that are impossible to dismantle on a busy school morning. I can't do this here, in front of the kids. And it's unfair to blindside Dwayne when "the sky is falling" for him at work. Plus, a dark, horrible part of me considers the letter's date—over a month ago. Could Roshi be dead already? And if she is, is it worth imploding our lives? Maybe Vernon, Dwayne's oncologist cousin, would test me for the gene without me having to reveal my past. Suddenly grasping for a cover, I mutter, "I don't know. Lost mail."

He picks up the envelope, studies it with a "hmm," and drops it. "It sure rattled you."

Tears spring up and I blink them back. "It's just so sad."

"Hey." He puts down his mug and embraces me, and I feel our boys' eyes. They're used to displays of affection, but this probably feels weird. I pull myself together and nod into Dwayne's chest, focusing on his smell. Soap and cologne, hints of sandalwood and citrus.

"I get it, babe," he says, kissing my head, then pulling back to look into my face. "That's gotta be weird for you—a family hunting for a daughter who doesn't want to be found. But you know you've got all the family you need here."

His dark eyes pierce through me, and I'm awed by his ability to deny the truth staring right at him, by the depth of his belief in that first lie he learned about me.

The late June evening we met, I was shelving copies of Barbara Kingsolver's *Poisonwood Bible*. I'd been working at the bookshop part-time for the discount and to avoid lonely evenings in my sterile apartment after my day job at a dental practice.

He interrupted me, asking, "Is that one any good?" I was used to being asked about books and to rebuffing occasional come-ons. But he struck me speechless with his looming presence. His bright smile and eager face shot a jolt through me; he seemed to glow.

"Um, yeah," I said after recovering. "We're discussing it next Friday if you want to join." My face flamed as the words left me. I'd chosen the book for that month's book club, and I looked forward to a serious discussion about colonialism with the educated housewives and retirees who usually attended. Why had I just invited this man, energy shooting off him like fireworks?

He laughed. "It's actually for my sister, Denise. I need a last-minute birthday gift."

"She'll probably like it. You might, too." Inwardly, I chided myself for the flirting, for breaking all of my rules. Men only ever threw wrenches into my life. By then, I'd earned my career as a dental hygienist by avoiding men. I'd bought a two-bedroom condo and a car without a man. I didn't need a man ruining things. I didn't need anyone. Still, I didn't want this man to leave. His absence would have created an instant vacuum. Even that day, I knew.

"Will you be there?" he asked, his eyes twinkling. "Next Friday?"

A smile took over my face and turned me into a fool. I nodded, allowing him, the first person who'd sparked me in over a decade, to meet the few people I called friends in Atlanta—a group of women already sullied with my falsehoods.

He and his sister showed up early, and by the time I sat down to lead the discussion, they'd swallowed the lies my book club regurgitated. They believed I spent my childhood in foster homes after being abandoned by a family I barely remembered—my stock answer to the "where are you from" question. They also knew I didn't like to talk about it.

Shockingly, Denise turned out to be deaf. And a local celebrity. Dwayne pointed out the children's books she'd illustrated that our store carried, and the group clamored to buy copies for her to sign. Wearing a nose ring, a headful of locs, and a dashiki, Denise looked every bit the part of the accomplished artist. She daunted me by requesting we face her during the conversation, to read our lips. Dwayne's fingers flew to interpret things, but Denise's eyes bored into me as I guided the group. When she spoke, I worked hard to bury thoughts of Roshi, who'd flickered up from the depths.

I knew I should return to the safety of solitude, where my past could stay firmly buried. But I was a moth released from the dark, and Dwayne was a flame I couldn't resist. When his brown eyes met mine, the air grew palpable. I couldn't say no when he invited me to their family's Fourth of July barbeque. "It'll be fun, our family does a huge spread, we have rocket launchers," he said, signing. Denise nodded behind him. Just a friendly dinner, I told myself, just this once.

The house was out in the suburbs on a massive property. Music played in the backyard, and I followed a flag-lined path toward it. Dwayne greeted me with a loud "Look who came," and introduced me to his parents, grandparents, aunts, and uncles, who interrupted their barbecuing and card games to shake my hand. I gushed my thanks at being included and added brownies to a food-laden table. Other family—siblings, in-laws, cousins, nieces, and nephews— were in the middle of a wiffle ball game, adults versus kids. They welcomed me on the adult's team even though I'd never played. It felt like a dream, being embraced by this interracial, intergenerational mélange of smiling faces after being alone for so long.

When we sat down to eat, the conversation meandered from food, to books and music, to work, a clear source of pride for the group. Dwayne's mother was a high school principal, and his father ran the investment firm where Dwayne and another sibling worked. Several family members ran businesses—restaurants and mechanic shops—and there was a doctor and lawyer among the cousins. They effortlessly added sign language to their speech to include Denise and two deaf cousins. They felt out of my league, but I was hungry for family. I wanted more.

The following weekend, Dwayne invited me to a concert, and I found myself on our first official date, sitting on a picnic blanket listening to jazz at the Centennial Olympic Park, the inches between us charged. He poured me a fizzy cranberry-ginger mocktail from a thermos and pointed to my ankle tattoo.

He twisted his head to read it. "'Begin again.' What's the story?"

"My motto, I guess. It's how I survived care. Shake off the negative stuff and move on."

I'd gotten used to speaking that way—revealing just enough truth to mask the lie. And in some ways, I believed the foster care lie. My family *had* sent me to grow up in other people's homes. Wasn't that the very definition of fostering? Semantics, really.

Dwayne studied me and probed, "Does it have anything to do with why you're dry?"

At the family barbeque, he'd confessed to giving up alcohol after a fraternity brother died in a drunk-driving accident. He felt guilty because they'd recently parted ways at a bar; it could have easily been him. I'd said I didn't drink either but hadn't offered details. Now, I said, "Yeah, I had some bad years. Blurry years. Drugs and the whole bit. But that's water under the bridge. This is all that matters, right?" I gestured to the scene, the musicians on stage, the people on blankets, and leaned back onto my elbows in what I hoped was a flirtatious manner. My sundress exposed the tattoo on my shoulder, a singing bird escaping from a cage. His eyes went to it, and he said, "Is that a reference to the Maya Angelou book? The *Caged Bird* one?"

"My favorite." I smiled. "Bookish tattoos are my thing. I have a couple of quotes. Here and here." I pointed to my ribs and hip. "I'm a total geek."

He laughed and reclined next to me. "Red hair and tattoos in secret places. A face made to break hearts. Your goody-two-shoes librarian act doesn't fool me. You're no geek. You're trouble."

I laughed to hide my discomfort. *Trouble*—the word stirred truths that had bubbled in my gut since I accepted his date. *I was never a foster kid. I came to this country illegally. Oh, and I have a deaf sister, too.* But these truths would have forced an excavation of even heavier stuff, stuff I'd spent over a decade sealing away, stuff buried under a life built on a clean slate. The truth wasn't something I could dip my toe into. There was a man out there who could destroy me, a man I couldn't afford to think about. I'd worked too hard to bar him from my mind.

Dwayne was right. I was trouble. But I told myself we were just having fun. The charge between us would burn out, the relationship would soon end, and no one would get hurt. I wiggled my shoulders in time with the music and said, "If you take me dancing, I'll definitely blow my librarian cover."

He laughed a ground-rumbling laugh, stood, and reached down a hand.

We danced right there. People cheered, and others joined, but we entered our own world, moving to jagged beats and reading each other in a way that felt like magic. In that moment, our chemistry was the only truth that mattered. After, he hugged my sweaty body and placed his forehead against mine. It felt more intimate than a kiss. "Please, please, let's do that again."

I met his smiling eyes, so close to mine, and reached my lips to his. Electricity shot through me. *Trouble.*

The truth didn't matter in crowded restaurants and bars, where he was the life of the party and the dance floor always beckoned, where we met friends or coworkers and the deepest thing anyone ever talked about was the basketball score or politics. It receded as he introduced me to spectator sports and the gym, where I embraced exercise, that exalted distraction, and we trained together for 5Ks and half marathons. It even ebbed around his family and Denise, who stopped reminding me of Roshi, though she taught me sign language. On quieter dates, those weekends spent in bed, our bodies fitting together like puzzle pieces, my past sometimes burbled up. But I always pushed it away.

Weeks melted into months, and time, working its charm, buried the truth beneath routines that entwined us—work calendars, race-training schedules, and nights out. A year in, when his lease was up, he moved into my apartment, adapting to my neatnik ways. I convinced myself that the person he knew and loved—me as "Maya"—was true enough and all that mattered. We'd been practically living together anyway, and he seemed to crave me as much as I craved him. Two years in, on a weekend trip to Charleston for a half marathon, he dropped to one knee on the beach at sunset.

"I cannot imagine life without you," he said.

We'd been headed there, of course, but I'd long mastered the art of self-deception. Fear flashed across my face, and I was grateful for the dim evening light. But I, too, could not imagine life without him, so I dropped to my knees saying, "Yes. Yes." My stomach filled with acid as he put the ring on my finger and called me love. We hugged, and I sobbed—tears of joy and tears of fear. How had I let things get so far? Could I marry a man who barely knew me?

That night, he asked, "What was it like growing up in the system? You never talk about it." Memories snapped from the murky deep. *Him. That last day.*

I was at a clear crossroads. The internet had arrived, and I'd briefly thought about looking for Roshi, maybe even for my pursuer. But it felt dangerous, like tempting fates and long-dormant jumbies, releasing the iron grip I kept on the reins of my life. Mine was a life I cherished, made full by Dwayne. I feared jeopardizing it. Even if I'd been ready to reveal what I'd done, to talk about the man with a vendetta, to discuss the father I'd come to despise, I knew I'd waited too long. The light in Dwayne's eyes would certainly dim. His trust might vanish, his love might diminish, and his family, especially Denise, would feel betrayed.

I'd already lost too much family. I couldn't risk losing them. Losing him.

I teared up. "I barely remember it. But it was the opposite of this, the opposite of love." And that felt like the truth.

He kissed me and said, "Maybe you should try therapy."

I shook my head. Therapy was for sick and broken people defined by things they didn't choose. People who dwelled in the past. I had refused to be defined by my past, had blossomed despite it. I'd healed myself and sealed away everything bad, and I would be fine as long as I didn't think of it, as long as the past stayed where it belonged. "I don't want to dig at a scar," I'd said, determined to never look back and to keep control of my life.

But there was no scar. There was a scab that refused to heal. And now, decades later, this letter has pried it loose, teaching me it's impossible to sever the past and control it. The past can persist through one indestructible thread. *Gene.*

Dwayne's phone buzzes, grounding us back into reality. I extract myself from his arms and motion for him to take the call. "I'm fine, babe. I don't know what's come over me. Let me take the boys to school. You've got all those fires to put out."

"No, no," Dwayne says, turning to answer the phone. "You deserve your day off."

And just like that, everything resets, giving me time to do this right.

I turn to Nico and Camden, who've barely eaten. I'm glad to see they're ignoring us. They're deep in a sign language conversation about a toy car Cam believes Nico lost, and I fill with wonder at their easy communication. What I would have done to converse with Roshi that way. I rap the counter to get their attention, then sign, "Chocolate prize—first to finish. Dad, lots of work, leaving twenty minutes. Don't worry—car, we'll find."

The boys turn from each other, and in Nico's smirk and Cam's pout, I see flashes of my lost siblings. I shake the faces from my head and pack lunch boxes. I sanitize the counter and fill the dishwasher while avoiding the letter, still face up by the coffee machine.

By the time they're ready to leave, the letter's grip on me has loosened. In the mudroom, I pull cleats and shin guards from Nico's cubby and tuck them into his soccer bag. I remind him of practice after school and hand him his chocolate prize. When he hugs me, I hold him an extra few seconds before letting him race through the garage door to claim shotgun, the coveted position in Dwayne's new car—a black SUV with heated front seats. Cam tries to escape without a hug, so I catch his shoulder and point to my cheek. He rolls his eyes with typical preteen surliness but kisses me anyway. I embrace him and hand him a chocolate, too, then sign, "See you, classroom. Volunteering later." He smiles and nods, then saunters off.

Dwayne comes behind me, phone pressed to his ear, uh-huh-ing into the mouthpiece, clearly listening to a client's rant. He smirks playfully, then presses his lips to mine, pushing me lightly against the washing machine. He lets out a soft "mmm" even as his client speaks, making me laugh.

As he backs the SUV out of the garage, my red convertible comes into view. It's no longer new but it still makes me smile, this impractical and flashy gift from Dwayne when I turned forty, fit for his "dancing queen." I imagine Roshi raising her eyebrows in approval, but I also remember I wasn't really forty that day. I'll have to admit that now.

Out in the driveway, Nico waves wildly from the front seat, which I'm sure is on full heat despite the sixty-five-degree morning. "Love you, good day," I sign, as I wonder how many more times I'll get to do this. Could I already have the cancer?

When they're gone, I sit on the bench, exhausted, and the letter's grip returns. *Ma pass, gene, dying sister.* What will I do?

Dwayne's earlier question echoes. *Who is Sunny?*

It's the question I must answer to move forward. And to do that, I must exhume her. Sunny—a shattered, unrecognizable mess buried deep inside. I need to face her before I can introduce Dwayne to her and everything she's running from. Before I can think about this gene. Before I can attempt to help Roshi, if I'm not already too late.

PART TWO

SUNNY-NEENA

SUMMER 1985
MIAMI, FLORIDA

9

Friendly Flowers

A MERICA. IT DIDN'T SMELL like apples. It smelled of gasoline and burnt rubber packaged in air that wooshed over her as vehicles sped past. It smelled like chaos.

As Sunny stood with Mr. Michael on the concrete island, cars zigzagging about them, she recalled the busy ferry station with its banana-seawater scent. How light that air seemed in comparison, how tame the traffic.

A car pulled up, and a woman jumped out to hug a man who stood next to Sunny on the island. The man pulled the woman close and kissed her on the lips. Sunny looked down, embarrassed. What would her family think? Then she smiled, imagining Roshi adding the kiss to her routine, hugging herself and puckering.

What was Roshi doing? Was it Sunday afternoon? Monday? Because she'd slept on the plane, Sunny didn't know. She pictured Roshi cross-legged in church, no one beside her to point out words in the prayer book. Roshi in the bottom-house after church, eating metemgee on the stoop, alone. Cleaning out the chicken coop, alone. Were they going about as if nothing happened? A rock grew in her throat. Had anyone noticed her missing yet, her family being so large? Annette would notice, certainly. Sunny pictured Annette's face twitching with jealousy.

Mr. Michael interrupted her reverie. "Here's Lila."

The kissing couple were gone, and a small gold-colored car sat at the curb. The woman inside glared at her without a hint of a smile. This was Lila. Her new mother. She'd pictured a warmer, younger version of Neena's nani. That picture dissolved as she met this woman's accusing eyes.

Lila did not exit the car, but Sunny could tell she wore pants. This surprised her as much as seeing the woman behind a steering wheel. Guyanese women didn't wear pants or drive cars. And they were bigger. The tiny woman didn't even look pregnant from Sunny's vantage. She looked about Sunny's size.

Sunny looked down, feeling stupid in her dress and ribbon. Her mosquito bites itched, but she resisted them.

Mr. Michael put their luggage inside the trunk, then opened the passenger door. Music on the radio poured out.

Sunny slid inside, running her palm along the velvety seat. A chemical scent filled the air, not quite that floral apple smell she'd craved but an improvement from outside. She expected Mr. Michael to introduce her. Practiced words flitted around her head as he took the front seat. *Hi. Hello. Nice to meet you. Sorry about your daughter. Thank you for bringing me to America.* But no one spoke, and her throat grew dry with this absence of words.

As the car flew from darkness into the blazing afternoon sun, an American song blared. In it, a man crooned for someone to take a look at the empty space around him. Tears filled her eyes. Annette, her family, Roshi—they should all take a good look at her now, speeding along a pristine ribbon of a highway, amid so many cars and gigantic buildings. She brushed away a hot tear, and her finger grazed the mole that had cursed her. She faced the window, trying hard not to listen to the music, praying for the song to end.

As if hearing her wish, Lila turned off the radio. "You fucking liar," she said.

Startled, Sunny looked at the adults, both staring forward.

"You said you'd bring my money," Lila continued. Her voice was unmistakably Guyanese, but so American, clearly book-talk. What lies and money was she referring to?

"I am not taking this girl," Lila said.

Sunny's insides clenched.

"Lila, how many times we confirmed this? Three? Four?" Mr. Michael's voice was steady.

"Everybody expecting my daughter," Lila shouted. "How can I explain this girl?"

"And that's *me* problem now? Look, if that's your worry, just call the girl Neena."

No, Sunny wanted to shout. She was not Neena and should not be called Neena. If this woman didn't want her, maybe she could go home, and no one would get jailed. Her father would be angry, yes, losing so much money in this gamble, and she might have to kneel on rice. But she'd be where she belonged—her crowded bottom-house, not this car.

"I didn't ask for this," Lila said. "I asked for my money back."

"Me ears hear you ask for this exactly," Mr. Michael said. "Just yesterday morning. You can't call the day we depart and say you change your mind, demanding money back. That money long gone. How you think I pay for things—tickets, passports, papers? That stuff not free. So how can I give back money I don't have? This transaction break me, you hear? Every penny sink with this ship, and you expect me to smile and walk away like some dancing monkey? Lady, me a businessman, and businessmen don't run they business like that."

"If you broke, you doing something wrong," Lila said, her book-talk faltering. "Me know what me pay you. You minting money and taking me for a ride."

Mr. Michael laughed, and Sunny prickled with sweat.

"I hired you to bring my daughter," Lila said, "and this girl is not my daughter. When I find out you expect more money, the deal was dead. You expect *me* to pay *you* to keep her? After all I paid? After her family probably paid you, too. You must take me for a fool."

"You must take *me* for a fool. You asked for help with your baby, housework, and farmwork. You expect that for free? I find a solution for you, so I expect the girl to pay her passage. And you're the one holding the purse. Now you're behaving like I lie to you? You lying to yourself, woman."

"You snake," Lila hissed. "You preyed on me. I was in shock, mourning Neena."

"Look, you keep running your mouth, and my sympathy guh run out. I give you a deal since your daughter died, but the price can jump."

"I ain't paying shit, and you can keep your girl."

Mr. Michael chuckled. "Girl or no girl, you still paying. So, if I were you, I would shut my mouth and take what I get. If I don't see my money, you can expect immigration authorities at your front door. I don't play games."

Sunny's head throbbed with sudden understanding. She wanted to disappear. What would her father say if he knew Mr. Michael had used them all? And what would happen now that Lila didn't want her? Would she work for Mr. Michael, or return home? Would they get jailed?

"You think your hands clean?" Lila said. "Deport me, fine. I guh go back. But you? You guh face jail time."

Mr. Michael emitted a shrill, high-pitched laugh that made Sunny jump.

"Jail time?" he asked when he composed himself. Then he slipped into book-talk that trumped Lila's. "For what, exactly? Do you know my given name? Do you know my address? You know nothing. Where's all your evidence? Cash transactions and phone conversations? Show that to the police. Look, the price just jumped to one thousand. Threaten me again, it guh be fifteen hundred. Expect me or my associate every couple months. At least two hundred every time till you pay up. And if you don't have it, pack your bags and watch your back. You can't hide from me or the INS."

Outside, a metal guardrail whizzed by. Sunny levitated as the world sped past.

"Exit here," Mr. Michael commanded.

Lila left the highway for a house-lined road. Squat homes pressed right to the ground, clearly never having to deal with floods. Green squares of lawn and gray squares of concrete fronted each house, and metal fences separated them. In one driveway, a little girl wheeled a pink bike with handlebar streamers. This might have brought Sunny joy and made her feel like she'd finally arrived in America if the air in the car hadn't turned yellow. If the air didn't feel like a weight on her chest, if sweat didn't drip down her back, if her dress didn't cling.

"Drop me off there," Mr. Michael ordered, pointing to a corner. "The girl, too, if you don't want her."

"Me promise to take you to you friend house, so that where we going. Me want meet this *associate*," Lila said, her Guyanese lilt exaggerating the last word.

"Here."

The car screeched to a stop along the sidewalk.

"Get out and take out the black bag," Mr. Michael ordered.

"You get out. Me giving you a ride. You should pay me and get the hell out!"

"You must really want the price raised again. You think me stupid? Me know you plan to drive off with me suitcase."

Lila jumped out, popped the trunk, and threw the suitcase onto the sidewalk. A latch popped open, and clothes protruded.

Shouting obscenities, Mr. Michael got out, and Sunny wondered if she should get out, too, or if she should wait for the woman to throw her out. But Lila marched back into the car and peeled off as Mr. Michael kicked the door.

Lila turned the music up as she reentered the highway. Sunny hoped the woman would return her to the airport. A nasally voice sang about girls wanting to have fun. *Fun.* That word belonged in Guyana, not here. Fun was running down dirt paths, dancing to soca, swinging hard in a hammock.

Lila turned down the radio and met Sunny's eyes in the rear view. "You can clean?"

Sunny nodded.

"You can talk?"

"Yeah."

"You should say, *Yes*, not *Yeah*."

Sunny nodded.

"Say it," Lila said.

"Yes."

"You have a lot of brothers and sisters?"

"Yes."

"So you probably did a lot of cleaning."

"Yes."

"Your sisters helped? How many sisters do you have?"

"Tree."

"It's *three*, not *tree*. *Tree* is the plant. *Three* is the number."

Sunny seized with shame.

"Say *three*."

She whispered, "Th-r-ee," turning the word into three syllables.

Lila laughed a manly laugh that belonged to a bigger body, and Sunny curled her toes in her sweaty sandals.

"I have a cleaning job, and you might as well start today. That snake wants his money."

Sunny nodded, then said, "Yes."

Lila exited the highway and drove past two-story houses, separated by bushes, trees, and wood fences. These had long driveways boasting bigger lawns, and Sunny felt stupid to have admired those earlier houses.

Lila sighed and said, "God, that mole. You look just like her."

Should she say yes?

"Seeing you, I thought Michael lied. My own mother, too. How could Neena be dead when she's right here? I still feel crazy looking at you."

Sunny looked down.

"I was foolish, opening my big mouth. Now, Janna, people at the farm, everybody expecting Neena. And then, I just couldn't . . . I still can't believe . . ."

Sunny nodded sincerely. She couldn't believe any of it either — where she was and all she'd heard the past half hour.

"You're a mouse. Neena, she was a lion. You should have heard her filthy mouth last time we talked. Telling off Prem after he cursed her for seeing that Muslim boy."

Storybook images of a mouse and a lion came to Sunny from something a teacher once read. She couldn't remember much of the story, but she didn't want to be the mouse.

"That snake," Lila resumed, her voice thick, "taking everybody for a ride — you, me, your daddy, too. Everybody expecting something they won't get. I was grieving. For Neena, yes, and for that damn money. It took so long to work. And look where it got me. Me stuck with you, you stuck with me, and Michael winning out."

Outside, the houses gave way to a wall of green as trees whizzed past.

"I was sixteen when I had her," Lila said. "Barely older than her, but just as wild. Ma did everything, so she was more like a sister than a daughter. When I left, I always thought . . . I didn't know . . ." Her voice cracked and she sniffled.

They passed farmland now. Neat rows of crops ticked past, so unlike the overgrown masses of sugarcane and clots of trees and plantings in Guyana. A metal contraption sprayed water like arcs of diamonds over a field, and Sunny imagined herself running in the jeweled drops.

They stopped at a stop sign and turned near a farm. On a sheet of plywood, painted letters said U-PICK STRAWBERRIES. Kids raced up a field carrying green baskets, laughing and eating fruit. *Fun.*

"You know about Prem?" Lila asked, her controlled voice returning.

Sunny nodded. She knew Lila's husband was named Premanand.

"Stay clear of him, you hear? He don't like when things don't go his way. He told me to end this thing with Michael."

Her stomach knotted even as the car drove past some of the most beautiful flowers she'd ever seen. It was like Annette's crayon box spilled and came to life. But she couldn't enjoy the sight with Prem now on her mind.

Lila pulled into a dirt lot adjacent to the colorful field. A hand-painted sign read FRIENDLY FLOWERS. It stood near a shaded wooden stand that sold rainbow-colored bouquets, arranged in staggered buckets. A smaller cardboard sign read GERBERA DAISIES.

Beyond, there was a tall fence. Green strips woven through the chain link hid what was behind it. Lila got out of the car and walked to the fence. She slid open a gate to reveal a compound of metal buildings.

As Lila returned to the car, a young, half-naked woman ran from the flower stand. "Lila! Lila! Hola! Is this Neena?" She looked about Ravi's age and wore the shortest pants Sunny had ever seen, exposing every bit of her sturdy, golden legs. Her T-shirt had been slashed from midriff to hem, and belly flesh showed through the gaps.

Sunny wondered if *hola* was an American word.

"Yvonne, don't you have work?" Lila asked.

Ignoring this dismissal, Yvonne waved. Red lipstick marred her teeth, but her skin was smooth and creamy and black hair swirled in waves about her face. Her brown eyes twinkled. "Hi, Neena, how was your trip?"

Sunny blinked at being called Neena. She nodded as if that answered the girl's question and looked away from the lipstick, her lips forcing the smile she'd given to Mr. Michael in the bottom-house.

"Yvonne, there's people waiting," Lila said.

"Sí. Sí. I'll show you around later, Neena. Adios y bienvenida." Yvonne ran back to the flower stand.

Lila left the gate open and crunched the car along a wide gravel path, passing rectangular homes propped on concrete blocks. No square patch of grass or walkway fronted these. Clothes fluttered on clotheslines between them, and cars sat in front of some. In front of one, a man glanced up from the wood table where he ate. Through gaps between the homes, Sunny spotted large shed-like buildings beyond, some covered with plastic sheeting. People moved about there, and men hoisted trays of flowers onto a truck that must have used a different entrance.

Lila stopped in front of the boxy home at the end of the compound. "Prem's probably in the greenhouse. Change into something sensible quick so we can leave before he sees you."

Sunny tugged the car door's lever, wondering what Lila meant by sensible. The door didn't budge.

Lila rapped on the window. "You're some kind of royalty? You need me to carry your luggage, too?"

Her body flared with heat as she tried the lever again.

Lila rolled her eyes and pulled the handle. The door was locked. She clicked a button to flip the lock and told Sunny to get out without apology.

10

Kool-Aid and Pop-Tarts

THE TRAILER WAS HOT and smelled of burnt oil. After her eyes adjusted to the dark, Sunny registered a brown plaid couch and an enormous TV on a wooden stand to the right, a tiny kitchen with white electric appliances to the left. She suppressed a smile thinking of watching *Knight Rider* as she cooked on an American stove. She slipped off her sandals but held her suitcase. The checkered linoleum floor under her feet was scuffed, but she dared not place the bag down until instructed. Lila flipped on lights and headed past the kitchen to a door.

"Change in there," Lila said, pointing to a door beyond the TV. "That's your room. And take out that stupid ribbon."

The lightweight door flew open to reveal a room that felt like a sealed box. A metal twin bed and a crib fit against one wall, both dressed in blue cartoon sheets. There was no mosquito netting, but the window was shut tight behind slatted metal blinds. A dresser, holding a digital clock and tiny lamp, sat adjacent to the door, leaving a narrow strip of floor to maneuver about.

Sunny shut the door and put her suitcase on the bed, her hands quivering as she undid her plait. She fingered the frocks, skirts, and blouses that made up her wardrobe, none of which seemed sensible. Neena's jumbie-imbued clothes might be the only clothes Lila approved.

"Hurry up," Lila called.

Startled, she grabbed stiff pants and a T-shirt.

When she emerged, Lila said, "Where'd you get that?"

"Nani," she said before shaking her head at the error. Her own nani hadn't given her a thing, hadn't even known she'd left Guyana. "Uh, Neena nani gimme this."

"Neena's nani gave it to me," Lila corrected before sighing. "Did she give you everything?"

Sunny shrugged slightly and looked down. She should have guessed Lila wouldn't want her in these clothes, fancy factory-made things likely sent from America. She hunted her brain for the right words. "You want I can change? I have skirts and tops."

"No. We don't have time. And leave that purse."

Use more *I*'s, she thought when Lila didn't correct her grammar. She returned her purse to the room, tucking it inside the suitcase. It contained her birth certificate and the peanuts from the airplane. She was reluctant to leave them both. Her father had said the birth certificate was an important document to keep with her always, until Mr. Michael needed it, and her growling stomach begged for the peanuts. But she couldn't argue with Lila.

Lila crunched along the gravel road faster this time. At the gate, Yvonne waved and smiled brightly. Sunny lifted her hand and found a half smile to return.

"That girl's wild," Lila said. "Barely works and full of talk. Stay far from her."

Lila wove the car through gridded streets as guitar-heavy songs played on the radio. Fifteen minutes later, she pulled into a semicircular driveway in front of a blue two-storied house. Sprays of purple flowers bordered the drive and lawn. Plastic flamingos sat in front of coconut trees, and flowering pots decorated the porch. It was a dazzling display of Americana.

Lila led her up a path to a wood-and-glass front door and pressed a button that rang a bell. Colored blobs swam behind the glass as someone approached. A golden-haired, blue-eyed woman opened the door, and Sunny glimpsed plush wall-to-wall carpeting for the first time. Goose bumps played across her skin.

"Oh, Lila. Is this Neena?" the woman gushed. She reached to hug Sunny. "Welcome, Neena. I'm Janna."

Sunny's body tingled with the unexpected hug. She wanted to melt into this flower-scented woman, but her body wouldn't comply. She remained rigid as Janna patted her back.

"She just arrived," Lila said. "Sorry, that's why I couldn't come yesterday and came so late today. She'll help me clean. Is that fine?"

"Yes, of course." Janna pulled back and looked at Sunny's face quizzically. "You're fifteen? You look so young."

Sunny nodded slightly, afraid to look to Lila for confirmation. But Lila said, "Yes. Almost sixteen."

"That's a great age for a summer job."

"I'll teach her, so today might take longer." Lila strode past Janna into the house without removing her shoes.

"Certainly." Janna clapped her hands together. "Hopefully my girls will get back in time. I'd love for them to meet you, Neena."

Sunny bent down to remove her sandals, but Lila said, "Keep them on."

It felt sinful to step on any indoor surface with shoes, let alone such creamy lush carpeting. But Sunny tiptoed behind Lila to a closet that housed cleaning supplies. Lila demonstrated how to make neat, wide stripes across the carpet with a vacuum and how to dust, then she sent her off. Sunny's heart soared, eager for a private moment to kneel and stroke the carpet. As she made stripes, she smiled knowing no one in Guyana could possibly guess what she was doing.

Vacuuming the living areas downstairs, she quickly learned to clear the floor of the family's things lest they clog the machine. She marveled at how many things they owned—multiple televisions, sofas, and display cabinets, and bookshelves so overloaded that books lay tossed on the floor. In a bedroom upstairs, a stack of pillows weighed down a bed, matching the curtains and a thick bedspread. She wished Roshi could see it, so unlike their bed with its thin sheet and meager pillows.

Unable to enter such a beautiful room with shoes on, she placed her sandals outside the door. The carpet felt more sumptuous than she'd imagined, and she grasped it with her toes as she vacuumed. Amber perfume bottles lined a vanity with an ornate trifold mirror, and as she dusted, she wanted to sniff the bottles, to find the scent Janna had worn, but she resisted.

In the adjacent bedroom, toys lay brazenly strewn across the floor. Her heart leapt at the sight of six unboxed Barbies—one naked and one missing a leg. She gathered them tenderly, along with some colorful ponies and a doll that puffed out a candy smell. She sat them on a paper-strewn desk, but after vacuuming, she decided they belonged on the bed. She smoothed the bedsheets, plumped pillows, and straightened the bedspread featuring smiling bears. She was proud to recognize the characters as those on Annette's lunch box—Care Bears. She lined the dolls, even the legless one, and the ponies along the pillows.

"Oh, here you are!"

Sunny jumped at Janna's voice. The carpet had muffled her approach.

"Sorry—" Sunny began, wanting to apologize for touching the dolls.

"Oh gosh, look at how neat you made everything. The toys and the bed. Nicole will love it! The girls just got back. Come meet them."

Sunny set the vacuum in the hall and followed Janna downstairs. Lila glanced at her bare feet as they entered the kitchen, and her face hardened.

Janna's daughters sat at the counter eating a sweet-smelling snack that overpowered the scent of cleaning solution. Sunny's mouth watered as Janna introduced her as Neena.

Leslie, the older girl, spun on her stool and said, "Hi," barely glancing up. She seemed about Baby's age, nine or so, with yellow hair and dusky blue eyes that matched Janna's. Her skin was distinctly pink.

Nicole, who was half Leslie's size, seemed about six. Her frothy hair looked almost white, like fresh ghee, and her eyes were a lighter, glassier blue. "Hey," she said, kneeling on her stool and throwing half her body onto the counter. She stared at Sunny.

"Nic, wait till you see how Neena arranged your dolls," Janna said.

Nicole shoved food into her mouth.

"Remember your Smurf bedding and towels, Les?" Janna asked. "Neena's the one we gave them to."

"Cool," Leslie said, still spinning.

"Neena, you must be hungry," Janna said. "And exhausted. Lila was telling me you *literally* just arrived. Would you like a Pop-Tart?"

Yes, she was hungry, particularly after smelling the sweets. But she didn't have to check with Lila to know she shouldn't accept this woman's food. She shook her head no.

"She ate on the plane, so she's not hungry. And she was sitting all day, so how can she be tired?" Lila said, pausing her cleaning of the stove.

"Travel is exhausting, Lila," Janna said, a reprimand in her tone. "Even if you are sitting. Neena, please. Sit and have a snack."

Janna placed a speckled rectangular pastry on a plate near

Nicole. She also poured a glass of blue liquid. "And have some Kool-Aid."

Who trumped who—Lila or Janna? Janna was Lila's boss, and it was her house. Certainly, Sunny had no choice but to eat this colorful food.

The jam-filled pastry was the sweetest thing she'd ever tasted, surpassing burnt sugarcane, hard candies, and the cake on the plane. She almost gagged on it. But she chewed and swallowed as everyone looked on, chasing it with the refreshing blue water.

"You ever had a Pop-Tart?" Nicole asked. "You like it?"

Sunny nodded and said, "It sweet. Taste like cake."

Nicole laughed. "You talk funny."

"Nicole!" Janna admonished.

"What? She talks funny."

Sunny stared ahead. Her last bite had become a paste on the back of her tongue that threatened to choke her. She forced herself to swallow.

"It's not nice to say that to someone. Up to your room," Janna said. "I'm sorry, Neena."

"But, Mom . . ."

Sunny had never heard such pleading, cloying words. *But, Mom.* Pop-Tart words.

"Now!" Janna commanded.

"You're so unfair." Nicole jumped off the stool and ran upstairs, each footfall producing sound even on the soft carpet.

Leslie grabbed Nicole's half-eaten Pop-Tart and shoved it in her mouth, then whirled in her chair as if nothing had happened.

Nicole slammed her door, and Sunny marveled at the audacity of American girls.

"I don't want she get in trouble," Sunny said. It was her fault she couldn't speak right, not the little Barbie owner's fault. She paused, pulling words together. "Me . . . I guh work on my book-talk. I still not used to it."

"You sound fine, Neena. Just fine," Janna said. "Why don't you help Leslie with her room after your snack. I'd like to discuss something with Lila."

She followed Leslie upstairs, staring at the girl's pink legs, displayed without an ounce of embarrassment. She thought of Yvonne's shorts and wondered if this was the American way.

Leslie's room was an explosion of pink. It contained even more Barbies than Nicole's, but hers were dressed and posed in an enormous dollhouse. Sunny sucked in a breath seeing the tiny bed with its ruffled cover, miniscule plates on a dining table, the luxury lavished on dolls.

Wordlessly, Leslie left Sunny to join Nicole. As Sunny tucked the ruffled pink bedding, the girls whispered and giggled in the other room. Sunny made out one word, *weird*. She hadn't heard the word before, but tone told her everything she needed to know.

She turned on the vacuum to drown out the girls.

Near the bedpost, she spied a tiny toy hairbrush and picked it up before it could disappear into the machine. It featured a Barbie logo, reminding her of Annette's doll's comb, and she thought of Roshi never getting to see such things. Her hand moved the brush into her pocket instead of the dollhouse where it belonged, and her body lit afire. She pushed the vacuum over the same stretch of carpet, the toy burning a hole to her skin. She should return it. God might punish her worse than he'd already done. The toy might be missed. Lila would . . . But as she turned the vacuum off and looped the cord the way Lila had shown her, she knew she'd keep it. Something deep inside her grumbled, insisting. Did she want it for Roshi? Was the ruined lion inside her fighting for something? Or had Neena's jumbie possessed her?

"Neena?" Janna called from the stairwell, startling her again. She hurried to the door, the little hairbrush weighing down her pocket. The girls stood in Nicole's doorway.

"It's all set," Janna said. "I'll help you with your speech for a half hour every time you accompany your mother. I happen to be a speech therapist at the school!"

Oh. Sunny wasn't sure what to say. Janna had lied. She didn't sound "just fine." She sounded funny just like Nicole said, just like she already knew.

"Would you like that?" Janna asked.

She wasn't sure she could handle the golden woman's piercing, expectant eyes. What if Sunny wasn't fixable? What if what was wrong with her was that she belonged in the cane fields instead of that carpeted room full of Barbies? But she smiled and nodded, her throat tight.

"Oh, good! It'll be wonderful for the girls to have such a lovely role model around. Maybe they'll even learn to make their beds!"

In the other doorway, Leslie rolled her eyes, but Nicole's face remained neutral.

Lila walked up behind Janna and said, "We're done for now. I'll take the laundry and see you Wednesday." She threw the contents of the girls' full hampers into large canvas bags and handed them to Sunny.

Sunny carried them out the front door as Lila returned the vacuum cleaner to the closet.

"Bye, Neena," Nicole said, running up to hug her from the back.

Sunny almost fell forward.

"Sorry about what I said." Nicole looked up with glistening eyes. "I didn't mean it."

"Oh." Sunny couldn't hide her shock. She was being touched by a white girl, who'd apologized, whose eyes were puddles capable of drowning her. What was expected of her now?

Nicole stood clutching her, so Sunny placed a laundry bag down and patted the girl's head. As her hand brushed Nicole's feathery locks, she thought, if only Annette could see me now, touching real-life Barbie hair.

11

Three's Company

The TV blared from inside the trailer when they arrived. Lila told Sunny to grab the laundry bags from the trunk as she walked to the front door. Soon after Lila entered, a man barreled out. He was short, but his shoulders spanned the door's width.

Prem.

He stood and stared at Sunny, then he stormed away from the trailer.

She felt shaky as she carried two heavy bags inside.

"Drop them there," Lila said, indicating that Sunny should leave the bags by the door. "Turn off the TV and get the other one."

A woman spoke about a famine onscreen. Photos of dark, naked children flashed as Sunny approached the TV. She had no idea how to turn it off. She stared; a potbellied child cried in front of a thatched home, his skin smudged with orange dust. An image from an alien land.

"I said turn it off."

A cord trailed from the unit to a plug. Hoping TVs worked like vacuums, Sunny pulled it.

"Are you stupid?" Lila huffed. "You can break the thing like that! I didn't say unplug it. Leave it. Go. Get the bag."

Sunny's ears went hot. She fled to retrieve the third laundry bag.

The bag was stuck in the back of the trunk. Sunny climbed inside to unwedge it. She curled up beside it and closed her eyes for a moment.

Dusk had enveloped the farm. Frogs croaked and crickets trilled, reminding her of home. A bird cooed, an eerie jumbie sound that brought gravestones to mind, those in the cemetery where she and Roshi had played. Was it also night in Guyana? A whole day had passed since she'd seen Roshi—a record. *Roshi, they have frogs here, too. They sound different.* She imagined Roshi feeling her thoughts across the miles and smiling.

"Where'd you go?" Lila yelled, silhouetted at the door.

She jumped from the trunk and heaved the bag out.

"You need to listen when I tell you to do something," Lila admonished.

Sunny walked in and placed the bag next to the others.

"We'll do laundry in the shed tomorrow. Go shower, then you can eat."

Sunny looked at her blankly. Was the shed an outside shower like the one she'd known and where she'd washed clothes in Guyana?

Lila sighed and pointed to a door in the small hallway. "The shower is there."

Sunny nodded slightly.

"That woman can only do so much. If you don't talk here, that time with her is a waste."

Sunny stared past her, waiting for more admonishments.

"Girl, move. Go to your room. Get your clothes. Walk in the bathroom and shower. When you're done, come out and eat. Then go back to your room, and sleep on the bed. You need me to explain like you're some two-year-old?" Lila's voice rose as she spoke.

 Lashed by the words, Sunny moved. She passed the silent TV and retrieved her nightshirt and fresh underwear, thinking Lila had used the word *bathroom*, not *washroom*. She'd have to remember that. Then she aimed for the door Lila indicated, passing the kitchen. Faint food smells filled the space, although nothing sat on the stove. Lila stood with crossed arms, staring into a glowing orange box, a bowl rotating inside.

 A dark closet of a room stood beyond the bathroom door, and Sunny stood there.

 "The light switch is on the right," Lila said from the kitchen. "And use the blue towel." It was the kindest she'd sounded all day.

 Sunny flipped the switch, and the room glowed white: white sink, white flush toilet, white floor. The toilet featured a fuzzy green seat cover. A matching green curtain partially hid the shower tub, and green towels hung from towel pegs. But one blue Smurf towel sat folded atop the toilet tank with a new, packaged toothbrush. It all felt so clean and cozy and American, so different from the rusty zinc-walled shower and outhouse she was used to. Staring at the toothbrush, Sunny wondered if Lila had planned to be kind to her before they met, when she thought she'd get Sunny for free.

 She undressed and folded her clothes, placing them on the sink counter. Standing on her tiptoes, she peered into the small mirror. Placed too high, it revealed only her anxious eyes.

 In the tub, Sunny felt proud when she turned the lever and cool water gushed from the spout. She turned the lever upward, expecting water to move to the shower head, but the water grew boiling hot. She'd never bathed with hot water before. She managed to make the water warm and accidentally closed the tub drain. Hot water rose in the tub—more water than she'd ever been rationed in her life. She turned off the water when the tub was half full, afraid Lila would get angry about the waste, and sat in the slick tub. She washed with a bar of green, perfumed soap that made the tub even more slippery, and she slid flat on her back. This turned out to be a good way to wash her hair. Looking up at the white ceiling and shower curtain, warm water lapping her face, she thought, Annette would be jealous. Roshi, too. It was the most luxurious thing she'd ever experienced.

Her head underwater, she heard footsteps, slamming doors, and muted arguments through the wall. She sat up and made out Lila saying, "He brought the girl, what was I going to do? I need the help."

She leapt out of the tub, fearing Lila might knock and say she was taking too long. When she unplugged the bath, draining water muffled their angry voices. Drying herself with the Smurf-covered towel, she suddenly felt Neena's jumbie. Somehow, she knew Neena would have hated the blue creatures and told her mother so, maybe even called them *weird*.

Dressed in her loose nightshirt, Sunny exited the bathroom, expecting Lila and Prem. But sudden silence greeted her. A plate of food—pumpkin and rice—sat on the miniscule dining table. Light shone from under the door to her left, and she felt Lila and Prem there, listening.

Sunny ran on tiptoes to her room, closed the door, and pressed her back to it. The stolen hairbrush dug into her ribcage.

She retrieved the toy and ran its stiff plastic bristles along a tip of her wet hair. When would Roshi see it? *Six years' time?* She hid the toy in her suitcase's zippered pouch, which contained some of Neena's underwear. The foreign clothes suddenly unnerved her, saturated as they were with the girl's spirit, and Sunny threw them in the chest of drawers.

Unthinkingly, her hand brought her white dress to her face, and the smell of home—smoky, earthy, and wet—opened a hole inside her. The room expanded around her, and she grew woozy, as if on a ferry miles from the bank. She wasn't used to this much space, should have never wished for it. She pictured her sisters in bed, tucked in by mosquito netting. *Oh, Roshi. They don't have netting here.* She buried her head in the dress, a portal to home, and she fell into the suitcase on her bed. Knees bent to meet her chest, she squeezed herself inside and pulled the top down like a blanket to cover herself, weeping as quietly as she could.

When she grew hot and could no longer ignore her hunger pangs, she found the tiny bag of peanuts. She wrestled with it but couldn't open it. Another Sunny-proof thing. Like America.

The room had returned to its normal size. She eyed Neena's clothes in the open bureau drawer. Neena would never hide in a suitcase, crying. Neena would walk about the house as if she owned it. She'd eat dinner and maybe even sit and watch the television.

She climbed from the suitcase, determined to channel Neena, the lion. Perhaps Lila and Prem were still in their bedroom, and she could eat quickly and avoid them. The living room was quiet, but when she opened her door, she walked right into Prem.

He cocked his head and stared at her.

Channeling Neena, she stared back. "Hi," she said, wondering if the jumbie had indeed possessed her.

Lila looked up from where she stood at the kitchen sink, surprised.

"Hi," Prem said, stretching out the syllable, a perplexed look on his smooth, round face. His black hair was cut so close to his scalp he looked almost hairless. "It's like me seeing a jumbie. You sure you're not my daughter?"

She shrugged, wondering what Neena would say. "Everybody calling me Neena here, but me think you know me name Sunny." She'd never spoken so brazenly to an adult before.

Prem laughed. "You even sound like my daughter."

Lila harrumphed and washed her plate.

"Nenwah husk," Prem said. "That's what I called Neena. Nenny 'cause she was rough like nenwah husk, telling me off every time we talk."

Sunny thought of the nenwah husks hanging in their outdoor shower, one for each person to scrub with. She liked the idea of becoming abrasive like the dried gourds, like Neena.

"I'll call you Husk," Prem said.

She smiled at this proper rum-shop nickname. An hour before, this man had seemed like a monster. Now, he seemed nicer than Lila.

"Come on, Husk," Prem said, turning to the television. "Get your plate and eat by me. Bet you never eat and watch TV before. That's the best thing about America."

"She needs to eat and go to bed," Lila said. "We got work in the morning."

Ignoring Lila, Prem said, "Go, Husk. Get your food. Lila, give she a beer for me."

Lila slammed the beer next to the waiting plate of food and marched to her room. Sunny floated over to the food. There was a fork beside it. She picked it up, determined to master the utensil. She placed the beer by Prem's feet, propped up on the coffee table. He opened the beer wordlessly, keeping his feet up. The table shook whenever he laughed at the TV show.

Sunny felt strange eating there in her nightshirt. She balanced food on the fork and carefully lifted it to her mouth. It tasted metallic and bland, like it needed salt and a wiri wiri pepper. But she ate every bite, grateful for the first normal food she'd tasted all day.

Onscreen, a couple scantily clad girls argued with a man in a living room. Though Sunny couldn't follow the story, she chuckled along with the laugh track and with Prem, clinging to the small kindness he'd shown.

12

Risky Business

THE FOLLOWING MONTH, SHE was startled from a nightmare when Lila threw open her door. In the dream, she'd hidden from a jumbie who shot seeds from an enormous touch-me-not pod turned machine gun. Seeing Lila in the dark doorway, she clutched her sweaty sheets and gasped.

"Get up," Lila growled. "No more of that useless TV."

This was the first morning Sunny had slept in, the first morning Lila had ever awoken her. She usually sprang up at Prem's footsteps as he left for the greenhouses or field, hurriedly made her bed, dressed, and beat Lila to the kitchen. But exhaustion had caught up with her, and Lila was right. Staying up to watch a horror movie with Prem probably wasn't a good idea. It'd become their thing, though, watching TV, and Sunny treasured it even if the two hardly spoke and Prem often fell asleep, snoring as the shows played on. When he spoke, it was usually to ask her to get him a beer.

On the evenings he quarreled with Lila, Sunny felt united with him against her. The previous night, Lila had started an argument, saying Prem's beer habit cost too much. Prem stood as if to hit her, and she slammed her room's door. He stayed awake during the movie, and during a scary scene, when Sunny squealed, he patted her shoulder and left his arm there. The heavy hand had felt like a hug from a proper American father. Sunny didn't want Lila taking this away.

She jumped into her daily routine, changing from bleach-mottled pajamas into the field workers' uniform of pants and a button-down shirt, hand-me-downs Lila had given her. Mornings, they harvested daisies and sunflowers for the flower stand, then they transplanted seedlings in the greenhouses. They usually worked apart from the others, who chatted in Spanish and whose field harvests were placed on delivery trucks. Midmornings and some afternoons, they left to clean houses. Other afternoons, they dug up and replaced spent rows of plants.

Prem and the second supervisor, Yvonne's dad, patrolled the farm in golf carts, assigning tasks, spraying fertilizers and pesticides, and filling in as needed. Their main job, it seemed, was to please the farm's owner, a man everyone called Jefe, who ran two other farms and came around twice a week. During Sunny's first week, the red-faced owner had said, "I'm a family man, but I don't usually hire children, especially girls. But Prem's a good worker, and if you're as hardworking as your folks, I have no issue with you being here." Sunny fought to meet the daily quotas on her log sheet, and soon, she began to exceed them.

In the kitchen, Lila said, "Hurry up." She left the trailer, slamming the door.

Sunny craved a Guyanese breakfast—dal, rice, and an egg—but she made a bowl of instant Cream of Wheat, the only breakfast Lila allowed. After, she retrieved bread and iceberg lettuce from the fridge. Lunch prep had become her job, and she'd mastered the art of the American sandwich. She felt pride as she operated the electric can opener, mashed mayonnaise into flaked fish, toasted bread, and assembled tuna sandwiches. Only weeks ago,

Lila had yelled at her for being slow and not remembering where the mustard was stored. Now her hands behaved as if she'd made tuna sandwiches her whole life.

In fact, the kitchen was slowly becoming her domain. She'd made a chicken curry the night before. It didn't taste like her mother's, but Prem praised it as the best meal he'd had in years. Now, she wrapped curry into a roti, burrito-style, and left it in the fridge for him. He usually returned to the trailer for lunch, and he'd requested these leftovers. When she suggested packing similar leftovers for their lunches, Lila had said curry stunk up the clients' homes.

Approaching the flower fields, Sunny savored the morning air. The rising sun illuminated a dewy mist that hovered over the daisies and the workers in the distance. Everything glowed angelically, even Lila, who hunched over a row of gerbera daisies.

Lila didn't acknowledge her arrival, and Sunny didn't speak as she donned gloves to protect her hands from the sandpapery stems. Filling a bucket with orange blooms, she wanted to apologize for the late start, but she didn't know how to overcome the silence and negativity that defined their relationship. Plus, she still hadn't addressed Lila directly, not knowing what to call her. She couldn't call her Ma. Calling her Lila was rude. And *Aunty*, the respectful term for adult women, felt off-limits, since it would reveal she wasn't Lila's daughter like everyone thought. Sunny suspected Lila grappled with the same problem. The woman snapped her fingers, saying "girl" or "hey" to get her attention. Sunny wished she'd call her Husk, or even Sunny, an easily explained nickname. Remaining nameless to each other widened the gap between them daily.

She moved to a new row, and Lila said, "You're cutting the stems too low. You ruined that plant."

Sunny didn't respond. Lila made false accusations like that daily.

At the stand, wearing ripped jeans and a cut-off T-shirt, Yvonne staged bouquets in buckets. "Que bonita, chica," she said as Sunny handed over the flowers. "I like these tall ones. I'll put them with these greens! What you think?" She placed a tall flower amid leafy stems.

Yvonne always spoke as if they were friends. But Sunny only ever smiled and nodded, fearful the girl might laugh at her accent. Now, she said, "Looks nice." Her face burned, but the words sounded okay.

"We're late," Lila said, pulling her away as usual. "Let's go."

Yvonne mouthed, "We're late, let's go," mockingly at Lila's back, and a smile darted across Sunny's face.

Lila dropped her off in front of the nurses' house, the first home on their cleaning schedule. Sunny got out, taking her lunch sack. She retrieved the key from under a planter to unlock the front door, then watched Lila drive off. Lila had been leaving her there alone since the week she arrived. The small, neat house — a three-bedroom, two-bath bungalow Sunny had come to realize was typical of America — was never dirty. But she carefully dusted, vacuumed, and mopped it each week.

At first, she felt like a jumbie haunting the empty space. She worried one of the nurses would show up or that she'd do something wrong. But she grew to prefer the solitude. She lingered in front of mirrors as she polished them, trying to find Neena in her face, darting away when the girl's jumbie spooked her. She glanced inside books, sometimes getting lost in their pages for full minutes. And she peeked into drawers and cupboards for a trinket, a thrill she now anticipated every time she cleaned a house.

Pocketing small things had never been her plan, even after taking the toy hairbrush. But a silver button got stuck in the vacuum wand at one house, a dazzling blue bead darted across the floor at another, and a chain of pastel paper clips peeked from under the curtains at Janna's. As she tucked them in her pocket, she imagined showing the things to Roshi. It was wrong, she knew, but they were things no one would miss, and they added a burst of joy to her long, draining days. Soon, the zippered pouch in her suitcase began demanding treasures.

Her favorite house to steal from was the old lady's. The lady often sat crocheting or sewing as Sunny vacuumed around her. Treasures, like bicycle-shaped buttons, lace tattings, and strings of sequins, littered her floor, and it was easy to pocket something. Only at the nurses' immaculate house did Sunny risk peering into drawers.

She took off her shoes and padded across the carpet. She opened the fridge to store her lunch and peeked into a slightly open red-and-white carton. The food released a mouthwatering smell, and she was tempted to taste it. But such a theft felt like crossing a significant line; plus, it couldn't be saved in her suitcase's pouch for Roshi. A banana magnet fell off the magnet-covered fridge when she closed the door, and she pocketed it. The thing had fallen off before, clearly wanting to be hers. She imagined Roshi pretending to eat it.

While cleaning the living room, she accidentally turned on the radio. Madonna's "Holiday" blared, a song she often heard in the car. She danced and sang into the mop handle as she'd seen someone do on TV, imagining Roshi as her audience. Pure joy shot through her, something she hadn't experienced since dancing in the van with Roshi that day. Perhaps she could dance like this every time she cleaned there. Perhaps she could even watch TV.

She had only the kitchen left to mop and Lila wasn't due for forty minutes, so she placed her sandwich and orange on the coffee table and turned on the television. A soap opera flickered on.

She took a bite and returned to dancing with the mop, occasionally glancing at the TV.

One song later, the garage door opened behind her.

She froze.

"Hello?" a voice called.

She turned around. A large brown-haired woman stood with her hand on her hips, wearing white scrubs.

Her stomach sank. Lila had told her to say her mother had left for a quick errand and would be back soon if anyone returned home while she was there alone. But Lila wasn't due soon. And here was Sunny doing everything wrong.

"Who are you?" the woman asked.

"Uh." She gripped the mop handle, digging her fingernails into her palms. She imagined the banana magnet flying out of her pocket, completing the scene.

"Are you the cleaning lady's kid?"

Sunny nodded.

"Where is she?"

"She's coming back. She had an emergency." She was pleased with her words, particularly *emergency*, which she'd heard on a sitcom. Janna would say "kudos" to hear it.

"And she left you here? Alone?"

Sunny nodded. "To clean. Yes. I was cleaning. She had to, uh, get her medicine. For the baby, she takes a medicine. She's expecting, and she forgot to take it, so she went to get it. She's coming back." This was the most Sunny had spoken to anyone other than Janna in a month. She felt proud of the lie that formed so easily and sounded like truth.

"Well, I'm Carol. I live here." The woman's eyes roved. "Looks like a party. The radio *and* the TV?" She clicked off the radio, and her eyes rested on the food in front of the TV. "I see you're having lunch. While cleaning? We don't normally eat in the living room."

Heat rushed up her body. Janna's kids ate popcorn while watching shows in their living room. The old lady ate microwaved meals in her living room. Prem and people on sitcoms ate in living rooms. She'd assumed eating in living rooms was the American way.

"I, oh, sorry. I, uh—" Tears formed in her eyes. Would this woman tell Lila everything? Would Lila beat her? Would Prem turn on her? Sunny laid down the mop and ran to turn off the TV and gather her lunch.

"What's your name?" Carol asked.

"Sun—uh, Neena. Neena." She threw her food into the paper sack.

"Neena. That's a pretty name. How old are you?"

"Uh, fifteen?" This lie sounded like one.

Carol cocked her head. "So, ninth grade?"

Sunny nodded. She didn't know the American system.

Carol smiled. "Bring your lunch to the table. We'll eat together. I forgot to pack my lunch. That's the only reason I came home."

Sunny placed the sack on the glass table.

Carol threw the boxed food on a fancy plate and microwaved it, saying, "Do you know when Lila will return?"

Sunny shook her head and picked up the mop.

"Leave that," Carol said. "You can clean when your mother returns. Let's eat."

Sunny placed the cleaning supplies in a corner and sat in front of her sack. Her hunger had vanished even as the savory smell of Carol's food permeated the air.

Carol pulled place mats from a hutch and lowered her plate atop one. She handed one to Sunny. Sunny spied the mats before but hadn't known their purpose. She pulled out her half-eaten sandwich and used her sack like a plate on the mat. Carol handed a paper napkin to Sunny before spreading one on her own lap. Sunny mimicked the motion, but her napkin fluttered to the floor.

She retrieved it and spread it out again, tilting her thighs to balance it.

Carol smiled and began eating. Sunny didn't touch her sandwich. She shouldn't be sitting at a table with Carol.

"So, how long have you been helping your mother?" Carol asked.

In her nervousness, her poor grammar snuck in. "Ah, just this month. Me had lived with my nani in Leguan, and then my parents send for me, so I just come. A month ago, now." She cringed at all the mistakes Janna would have corrected.

They ate in silence, Sunny peeling her orange self-consciously. It seemed like forever before Lila showed up.

"Oh, Carol. Hi," Lila said, closing the door behind her. Her face was tight with surprise. "I didn't know you'd be home today. I left to, uh, go get, uh, something."

"Yes, that's what Neena said," Carol said. "How are you, Lila? Neena mentioned that you're pregnant?"

Lila nodded and patted her belly, which was still not very big. Her eyes hovered over the cleaning supplies.

"Sounds like you're lucky to have Neena around, helping this summer?"

Lila smiled tightly.

"I wish you'd told us. I'm sure you understand that we need to know who's entering our house when we're not here, even if they're your children. There's liability, you know, especially with children. You should have called."

"Sorry, Carol," Lila said, sounding heartbroken. "But things got busy."

"Hmm," Carol said, eating her last bite.

Lila entered the kitchen, and Sunny swept the crumbs and orange peel into her paper sack with the side of her hand. She folded the napkin and placed it on the placemat, then stupidly bowed her head before leaving the table.

"I assume Neena will be in school come fall?" Carol said, standing with her empty plate. "That this is temporary?"

"Oh, yes," Lila said, although she'd never mentioned school.

"Well, I'll let you guys finish up. It was nice to meet you, Neena," Carol said, placing her dish in the sink. "The house looks and smells great, by the way."

Sunny didn't dare meet Lila's eyes after Carol left. She mopped in silence and washed Carol's plate, the salty-sweet smell nauseating her.

In the car, Lila said, "When did she come home?"

"Twenty, thirty minutes ago?"

Lila sighed. "They'll fire me. I would put money on it. And with Michael due next month. Carol, she's the nice one. The other one, Betty, she's the bitch. Let's just hope they don't talk to the old lady. They gave her my name, but she's not picky like them."

It felt like Lila was confiding in her, that they were finally a team. "I'm sorry," Sunny said.

Lila stared ahead. "You should be."

13

Disappearing Milk

The nurses did fire them. For weeks, Sunny worried Lila would tell Prem about it, blaming her. One evening, as she waited for a load of Janna's laundry to dry in the laundry shed, she heard them arguing. But it wasn't about the nurses.

"One grand?" Prem shouted. "I told you I'm done paying that man."

The laundry shed stood adjacent to their trailer, buffering their unit from the four others in the compound. Sunny was alone, but all three washers and dryers were in use, and she worried someone might show up at any moment. The Spanish-speaking workers might not understand Prem—even she had a hard time making out his words over the machines' whirring and the distant mariachi music—but his tone spoke volumes.

She edged closer to Lila's bedroom window.

"Why you only telling me this shit now?" Prem yelled. "You said the girl family paid."

Had Prem not known about Mr. Michael's blackmail? Had he thought she was free? Would he stop calling her Husk? Stop hugging her?

"The man threatened INS whether we keep the girl or not," Lila said in a low growl. "And she already make back most what she owe. But if you don't want the girl, why you sitting with her like she your whore."

Whore—clearly a dirty word. What did it mean? Her body flamed.

A slap reverberated. Had Lila slapped Prem? She ruined everything.

"Motherfucker," Lila said.

More slaps followed, and the walls shook.

Lila moaned in pain, and it became clear Prem was doing the hitting.

Sunny found herself guiltily rooting for Prem even as he morphed into the worst version of her father. Even if the fight could never be fair, Lila being so small and pregnant.

Laughter and chatter from the other trailers rose above the lively music as theirs quieted.

Sunny returned to the shed and emptied the dryer, amazed at how quickly the magical machine dried clothes. Not daring to reenter the trailer to fold in front of the TV, she folded the clothes on a scuffed plastic table, creating small piles of Leslie and Nicole's cartoon-printed underwear. A surge of emotion overcame her, and she spat on a pair. Guiltily, she wiped the spittle-stained underwear against her shirt. Who was she becoming? A whore? Was that something a whore did?

She was glad to hear she'd earned most of what was owed, but she worried Prem would now see her as a burden the way Lila did. They housed and fed her, and though she did all the cooking and cleaning, she feared she wasn't earning her keep. If she weren't there, she knew they could house migrant workers in the spare room and reduce their rent.

Someone laughed from the first trailer where workers often played cards at night. Yvonne's family's place. Yvonne's father and brothers were supervisors, like Prem, and they lived permanently at the compound, too. But unlike Prem and Lila, they socialized with the temporary workers who filled the other units, their common language turning them into one enormous family. Sunny had never felt more jealous of their world than in that moment.

She mentally willed a feeling of family inside the trailer as she approached with the laundry basket, hoping to see Prem and Lila eating the potato curry she'd made earlier. But Prem stormed past her and slammed the door. And Lila was locked in her room.

Nothing looked amiss until she stepped into the bathroom. The plastic shower curtain had been ripped off the hooks and towels had been knocked onto the floor. Shampoo bottles and cleaning products lay strewn about. Sunny hurriedly cleaned up as best she could.

She'd eaten her dinner and was washing her plate when Prem returned.

"Make me a plate," he ordered.

She heaped some food onto a plate for him, leaving a little behind for Lila. The woman barely ate, defying what Sunny's mother always said about pregnant women eating for two.

Sunny placed Prem's dinner in front of him as he watched *Sanford and Son*. Onscreen, Sanford and Esther, sworn enemies, were accidentally handcuffed together. She'd seen this episode, and their antics triggered her laughter. She sat tentatively, chuckling.

Prem silenced her with a stare and said, "Get to bed."

She awoke later that night to a shriek. At first, she thought she'd overslept again and had made Lila angry. But when her disorientation wore off, she realized the shrieks and groans were rooted in pain. Lila's pain.

Sunny peeked out from behind her door. The bathroom and bedroom lights glowed yellow, and guttural groaning filled the trailer.

"Lila, stop fighting me," Prem said.

"I need the doctor!"

He gripped her, his hands under her armpits, her body limp. Sunny had only ever seen that much blood when her mother gave birth to Indy. Blood covered Lila's legs and nightdress. It flowed.

Falling out of her book-talk, Lila cursed in a wracked voice. "You dog, you mother skunt. You did this. Call the hospital."

"What, so they can deport me? And you? You want live with your mother again?"

She shrieked and twisted, slipping from his hands to the ground. "When me dead, they guh put you in jail where you belong."

He picked up Lila, who'd lost her fight. Glaring at Sunny, who stood in her doorway, he ordered, "Clean up this mess. And put some garbage bags on the bed."

Sunny placed clean towels atop garbage bags to protect Lila and Prem's mattress, remembering how they'd used cloth and plastic to deal with her mother's bleeding, too. Then Prem moved Lila onto the bed, where she bled and sobbed.

Cleaning the floor, Sunny battled waves of nausea. The rank metallic air reminded her of the time her family slaughtered a goat, draining its blood into a bowl. Prem exited the bathroom with a heavy-looking garbage bag, and she swallowed back vomit, thinking of what the bag contained.

Redness screamed against white porcelain as she rinsed bloodied things in the bathtub, and she retched. She chased her vomit and the blood down the drain with bleach.

She dropped sodden, hand-washed towels into a dryer, feeling renewed awe for the machines, doing the work of sunshine under the shroud of dark. Lila normally insisted on using a clothesline to dry towels, but the machines, which cost a quarter to operate, were not luxuries that night.

The darkened trailers droned with air conditioners and snores, while theirs glowed garishly yellow against the black night. It reminded Sunny of a Guyanese wake she'd attended when a neighbor died, that sad and festive night of staying up to help the jumbie pass. She wondered if this counted as a wake, if the baby was big enough for a jumbie, one that could haunt. Then she worried Lila would die and become the haunter. How complicated would life become then? *When me dead, they guh put you in jail where you belong.*

She'd rooted Prem on, so she was guilty, too. Looking up to the scattered stars, she asked for God's forgiveness and muttered the Shanti Path, a prayer she hadn't chanted since leaving her sisters.

In the kitchen, she retrieved ingredients to make metemgee. Sunny's mother always made metem when someone was sick, and because it was after-church food, it also felt like prayer food. Sunny had found the cassava and plantains at a Cuban market, and Lila hadn't objected, since the provisions were cheap.

She sautéed onions, garlic, and pepper as Prem snored on the couch. Her hands became her mother's as she peeled and chopped vegetables and squeezed creamy white milk from a grated coconut into the pot. She stayed awake humming prayers, stirring the simmering soup and checking the dryer, wanting to gather the towels before any of the workers rose.

By sunrise, Lila stopped bleeding. Sunny offered her a bowlful of coconut milk broth, and she didn't push it away. It seemed she'd live, and Sunny felt certain the prayer and metem had helped.

Buzzing with exhaustion, she went through the morning routine. She made sandwiches for lunch and picked flowers for the stand. She smiled at Yvonne and said, "She's sick," when asked where

Lila was. When Yvonne asked, "Wanna make a bouquet?" she shook her head no. She needed to race through the morning quotas, filling both hers and Lila's. Prem drove up to the trailer in his golf cart just as she returned from the greenhouses.

She served him soup for lunch, then worked up the courage to say, "Janna needs her laundry. If you take me, I could clean her house."

Prem scowled but after he ate, he said, "Get in the car. Let's go."

She climbed into the back seat where she normally sat, but he barked, "Sit up front."

It felt strange sitting so close to him after what had happened. *Whore.* The dashboard, with its myriad dials and vents, closed in on her.

"Where's this house?" Prem asked, pulling out.

She gave directions, saying "turn here, no over there," and soon realized Prem had no idea where Lila spent half her days.

When they arrived, he said, "Tell the lady you have to miss today. Tell she Lila's sick and you need to care for her. I don't have time to come back. And ask if she can pay what she owe. Michael showing up for your money this afternoon."

Sunny flushed. Everything was her fault.

Nicole answered the door dripping in a bathing suit, holding a bag of chips. Sunny assumed she'd been playing on the slip-and-slide in the backyard and had run in for a snack. All the girls ever did was play, eat, and make messes.

"Hi, Neena," Nicole said, pivoting away from the door. "Come check out our new pool!" Nicole ran toward the kitchen, leaving wet prints on the carpet. Sunny gritted her teeth.

She took off her shoes and placed the laundry bags near the staircase. She walked through the kitchen to the patio door, and she almost gasped. An enormous above-ground swimming pool had taken over the yard. Janna sat reading on a lawn chair beside it, shaded by an umbrella. Nicole climbed a short ladder before jumping, grabbing her knees, and splashing into the water. It was like something out of an ad. That this luxurious scene existed simultaneously with her reality made her feel faint. She grasped the patio door.

"I brought the laundry," Sunny said, when Janna greeted her. "My mother is sick, so we can't clean today."

"Oh, no," Janna said, scrunching up her face and putting a hand to her heart. "It's not the baby, is it? Is she in the car?"

Sunny wasn't prepared for direct questions. Yes, it was the baby. And no, she wasn't in the car. Prem, the man who'd beaten the baby out of her, was in the car. "Uh . . . she . . . my . . ."

"Say it how you would in patois, Neena," Janna said. Whenever she got stuck, Janna made her say it "in patois" before marveling at the terrible words, writing them down, and correcting the grammar. Sunny became an alien under a microscope, stupid and judged, even if Janna insisted her house was "a no-judgment zone." If there were truly such a zone, Sunny could say, "Lila's husband, Prem, beat her shitless, because of me. Lila lost the baby, and she's half dead right now. I need to nurse her back to life so we don't get jailed and deported because we're all illegal. Especially me, who isn't their daughter and who she hates." How could Janna not judge that?

She'd never felt ill will toward Janna before. But bitterness rose inside Sunny as Janna waited for her to speak patois, as the girls shrieked and splashed in the pool.

"Go ahead, Neena," Janna said, smiling. "You can do it."

"She is resting," Sunny finally said. "She's in bed. Maybe she ate something bad."

"Listen to that diction." Janna beamed as if Sunny had done something miraculous. "So, who drove you here?"

"My dad." The words came out easily. Too easily.

"Oh, I haven't met him. I'd come say hello, but I don't like leaving the girls unattended in the pool. Nicole isn't the strongest swimmer yet."

"That's okay," Sunny said. Nicole was so precious she couldn't be left for a moment. Angry words flashed through Sunny's clouded head—*not worry about me, me not your problem, go back to your brats*—and she instantly regretted them. Still, a strange brew of anger and envy bubbled inside her. She desperately wanted out of there.

"We are in a rush," Sunny said. "We need, uh, medicine for . . . Mom."

"I have to say," Janna said, grinning, "your speech has gotten so impressive. I can hear the flavor of your beautiful accent, yet the grammar is perfect. Kudos to you."

Sunny smiled tightly, hung up on the "flavor of your beautiful accent." The hard line between their worlds continued sharpening itself. Even if Sunny's speech became unflavored, she could never become Janna. She'd never be Leslie's or Nicole's equal. They could clap and say, "Kudos," but she'd never be anything more than an alien.

"Tell Lila, 'Feel better,' for me," Janna said, "and have her call if she needs something."

Sunny nodded and turned to leave before remembering Prem's request. Flushing, she forced the words out. "My dad said that, uh, if you owe money for the work? The medicine is expensive."

"Oh, Neena, tell your father, we're all paid up. But I can give you an advance if things are tight. Let me grab my purse." Janna stepped into the kitchen, adding, "You brought the laundry?"

"Yes."

"Do you mind putting it away while I write a check? You know how much I despise laundry, and the girls are too good at making it." She laughed. "Would your dad mind waiting? And do you mind taking the dirty stuff, too?"

The bitter brew inside Sunny bubbled over as she said, "Of course." No, she didn't mind doing laundry even though Janna owned perfect machines in her garage. No, she didn't mind putting it away even though Janna was just sitting there reading. No, Prem didn't mind waiting. Mr. Michael didn't mind waiting for his money. Nobody minded. All that mattered was that Janna was happy.

"Thanks so much, Neena."

She broke her one-item rule and pocketed three things as she put away the clean clothes and collected new laundry. She picked up a Garbage Pail Kid card from Leslie's floor and a glitter-water bracelet from Nicole's floor. She was going to leave it at that, but she spied Leslie's charm bracelet draped across her inside-out T-shirt and crumpled shorts on the bathroom floor, abandoned where Leslie undressed for the pool. The plastic chain was full of colorful bell charms, which Leslie loved to jingle. The baby bottle charm was especially prized, and Nicole often whined for a turn to play with it. Sunny usually only took things no one would miss. This would be missed. As she clicked the charm off the bracelet, the girls squealed with joy in the backyard. The minuscule bottle was filled with milk that disappeared when turned upside down. It was magic. A tiny bell next to the bottle made a tinkle as she pocketed it.

"The check's on the foyer table," Janna called from the kitchen as Sunny descended with the laundry. The check, made out to cash, was for thirty dollars—a generous sum, the payment for a full day's work including laundry.

Her pockets weighed her down as she called back, "Thank you, Janna."

Janna glanced around the corner. "Of course, Neena. Anytime. And let's not call it an advance. Let's just call it a get-well gift for Lila. She's always taken such good care of us, and you've become so dear to me. Please give her my best."

Sunny nodded, feeling sick now and fearing the charm would jingle in her pocket. She was a terrible, terrible person who deserved punishment. Maybe Janna got her perfect life because God knew she was kind and generous, not garbage like Sunny.

14

Sweet Deal

Prem stared at the check without comment. He remained silent as he drove to the grocery store that contained a check-cashing counter. Sunny stewed in guilt as she waited in the car, knowing the money was for Mr. Michael, hoping this would count toward what she owed.

Before getting back in the car, Prem turned into the adjacent liquor store. He returned with a brown bag and uncorked a hidden bottle, releasing the heady scent of rum. He took a swig, and Sunny's sinuses filled with pressure.

They drove back to the compound, Prem drinking the whole way. As the car crunched along the path to their trailer, Sunny spotted Mr. Michael and a stranger on the tailgate of a white truck parked near the laundry shed.

Prem sucked his teeth. "Fucker," he muttered, his alcohol breath fouling the air.

Mr. Michael stared at them, his eyes naked without his signature sunglasses. His gaze slid over Prem, then over her, then back to Prem. It suddenly felt wrong to be sitting in the front seat, next to Prem. *Whore.*

Mr. Michael scratched his cratered cheek with one hand. His tall, wiry friend, a Black man, wore a backward baseball cap and a scraggly mustache. He winked at Sunny.

Her eyes fell to her lap.

When Prem got out, she eased open her door and crept toward the trailer.

Mr. Michael exaggerated bringing his gold watch up to his face. "Your watch must have broke, buddy. I told Lila one o'clock. I been waiting here half an hour, and nobody answering your door."

"Lila's sick," Prem said.

"Well, me not feeling too good either, brother." Mr. Michael jumped off the tailgate and shouted toward the trailer. "Lila! You better have my damn money."

"You got some nerve," Prem said, "yelling for money we shouldn't owe. You should be paying me to house and feed this girl."

Mr. Michael spat in the gravel and stepped toward Prem. His scowling friend leapt down.

"You must like things messy," Mr. Michael said. "Me, I like things simple." He punched a fist into a palm. "Me and Lila come to an agreement, a plain and simple agreement. I done my part. Now you have to do your part. But if you cross me, things guh get messy."

Prem harrumphed, as if calling his bluff.

Mr. Michael snapped his fingers. "That's all I have to do, you know? This." He snapped again. "And you guh lose a few teeth." He snapped. "And you guh lose your job." He snapped. "And you guh lose this country."

His friend laughed.

Mr. Michael's eyes landed on Sunny, and he snapped his fingers again. "This girl, too. Gone, just like your daughter. Free labor for life—that's one sweet deal you giving up."

Heat flashed through her body. *Free labor for life. Sweet deal.* Was she meant to live on the farm forever?

"Keep me daughter out of your filthy mouth," Prem said, taking his turn to spit on the ground. "You snake."

Mr. Michael laughed, hissing a little. "Take a snake to know a snake."

Sunny expected them to attack each other at any moment. The future became a many-fingered thing, slithering out before her. She imagined vague beatings, uniformed authorities, jail, deportation, kneeling on rice, her father's angry face, her family's disappointment.

Then she pictured Lila inside the trailer, listening. Or worse, not listening. Had Lila died? Perhaps Lila bled while they were gone. Neena's jumbie shot into her. She met Mr. Michael's eyes and said, "I'm going inside. Excuse me."

Mr. Michael's eyebrows arched. "Ho, ho! Listen to *this* book-talk."

She walked toward the trailer, laughter at her back. As she opened the door, Mr. Michael's friend said, "If you tired of the girl, give me she. I know how to work that."

"Who work the girl don't affect me," Mr. Michael said. "But I still expect my pay."

Sunny closed the door as Prem threw an envelope at Mr. Michael and told him to get off the property.

That night, there was little conversation and no television. She emerged from the shower to find Prem asleep on the couch. A blue-and-red-striped envelope sat on the floor by her door. It had already been ripped open.

In her room, Sunny stared at her proper name, Sunita Kissoon, written neatly on the outside of the envelope in Raj's block lettering.

The trailer filled with Prem's snores as she opened the letter.

Dear Sunny,

We hear the good news from Michael that you got to America safe and started enjoying your life by Lila and Prem. Daddy say to tell them thank you, and Ma say to listen to the lady and help her cook. We all look forward to hearing about where you live. Everybody want to know how you like your own room and the flush toilet and if you watch TV every day.

Michael says Lila had work lined up from day one, so the debt will pay off soon. We are looking forward to whatever money you can send after that. Work been drying up here, and inflation on the rise. Basic things like rice and dal getting dear, and flour got scarce. Otherwise, things the same, and everybody doing good.

Especially Roshi and Pappo. We got some good news with them. Some overseas people came to Canal, and they promised hearing aids. For free. Soon, Roshi might hear as good as you! They even starting a program for deaf children in town, also free, and we won't even have to pay for travel. Now everybody want to be deaf to get free schooling. Laugh.

Everyone miss you here. In particular, Roshi. She kept asking about you, but she is happy to reunite in America in six years or so. By then, who knows, she might talk as good as you. Laugh.

Hope to hear from you soon. You can send a letter back with Michael, or ask Lila and Prem about stamps.

Your loving family.

Everyone had signed their names. Roshi had added: *Dear Sunny, Miss you. See you six years, your ever-loving sister Roshini.*

She touched the signatures and Roshi's words. Tears rolled down her cheeks. The tears were for missing her family, yes, and finally hearing from them. But they were also for the pressure the letter placed on her shoulders, the worry that her family believed something false. Shamefully, they were also for the realization that Roshi no longer needed her, that life went on without her. The tears came on stronger, and she buried her head, crying for everything she bore that day—the baby that died, Lila's pain, her jealousy of Janna's girls, stealing the charm, and her fear of Mr. Michael and his friend. A conflicting tangle of emotions swirled through her.

Spent, she clutched the letter to her heart and lay facing the crib that would remain empty. She felt Lila's weighty presence on the opposite side of the trailer as Prem's snores vibrated the walls, the whole place like a seesaw about to tip.

A letter formed in her mind. *Dear Roshi, I'm glad you'll get to hear soon. But not everything you hear will be nice.*

The next morning, she placed a breakfast of porridge on Lila's nightstand as Prem entered the room. She wanted to ask about stamps and mailing a letter, but it was the wrong time.

"You need to pick up the phone, Lila," Prem said. "Your mouth works, right? So call the people and tell them you're sick. If they want their house cleaned, they guh wait. But if you stop going, they guh get somebody else, and how will this girl pay Michael?"

Sunny stiffened as Lila turned onto her side, closing her eyes and ignoring the food. It was as if the baby took her bark and bite with it.

Prem kissed his teeth and left.

They were due at the old lady's place later. They needed to make a good impression since the nurses' firing. Prem was right—Sunny couldn't afford to have Lila lose any of her remaining clients. Sunny didn't fear returning to Guyana or even jail. She feared Mr. Michael's friend's offer to take her. *Free labor for life. Sweet deal.* She pictured the sneering man throwing her into the back of their white truck. Would they make her clean their houses? Cook and wash clothes? And what? *Whore.*

"I can clean the old lady's myself," she said to Lila's back. "And the houses tomorrow."

Lila didn't react.

After her morning work, Sunny found Lila still in bed, her food untouched. Determined to clean the old lady's house alone, she intercepted Prem in one of the greenhouses to ask for a ride. He and Yvonne's dad, Don Hernandez, were directing workers as they loaded trucks.

Not wanting to lose her nerve, she approached him and called, "Dad." She'd practiced the word in her head, but it still came out strange.

Prem turned to her, his face twisted with surprise. Don smiled.

"I need a ride," she said. "For work."

"Sí, sí, go," Don said. "Take care of what you need. I got this."

Prem vibrated with anger as she instructed him to the old lady's house, and he peeled off as soon as she exited the car. She'd resigned herself to the full forty-five-minute walk home after work. So she was surprised when Prem intercepted her a few blocks from the trailer.

"If you make fish curry," he said, "Lila might eat."

He smelled of liquor and swerved as he drove to the Cuban market, talking about green mangoes being a curry's secret. He sent her inside with a few dollars to buy mangoes and fish, and as she shopped, an idea that had simmered in her mind that afternoon solidified.

Back in the car, she said, "If you teach me to drive, I can clean the houses myself until Lila gets better. I'll keep up with the farmwork, too."

Prem laughed. "Drive? You?" Then, realizing she wasn't joking, he said, "All right, Husk. That make sense. You almost sixteen anyway."

No. She wasn't almost sixteen. Neena would have been almost sixteen. Sunny wouldn't be thirteen for months, not until around Diwali in October. But why did that matter? She was as big as Lila, and if Lila could drive, why couldn't she?

He told her to take the wheel, then instructed her to adjust the seat to reach the pedals and peer into the necessary mirrors. She turned the car on and revved the engine.

"Woah," she said, feeling a thrill at the car's power.

Prem laughed and looked at her as if seeing her for the first time.

She drove jerkily around the parking lot until she got the hang of things, pressing this pedal to speed up and go, that one to slow down and stop. Prem told her to drive home, and she stopped at all the lights and signs, waiting her turn when other cars showed up. Soon, maneuvering the grid of streets began to feel as easy as vacuuming straight lines into carpet, and she wondered why Guyanese people considered driving men's work.

"You driving like a pro, Husk," Prem said as she turned into the farm's gravel lot two hours later.

She shot Yvonne a bright smile as she opened the gate. And she thought, *Dear Roshi, Forget flush toilets and TVs. Guess who's driving a car like Knight Rider?*

Still buoyed by the thrill of driving earlier that day, Sunny served Prem a bowl of curried fish and took a tentative seat beside him on the couch.

Prem took a bite and said, "Damn good fish, Husk. You proving your worth around here." He laid a heavy arm on her shoulder as they watched *Three's Company*. She procrastinated doing the dishes to indulge in that warm weight, which she'd missed.

That night in bed, as she wrote a mental letter to her family, her door opened. Through slitted eyes, she saw a figure silhouetted by murky light. Lila, finally feeling better, she thought, groggily. But it was Prem, reeking of liquor. He walked toward her, and the bed creaked as he sat. His bottom pressed against her shins.

She stiffened and closed her eyes. Perhaps he was sleepwalking. Pappo did that once. Raj found him trying to climb the fence at 3:00 a.m., thinking they were stairs. Raj had said Pappo looked like a jumbie possessed him, that he wouldn't wake up. Raj had to guide Pappo up the real stairs and back into bed.

Prem leaned back, nudging Sunny against the wall, trapping her in a triangle of space. She tried to appear dead asleep, limp. A heavy hand landed on her legs. The hand stroked her through the sheets, running up her thigh and stopping on her hip. It moved across her bottom. Up and down. Her body tingled, and she feared he could tell she was awake. She held her breath.

His palm cupped her bottom and grasped it, and she clenched her jaw to keep from shrieking. The bed shook, and the springs sang rhythmically as Prem bounced his backside.

He was not sleepwalking. *Whore.* This was what the word meant, she suddenly knew.

She feared the squeaking would awaken and anger Lila. The noise and movement grew until Prem grunted. He sat a minute more, then rose and left.

Through the thin wall, she heard him rustle and settle on the sofa. Minutes later, his snores trembled the trailer.

She remained wide awake, a deep hollow forming inside her as the feeling of his hand remained on her bottom. *Dear Roshi . . .*

15

Red Delicious

SUNNY PRESSED DOWN ON the accelerator and blared Top 40 music as she drove to and from Lila's clients those last weeks of summer. Navigating the gridded suburban roads, with its clear-cut stop-and-go rules, felt easier than everything else in her life. Singing in the car, she forgot about Lila holed up in her room, Prem's sleepwalking hands, Mr. Michael and his friend, and her parents' expectations.

She still hadn't responded to the letter. She'd tried to pen the lies she knew her family hoped to hear—*Lila and Prem are nice, the work is easy, Mr. Michael is a good man*—but she couldn't bear to write them. If she complained, they'd think she was lazy and ungrateful, unwilling to sacrifice for them while they counted on her. She couldn't imagine writing the truth.

Today, the impending threat of school consumed her. She was to spend the afternoon watching Janna's girls as Janna ran errands, and she knew Janna would bring up school again. She parked the car a block away from the house because Prem had warned, "You don't want people asking to see your license."

Inside the house, Janna handed her a pair of Leslie's shorts and a T-shirt. "I thought you might want to join the girls in the pool."

Sunny thanked Janna, touched by this kindness. She'd been dying to try the pool. When she and her sisters swam in the conservancy's dark water, they wore their brothers' outgrown T-shirts, stretching them to reach midthigh like dresses. The pink shirt and black running shorts Janna handed her would reveal more skin than a large T-shirt, but the clothes were still more modest than the girls' swimsuits.

In the bathroom, a full-length mirror hung behind the door. In the past, she'd snuck glances at herself while cleaning, but she'd always been cloaked in baggy clothes. As she changed, a stranger stared back at her. Her skin had lightened from being covered and spending so much time indoors. The tiny shorts exposed lengthening legs and a curvy waist, and the butterfly print on the snug T-shirt accentuated mounds on her chest. When had those grown? In mere months, she'd transformed.

As if speaking to Roshi through the mirror, she posed like Kimberly Drummond in a *Diff'rent Strokes* episode, one hand on her head and one hand on her jutting hip. She imagined Roshi mimicking the pose, wherever she was. Then the hand on her hip morphed into Prem's, and she darted away. She tiptoed down to the pool, wrapped in a towel.

The girls were in the pantry fighting over cookies when she slipped into the cool water. She sat low, letting the water protect her bare skin from their eyes.

"Yay, Neena's swimming," Nicole said. She cannonballed into the pool, splashing Sunny.

Leslie slid down the pool slide their father had recently erected, then promptly performed an underwater handstand. Sunny scooted back, worried Leslie would assess her bare legs.

But if the girls had opinions about her exposed skin, they didn't share them. She let herself sink underwater, mesmerized by the glittery sunlight on the pool's floor. Guyanese black water obscured everything. This water bent light to create beautiful patterns.

The girls began role-playing with Barbies, making the dolls say things like, "Cool pool party, is Ken coming, he's totally tubular."

Nicole handed Sunny a Skipper doll. "Here, Neena. Play with us."

Perhaps the water had dissolved the guard Sunny usually kept up because she heard herself saying, "Yes, Ken is super awesome," as she twisted the doll side to side the way the girls had.

Leslie spurted out a laugh, and Sunny's face heated up. She'd hoped to mimic the girls' casual tone, but stiff words had left her mouth. Stiff words with a singsong lilt.

"Say more," Leslie said.

She shook her head no.

"Aw, come on," Nicole said. "Make her say Guyanese stuff."

Sunny's body blazed and her tongue felt heavy. She'd worked so hard to stop saying Guyanese stuff, but she still sounded Guyanese. She quaked at the thought of school, supposedly starting in a week.

That afternoon, Janna handed her five extra dollars for "fun school supplies" and asked if Lila felt healthy enough to return to cleaning when the term started. Sunny nodded yes even though Lila hadn't said any such thing. In fact, Lila seemed oblivious to the start of school, content with the new arrangement—Sunny doing all the work while she slept.

Sunny got up extra early to cut and deliver the morning flowers before transplanting seedlings in the greenhouses, filling out both of their log sheets. She cleaned houses alone and raced through plantings in the field, if there were any, sometimes working until sunset. Then she made dinner and ran laundry before heading to bed.

She was meant to grocery shop with the money Janna paid today. She stared at the five-dollar bill in her hand. Lila would examine the grocery receipt and the change, but she wouldn't know about these extra dollars.

When Sunny spotted a garage sale sign on her way to the store, she turned down the unfamiliar street and followed the arrows. A lady and a young girl stood amid cluttered tables and boxes, but there were no customers.

"We're packing up," the lady said, "so everything's half off."

Sunny perused a box of books, advertised at fifty cents apiece. She picked one featuring a buxom real-life Barbie woman. Books qualified as school supplies, and these were cheap.

A scuffed plastic *Sesame Street* lunch box sat open with a mismatched *Super Powers* thermos. She traced the raised pattern on the lunch box and studied the strange characters.

The girl called, "You can have both for a dollar."

Sunny paid the girl with shaky hands and stowed the change in her pocket.

The lunchbox screamed for an apple, so after she shopped Lila's list, she returned to the grocery store and casually picked up two shiny Red Delicious apples. Lila had said they were too expensive, and Sunny had passed them enviously ever since. She paid a dollar for them and threw away the separate receipt the clerk handed her.

In the car, she sniffed the flower-scented fruit deeply and drifted to that day with Annette. She bit into one. The crunch surprised her, and a candy-like sweetness filled her mouth. She wanted to transport the taste to Roshi. It was so much deeper than the smell. Among the Guyanese fruits she loved and missed, she tried to think of a cousin to this apple. *Dear Roshi, apples taste like mamee and cashew mixed together, and crunchy like green gooseberry. But not really.* She placed the second apple inside the lunch box. Thinking about eating it at lunch on her first day, she felt excited about school for the first time.

At home, she unpacked milk, vegetables, and fish as Lila studied the grocery receipt. She steeled herself before saying, "Janna mentioned school is to start next week." She felt proud of her proper words.

Lila harrumphed. "What do you need school for? School won't pay Michael. And you're illegal. All you can ever do is house or farmwork. You don't need school for that."

Sunny hadn't expected this. Janna made school seem inevitable, and her parents had said she'd get free schooling. Her eyes slid over to Janna's laundry bag where she'd hidden her loot. She didn't need the lunch box after all.

Lila continued, "Who's gonna know you're not in school?"

"Janna will," Sunny said, surprising herself.

Lila sucked her teeth. "Janna needs to mind her own damn business. She's starting school, herself. How's she going to know who's cleaning her house when she's gone all day? Once school starts, she leaves the key under the flowerpot like everyone else. And she won't be thinking about you."

Sunny's eyes watered inexplicably, but she persisted. "What about the old lady?"

"That lady only sees her sewing. I can tell her you're twenty, and she would believe it."

A mixture of relief and sadness overcame her. She was glad to avoid the Leslies and Nicoles of the world, but it felt like their America had just been snatched from her reach.

That week, she stole bigger things, unsure why, unable to pretend they were trinkets for Roshi, certain they'd be missed. She took a silver spoon from the old lady's curio cabinet while dusting, a mug with a mountain scene from the accountant's shelf, and a water globe with two floating figurines from the businesspeople. The last two didn't even fit in the zippered pouch, and she felt dread as she stowed them in her suitcase. *Dear Roshi, imagine if they made a water globe with a sugarcane field inside. Shake it, and two girls would swirl through the water, flying over the cane.* Maybe she wanted to be caught and sent back home, where she could fly through cane fields with Roshi.

At Janna's the following week, she found the door key under a planter just as Lila had predicted. She placed the laundry bags by the stairs and thought of the Baby-Sitters Club book she might take—the soft paperback with girls having a pillow fight on the cover. She might even lay on Nicole's bed and read a bit.

Janna's voice came from behind. "Neena?"

Sunny jumped.

"Neena," Janna exclaimed, "why aren't you in school?"

Her whole body flushed.

"Neena, please tell me your parents registered you."

She lowered her eyes, her insides dissolving.

"I was expecting Lila. I'm only home because resource teachers get an extra prep week. I had no idea she hadn't registered you."

Sunny nodded, her head beginning to throb.

"We must fix this." Janna grabbed her keys from the foyer table. "I'll drive you home."

"I can tell her myself," Sunny said, a bit too loud. "I'll go home and tell her now. She's still not feeling too good."

"No, Neena. Lila might not be aware, but it's illegal in this country for you to work instead of attend school. Come on, let's go."

Sunny's face flamed anew. "I drove here."

"You what?" Janna's eyes bulged, but she didn't say that was illegal, too. Instead, she said, "Fine. I'll follow you."

Feeling lightheaded, Sunny walked to the little gold car, parked across the street.

Janna backed out of her garage in a black sedan, looking formidable. Sunny sat as tall as she could in the car, keenly aware of Janna's judging eyes.

At the flower stand, Yvonne's face fell when it landed on the car following Sunny. Sunny barely breathed as the cars crunched closer to the trailer.

The shabbiness of their home became apparent as Sunny parked. She'd never noticed how dingy the trailer was. Green and black mold stained the concrete blocks and crept up the base of the unit. Drip marks ran from the air conditioner, towels hung limply on a clothesline, and slippers sat haphazardly around the doorstep. They were in the middle of a flower farm, but not a single flower decorated the place. Gritty gravel and bare dirt marked the trailer as woefully inferior, perhaps even un-American.

"Let me get her." She jumped from the car, not wanting Janna to go inside the trailer.

Janna nodded. Her face had softened.

"Uh, Lila. Janna's here," Sunny said. Lila sat on the couch watching a soap opera, and Sunny swallowed her surprise. Lila never watched TV with her and Prem, so she assumed Lila disliked TV. Now she wondered if this was what Lila did all day.

"Who?" Lila seemed disoriented at Sunny's intrusion. "Why?"

Sunny stared at her feet. "Um. About the school?"

Lila stood and turned off the TV. "I'll deal with her."

Sunny peered through the blinds, as Lila limped up to Janna, clutching her stomach. Janna hugged Lila, patting her back, presumably lamenting the lost baby. Lila brushed her eyes. Their conversation was too low to hear but Sunny explicitly heard Lila say the words, "I didn't know."

They talked more, Janna gesticulating, Lila nodding. When Lila turned back to the trailer, Sunny rushed to sit at the kitchen table.

"She rass," Lila said, cursing and reverting to the crudest version of her mother tongue. "She can't mind she own business. Now she want register you at the school she work at so she can oversee you. And she saying you need a proper permit to drive. Like you're some precious thing she need to save from me. Mother scunt."

This version of Lila emerged whenever she was cornered, but it also meant Lila had lost. Sunny smiled inside.

"I need the paperwork," Lila said, walking toward her bedroom.

"I have my birth certificate," Sunny offered.

"You pagli?" Lila stopped at her door and stared at Sunny. "Not *you* paperwork. She think you name Neena and me your mammy, remember? She want *me* papers, the bills and everything."

Minutes later, Lila stormed from her room shuffling papers and stewing her teeth. Sunny followed her to the gold car and slid into the back seat, afraid of making eye contact with Janna, who'd remained in her driver's seat.

As Lila followed Janna's black car away from the compound, she said, "This better not get me deported."

Sunny stared from the back window, her body tight. Would Janna do that?

"Same thing happened with Yvonne when they moved here," Lila said. "Somebody like Janna, who couldn't mind their business, reported underage workers. Next thing we know, the boss is here, yelling. I never seen Prem that scared, ready to run. But nobody checked for paperwork. Maybe Jefe paid off people, I don't know. All that happened was Yvonne started school. But Prem can't stand anything to do with the authorities. Wait till he hears about this."

Sunny tried not to think of Prem. She studied the houses flashing past. They hadn't driven that route since the day she arrived months ago, and she noted how dull and unappealing everything had grown in that time.

Lila laughed. "Foolish Yvonne. She lasted two years. Then she was so big, no one could call her underage. We'll see how long you last."

They pulled up in front of a large building and parked beside Janna's car in a full parking lot. Sunny's stomach fluttered.

"This is the best junior high, Neena," Janna said, leading them up concrete stairs to double doors. "It has a magnet program, so you'll be introduced to the arts—music, theater, dance, you name it. Some rare variances opened for general ed. I only found out about them yesterday, that's why I want to jump on this. You're the sort of student they want. Hardworking, intelligent, bringing a different cultural point of view."

Sunny smiled at the compliment of being called intelligent and the absurdity of dancing at school. Lila remained silent.

"I'll drive you tomorrow. But generally, you'll take the bus. One comes out by your place for the magnet students. It'll be good for you to socialize with kids your age."

Inside, raucous children filled the hall, and Janna explained that it was lunchtime. Kids laughed, ran, and slammed lockers. Most carried backpacks and some held brown sacks. No one carried a plastic cartoon lunch box. The place felt a world away from the one-room schoolhouse that had defined school for her, where classes were separated by rolling blackboards, where students marched single-file in blue uniforms to lunch, where they'd be beaten with rulers for shouting.

Janna hugged a gray-haired lady whom she introduced as Mrs. Martin. They entered her office, and a blur of conversation followed during which Sunny got so used to being called Neena that the name truly felt like hers. They discussed Neena's age, still fifteen at the September cutoff, and the deficits Janna discovered during speech therapy. They decided that although she belonged in ninth grade, she could benefit from eighth grade before entering high school. She looked young enough, and she'd graduate by age twenty, which the law allowed. They asked if Lila objected, and Lila shrugged.

Lila wrote down Prem's name when Mrs. Martin asked about Sunny's father, and she offered her driver's license and Neena's birth certificate when prompted. But she barely spoke.

An amber-haired, green-eyed girl rapped on the door. "You sent for me, Mrs. Martin?"

"Bianca, yes. This is Neena. She'll be starting tomorrow. Do you mind showing her around? Here's her locker combo." Mrs. Martin handed Bianca a piece of paper.

"Hey, Neena. That's such a pretty name," Bianca said as she led Sunny away.

Bianca's feathered hair bounced, and Sunny touched her own plaited hair self-consciously. She wanted to say that *Bianca* was the most beautiful name she'd ever heard, that Bianca might be the prettiest person she'd ever met in real life. But she was incapable of speaking around this girl. She grew keenly aware that the khaki pants and long-sleeved shirt she wore were out of place.

"Eleven-twenty-four. Your combo is super easy!" Bianca exclaimed, staring at the paper. "Mine's thirty-four, twenty-seven, thirteen. Ugh. Can you get any harder?"

Bianca demonstrated opening the locker and asked Sunny if she wanted to try. She shook her head no. Bianca's chipped pink nail polish, stack of woven bracelets, and silver ring had distracted her. She had no idea how to open the locker, or what it was even for. And she didn't want Bianca to see the greenhouse dirt that stubbornly remained under her fingernails.

She followed Bianca up and down stairs and in and out of mazelike, fluorescent-lit hallways. Without windows or the sun to orient her, she quickly lost her sense of direction, and the tour became a nonsensical blur. Bianca pointed out the cafeteria, the PE locker room, and the science lab, then entered a large red auditorium that made Sunny think of the apple in her lunch box.

Plush seats faced a stage where pink girls twirled and leapt in skirted pink leotards, their legs long and bare.

"This is the auditorium," Bianca said before calling out to a friend. "Hey, Dana."

"Hey, Bee," Dana called back before twirling like a Barbie, her pink skirt spinning around her like a plate, exposing her panties. Sunny looked down at the small blue tag on Bianca's white shoes.

Dear Roshi, American schools are fancier than anything in Guyana. Kids even dance there. She felt relieved when Bianca led her out of the red room and back to the office.

"See you around, Neena," Bianca said, walking off. "Don't be a stranger."

16

Such a Pretty Name

That night, Prem and Lila argued as she showered. Sunny let hot water flow over her head to drown their words, but they reverberated. *School, work, owe.* It was quiet as she dried herself and dressed in her bleach-stained pajamas. She emerged to find Prem in front of the TV. An old *All in the Family* episode played, but his fixed stare told her he wasn't really watching.

She'd have to walk past him to enter her room, and she feared his barely suppressed rage. She placed her folded dirty laundry on the counter, plated some of the dinner she'd made earlier—spinach with dal and rice—and sat down at the small dining table.

"You too good to sit by me now," he said.

She moved her plate to the coffee table, her appetite gone, and cautiously took a seat beside him. He smelled like beer.

"I hear you starting school."

Would he beat her? It felt like he might.

"You lucky you have that lady Janna on your side, Husk," Prem said, throwing an arm over her shoulder.

The arm pressed her wet hair against her pajama top, and water slid down her back. She nodded and smiled tentatively. His touch didn't seem angry. It seemed almost paternal. Maybe he was happy she'd go to school. Maybe he'd begun to see her as his daughter. Maybe he'd start acting like a sitcom dad, like Steven Keaton on *Family Ties*.

"You sure luck out. You come to America, with a house and food waiting for you, free clothes and things, with you doing almost nothing." He laughed. "You got *me* working for *you*, me paying Michael while you gallivant off at school, like *me* owe *you* something."

His hand became a stinging weight.

"How you guh earn what you owe, Husk?" he asked. "Now that you can't work?"

Sunny shook her head slightly. She didn't know.

He moved the hand from her shoulder onto her thigh, near her crotch.

She jumped aside.

Prem laughed, and Sunny's eyes darted to Lila's door. This was the first time he'd touched her outside of her room, breaking the sleepwalking delusion she'd clutched.

He stood. "Seem to me, with all you got, you still ungrateful. Seem to me you think we don't give you enough. Come. Me want talk to you about something me find in your room."

She shook her head no.

His eyes grew possessed. "Don't shake your head at me, you hear? You my property. *My* property. I pay to bring you here. I pay for you. So you better listen."

Lila's door opened.

Prem pointed at Lila. "You stay out of this. Get back inside."

Lila crossed her arms, and all of Sunny's hatred for Lila evaporated. Lila could save her. A switch had flipped, and Prem became the raging monster Lila always promised.

"Fine. Stay and watch, Lila, because me want you see the thief we take in."

Prem barged into Sunny's room and returned with her open suitcase. He threw it onto the coffee table, sending her plate crashing to the floor. Her cache sat exposed—all the stuff Roshi would never see. The open lunch box revealed the garage-sale book, apple, and a few dollars she had left over from Janna's gift. Her stomach dropped.

"Where you get this stuff? This money?"

A hot tear dripped down her face.

"You been stealing from people? From me?"

Her heart hammered and the pressure in her skull rendered her mute. She shook her head.

"They fire people for this, you know that? Or call the police! You want Lila get fired and deported? That your plan, after we take you in? Get everybody deported?"

She shook her head, and words finally came. "Janna," she whispered. "Janna gave me."

"Janna give you *this*?" He grabbed the mug from the suitcase. "A *cup*? What you need a cup for? This spoon? This . . . whatever the hell this is?" He held up the doily.

She nodded.

"You must take me for a damn fool."

She took a shuddering breath and whimpered, "Janna."

Prem threw the mug at the wall, and it shattered. "You not guh take advantage of me, you hear? Prance around school and have me work off you debt. Steal stuff and get me in trouble. While me break me back all day and nobody doing me no favor."

He picked up the glass globe and threw it. It bounced and cracked, and water leaked from it. "You not getting me deported, you hear? You put me at risk today. Them school people force Lila to show papers and give me name. My name! They got my name in their files. What if somebody question the Social Security number and called immigration? You think about that?"

Sunny stared downward. She had been content not to go to school. But she had no choice. She started to speak, "Janna—"

"Janna nothing! I don't want to hear that lady's name." He threw the lunch box, and the apple flew toward Lila.

"Lila, clean up this mess. I guh give this thief what she deserve."

He grabbed her shirt, and she steeled herself, remembering Lila's blood.

"No," she said as he dragged her into her bedroom. She looked back at Lila, who only stared at the apple near her feet.

He pushed her onto the bed and slammed the door shut with his leg. The book from the garage sale was in his hand. She hadn't noticed him pick it up. She hadn't looked at it since buying it, that book about a beautiful woman.

"I flip through this book. Very interesting thing you steal here, Husk." His voice had changed. It teased, and she hoped he was calming down.

She righted herself and edged toward the headboard, fingers gripping the mattress.

"You testing me. After everything me do for you, you really testing me, Husk."

"That's not my name," she heard herself say.

"Oh-ho. Then what your name?"

Her tongue blurted, "Neena," believing he'd spare her if he saw his daughter inside her.

He slapped her with the book. "Shut your mouth."

She stared ahead as if he hadn't just lit her cheek afire. He'd beat her whether she was Sunny, Husk, or Neena, she realized. He'd probably beat Neena if she were there. Neena's spirit roared inside her. She'd never asked for the name. They'd given it to her, and she had no choice but to answer to it. Knowing she was playing with fire, she shouted, "Neena!"

He slapped her again and pushed her face down, hitting her

head on the metal headboard. He pressed her nose into the pillow. "I don't want to see your face."

She struggled to breathe. Holding her head tight, he kneed her back and tugged at her pajama bottoms.

She twisted and shouted a panicked "get off" into the pillow. But she was pinned. She grew lightheaded when air touched her bare bottom.

He pressed harder. "This what you want, Husk? This what the white people in your dirty book do. You want know how it feel?"

What was he talking about?

"Me the one in charge here! You hear that? I am in charge." His sweaty body pressed against her, and he began thrusting, that sickeningly familiar rhythm she'd never felt against naked skin. Something hard rubbed between her legs, and then a knife pierced her.

The pain was so intense, she saw stars. Her throat released an animal sound she didn't know she was capable of making, but the pillow muffled it. What had the people in that book done? What was he doing to her?

Unable to breathe, she numbed and levitated away from the pain. To Guyana. To kneel on rice. That should be her punishment, not this. She leaned into the dry grains, feeling them pierce her kneecaps, as she prayed to her flag. She was a bad person, taking things that didn't belong to her. And she hadn't prayed enough. God was angry. Dark water edged in, and she searched for light but found only ink and sludge. Through the mud, she heard a grunt. She felt a wetness, as if she were really face down in the mud, a torn rag doll with stuffing coming out of her spine. God had left her.

The pressure on her head eased, and normal noises broke through a ringing that filled her ears. A shuffling, a zipper, a clearing throat.

"You ask for that. Don't try me again, you hear?"

The door slammed.

Air seeped into her lungs, and a musky smell assaulted her, reminding her of blood and frogs. She spasmed to contain a wave of nausea and a twisting pain seared through her.

She stayed motionless, trying to distance herself from the pain, trying not to gag, wondering if she'd die. But she kept living. The wetness below her grew sticky, and the burning between her thighs grew insistent. She needed to pee. She needed to fix herself.

The living room was dark when she eased the door open, the floor still littered with her stuff. Low snores rumbled from Lila's room. Prem wasn't on the couch.

She stepped forward and her foot landed on a glass shard. She walked to the bathroom, purposely stepping on glinting glass, wanting to feel pain she understood. She didn't turn on the lights, afraid of what she'd see in that glaring room. She filled the tub and slid into the black water, letting her head go under. Sobs racked her body, and she choked.

Prem's snores vibrated the wall. He wouldn't hear her, but if Lila were awake, she'd hear the sputters and coughs, and Sunny wanted her to hear.

Wrapped in a towel after the bath, she flicked the kitchen switch. Blinding light exposed her bloody footprints on the linoleum. This time, she avoided the glass shards as she walked.

She found her old sleepshirt, something she hadn't worn since Lila insisted on the bleached pajamas, now soiled. The shirt still smelled of mosquito coil and damp wood. Dressed in this and her work pants, she returned to the living room to clean, despite the pain. Janna would arrive in the morning, and Sunny needed to spare Janna the mess in case she came inside. Her hands trembled as she dropped the bruised apple and book into the trash. She kept the baby bottle charm and toy hairbrush to return to Leslie, and some buttons and the spoon to return to the old lady. She pledged not to steal again.

She wiped the food-soiled suitcase and carried it back to her room. When she stowed it under the bed, she tucked herself in the space beside it. She couldn't return to the bed, those cartoon sheets stained with blood and rank fluids. Inside her purse, she felt for the birth certificate and packet of peanuts. The soft, worn-out certificate that seemed so precious when her father handed it to her now felt shabby and meaningless. She rubbed her finger where she knew her name was scrawled in blue ink. Sunita Devi Kissoon. Who'd assigned that random string of letters to her when she was born—that name she'd never been called? Her mother or father? And what had they expected, calling her Sunny, that she'd be joyous and happy? Perhaps the name fit her once, but she was not Sunita or Sunny anymore. She rubbed the birth certificate, wanting to remove the name. She could never return to being the girl full of light and cane juice, leaping across bridges. She could barely remember what that girl looked like. She couldn't even bring Roshi's face to mind.

Dear Roshi, Sunny is gone.

Neena Das. That name no longer felt foreign, and that girl's face, laughing over her shoulder, was burned in her memory. She no longer flinched when answering to the name, and Neena was who she saw in mirrors. Perhaps the jumbie had eased into her without her realizing it and pushed out her old self. Perhaps that was why she'd blurted the name. The jumbie was trying to tell her she'd become Neena. Had for a while.

She stroked the mole under her left eye with the edge of the paper.

Neena—it was such a pretty name. She ripped her birth certificate to shreds.

MAYA

ATLANTA, GEORGIA

Since Dwayne left, I've been paralyzed, staring at the letter. It's still on the counter where he dropped it, near the envelope, out of place in the sparkling kitchen. I can't bring myself to touch it, to see *Sunny* written in Roshi's handwriting.

Sunny. The girl who was cleaved out of me so long ago. The girl I buried.

Memories churn in my mind. Gerbera flowers and apples. A gold car, a white truck, a brown suitcase. A birth certificate, shredded.

Outside the window, blossoms flutter as the dogwood quakes in a gust of wind.

I turn from the letter and head upstairs in a fit. I need a proper plan. I need more time. I need a long run to clear my head.

But words shout from the paper. *Ma pass last year. Gene. Dying sister.*

I'm out of time.

A faintness comes over me as I reach the landing, and I collapse on the floor. I live on a planet that no longer contains my mother. Even Roshi might be gone. And *I* might soon follow. I'd lived all these years essentially motherless, sisterless, but they'd been some sort of grounding wire, I realize. Their dim existence in the back of my mind—my mother forever cooking at that fireside in a housedress, Roshi forever smiling and miming her apple crunch—made the world real. It made time stop. It made any reckoning with the past a thing to save for the future. Now everything feels illusory.

The space around me grows foreign. The room, dominated by a palette of blue, gray, and cream, is like something from a magazine. Striped navy drapes frame a Palladian window. A cracker-thin television sits on a painted shiplap wall. Leather, wood, and metal furnishings surround me. It strikes me as exactly the opposite of everything from my past, as if I picked a color scheme to hide behind, one in which my mother and Roshi could never belong, perhaps one in which I've never truly belonged.

What is happening to me? I am not someone who falls apart. I am someone who handles things. Who makes lists and plans. I have to get tested for a gene. I need to contact Vernon. I need to help Roshi, if I still can. I need to figure out how to tell Dwayne.

Clutter within my reach offers a chance to collect myself. I crawl to gather remote controls, toy cars, and stray LEGO pieces. I stand to return them to shelves and cubbies, to heal myself with busyness and cleaning, like always. But I'm quaked by another memory. It pushes through, transferring me to another moment of cleaning. A room with shattered glass and blood on the floor. A room that doesn't belong in any magazine. A room my mother was spared from seeing. A scene I could never relay to Roshi. I drop onto the couch, my breath coming hard.

Shame floods me. It's as if I'd been floating outside my body all these years, sprinting on a treadmill to distance myself from this pain, and I'm jerked right back there. To a moment I've never properly dealt with.

I sob myself to exhaustion, reliving my helpless terror.

Then a rage builds inside me. Rage at my mother, who'd been spared. I picture her walking away from me the last time I saw her, Indy on her hip and Roshi running behind like chosen children. She died never knowing what I'd endured. She had an obligation to protect me, and she turned her back, discarding me. While I lived with a beast and my life spiraled out of control. While I became someone unrecognizable, the whole time thinking I owed her something, owed my family something. Did she ever care about me?

I was a child!

I swipe away tears and deflate.

She is dead. Roshi is sick. There's a gene. Everything has changed.

Framed photos decorate the wall and the console table across from me. In them, my family skis, hikes, and snorkels on vacation. We hold hands and laugh, following a photographer's silly instructions, and we sport coordinated costumes at the Halloween bashes I hosted yearly. In one picture, I'm clinking glasses and dancing, a sweep of bangs—dyed my signature auburn color—obscuring my mole. I was having fun, I'm sure. But I was also aware of the camera. Had I playacted my whole life on some level? Curated and faked it for the camera? For Dwayne?

No.

In my favorite wedding photo of us, our eyes are locked, both of us half smiling. I felt such wonder in that moment, knowing our electricity ran two ways, feeling safe in his arms. It was all that mattered. Even today, the photo sparks a love inside me that has never dimmed.

But though his eyes radiate love, they study me, like I'm a mystery. By then, I'd doled out a smattering of truths. He knew I'd seen a *foster* mother get beaten, then watched her bleed out a child. He knew I'd felt like an ugly misfit in junior high. I told him I'd lived out of a car in St. Augustine for weeks after escaping Miami. That

I'd quavered when a cop banged on the glass, pulled me out and threw me on the hood, asking for my license and registration. That I waitressed to put myself through a dental hygiene program in Jacksonville. He knew just enough to paint a picture. Blurry, but not fake.

I never faked it with the boys either. In a photo of Nico as an infant, I'm nuzzling his chubby cheek while Cam is draped across my body, laughing. Dwayne took the picture as we lounged in bed, and I can almost see him making faces at Cam. I'm disheveled—roots showing, plain-faced, wearing misshapen nursing clothes—but I've always loved that picture. It felt like my heart on display. And in it, I'm no one else but Maya.

Dwayne's words come back to me—*You have all the family you need.* I believed this once, certainly in that moment, but it's untrue.

Roshi's missing from the wall. My siblings and Ma, too. They should have watched me marry Dwayne, walking barefoot toward him on the beach where he proposed.

My eyes settle on a photograph that includes Vernon, who researches cancer at the university. He'll be at Denise and Dwayne's parents' fiftieth anniversary party this weekend. I need to be ready to talk to him about Roshi, about the gene. He might be able to help her. And me.

Feeling lighter with a plan forming in my head, I pull out my phone to cancel the nail appointment and my commitment in Camden's class. Then I text my cooking group: **Bad headache, feeling sick. Gonna skip.** It'll be the first one I've missed in years.

My friends respond with **feel better's** and **miss you's**.

Denise responds with **rest up before the party** along with a dance emoji.

I ditto her emoji and my heart flutters with guilt. She, who's been a surrogate sister to me all these years, who was matron of honor at my wedding, who watched my children enter this world—will she understand? Would my fingers even cooperate if I tried to sign an apology? *Sorry I lied to you all these years even though every time we spoke, my own deaf sister glimmered from inside you.* Denise would have every right to never speak to me again. I try to picture her meeting Roshi, the two of them signing, but I can't. I've spent too long pushing them apart in my head.

When Camden was born and pronounced deaf eleven years ago, I wanted to confess everything. I'd sobbed, and Denise hugged me, saying, "It didn't hold me back." Dwayne pointed out our good fortune—an extended family fluent in sign language and familiar with the deaf world. They thought my tears were those of a hormonal mother adjusting to difficult news. They couldn't know of my shame for keeping Roshi and Pappo a secret, of the words jammed in my throat—*Oh, by the way, deafness runs in my family, too, the one I never told you about*—of the feeling of God screaming at me, punishing me through Camden for every sin I'd committed.

But I didn't speak because the moment Cam's eyes locked onto mine, I felt the deepest love I'd ever felt and a fierce urge to protect him. Long-buried memories flashed, and I vowed to give him the unconditional love I'd never received. To keep him safe from my father who would have called him Dougla, or worse, and looked at him with scorn. And to keep him hidden from the man who would gleefully turn me in for obtaining legal status with a dead girl's name. The stakes were suddenly higher. I couldn't risk exposing my alias. It would mean risking deportation, even imprisonment for the crime, and leaving Cam motherless.

So, I dug in and threw myself into motherhood. Dwayne jokes that I invented "Maya 2.0" then. I joined a deaf infant mommy-and-me group where I met my best friends. We bonded during nature hikes and craft playdates, then started a cooking blog to share recipes for fusion baby food. At the library's story time, we signed in synchrony to the librarian's story, and we grew a small following. Denise joined us when her daughter Simone was born, just months after Nico, and our following took off.

There's a photo of my boys signing "Happy Birthday" to Simone on her first birthday, huge grins on all their faces. Nico, barely a year old, is clapping his chest with both hands, looking up to Cam, who's guiding him. Born in an immersive deaf world, Nico signed before he spoke. I tear up remembering his little hand grabbing his cheek, saying apple.

Daily, my life grew ever more precious. A chest-tightening panic often gripped me when I imagined losing it, so I insulated us with my lie and prayed my buried past would decay.

But the past has come roaring up from the grave.

Gene.

I pick up a photo from the console: Dwayne and the boys at an amusement park a few years ago. I was sick and couldn't go. Denise likely took the photo. Dwayne holds Cam up like a trophy while Nico sits on his shoulders. Just the three of them. That's how it'd be if I died.

I can't die. The boys are too young; they still need me. And I still have too much life to live—graduations, trips, birthdays, weddings. I'm scared to come clean, but it might be the only way to save what I've built.

Inside our family office, boxes line the closet's top shelf. Most are Dwayne's, packed with school memorabilia. One is labeled "Maya's Dentistry Books." Textbooks and notebooks do indeed fill the top half, but they hide a bag. I use a stool to retrieve the box, heavy and coated with dust. The tape is still intact, proof that Dwayne hasn't looked inside in the twelve years we've lived here.

I unpack books and papers to find the faded backpack near the bottom. It's smaller than I remember, but it still smells faintly of crayons. The evidence of my past selves is crammed inside. Letters and photographs. Documents. Clothes. Artifacts packed that last day in Miami.

Memories surface, threatening to derail me again. Notes from a boy, my first love.

To push them down, I clutch the backpack to my chest and review my plan. I'll look up Roshi's website, and I'll email her to figure out her status. Will we reconnect, speaking in sign language? God, that'll be strange. I'll research her cancer and the gene. Then I'll hunt for my hunter. Instinctively, I shake my head to expunge him—just the thought of googling him makes me sick. But maybe he's no longer a threat. Maybe he's just a jumbie I've been needlessly fearing. I need to know where he is before I talk to Dwayne, how much of a threat he still poses. Then, perhaps in a few days' time, I'll lay out the bag's contents for Dwayne, to reveal every secret I've kept, from that first day in Miami to that last one, the day I won the revenge that forced me into hiding.

My phone dings, bringing me out of my head.

It's a text from Dwayne: **You're Sunny, aren't you?**

PART THREE

NEENA

1985–1986
MIAMI, FLORIDA

17

Back to School

She barely slept that night, huddling near the suitcase until the digital clock said three thirty. The soreness between her legs made movement difficult, but she pulled on loose jeans that once belonged to a dead girl and braided her hair into a waist-long plait.

My name is Neena. I'm Neena. Thinking these words gave her confidence as she tiptoed into the kitchen to make lunches as Prem and Lila slept.

Out in the fields, she cut sunflowers and daisies as the sky pinked. She filled out her log sheet and left the flowers in buckets of water at the stand for Yvonne. Then, gripping her lunch box, she walked a block past the gate to wait for Janna.

Janna arrived alone.

As she entered the car, she formulated proper words. "Thank you for picking me up. Are the girls missing school today?"

"Oh, no. Elementary school doesn't start for another two hours. David's with them."

David—Janna's husband, whom she hadn't yet met. Photos on their walls made him look like a TV dad. A perfect match for Janna, who had long proved to be a TV mom.

"I brought you a backpack," Janna said as the farm vanished in the rearview mirror.

A multicolored canvas bag sat in the back seat. A large pink pocket on the front featured a smiling sticker and a peace-sign button. She'd seen this bag in Leslie's room.

"It's Les's from last year, but it's still in good condition. There are some supplies inside, including deodorant for PE. Go through it and let me know if you need something else."

The pink pocket contained pencils, pens, and erasers, but it smelled of crayons. The main compartment held paper, notebooks, folders, and the deodorant Janna mentioned. She recognized it from a TV ad. The jingle, "Raise your hand if you're sure," popped into her head.

Her eyes watered at this extravagant gift. "Thank you," she whispered.

"You're welcome, sweetie. I'll show you to your classes today."

As a guitar intro played on the radio, she snuck Leslie's toys from her pocket and wedged them in the seat crevice for the girls to find.

Janna turned up the volume. "I love this song," she said. "U2's 'Bad.'"

The car sped toward school, and evocative lyrics about letting go, fading away, and being wide awake filled her gut with butterflies.

I'm Neena. Neena can do this.

As she climbed the stairs beside Janna to the school's main entrance, each step triggered a shooting pain. Kids bounced by like balls, some calling out, "Hey, Mrs. Parker," but she kept her eyes cast down, worried they could see the damage inside her.

Janna showed her how to open her locker, and she stowed her lunch box. Nearby, kids slammed doors on lockers decorated with photographs and mirrors. Her lunch box looked childish and pathetic in her empty one.

Walking to first period required two sets of stairs, prompting more pain. Janna explained the bell system, and she tried to understand. But she was distracted by the chaos—kids rushing in every direction, shouting greetings at each other. She spotted Bianca, who looked past her as she giggled with a friend.

"Here's your homeroom and first period," Janna announced.

They stepped into a windowless classroom, illuminated by rectangles of overhead lights. Rows of chairs faced a teacher's desk, a setup that felt familiar. But familiarity ended there. Packed bookshelves and tables lined the periphery, and poster-covered walls threatened to close in on her. *I am Neena.*

"Flora," Janna said, approaching the teacher who stood beside a glowing machine.

She waited just inside the door, hoping to remain invisible. Students streamed in, talking loudly and bristling with energy. Chairs squealed, backpacks thudded, and papers rustled, preventing her from hearing anything Janna said to the teacher.

Janna motioned her over. "This is Mrs. Bly, your homeroom and history teacher." Janna turned to the teacher and said, "Neena just joined her family here, from Guyana."

Mrs. Bly's face lit up. "Oh, Guyana! Jim Jones's Guyana?"

She'd never heard of Jim Jones, but Mrs. Bly's tone made the man seem like a good thing. So, she smiled and nodded reflexively.

Mrs. Bly faced the classroom. "Oh, class. Everyone. Settle down. This is our newest student, Neena Das. She's from Guyana, a fascinating little country."

Her head swam under the gaze of so many eyes. To keep her face forward and placid, she channeled her namesake and repeated *fascinating little country* in her head.

A GIRL WITHIN A GIRL WITHIN A GIRL

Janna left, and Mrs. Bly pointed her to an empty seat before recounting the story of Jonestown and Jim Jones. It wasn't a good thing. Kids gasped and guffawed as Mrs. Bly told them of a temple run by a madman who'd poisoned one thousand people, three hundred of them children, with Kool-Aid. Upon learning this truth about her *fascinating little country*, her face flamed. Eyes lit on her as if she'd had something to do with the poisoning. She thought of the blue Kool-Aid from that first day and wondered why Janna hadn't mentioned Jim Jones.

Her science teacher, also excited to hear she'd come from Guyana, asked if she knew anything about the jaguars, tapirs, and giant anteaters that lived there. Shaking her head no, she felt as if she'd failed at being Guyanese.

As the morning went on, she felt more and more stupid. The kids around her, though only slightly older, seemed light years ahead. They spoke to the teachers as equals and discussed things with a level of sophistication she feared she'd never match. The English teacher pulled down a map to point out Guyana and other countries the British had colonized, saying "after slavery ended, they created a vast diaspora of people from India with indentured servitude." Someone asked, "Like how the Jews were displaced?" The conversation veered to war and a diary written by a girl named Anne Frank, a book everyone had read the previous year.

Her backpack grew heavy with books, and around noon, Janna sent her to swap the books out for her lunch box. As she fumbled with the locker, a girl behind her said, "Is that braid like cultural or something?"

Braid. Americans said *braid*, not *plait*, she'd recently noticed. She turned, touching her hair, wondering if the question was genuine. But the girl's laughing eyes told her it wasn't. The girl touched her own forehead. "Don't you need like a dot right here to go with it?"

The girl, her bangs in a stiff wave above her head, walked off with her giggling friends, confirming what she suspected. She was in a sea of Annettes and Navis. And like those rich girls, her peers traded in currency she couldn't access. Theirs was a world of cool clothes, glib mannerisms, and gravity-defying hair.

The chaotic lunchroom smelled like a dirty microwave and rang with the din of too many kids talking at once. Janna introduced her to three girls—Heather, Tiffany, and Wendy—and asked if she could eat beside them. They seemed genuinely glad to welcome her. After Janna left, they smiled and asked how she liked the school. She nodded and tilted away. Even if their kindness wasn't fake, it was forced, and she didn't want to be beholden to them. Plus, she didn't want to *sound Guyanese*. They exchanged confused looks before returning to their conversation, and she felt a small surge of power. Silence was a weapon.

After lunch, Janna escorted her to the girls' locker room, a stuffy, wet-smelling place. Girls flashed bras, pale skin, and underwear as they changed into tiny black shorts and green T-shirts for PE. "You don't have to change out today," Janna said. "You have your placement tests. But I'll introduce you to the teacher."

Outside, Janna chatted with the gym teacher as girls began doing jumping jacks and push-ups in the skimpy clothes. She prayed hard to the jumbie, the only spirit she felt anymore. If the jumbie had any power, she pleaded with it to help her avoid the fate of PE and having to change in front of a bunch of girls.

The jumbie answered. She failed the placement tests.

"That's okay," Janna said. "We'll pull you from PE for a little tutoring instead." They walked to the library to meet the resource teacher, Mrs. Macy. "You'll meet here during lunch and fifth period for remediation. Just a little help so you can catch up."

The low-ceilinged library smelled of aging paper, warm and smoky. That she could hide in that cozy space instead of sitting next to girls forced to eat with her or running around half-dressed at PE felt like a blessing from the jumbie.

The trailer was empty when she got home, and Lila's car was gone. Heart racing, she rushed through her chores, hoping to be done before anyone returned. In the greenhouse, she transferred seedlings and filled out her log sheet in record time, grateful to not see Prem. She whipped up a quick meal of rice and egg curry while washing and drying Janna's laundry on the rapid cycle. After a three-minute shower, she stood in her bedroom, her back against the door.

Her gaze slid to the bureau. She ran around it and pushed hard. It barely budged. Panicked, knowing Prem would be home soon, she removed the drawers to lighten it. Then she shoved it in front of the door. Minutes later, his footsteps shook the trailer.

She dropped to the floor and waited, her whole body pounding out her heartbeat.

She expected him to hammer the door with his fist, to yell and push past the bureau. But she only heard cutlery against plates and a sitcom's laugh track. She was folding Janna's dry laundry, which she'd deposited in her room, when Lila returned. No one mentioned her. Drifting off to sleep, she chanted thanks to the jumbie, certain it was guiding her. She was Neena.

But Prem's eyes followed her as she made dinner that Saturday night. She'd spent the day cleaning houses and rooting poinsettia cuttings in the greenhouses with Lila, doubling her quota to make up for being gone during the week. Her body ached, and she was eager to escape to her room. But the bureau wouldn't budge this time. Prem had nailed it to the wall.

Terrified, she stacked the full drawers against the door. When she heard footsteps, she thought, *I am Neena*, and added her body to the weight against the door.

The door jangled against the drawers, and Prem peered through a crack, laughing. "You think you're in charge, but I'll show you who's boss. This is my house."

Later that week, he drove screws into the bureau, making the drawers difficult to remove, so she shoved the crib against the door. When he tossed the crib into the dumpster, she used her bed as a barricade. He secured that to the wall a week later, and she pressed her mattress against the door, determined to stay a step ahead of this terrifying game of hide-and-seek.

The late September day the real Neena would have turned sixteen, she stood at the bus feeling sore. Prem had pushed past her mattress, and she'd awoken under his weight. "I'm in charge," he'd hissed before leaving. She was thinking about some concrete bricks she'd spied behind the laundry shed, imagining sneaking some under her bed after school when Janna pulled up.

"Good morning, birthday girl," Janna said. "Thought I'd take you to school to celebrate. Hop in."

She'd forgotten about the birthday.

"How's it feel to be sweet sixteen?" Janna asked.

She buckled her seat belt and shrugged at this absurd question. In some ways, she felt much older than sixteen, though she was not quite thirteen. Did anyone feel their age?

"That's for you."

A bow-tied journal and marker set sat on the center console next to a plastic-wrapped Little Debbie cake. Her eyes watered at this unexpected thoughtfulness.

"Gosh, Janna, thank you," she said. "It's so nice." She'd never received a wrapped birthday gift. Her family had celebrated with food, she and her sisters working with their mother to make the birthday child's favorite dessert. Would her family celebrate her birthday when it arrived that year, October 31, sharing salara, the cinnamon coconut bread she loved? Even though she hadn't written? How could she possibly write about what she was enduring?

That night, she wedged her box spring between the door and bed frame, then she nibbled the Little Debbie cake on her mattress, which now sat on the ground. *Dear Roshi, today was a good day and a terrible day. Maybe he'll leave me alone now that he's won.*

Near midnight, the box spring landed atop her, startling her out of a dream. She propelled herself from under the thing and stumbled into the living room, shrieking, half inside a nightmare.

A light flicked on, and she saw Lila in the kitchen.

"You must really want me call the police," Lila said, grabbing the wall-mounted phone.

Prem stepped from her room, holding a screwdriver. Her doorknob now dangled from a hole. "This girl thinks she can control where I go in my own house. She needs to know better."

Lila began dialing, and Prem leapt at the woman. He yanked the receiver and slammed it down. Then he held the screwdriver to Lila's neck.

I am Neena. Courage surged into her. Neena sprang for the front door. She'd just touched the knob when Prem gripped her shirt and pulled her back, choking her. He threw her like a rag onto the coffee table. She screamed as the table's corner connected with her pelvic bone. She righted herself and crawled behind the table just as a loud whack met a different body.

Lila had swung a broom at Prem's back. She looked possessed, clutching the broom stick, her knuckles white.

"You guh pay for that." Prem wagged a finger at Lila. With the screwdriver, he pointed at Neena, still on the floor, and hissed, "Get in that room." Both arms out, he looked like a cross.

She spat at him, but nothing came from her dry lips.

He stared at her even as he addressed Lila. "See how she disrespect me? You teach the girl this, so you both guh pay. You want call the police? Call, and they guh take all of we away."

A knock on the door startled them all. Were the police somehow at the door? If they were, was it a good thing?

She stood as Lila placed the broom in a corner and Prem opened the door.

Yvonne's dad stood outside, his sons and a few workers peering from behind him. "Todos bien, Jefecito? These guys hear some noise and screaming."

She knew Prem hated the nickname, Jefecito, little boss. He was much shorter than Don.

"Sí, amigo," Prem said, "everything all right. A little argument, that's all."

Don nodded and took a step forward. He looked from Lila to Neena, his eyes pausing on the broken doorknob. "Javier can fix that, mañana."

Javier, Don's son, served as the farm's handyman. He leaned forward to look.

"Okay. Thank you," Lila said, and Neena looked down, embarrassed.

Don chuckled. "Sí. All right. Just making sure the señoritas are okay. Buenas noches."

After Don left, Prem seethed, "Get to your rooms."

She propped her box spring against the broken door as Prem settled himself mere feet away. She stayed awake on her wedged mattress all night, listening to him snore on the couch. Her body ached from the hit she took, but she felt strong. Like a lion, not a mouse.

The next morning, she came out of her room after she heard him leave. As she prepared breakfast and packed lunches, Lila helped, and when they walked out to cut flowers, Lila looked at Neena with something close to a smile.

18

Hermana

Javier installed a locking doorknob while she was at school. That night, Neena sat on her bed and stared at her locked door, listening for Prem. Her heart pounded as she heard him heating food in the microwave and turning on the TV.

Just as she began to relax, he shouted, "Get out here."

She stepped into the living room and was grateful to see Lila in the kitchen.

He shoved his dinner plate to the edge of the coffee table. "This shit's tasteless. And your hair is in it. Throw it away and fix me something else."

His retaliation continued the following days. He sought her out in the greenhouse and made her redo tasks. She barely met her quotas, but she was grateful he stayed away from her door. For good measure, she snuck in half a dozen concrete bricks from around the property to help barricade her room.

To keep up with the extra work, she set her alarm and rose even earlier to complete her log sheet before catching the school bus. In her seat, she cleaned dirt from her fingernails with a broken pencil tip and applied extra deodorant to mask the earthy smell that clung to her clothes. Then, amid the roar of kids who ignored her, she tucked in to read, almost happy, grateful for the long school days that buffered her from the farm.

She raced through every easy book series her resource teacher recommended, and she savored the more challenging ones the librarian handed her: *Tiger Eyes*, *Stranger with My Face*, and *Heaven*. The books transported her to other kids' worlds and problems, allowing her own problems—Prem, Mr. Michael, and her insane workload—to briefly disappear.

By the time her actual birthday arrived, she'd eased into feeling occasional moments of joy again. She understood the day was a holiday, Halloween, that involved costume contests, something called trick-or-treating, and candy. Kids boarded the school bus wearing wigs and strange clothes, and though she felt more out of place than usual in her loose jeans and blouse, she reveled in the festive air. When teachers passed out candy, she pretended they were celebrating her.

But her joy dimmed that Sunday when Mr. Michael arrived for his second installment. Lila sent her outside to wait for him with an envelope containing less money than he expected.

The white truck pulled up, and his associate winked from the driver's seat.

Mr. Michael got out, and Neena approached him, holding the envelope in an outstretched hand. "I, uh, um, since I started school, I can't work as much. So it's less."

Mr. Michael riffled through the bills, then he spat on the ground and looked at Lila, who'd appeared in the trailer's doorway with crossed arms. "You must be paying yourself before you pay me," he said. He spat again and addressed Neena. "You lucky I know your daddy so good. But at this rate, you might still owe me by the time I find a man to marry you."

"I don't need a big dowry," Mr. Michael's man announced, and the men laughed.

The day before winter break, at the Christmas recital in the auditorium, two girls, one in a green velvet dress and the other in a red flounce skirt, sat on stage and played a violin and a piano, evoking magic from the complicated instruments. Their beautiful, haunting music untethered something inside Neena. She felt goosebumps in places goosebumps shouldn't exist. Her esophagus, stomach, intestines. Her vagina, urethra, anus. Embarrassing words that labeled embarrassing places she'd learned about in science class. Her insides quivered and cramped as if the girls onstage strummed and bowed her instead of their instruments.

She clutched the soft seat and dug her finger into a hole, scraping the hidden foam with her nail. Sweat pricked her skin and she felt herself growing into a wet, slimy thing. To escape the affecting music, she scrambled down the aisle, tripping across legs. Kids snickered and recoiled from her touch. She tumbled from the suffocating velvet-walled room, gasping for air.

Her pants felt damp, as if she'd peed herself. She wanted to find a bathroom, but the hallway—home to drama, music, and dance students—was unfamiliar. She stumbled through the halls, weaving away from the vibrations until she reached the library.

Nestled between two bookshelves, she hugged her knees to her chest. But even the hush of that dark refuge couldn't quiet the haunting chords. Music continued to reverberate through her body, making her abdomen ache. Tears slid down her cheeks, and her crotch grew wetter. She was leaking everywhere. She pressed her knees painfully against her eyeballs to stop the crying. She hadn't cried at school once, no matter her anguish. But a strangled gasp escaped her.

"Neena?"

She looked up, startled to find Mrs. Fredrickson, the librarian.
"Are you all right, darling?"
She nodded vigorously, salt crusting on her cheeks.
"Are you certain? Why aren't you at the theater for the show?" Mrs. Fredrickson asked, showing off her British accent.
Neena marveled at the phrasing *theater for the show*, words to pocket. Her homeroom teacher had said they were going to the "auditorium for the recital," which seemed dull in comparison. She stared at the librarian; how could she explain that the music was too beautiful, that it hurt? Her overloaded brain formulated an improper sentence, *the music pain me*. She didn't want the librarian's eyes to dim with pity as patois tumbled past her lips.
"Oh, come now, darling," Mrs. Fredrickson said, reaching out a hand.
Neena didn't want the hand. She'd never touched a teacher before. Still, she allowed Mrs. Fredrickson's impossibly soft hand to pull her up. When she stood, her stomach seized. She gasped and clutched her sides involuntarily.
Mrs. Fredrickson said, "Ah. I see, darling. That's nothing to be ashamed of. You've got your period. It happens to all of us ladies. I'm sorry it ruined the show for you, but it's easy enough to manage. You're a young lady, now."
Those words echoed tauntingly in her head. *Young lady now. Young lady now.* She looked down. Blood bloomed across the crotch of her gray pants. She stared at it uncomprehendingly. She'd only ever bled after Prem tore into her.
In the school clinic, an antiseptic, blue-walled room, a nurse handed her a rectangular wad of cotton and a printout with embarrassing cartoon instructions. Clean clothes made their way into her hands. Pink underwear, a pair of black shorts, and a green T-shirt, which she recognized as the PE uniform. She strategically folded her soiled pants and underwear to hide the blood and placed the flowered shirt she'd been wearing on top. She inserted

the bloody pile in a thin "Thank You, Come Again" plastic bag the nurse gave her. The package felt explosive.

She'd worn shorts only that one time in Janna's pool. She felt almost naked and worried the cotton wedge would protrude if she moved too fast.

"Your family should be here soon," the nurse said in a sympathetic tone, handing over her backpack, somehow retrieved from Mrs. Bly's classroom.

Her *family*, meaning Prem and Lila—the last people on earth she wanted to see. Her real family felt out of reach and blurry. After she stopped being Sunny, she'd pushed them from her mind. Even Roshi. She hadn't received another letter, and she worried it was because she hadn't returned one. She had filled a sheet of paper with lies—*I'm doing well. I'll send money. I'll see you in six years*—but she couldn't bring herself to mail it.

She wished Janna were there. Her lower abdomen ached as she pictured facing Prem, whom the school likely contacted since Lila would be cleaning a house. Trembling, she stared at a poinsettia in the corner to ground herself. The plant was grossly red. A lady plant, she thought. Mrs. Fredrickson's embarrassing words returned to her. *Young lady. Us ladies.*

Lady. Woman. Miss. Ma'am. She didn't want any of those words associated with her.

The nurse interrupted her thoughts. "Your sister's here." Sister? She must have looked perplexed because the woman added, "Your father sent her."

She imagined Roshi somehow awaiting her. *Roshi, has this happened to you, too?* Rounding the corner, she saw Yvonne, heavily painted and scantily dressed as usual.

"Hola, Neena."

Despite the crippling cramps, Neena smiled widely, grateful for Yvonne's beautiful, light-filled face.

As she climbed into the passenger seat of the rusty yellow coupe, Neena imagined saying, *This is weird.* She'd been dying to use that American phrase, and it fit. It felt weird to enter a car with this magnetic girl she barely knew, to slide low into a front seat reclined almost flat, and to see the ground through a hole in the car's metal floorboard.

Her shorts rode up, and her bare thighs spread out like chicken drumsticks on the cracked leather. The pad was a monstrous lump in her crotch. She covered her lap with the backpack.

"Jefecito's busy," Yvonne said, smiling brightly. Her front teeth flashed under candy-red lips, and her eyelashes sank, heavy with mascara. A crop top stretched against her ample chest, and rips in her jeans exposed swaths of soft flesh. "So Papi sent me, said to say I'm your sister. Hermanas—you and me!"

She giggled, and Neena smiled shyly.

"Papi said you were sick and need medicine, and your dad gave me money. But the teacher said you got your . . . you know." Yvonne whispered the last words and giggled again.

Neena flushed. She couldn't even think the word Mrs. Fredrickson and the nurse had uttered so casually. Yvonne's whisper made it clear those women were the weirdos.

"I got you. Okay, chica?" Yvonne rummaged in her purse, then handed Neena a stick of gum and two white pills. "Take those—for the dolor," she said, patting her belly.

She turned the car on, and Tina Turner's "What's Love Got to Do with It" screamed over the radio. Neena's insides reset. It felt good to hear pop music, the opposite of what those primped girls played onstage. And it felt good to be called *chica*. It sounded like the opposite of *lady*.

"We got Javi's car and Jefecito's money, so let's go have us some fun." Yvonne smiled. Both of Yvonne's older brothers, Javier and

Oscar, owned cars. They often worked on them, playing loud music and laughing, making her miss her own brothers.

Yvonne revved the car out onto the too-quiet street, and Neena thought, this is so cool, another American phrase she'd wanted to try. She swallowed the pills, then popped the minty gum in her mouth. She felt like a kid in a TV commercial, leaving school with a pretty teenager in a sports car, chewing gum, windows down, blaring fun music in the middle of the day.

"I was so scared my first time," Yvonne shouted above the music. "Thought I was dying. But you get used to it, chica. You're lucky you got it so late. Sixteen? I was eleven. So little, and I didn't know nothing. And I already had these." Yvonne jiggled her boobs and laughed.

Neena smiled, feeling younger than she'd felt in months. "How old are you?" she blurted.

Yvonne looked startled to hear her voice. "Seventeen. One more year, and I'm gone. Fin. Adiós." She laughed and sang the chorus, "Who needs a heart when a heart can be broken."

Surprising herself, Neena joined in, as if Yvonne had magically unlocked her old self.

They drove and sang until Yvonne pulled into a strip mall parking lot. "Vamos."

Neena exited the car and tugged her shorts down to cover more of her legs.

"Chica, look at you, you look good!" Yvonne said. "Why you always cover up under those ugly clothes? We got to fix that!"

Neena felt herself go hot at this compliment and insult.

"It's Goodwill," Yvonne said, leading her into the overstuffed store. An assortment of furniture sat in the entrance, but the store was empty of people. "Rich people donate this stuff for people like us, sometimes even *girl stuff*. And they sell it. But I know the people that work here. They're probably in the back, so let's get shopping." She winked.

People like us. Neena liked being lumped into whatever group Yvonne belonged to. And she liked the store. It was like a thousand garage sales in one.

In the clothing area, Yvonne handed her a pair of jeans from a box on a messy table and whispered, "Put it on, and don't take it off."

Neena understood this game instantly. She ducked and pulled the pants over her shorts. At Yvonne's urging, she slipped a cropped T-shirt over the one she'd worn into the store and tied a man's plaid shirt around her waist.

Yvonne tucked a pair of tights into her own waist and threw on a blazer.

A worker walked out from the back, and Yvonne called, "Cara, mi amor, how you been?"

Neena's heart raced. If Cara recognized the clothes on Neena's body, would she call the police? Could they get deported? What would Prem do?

But Cara waved back. "Good. You?"

"Real good," Yvonne said. "Y'all got new stuff in."

"Yeah," Cara said. "And everyone called in sick, so I'm on my own. Pain in my ass!"

Yvonne laughed.

After an hour of sifting through boxes and Yvonne saying, "Oh, sí, sí," or "Dios mío, no," they approached the counter with a pile of clothes, worn jelly shoes, and a roll of mesh fabric Yvonne planned to convert into clothes.

"This stuff's on discount, no?" Yvonne asked, before adding in a pseudo-whisper, "And you got any girl stuff?"

Neena averted her eyes as Cara plunked a half-full box of pads and an opened box of tampons onto the counter. "I saved them for you."

Miraculously, the total for their loot only came to five dollars. Neena felt giddy, but she was also terrified of what Lila and Prem would say about the new clothes. Would Prem know she'd stolen some of it? Would he punish her?

"Maybe you can keep it for me?" she said as Yvonne threw the bags into the trunk.

"Nah. Tell Lila this shit's from me. And I got more, stuff that don't fit me no more. It would look cute on you."

Inside the car, Yvonne reached for Neena's face. "Come here, let me see." Yvonne gripped her jaw and twisted it side to side with rough hands. Then she pulled the rubber band from Neena's thick braid and said, "Take that shit out."

Neena undid her hair as Yvonne retrieved a lipstick from her purse.

"Do this," Yvonne commanded, puckering up.

Neena tried to mirror Yvonne's pout as Yvonne dabbed lipstick onto her lips. And she mirrored the pressing, smearing motion after.

Yvonne then applied powder, blush, eyeliner, and mascara. It was strange to feel hands on her face and to smell Yvonne's minty breath so close. But she didn't flinch, even when Yvonne almost poked her eyes. She was reminded of how easily and often Roshi used to touch her. She wished Roshi could see this makeover. *Roshi, you'd like Yvonne.*

After, Yvonne sat back and assessed Neena's face. She fluffed her waist-long hair and tsk-tsked. "Wait here. And don't look yet."

Yvonne darted back into the store and emerged with a pair of scissors. "I saw this layer cut in a magazine. It would look so good on you. Can I try?"

She nodded.

"Javi will kill me if we get hair in the car. Let's get out."

Outside the car, Yvonne finger-combed Neena's hair and snipped. Long chunks of black hair circled her feet, and Neena grew lightheaded wondering if she was tempting God again. This was not something she could hide. But she didn't want Yvonne to stop. She wanted Yvonne's hands in her hair, coaxing dead parts within her to life.

Yvonne teased, flipped, and fastened her hair, which now skimmed her shoulders. "Close your eyes," she said, holding up a can of hairspray. After spraying, she said, "Mira," pointing to the car's side mirror.

Neena peeked into the mirror and couldn't help the "Oh!" that escaped her lips. She didn't recognize herself.

Yvonne emitted a shrill laugh that echoed through the parking lot.

Neena couldn't stop staring. She'd been transformed. Heavy bangs covered her forehead. A puffy half ponytail spouted on top of her head while the rest of her hair grazed her shoulders. Her eyes were lined black and powdered in blue. And her lips were absurdly red. Yvonne red.

"You look hot, chica!" Yvonne said. "Ay, ay, ay."

She blushed. She was a mini Yvonne. Too loud. "Lila won't like it. I mean, my mom."

"No offense or anything," Yvonne said, "but your mom's a puta."

A strained laugh escaped Neena's body. She looked at Yvonne, who erupted in contagious laughter, and the two fell to the ground.

When they finally calmed down, Yvonne handed Neena a lipstick. "You look good, girl. Here, you take this one. Wear it at school." She winked.

19

Hot Tamale

Neena hid the makeup and clothes in the bureau and tucked her hair in a small ponytail. She wanted to hide her period, too.

But after she barricaded herself that night, Lila rapped on her door and said, "Open up."

Neena pushed the concrete bricks aside and opened the door.

Lila's eyes moved from her haircut to the bricks on the floor as she stepped inside and closed the door. She spoke quietly. "Yvonne got you what you need?"

Neena nodded. If Lila knew about her period, that meant Prem knew, too.

"You know what this means?"

A picture of the uterus from science class invaded her mind. *Menses. Ovaries. Gestation.*

"You know how to use the stuff?"

Her face heated up as she recalled Yvonne miming perverse tampon instructions.

"I don't want stains all over the sheets."

More vile images flashed through her mind. Blood on Lila's sheets. Blood on Papa Smurf's face.

"I have half a mind to send you back right now," Lila hissed.

Neena stared at the floor. She shuddered to think of being sent to Mr. Michael, or his man. She tried to imagine returning to Guyana, standing in the bottom-house with her suitcase, but she couldn't.

"If not for Janna, I would," Lila said.

Neena nodded at the ground. Janna was Lila's highest-paying client. Lila wouldn't risk losing that job by upsetting her. Plus, Mr. Michael would still demand his money.

Lila leaned forward. "But if you get pregnant, you'll be on the street, Janna or not. If he comes anywhere near you, you better kick and scream for Don."

Neena nodded, filled with shame.

School was out for two weeks, so Neena helped Lila clean houses during the day and tripled her quota in the greenhouses. Perhaps because Jefe was around more, Prem left her alone.

At Janna's house midweek, Neena stood transfixed by the twinkling Christmas tree in the living room—a real tree, smelling of pine—as Nicole gushed over her haircut.

Janna led them to the refrigerator, where Neena's report card had been printed and magnetized next to all the girls' straight As.

"As in math and art, and Bs in the rest," Janna said. "Aren't you proud of this girl? After such a bumpy start?"

"Yes," Lila lied before turning to gather the cleaning supplies.

Neena never thought to show any of her report cards to Lila, certainly not the ones with Cs and Ds. She was embarrassed to see her still inferior grades adjacent the girls' perfect ones.

Janna's husband walked in from the garage, carrying a box of lights. "So this is the famous Neena! I'm David. So nice to meet you."

David reached out a hand, and she took it. He was tall with sandy blond hair and grayish blue eyes. Like Janna, he struck her as a grown-up version of the popular kids at school.

"Merry Christmas, Lila," David said. "Good to see you. I was hoping you could get the garage floors and shelves today. I made a mess pulling out Christmas things."

"Yes, Mr. Parker, I'll do that first," Lila said. She pushed the vacuum and duster toward Neena. "Go get started upstairs."

"Lila," Janna pleaded in a sugary voice, "I was hoping Neena could help the girls make ornaments today. They never see her anymore. Skip the girls' rooms today if that's too much."

So, Neena cut, glued, and glittered ornaments with the girls, listening to carols on the radio, the whole time feeling guilty and fearing Lila's wrath.

When they were to leave, Janna handed her a festive paper bag full of wrapped gifts.

"Open mine now," Nicole said, clinging to her hand.

"Nic, maybe their family opens gifts on Christmas," Janna countered.

"We don't celebrate Christmas," Lila snapped, and Neena considered declining the gifts.

"Oh, but we celebrate, Lila," Janna said, "and we feel blessed having you in our lives. The girls loved shopping for Neena, and there's something in there for you, too. Along with your bonus. You won't object to that, will you?"

Lila tightened her lips into a strained smile but didn't say anything.

"Open this first." Nicole pointed to a Santa-covered box. "I picked it out."

Neena sat on the soft carpet and carefully undid the colorful paper to reveal a tanned, brunette Barbie knockoff.

"She's like you," Nicole exclaimed. "You even have the same bangs now."

"Thank you, Nicole," Neena said, smiling. Did Nicole truly believe she looked like this perfect chestnut-haired doll?

Leslie's gift was a box of chocolates—twelve beautifully molded shapes in a yellow box.

"Try one," Leslie said.

Neena picked a rounded confection. Her mouth filled with saliva as the overrich scent filled her nostrils. *Roshi, oh my god!* She held the box toward Lila, who shook her head no.

The third gift, a light blue denim jacket, took her breath away. "Oh," she said, in shock.

"It'll get chilly soon, and I figured you didn't have a jacket." Janna winked and added, "The girls said this one's cool."

It was cool. Very cool. All the school kids wore jackets like it, even on warm days.

"She has a jacket," Lila said, although it was untrue. But Neena understood her reaction. The gifts were overwhelming, and two others remained in the bag.

"Save those for Christmas Day," Janna said. "One's for you, Lila, and the other is something the girls got for Neena. It's her first Christmas here, and we wanted it to be special."

In the car, Neena felt Lila bristling. "You're not coming back. I can't stand that lady, acting like she owns you because she gives you one or two things. She doesn't feed you and give you a bed. She doesn't pay Michael. I pay!"

Neena pressed herself into the back seat, clutching the gift bag.

Christmas approached, and the compound grew festive with twinkling lights and music. But a hole opened inside Neena. She hungered for pepper pot, black cake, and soca music, things that had marked the holiday for her in Guyana, a holiday her father always said was "the best thing the British give us, besides rum."

Christmas Eve, she pictured her family eating chicken curry, drinking soda, and dancing. They usually butchered an old hen for the holiday, and everyone got a sip of Pepsi. Had they talked about her as they plucked feathers the day before? Could Roshi join in now that she'd gotten hearing aids? Neena couldn't imagine this. What she could imagine was her mother stewing that she hadn't written back. She'd come close to asking Lila for stamps to mail her letter full of lies, but the question always caught in her throat.

She tried to capture some Christmas feeling by currying some chicken and making a batch of mithai, the crunchy fried dough they always made for Roshi's birthday in December.

Dear Roshi, I didn't even think of you on your birthday. I'm sorry. Things are so hectic, and I'm . . . different.

The curry tasted wrong, since the grocery-store chicken couldn't match the flavor of a fireside-roasted homegrown hen. And the mithai came out too soft since she misremembered the flour-butter-milk ratio.

Lila took a bite and called it garbage.

"I'll throw it out," Neena said. She tossed the treats into a paper bag and strode out. She'd intended to pretend to throw it away in the dumpster, then hide it in her room because they tasted great even if the texture wasn't perfect. But she found herself walking toward Yvonne's.

Yvonne and her brothers were lounging on chairs, listening to music and playing cards.

"Hey, Neena!" Yvonne waved to greet her.

"Hi." Neena held out the bag. "I made this. Happy Christmas."

Happy Christmas. It was what they said in Guyana, and aloud, the un-Americanness of her words hit her. Everyone said *Merry Christmas* here.

"Happy Christmas," Javier said, "I like that."

He was the one who'd fixed her door, and though she felt grateful for him, she couldn't meet his eye.

Yvonne's other brother, Oscar, said, "What's up?"

She nodded at him. He was the farm's mechanic and driver, repairing machines and delivering plants.

"Ma, look what Neena brought," Yvonne said, taking the bag and ushering her to their trailer. Yvonne's mother, Estelle, greeted her at the door. "Hola, chiquita. Your mami here?"

"No." She shook her head. She knew Lila wouldn't want her there, but the sweet air escaping the trailer drew her. She let Yvonne nudge her inside.

It was the same layout as her trailer, but the interior exploded with color. Haphazardly placed religious art and figurines filled the walls, including a frightening one of a bearded man on a cross. A small plastic Christmas tree sat in a corner, propped on boxes. Lights twinkled near the ceiling along the back wall. A sofa sat adjacent to a bunkbed, and a small TV sat on a low, cluttered bookshelf. Food covered two tables and the kitchen counter. Bags and boxes unabashedly filled corners and narrowed the walk space.

"Look, she brought this." Yvonne shoved her nose in the bag. "Dios mío, this smells so good. *You* made it?" She took out a soft mithai stick, ate it, and closed her eyes. "Oh, it's like sopapillas." She handed one to Estelle.

"Mmm," Estelle said, taking a bite. "Neena, you are such a good cook, you should teach Yvonne. Ven, I made empanaditas. Take some." Estelle pressed a flaky pastry into her hand.

She took a bite of the sugar-dusted dessert even though she worried Lila had already noticed her missing. The taste transported her back to a day she and Roshi gorged on overripe guavas until their stomachs ached. *Roshi, you need to try this.*

"It's amazing," Neena said. "Thank you. But I have to go. I just wanted to give you something. For Christmas."

"Come for tamales," Estelle said, returning to the stove. "Ask your mami. Es Navidad!"

Neena nodded.

"I have something for you, too," Yvonne said, tugging her into a bedroom.

Tousled pink covers tangled with sheets and pillows on Yvonne's bed, and magazine pages covered the wall. A small scrap-covered table held a sewing machine. But the room was mostly storage. Boxes and bags filled one side, and clothes hung from open racks and pegs.

"You have your own room?" Neena asked, surprised Yvonne didn't share with her brothers.

"Por supuesto," Yvonne said. "The boys have the bunk. I'm the girl. I need my space."

She handed Neena a plastic bag containing a stack of teen magazines and a mesh shirt constructed from the fabric from Goodwill. Yvonne made her try on the shirt over her clothes, then showed her the results in a warped mirror behind her door. The mirror stretched Neena's torso out, but she looked edgy and cool.

"Chica, you look like Madonna," Yvonne said.

"Thank you." Neena blushed. She took off the shirt and tucked it back into the bag.

"Come tonight. Puta madre doesn't have to know, right?"

It was true. Her bitch mother didn't need to know. She knew a way.

That night in her trailer, on her bedroom floor, a small feeling of Christmas flickered in Neena as she opened Janna's last gift. She wished her sisters were there. She'd give Roshi the gift because she'd already received so many. Indy would get the pretty paper. And Baby would get the ribbon.

It was a makeup set, complete with a small stand-up mirror. Her heart leapt. One of Yvonne's magazines featured an "ultimate styling tips" article she could now try.

She set the mirror up and teased her hair "for maximum body" before pulling it into a side ponytail. She applied gold powder to her eyes and maroon shades to her lips and cheeks. When she was done, only the tear-shaped mole linked her to her old self, and even that looked like jewelry on her new face. She pin-rolled her jeans, following the magazine's instructions, knotted her T-shirt, and threw Yvonne's mesh shirt over it.

When Prem thudded to the bathroom and turned on the shower, she squeezed through the window, leg first. Dangling half inside her room, her heart pounded. The room looked strange and messy from that angle, the mirror propped up on bricks, the makeup still out. She lowered herself onto some crates she'd stacked there earlier—a makeshift ladder. One fell with a clatter, and she crouched, her heart hammering. But water continued to rush through the pipes, and a burst of televised laughter sprang from Lila's room, blending with the music that drifted over from the other trailers. Neena crept around to the front door to retrieve her shoes. Then she ran toward the Hernandezes' glowing trailer.

"Hot tamale!" Yvonne shrieked when she saw her. Neena knew then that she'd discovered an escape hatch from her life.

20

Pink Carnations

Encouraged by Yvonne, Neena unveiled her new look after Christmas break. On a crisp January morning, she threw her jean jacket over Leslie's butterfly T-shirt, pin-rolled her pants, and heightened her bangs with hairspray. She cut carnations and chrysanthemums in this attire, and Lila looked at her funny but didn't say a word. On the bus, she applied eyeliner, mascara, and a smudge of wine-colored lipstick, all of which she planned to remove before returning home. Her goal was to look less weird at school, maybe even pretty.

In math class, someone asked, "Who's the new girl?"

And, that afternoon, a popular kid named Marcus smiled as he passed her seat on the bus, sending a current through her.

The attention disoriented and exhilarated her. But, like silence, her look felt like fresh armor. There was no going back.

A new routine began even as she continued meeting her quotas and finishing her chores. At school, she transformed herself into someone who walked taller. Weekend evenings, she snuck out her window to play gin rummy with Yvonne and Estelle. Sometimes, she lounged on Yvonne's bed, listening to the radio, flipping through magazines. Or she organized her friend's disheveled room while Yvonne altered clothes from her latest Goodwill haul.

"Where'd you learn to sew?" Neena asked one night.

"At this clothes factory I worked at with Mami, before the farm."

Neena learned that, as a child, Yvonne lived with her grandparents in Mexico while her parents worked under migrant visas in the States. When she was seven, her parents paid coyotes to smuggle her and her brothers into Texas, hiding them in busses and vans. They learned English at school, but the family moved to Texas, Alabama, Georgia, and Florida to find work. When Yvonne was thirteen, Don found work at Friendly Flowers, and he took the boys. Yvonne stayed with Estelle in Georgia, where they worked at a clothes factory, hemming skirts and blouses after school. It was grueling work, but Yvonne loved the fabric and clothes. At the farm, Don and the boys moved up, earning supervisor positions and securing the trailer. Don proposed the idea of the roadside stand to Jefe, saying his daughter and wife could run it, and when Yvonne and Estelle arrived, they made the stand a success. But Yvonne had bigger dreams. "One day, I'm gonna sell the clothes I make in a fancy store."

"What, like Goodwill?" Neena joked.

They cracked up. But Yvonne's fantasies made Neena realize that she, too, could one day leave the farm.

Dear Roshi, I have a new sister. And she makes me look cool.

On Valentine's Day, Mrs. Bly handed out "Valentine grams," pink and red carnations kids bought for each other to celebrate the strange holiday. Piles accrued on the popular girls' desks, and Neena wondered if the flowers grew from seedings she'd transplanted. She hadn't expected any, but two landed on her desk, their dewy smell filling her up. The pink one was from Janna, with a note reading, "Meet me after school! Girls have a gift!" The red one said, "From a secret admirer." Neena read those words with a forced nonchalance as her insides blazed.

She couldn't concentrate after that, worried the sender would reveal himself, that she'd have to break the stony silence she maintained, that nervousness would resurrect the lilt she'd worked so hard to diminish with Mrs. Macy. A part of her feared it was a practical joke; she'd seen something like that on a sitcom.

When she entered the library at lunch, Mrs. Fredrickson handed her a Valentine's Day recommendation, *Jane Eyre*. Her reading level had soared during remediation, and she looked forward to this new novel, having already reread *Pride and Prejudice* twice. She studied the back cover as she walked to the enclosed patio outside the library's back door, where she often worked with Mrs. Macy. She considered the picnic table her personal space, so she didn't expect a boy to be sitting there. He looked up at her with striking, light brown eyes, and her heart seized as he leapt to open the door.

Marcus. From the bus. An afternoon rider. One of the rare Black kids at school. A fellow minority. But unlike her, he was the sort of kid other kids called to in hallways, the sort of kid who was never alone. Yet, there he was, alone, in her spot. Was he her secret admirer?

"Hi," she said, her insides melting.

"Neena, right?" His voice betrayed a faint, unexpected lilt.

"Yeah," she said. She placed *Jane Eyre* on the table and retrieved her lunch box, which appeared like a toy in her hands. A small shame mingled with every other complicated thing she felt, and to push the feelings away, she asked, "Did you send the flower?"

He looked down and smiled. "Yes. I'm Marcus. We ride the same bus. But looks like you got two admirers." His eyes darted to the flowers peeking from her backpack.

A smile broke across her face, and she looked down at her shoes, a pair of Goodwill sneakers she and Yvonne had decorated with markers to cover up stains. She shook her head, feeling woozy. "That's from a teacher."

"Oh, phew," Marcus said. "So, there's this dance . . ."

She shook her head. "I can't." She'd seen flyers about the spring fling, but it felt like an event for other kids, not her. She'd never be allowed to go.

"Oh."

"Sorry, it's just . . . I can't . . ."

"No, I get it. Well, maybe we could hang out another time."

"Okay," she said, unsure of what she'd just agreed to.

"Wanna swap numbers?" he asked.

She shook her head no, feeling faint. What would Lila and Prem say if he called? She was an idiot for saying, "Okay." What did he expect now? "I was just gonna read," she blurted, touching *Jane Eyre*.

"Right," he said, his voice low. "You're a pretty big reader."

She nodded, feeling hot and stupid and sick.

"Well, okay. See ya." He walked past her, the space between them thick.

She'd ruined everything. "Thanks," she called to his back. "Thank you. For the flower."

"You're welcome." He flashed his smile.

She forced herself to keep his gaze and smile back. "I'll see you on the bus?"

"Sure. Save me a seat."

She floated through the day wondering how she was supposed to act if she saw Marcus in the hallway and wondering if he'd take someone else to the dance. In this daydream state, she approached Janna's car after school.

"Wow, look at you," Janna said, hugging her.

Neena smiled. "Thanks for the flower."

"Looks like you got a couple." Janna eyed the carnations poking out from her backpack.

"Yeah," Neena said. "This stupid boy." Her mouth had blurted the opposite of what she felt. Marcus was absolutely not stupid. He was the most beautiful boy she'd ever met.

"Well, the stupid boys are smartening up. They're realizing what I've always known. That you're awesome!" Inside the car, Janna added, "I have to say, I'm just in awe of this sassy look, this new you."

"Thanks." She felt shiny and new. She had friends—Yvonne, and maybe now Marcus. She had makeup and a new look that gave her wings. She had a locked door that let her sleep. She was even grateful for Lila who'd quietly paid Mr. Michael's associate while she was at school the previous week, saving her from having to hear the man talk about marrying her and saving them both from Prem's wrath.

They drove to the elementary school to pick up the girls, flush with candy and Valentine's Day cards. Janna produced a box of chocolates and a small teddy bear from the back seat for the girls to hand Neena.

"You look just like the Barbie," Nicole gushed. "That one I gave you."

"Can Neena do my makeup, Mom?" Leslie asked. "I want to look pretty like her."

"You're already pretty," Janna said, "and Neena's pretty without makeup, too. You can wear makeup when you're older."

"But it's Valentine's Day. You're no fun," Nicole whined.

Janna exchanged glances with Neena, as if conscripting her into some adult world.

"Maybe if Neena has time," Janna conceded. "She's definitely more of a makeup expert than me. Do you have to get home right away? Lila won't mind if I steal you for a little, will she?"

She shook her head even though Lila would definitely mind.

Plus, Yvonne had warned her that this was the farm's busiest day. But Neena didn't want this perfect day to end. Her chores could wait an hour.

The girls dragged her upstairs the minute they arrived. As she transformed them into living Barbie dolls, her mind replayed her conversation with Marcus and the feeling of receiving his carnation. It was only when David walked upstairs and said, "When did princesses take over my house?" that she realized over two hours had passed.

"Oh, Mr. Parker!" She scrambled up from the floor. She'd lost track of time, daydreaming and playing.

The sun was low when Janna drove her home, but there was still a long line of cars waiting for the flower stand. Yvonne, Estelle, and a couple others were busy taking orders, as Prem deposited cut flowers into empty buckets. Janna parked away from the stand's bustle.

When Neena emerged from Janna's car, Prem stared at her. She'd forgotten to take off the lacy overlay, and the girls had made her makeup even heavier.

"Well, look who decide to show up," Prem said. "You got lost walking the streets or something?"

"You must be Prem," Janna said, exiting her car. She mispronounced his name, rhyming it with *phlegm*. "I'm Janna. We haven't met. I hope you don't mind, but I picked Neena up from school today. The girls really wanted to play with her for Valentine's Day."

"Well, how nice," Prem said. "She got to play while we here working and wasting time looking for her. Yvonne said she never came off the bus, so everybody going crazy here. On the busiest farm day, too. I still got work, but I was about to drive around to search for the girl."

"Oh, I'm so sorry," Janna said, placing her hand on her heart. "It's my fault. I should have called. She and the girls were having so much fun with the makeup, though."

"I was wondering what the hell was on her face." Prem laughed, twisting his head side to side, surveying Neena. "You sure it's not clown paint? Or tramp paint!" He laughed loudly.

"Now, that's uncalled for, Prem," Janna said.

Prem bugged out his eyes. "If you gonna use my name, lady, say it right. *Praay-em*, like *game*. But I ain't playing no game here. Don't tell me what is called for and uncalled for. This girl here is my daughter. *My* daughter. Not your daughter. You can't go picking her up, taking her here, there, every which where you please, disrespecting me. I don't care if you're a teacher."

"I'm sorry. You're right."

"Damn right. And you know what? She done going to your fancy school and your fancy house. From now on, she going to the school down the street so she can get home in time and learn she no better than anybody else."

Heads turned their way. Neena hoped he wasn't drunk.

"Now, let's calm down. There's no need to overreact," Janna said.

"Lady, you bring my daughter home late, looking like some whore, and you telling me how to act?"

Whore.

"Neena, get back in the car. I've heard enough. You'll spend the night with me."

"The hell she will," Prem said. "Husk, get over here."

She looked from Janna to Prem. What had Janna meant by *spend the night with me?* Where would she sleep? And what about school? All of her things were in the trailer. But she didn't want to go anywhere near Prem in his agitated state. "No," she said.

"What the hell did you say?" Prem marched toward her.

"Get away from her." Janna moved to shield her.

"Lady, you didn't meddle enough?"

"I am this close to calling child protective services. And that's something you do *not* want me to do."

"You threatening me?"

"I'm educating you. Children have rights in this country. As an educator, I'm obligated to inform the authorities when I witness abuse."

"Woman, you haven't seen abuse yet," Prem said, stepping toward Janna.

"Hey," Don shouted. "What's happening?"

Prem looked at him and only then seemed to remember where he was.

"You loco, man?" Don said.

"Stay out of my family business," Prem said, pointing a finger at him. "I don't work for you. This is my family. My business."

"Tranquilo, hombre," Don said, raising his hands. "We were busy, and Neena was missing. You got stressed. But she's safe now, so relax."

Prem looked at Neena, spat on the ground, and strode away.

Janna addressed Don. "Is Neena safe here?"

"Yes, yes," Don said. "Jefecito. He gets a hot head and talks. Only talk, sí, Neena?"

Neena felt Don's mistrust of Janna in his false words, *only talk*, and nodded.

Janna turned to her. "Sweetheart, I must ask. Do you feel safe?"

She forced a smile. "Yes. Yeah. I'm fine, Janna. Really. He just talks crazy when he's mad."

Janna stared at her hard. "Okay, honey. Call if you need me."

"Thanks, Janna. Thanks for everything." She held up the bag of goodies as Janna returned to her car. "Happy Valentine's Day."

After Janna left, Don placed a hand on her shoulder and said, "Help Yvonne, sí? I can talk with Jefecito. He was worried, that's all."

Yvonne hugged her when she stepped behind the stand, and as Neena began exchanging bouquets of flowers for cash, her hammering heart quieted. But it resumed its pounding when Lila returned home near sunset, driving past the few remaining cars in line.

Just then, Don returned to the stand. "Neena, stay with us tonight. Your papi needs more time, okay?"

She tried to smile as Yvonne gripped her arm and squealed, "Sleepover!" She was glad to avoid Prem, but she wondered what he'd said to Don. What he'd say and do to Lila.

In Yvonne's trailer, Neena ate caldo de pollo, a buttery chicken soup that had simmered in a Crock-pot all day, and tortillas, which reminded her of rotis. A Spanish show played in the background as they ate. Yvonne's brothers and father watched from their bunks and the sofa, and Neena sat with Estelle and Yvonne at the kitchen counter. She couldn't follow the show or their conversation, which often fell back into Spanish, but as they laughed and joked, she felt at home.

As she got ready for bed, borrowing Yvonne's clothes, she showed Yvonne the gift bag.

"Qué lindo," Yvonne said, pulling out the red-hearted teddy bear. "Where'd you get it?"

"Marcus."

"Marcus? A boy? And you didn't tell me? I thought we were hermanas." Yvonne play-slapped her. "Puta."

"It was today. At school."

"He gave you all this? Chocolates, flowers, a teddy bear? He must like you a lot."

Neena nodded, opening the chocolates for Yvonne to try. She didn't know why she lied. But it felt good to pretend that Marcus had given her the gifts, instead of Janna and the girls. Thinking about Janna forced her mind toward Lila and Prem, and she wanted only to think about the boy who made her feel like a Barbie doll.

In bed, her body inches from Yvonne's, she imagined she was next to Roshi in Guyana. When Yvonne started to snore, Neena hugged the bear close and kissed it. *Dear Roshi, it's from a boy. He looks like a movie star.* For a minute, she felt like Sunny again.

21

Bubble

At four thirty in the morning, Neena left the warm protection of Yvonne's trailer to complete her chores before school. Just as she reached her trailer, Prem barged out. There was no escape.

He gripped her arm. "Show up looking whorish again, and I'll send you to Michael. He'll teach you about whoring." He pinned her against the trailer, his arm vibrating with rage.

Neena considered shrieking for Don, but this punishment felt inevitable. She kept her eyes down, expecting Prem to haul her to her room.

But he launched her to the ground, hissing, "Ungrateful, fucking bitch."

She fell hard.

"Quit testing me," he seethed, as he stalked off.

Disoriented and aching, she stumbled inside to change her clothes and pack lunches. Lila stood at the kitchen counter with empty eyes, a fresh bruise blooming on her neck.

On the bus, Neena applied makeup with shaky hands. She was glad Marcus didn't ride the morning bus. A fragile wall held her together, and too much lay fresh beneath it.

The rhythm of school dulled her enough so that when Marcus smiled at her that afternoon as he boarded the bus, she smiled back reflexively. She felt both sad and relieved as he walked past her to his usual spot in the back. But, even from there, his energy tugged at her. His laughter, whenever it rang out, felt as if it was meant for her.

Minutes before his stop, the bus mostly empty, he slid into the space beside her, dropping his trumpet case and backpack on the floor. His scent, a mixture of deodorant and sweat, washed over her. "Saved this seat for me?" he asked.

She chuckled to hide her nerves and returned to *Jane Eyre*, propped on her knee at a random page. She hadn't read a single word.

"You got far in that book," he said, his voice once again betraying a Caribbean lilt.

She shrugged and smiled, the air between them too charged for eye contact. She wanted to ask, "Where are you from?" but she said nothing.

"What's it about?"

"A girl," she said. "Named Jane."

He laughed. "Jane. She as pretty as you?"

She blushed at his brazen words. Was she pretty? Or did he only like her mask—the hair and makeup. He hadn't noticed her before. Still, his words lit her up.

"I want to hear more about Jane tomorrow," he said, getting up for his stop.

She nodded and smiled, wishing time would slow down,

wishing he could stay next to her a little longer, wishing she never had to leave the bus.

She expected her room ransacked, her lock broken, and Prem awaiting her. But the trailer was quiet when she got home. She hurried through her chores and daydreamed about Marcus as she stirred a chickpea curry on the stove.

When Lila arrived, she tossed two full laundry bags on the floor. "Run that tonight," she ordered, as if nothing had happened.

Later, Prem walked past the shed as Neena folded clothes. She waited as long as possible before returning inside, folding and refolding each piece of clothing with unsteady hands. At the sound of the shower, she rushed into the trailer with the clean laundry. She tiptoed to her room, locked the door, and barricaded it, trembling with relief.

The following afternoon, Marcus once again came to her seat near the end of his ride.

"So, it's good?" he asked, referring to *Jane Eyre*, propped on her knees.

"Not as good as *Pride and Prejudice*." She spent the rest of his ten-minute ride extolling the virtues of that novel, not knowing what else to talk about.

Marcus laughed as he rose for his stop and said, "I need to expand your horizons."

The next day, he pulled *Ender's Game* from his backpack as he slipped into the seat beside her. "To get you away from those romances," he joked. "It's about aliens and outer space, boy stuff, but you'll love it."

"You read?"

The book hovered between them, and he said, "I'm offended."

"I just . . . you don't seem . . . like a nerd, like me."

He laughed. "Believe it or not, I spent the last ten years with my nose in a book." He pushed the book closer. "Here. It's my favorite."

"I can't take it," she said, shaking her head.

"Borrow it. We have tons of books. My mom goes through them like water. She was a schoolteacher in Haiti."

Neena wanted to ask about Haiti, his mom, and the houseful of books. Their hands touched as she took the book, and a current shot through her.

That month, their friendship unfolded in ten-minute flashes, discussing books on the bus. It felt like playing Barbies, escaping into an imaginative little world contained in a pretty box, a world away from Prem and Lila and Mr. Michael and everything else she tiptoed around.

Spring break arrived, and Marcus handed her *The Clan of the Cave Bear*. Getting up for his stop, he said, "Call me. My number's inside."

He'd tucked a note in the book. She unfolded it with shaking hands. "Neena, I really like talking to you, even if you are a nerd. Meet at the mall? Or library? Your friend, Marcus." His number was scribbled below.

She kept the folded paper in her pocket, a talisman as she cleaned houses or transplanted seedlings beside Lila, a bookmark as she read the thick novel at night.

Midweek, she showed Yvonne the note. She'd shared only tidbits about the boy who sat next to her and gave her books. Now she hoped to call him from Yvonne's trailer.

Yvonne yelped in delight. "Ay, but Jefecito and Puta Madre would never let you meet."

"I know."

"Be careful with him, okay? Remember that pendejo I told you about?"

Neena nodded. Yvonne's first boyfriend, a guy she met at the stand, had taken her to the movies and to restaurants regularly for several weeks. Then, he suddenly stopped calling.

"He kept pushing me, you know, to do *that*. And I told him I want my first time to be nice, not in some ratty car. And he said I wasted his time and money. They only want one thing, you know. But maybe Marcus is different."

First time. One thing. She forced a smile and pushed away the vile memory of Prem. Yvonne's words made her see how naïve she'd been. She'd hoped to discuss *Clan* with Marcus, about how it opened her eyes to a history she'd never considered—early humanity with its strange tribes and peoples. But he might want to talk about other things. *That.*

She couldn't call him. She couldn't break their protective school bus bubble.

That Saturday morning, Yvonne's birthday, Neena delivered flowers to the stand with a cassava pone, a thick pancake-like dessert she'd made the day before with leftover cassava and coconut Lila had bought for provision soup.

"Ay, que rico," Yvonne said, closing her eyes and chewing. "Come tonight to dinner, okay? We're going to a restaurant."

She shook her head. "They won't let me."

"Papi will ask. Don't worry."

Don was overseeing the greenhouse when Neena arrived. Lila, who was cleaning Janna's house without her, had instructed her to work there until dinner.

"Neena, my hardest worker," he said. "All week you been hustling. Go to the stand with Yvonne, okay? It's more fun, and it's her birthday. And come with us tonight. I'll talk to your papi."

At the stand, Yvonne blasted music as she arranged the bouquets. She squealed when Neena arrived and taught her how to use greens to create complex arrangements. A Spanish song came on and Yvonne turned up the music. "Es mi cumpleaños. Let's dance."

Business was slow, so Yvonne taught her how to dance cumbia and salsa. For the first time that week, Neena didn't miss the refuge of school.

Neena was midtwirl, a smile on her face, when Lila drove up that afternoon. "What the hell are you doing?"

"Uh, Don sent me here," Neena said, feeling herself go hot. "We were making bouquets."

"Well, get yourself home. You have real work."

"Puta madre," Yvonne muttered as Neena left the stand. "See you tonight?"

Neena shrugged.

Inside the trailer, Neena retrieved a pot of leftover soup from the fridge to reheat, and Lila waved some school registration forms Janna had handed her. "That lady is out of her goddamn mind. She thinks I'm going to send you to her fancy school again so you can be gone all day, like you have nothing better to do. I told her you'll go down the street so you can get work done, and she said that should be up to you. Up to *you*. Like *I* don't get a say."

Lila sucked her teeth and shoved the fancy-school forms in the garbage, leaving one sheet on the counter. "You go where *I* say you go."

Neena stirred the simmering soup as Lila ranted on and Prem arrived home. "Sign that school form," Lila said as Prem glanced at the paper on the counter.

"I ain't signing shit," he said. "What's she need school for anyway? She needs to pay us back, that's what she needs to do. And that lady needs to stop minding other people's business. I have half a mind to drive over there and tell her off right now."

Neena clicked off the stove and turned to exit the kitchen.

"Where you going?" Prem asked. "Walking off while I'm talking, disrespecting me?"

She stopped.

"You think you're untouchable with this lady, this *Janna*, telling me do this, do that?" His tone shifted to that angry pitch. "And Don acting like some boss man, telling me I should let you go to some restaurant for his daughter birthday, that you and she became good friends? How the two of you become such good friends when you at school all day and supposed to be working the rest of the time?"

She stared at her feet.

"Answer me!" Prem stormed her and grabbed her arm. "Me the one in charge here, you hear? Not you, not *Janna*, not Don. Me the one who pay Michael."

She stiffened in his grip. *Roshi* . . .

"I should pull you from that school right now."

Could he do that?

"Janna will fire me," Lila said.

"I don't want to hear about no Janna," Prem yelled, shaking Neena's arm as if she'd uttered Janna's name.

He shoved Neena toward her bedroom.

"Prem, stay away from that girl," Lila squawked.

"Lila, me done listening to you. This girl needs to know who's in charge."

He kicked the door shut and locked it before throwing her onto the bed. It had been so long since he violated her she'd thought herself safe from it. That the threat of pregnancy, Don, and Janna would protect her forever. That maybe he even regretted that violent act because he was a monster, but not that kind of monster. The world spun.

Lila banged on the door. "Prem, leave the girl!"

He pressed an elbow on Neena's back and yanked her pants down, as she flailed against his weight.

A scene she'd recently read in *Clan* came to her—the violence on the ancient steppes where nomadic tribes roved. Perhaps this was just the way the world worked, the way men were wired since the dawn of time. Perhaps all women endured this pain. Perhaps even Marcus would do this to a girl.

No, Marcus would never do this.

She returned to herself as Prem released his hold to unbuckle his pants. A surge of rage filled her. She twisted from under his arm and kicked. He stumbled back.

Without thinking, she heaved one of the concrete bricks from under her bed. It hit his chest, and he fell. She grabbed the other brick and launched it with a yelp. It hit his head, knocking him out.

Maybe it was the high she rode from this attack or the rage she'd unleashed, but something made her stomp on his groin, unzipped and limp. "Leave me the fuck alone," she shrieked. "Leave me alone."

Lila hammered on the door, shouting, "Open up," and Neena saw that Prem was bleeding. Who had she become? Had she killed him?

Panic bloomed inside her. Quavering, she fixed her pants and opened the door.

Lila barged in and knelt down to feel Prem's chest.

What would happen if he died? Would they get deported? Would she go to jail? Her body shook.

"Go to Yvonne's," Lila said. "Sleep there. And stay out of his fucking way."

Neena threw some clothes into a bag and grabbed her backpack, fleeing the trailer just as Prem moaned, feeling a mixture of relief and dread that he'd lived.

Yvonne's birthday dinner was at a Mexican cafeteria. Sitting at a table with Yvonne's family, choosing meals from pages of options, discovering shredded pork—smoky and rich and like no other meat—Neena's head spun. She thought of Nicole cannonballing into the pool the day that Lila bled. It felt like déjà vu, eating and smiling amid this family while Prem bled.

People chatted at nearby tables, and she wondered what their lives were like, what Janna was doing, what Marcus was doing, what Roshi was doing. She imagined Roshi carrying a posey upstairs in a circle of lamplight, and exhaustion overcame her. She'd been gone so long things had certainly changed.

Dear Roshi, I almost killed Prem . . .

Neena leaned toward Yvonne and asked, "Can I sleep over? I had a fight with, with . . ."

"Your papi?" Yvonne asked. "Sí, of course. Stay as long as you want."

She wished she could sleep there forever. But as much as she loved the Hernandezes, she wasn't one of theirs. She was Prem and Lila's because they'd paid for her. Would they finally send her to Mr. Michael as they always threatened, even if she still owed them money?

Oscar was saying, "It's old, but when I get done, it'll run like new." He'd found a beat-up truck for fifty dollars and was fixing it as a gift for Yvonne in his spare time.

Yvonne shrieked and ran around to hug everyone, saying, "Ay, gracias."

Neena batted back tears, happy for Yvonne, recalling her own brothers' kindnesses. Raj insisting she buy new shoes, Ravi teaching her to swim, Mo taking her to fish. Had she ever thanked them?

"Now you can find a job and get off 'this damn farm,'" Don said as she hugged him.

Everyone laughed. At least once daily, Yvonne said, "I need to get off this damn farm."

An ice-cream parlor near the restaurant sold thirty-one colorful flavors. They sampled from doll-sized plastic spoons, and Neena experienced a world of new "sabors" before she selected pralines and cream. It reminded her of peera, Jeeve's birthday dessert, a milky fudge.

They licked their cones and walked toward a bar that played salsa at the end of the strip mall. Yvonne grabbed her free hand, and Neena pushed Prem from her mind as they danced.

A sign outside the bar said it was Latin night. "Can we come in?" Yvonne asked the guy at the door.

"Eighteen and up," he said, shaking his head at Neena.

"But it's my birthday," Yvonne implored, batting her eyes.

Through the partially open door, Neena glimpsed a couple sitting at the bar, drinking and talking, in a world all their own. She thought of Marcus and the school bus, and she touched his note in her pocket. Had she ruined their friendship by not calling? Would he stop bringing her books and writing her notes? She told herself if he did, it was probably for the best. Their bubble was always meant to burst.

22

Bailamos

THE NEXT MORNING, SHE waited until six thirty when she knew Prem and Lila would be gone. The trailer seemed its usual self, but the bricks had been removed from her room and there was no blood residue on the floor. Her bed remained mussed, so she fixed it before taking a quick shower. Then she washed two bags of laundry, packed lunches, made dinner, and filled out the local school registration form, rescued from the trash. Sunday mornings, she usually worked beside Lila in the fields and greenhouses, but she didn't join her until noon.

As they drove to their afternoon cleaning job, Neena felt Lila's thoughts—*I have half a mind to send you back.*

That night, she slept at Yvonne's again, and a new routine began, one in which she spent nights at the Hernandezes' to avoid Prem and days trying to prove her worth, praying they wouldn't send her to Mr. Michael or his man.

Marcus didn't board the bus the afternoon they returned from break, and Neena feared it was a message. He was absent the following two days, and her chest hurt from missing him.

When he finally boarded that Thursday, her heart fluttered. He sat beside her at his usual time and nodded his chin at *Clan*, which was open on her knees. "Thought you'd be done."

"Rereading my favorite part," she said, unable to meet his eyes.

"I thought you'd call."

"I couldn't. My dad's strict." She'd rehearsed this answer, something close to the truth. Prem's gashed head sprang to mind. That morning, he drove past her in his golf cart as she waited for the bus. He'd stared her down, pointed to his unbandaged forehead, and said, "You guh pay for this."

Marcus was quiet a while before saying, "My dad's strict, too. But my mom's worse!"

He told her he'd spent the previous afternoons auditioning for jazz bands at top high schools. His mother, who'd encouraged him to play trumpet to get into their junior high's magnet program, now expected him to get into a magnet high school. But he wanted to go to the local school where he could play basketball and hang out with people who were "more like us." Neena couldn't imagine such a place. Who was like her?

"You staying here for ninth grade or moving on?" he asked.

She thought of the forged signatures on the registration form she'd handed to Janna. "Moving on."

As he rose to leave, she held *Clan* out to him. Inside, she'd tucked a note of her own. "Even though you're not a nerd, I like talking to you, too."

They exchanged daily notes after that, mostly about *Speaker for the Dead*, the sequel to *Ender's Game* they argued about, but some of his were blushingly flirtatious. "Spotted you in the hall this morning, prettiest girl there." He sat closer and complained about his too-strict family. His parents had traded good jobs and upper-class status in Haiti eight years prior for lunch lady and janitor positions in Miami's public schools. They pressured him, saying they'd sacrificed everything for him and his brother. His mother checked his homework, and he was expected to make straight As, go to college, become a doctor.

When pressed, she offered little more than lies: "I came with my family a few years ago." "My dad runs a flower farm, and I help out a little." "My mom wants me to be a doctor, too."

"My mom kept me back a year when we first got here. So, I'm fifteen actually," he confessed one afternoon.

She nodded, wishing she could reveal the complicated truth of her age. Thirteen, but pretending she was sixteen.

Mr. Michael's associate had said, "You almost sixteen, nuh?" when he showed up for a payment that week. Lila had sent her to meet the man near the flower stand, to avoid triggering Prem. When Neena handed him the envelope of cash, he'd gripped her hand and said, "Fine gal, you looking like a grown woman. You need a real man like me." She'd pulled her hand back and said, "Fuck off," surprising herself, and he'd laughed.

"That's my house," Marcus said as they approached his stop. He pointed to a blue and white bungalow on a street of almost identical houses. Envy pierced her. A chain-link fence enclosed a green postage-stamp front yard. A basketball hoop hung from the eaves. A bike leaned against the house, and a rope swing dangled from an oak. Flowered curtains draped a bedroom window, and frosted bathroom windows obscured shampoo bottles. It was a perfect house with a proper family inside, not a dingy trailer hidden behind a tall fence. It was full of books and held a boy and his brother and their caring mother and father, not people attacking each other. She imagined his perfect life behind the thick walls, and she knew her flimsy trailer life could never collide with it. That he could never know the truth.

The end of school loomed like a gathering storm, and her heart ached knowing their school bus days were numbered. In mere weeks, her life would be defined by the farm and Prem, who'd been making her pay with small abuses—work that kept her in the fields or at the greenhouses, pushes and shoves when she encountered him at the trailer. More than ever, she relished Yvonne's bed, which she often fell into well after 10:00 p.m., waylaid by chores.

One afternoon, Marcus sat next to her immediately after boarding the bus. The kids in the back oohed at this move, and he flashed a middle finger at them.

"I got in," he said. He'd been accepted by an elite school. She thought of Bishops or Queens in Guyana, schools she'd dreamt of a lifetime ago. A twinge of jealousy shot through her. Pain, too—she'd secretly hoped to continue their friendship at the local school, writing notes and talking about books.

"I wish I didn't have to go," he said. "I'd rather be with you."

His words made her limp.

He took her work-battered hands in his soft ones and twined their fingers into shades of interlaced brown. Then, he pulled out his Walkman and shared his headphones. They seat-danced to Run-D.M.C's *King of Rock*, thumping shoulders and playing with each other's hands.

"See you tomorrow," he whispered, before he left.

She nodded, unable to look at him, feeling too much.

Days later, he drew her closer and his lips found hers. A tingling warmth shot across her face, down her neck, across her body, *there*. The pleasure levitated her, shattering the illusion of the game she'd been playing. She couldn't keep him in a bubble she visited on the school bus. He was real, and he wanted something real.

That. She pulled back a little, but he nuzzled her neck, drawing her back in.

Dear Roshi, have you ever been kissed?

The kiss transformed her into a girl who played with fire. When Marcus sought her out in the hallways, she hugged him, not caring who saw. They met at the library for lunch, sneaking kisses behind Mrs. Fredrickson's back. As time sped up, leaving just a week of school, she embraced him more urgently.

"I could visit when your dad's not around," Marcus said, twining his fingers with hers.

She wanted that, too. But when was Prem not around? He'd cornered her recently, saying, "This summer, you're going to work back every penny you owe. And I'm going to watch you like a hawk, morning to night. You think you been working? You haven't been working."

She studied their hands, that braid of color. She should have never let things get so far. "He's so strict."

"Well, I can't just *not* see you again." He laughed an exasperated laugh.

She shook her head, unable to imagine that either.

A pit formed in her gut the last day of school as Marcus asked, yet again, for her number and she shook her head.

"I don't understand," he pleaded.

"He would . . . hurt me." Her eyes brimmed.

"Fuck, Neena." He held her close until it was time to leave.

At his bus stop, he kissed her cheek and handed her a note. "Call me. Please."

She unfolded the paper. Under neatly printed digits, a phone number she'd long memorized, he'd written, "I miss you already. Love, Marcus."

"I know just the thing," Yvonne said as Neena cried in bed that night, unable to contain her heartbreak. She'd said Marcus broke up with her.

"Bailamos! You need to dance." Yvonne grabbed her arm and danced it.

Neena smiled weakly. Yvonne had gone dancing at the club several times, and she was determined to take Neena. As they lay in bed, Yvonne concocted schemes to sneak her inside.

She settled into her heavy summer workload with a grieving heart. Only when Mr. Michael arrived for his final payment two weeks later did Marcus leave her thoughts.

The white truck rumbled into the grocery store parking lot where she and Lila waited for him. Lila handed her an envelope. "Tell him it's everything. And I don't want to see his face again."

Mr. Michael parked to face the gold car, smiling mockingly. He was alone. Neena held the envelope on her lap, shaking. Seeing him after so many months, his glinting sunglasses, that rutted face, she was transported back to her family's bottom-house. Had he visited them again, and did they send a letter? Did they complain that she'd never written back?

"Go!" Lila said.

She walked to his driver side and held the envelope out without a word. No matter what Lila said, she knew this wouldn't be the last time she saw him.

Lila rolled down her window and said, "I better not see your ugly face again."

He laughed. "Or else what, Lila? Our business may be done, but this girl's daddy hire me to find she a man. So, if you keeping her and her money, you guh be seeing me."

"She owe me before she can pay you another dime," Lila said. "And that can take years."

Mr. Michael laughed again. "And you accuse *me* of highway robbery."

Neena's gaze snapped to Lila. *Free help for life.* How much did she still owe?

"Sunny, I plan to see your daddy soon," Mr. Michael said. "Expect word from him. And see if you can get the farm boss to pay you directly." He winked at Lila. "Otherwise, this lady might give you the runaround. Your family counting on you." He started the truck and revved off.

Neena stared at the retreating truck, and Lila said, "Come. We got work, and that man made us late."

As Lila drove them to the next housecleaning job, Neena's gut knotted in confusion. Did Lila now own her? Her English teacher's words popped into her mind: *indentured servitude.*

"How much do I still owe you?" she wanted to ask but didn't. She'd have to accept any answer Lila gave because she had nowhere else to go. Instead, a fantasy entered her head. Marcus arriving to whisk her away. Marcus marrying her and freeing her from Lila, Prem, and Mr. Michael. From her family, even, whose expectations she still did not understand.

Yvonne had come up with plan to sneak her into the nightclub, but she'd been reluctant. Now, she felt an urgency for this escape. If it worked, Marcus could meet her there, and in time, she could tell him the truth. Maybe her fantasy could become reality.

Friday was pop night at the club. Since Yvonne's brothers went only for Latin music, Yvonne swiped Oscar's car keys and a couple beers from the fridge. In the bedroom, they applied thick lines of jet-black eyeliner and dusted their cheeks with gold bronzer as the rest of the family settled into bed.

They wore identical black minidresses Yvonne had made from an elastic material, and they curled their hair with face-framing tendrils. One large curl obscured Neena's mole.

"We're like twins," Yvonne declared, sipping her beer.

Neena sipped the bitter-sour liquid cautiously, worried she'd transform into her father or Prem. But as she drank, her insides loosened, and she found everything funny. By eleven, when a cacophony of snores filled the trailer, making it safe to leave, Neena battled fits of giggles.

"Ay, you're like a fucking hyena," Yvonne hissed, as Neena fumbled out of the bedroom window onto a prickly bush, snorting with laughter when her dress snagged. They put Oscar's car in neutral and pushed it out the gate. Neena stifled giggles as the car crunched on the gravel.

"Jesus, you could have gotten us caught," Yvonne said, driving off. "Thank god for that loud-ass air conditioner." This only made Neena laugh harder. They sped toward the club, singing to the radio, whooping out the window, and sharing a cigarette from Oscar's stash in the glove box. The smoke burned her throat and triggered a coughing jag, but her head floated on her shoulders.

A small group stood at the club's entryway. From the speakers inside, Janet Jackson's "What Have You Done for Me Lately" blasted.

Neena crouched low, her mirth quelled, her throat raw.

"I'll be back," Yvonne said.

Neena peered over the car's dashboard to watch Yvonne chat with people in line before handing the bouncer her ID. The bouncer studied it with a flashlight and returned it. Yvonne paid five dollars and walked inside. Fifteen minutes later, she emerged from the exit and got a stamp on her hand. Back in the car, she handed Neena her ID. The plan was for Neena to enter with it and for Yvonne to re-enter using just her hand stamp.

Neena felt nauseous. Surely the bouncer would see that she looked nothing like Yvonne, that Yvonne didn't have a mole. Surely, he'd know that Yvonne had just left. She pictured him calling the police, who'd call Prem, and then what? Could this get them all deported?

"I don't know," she said, sharing a cigarette with Yvonne.

"Chica, it's so easy. When it's busy, he just lets everyone in. And the music is so fun. Just try. Worst he'll do is say no."

Neena got out and stood in line behind a group. She held her shoulders back, trying to look older. By the time she handed the bouncer her ID, sweat had soaked through her dress, and she was grateful it was black. The bouncer flashed the card with his light, barely glancing at her. He took her money and waved her in.

After Yvonne joined her, they ran to the bathroom, locked themselves in a stall and shrieked with joy.

On the crowded dance floor, an older man sidled up to Yvonne and offered her a rum drink, which she shared with Neena. Sweet and bubbly, it was infinitely better than beer.

The liquor hit fast, wrapping her in a hazy blanket. It erased every worry from her mind. It freed her to jump on stage and match Yvonne's hypnotic movements, not caring who watched. And it allowed her to let men come near without thinking about Prem, Mr. Michael, or even Marcus. *Dear Roshi, this is freedom.*

Yvonne got them a second drink, and Neena wondered how such a lulling, elevating substance could make anyone violent.

The girls snuck back home in the early morning hours. When Don and the boys rustled at five, Neena's head throbbed. But she rose to start her chores. She needed to behave as if nothing had changed, even if everything had. She had hope, even if it was lodged in an irrational plan.

23

Boyfriend

They successfully snuck out twice more before Neena showed Yvonne Marcus's notes and confessed he hadn't broken up with her. Yvonne immediately dragged the phone with its extra-long cord from the living room and handed it to her.

Sitting on Yvonne's bed, she dialed. Her insides liquified when his voice said, "Hello?"

"Marcus? Hey. Hi. It's Neena."

"Neena! Oh my god. I was losing hope."

She laughed. "I, uh . . . sorry."

"No, I know, your dad. Are you at your house?"

"No. My friend Yvonne's."

Yvonne brought her mouth to the receiver. "Marcus, qué pasa? Come dancing with us."

"Sorry, she's a little crazy," Neena said, pulling the phone away, staring hard at Yvonne.

Marcus laughed. "Yeah, let's go dancing. I'd like to meet this crazy Yvonne."

A GIRL WITHIN A GIRL WITHIN A GIRL

Anticipation electrified Neena as she waited for Marcus at the club. She'd given him instructions on how to sneak in, using his older brother's ID, and he said they'd meet her and Yvonne there. She played out the scene in her head. Marcus would enter, watch her from afar in the skin-tight fuchsia dress and yellow heels she'd borrowed from Yvonne. He'd stride toward her, keeping eye contact, and they'd connect in a blaze.

She glanced at the door as she danced on stage with Yvonne. Yvonne had found a liquor store that didn't ID, and they'd shared a small bottle of vodka in the car. Feeling well past buzzed, Neena's head swam and her body pulsed to the club's strobing lights. Suddenly, a shorter version of Marcus hurried toward them.

He motioned them down, shouting over the music. "You Neena and Yvonne?"

They nodded and led him to a quieter corner.

"I'm Mo, Marcus's brother," he said.

"Hey, Mo," Yvonne said as Neena resisted the urge to say, "I have a brother named Mo, too."

"Look, this is not gonna work," Mo said in a lovely Caribbean lilt. "That bouncer stared at my license pretty hard. No way he let Marcus in."

"But you look alike," Neena said.

"Nah, man. He laughed at my name, called me 'Moist.'"

"Moist?" Yvonne shouted.

"Moise," he said with an injured tone, showing them his ID. "Mo, short for Moise."

"But I always get in with Yvonne's," Neena said. "And she has a weird name."

Yvonne shoved her. "It's not weird."

"You're girls," Mo said, exasperated. "They don't care if you sneak in. You attract men."

She shook her head, not believing it. "Where's Marcus? I have an idea."

She ran to the exit and extended the back of her hand for a stamp. She found him leaning against the side of the building. "Quick, give me your hand," she said, her insides somersaulting at the thrill of seeing him after so long, looking so cool in his acid-washed jeans and blue shirt.

"Hey." He held out his hand, warm surprise in his voice. "What are you doing?"

She pressed her stamped hand on the back of his, hoping to transfer the wet ink. "They don't ID if you're already stamped."

A faint smudge appeared on Marcus' dark skin.

"It might work," she said, examining the hand up close.

"It's working great," Marcus said, wrapping his arms around her, "'cause this is all I want. You look amazing."

She looked into his face and melted into him. The building hummed with the music, and the vibrations passed through him to her. She didn't want to go back inside. She wanted only to be alone with him, feeling his embrace. Their lips met and his soft kiss washed through her.

"I missed you," he whispered, brushing his cheek against hers.

"Hmm." Wanting his lips on hers again, she bridged the small gap between them. Her body rippled with pleasure as he tightened his grip, and she suddenly wanted more. *One thing.* Realizing the alcohol had dropped all her walls, she pulled back slightly.

"I missed you so much," he repeated, and they kissed again.

"Neena!"

She jerked back. Yvonne had come around the corner. When Neena saw the fear on her friend's face, pleasure drained from her body.

"Hide," Yvonne said.

"Why?"

"Shh. Go. It's Jefecito."

Prem? Neena grabbed Marcus's hand and ran into the alley behind the building. Light streamed from a door, illuminating a dumpster. She scurried around it, pulling Marcus out of the light.

"What are we doing? This doesn't feel safe," Marcus said.

Fear and shame bubbled inside her. What had she been thinking? She shouldn't have brought him into her rotten life. She dropped his hand. "You should go back. Go without me."

"What? No. What's going on . . . who's Jefecito?"

He took her hands again.

"Nobody." How could she explain any of it?

"Neena, we wouldn't be in this alley if he was nobody. You in some kind of trouble?"

He didn't deserve this. "Really, Marcus. You should go back." She tried to drop his hands again, but he held tight. She was so stupid to think he could marry her, save her.

"Quit saying that," he said. "I'm not leaving you. Look, whoever this guy is, *Jefecito*, he's no match for me and Mo. It'll be okay."

She teared up at this kindness.

"You're shaking."

Faint music thumped in the background, and distant chatter added a warm layer above the rhythm. Was Prem really out there?

"Look, Marcus. Jefecito's my father, and shit's gonna hit the fan when he sees me. I snuck out, and the last thing I need is him seeing me with my boyfriend."

A madness overcame her after she uttered those words. She'd become something impossible—an American girl holding a boy's hand in an alley, saying cool things like, *shit's gonna hit the fan* and *boyfriend*.

Marcus pulled her to him. "Okay. I get that. But can I kiss my girl one last time?"

Her heart skipped, and she nodded.

He held her face and brought his lips to hers, so gently. Her pooled tears fell.

"Marcus!"

Mo appeared at their side, and she pressed her face into Marcus's chest to stanch her tears, knowing she might be staining his shirt with mascara.

"Come, we're taking Neena home. Her dad's a raving lunatic. He's looking under chairs and shit, saying he'll call the police and shut the place down if he don't find her." To Neena, Mo added, "Yvonne said you should sneak home, say you were in your room the whole time."

Marcus hugged her shoulders as Mo led them around the building. They were halfway across the parking lot when she heard him. "Husk!"

She jumped but kept walking, hoping to reach the car before Prem figured out it was really her.

"Husk! I see you with them niggers."

Marcus flinched this time, and the flinch rippled through her. Her body went numb as they sped up.

"You want to whore around, don't come home. Your father's gonna hear about this, too."

Mo opened the back door, and she slid inside, picturing Prem calling her father on the phone. Except her father had no phone.

"Get back here," Prem shouted, as Marcus jumped in next to her and locked the door.

"Oh, god. He's coming," Mo said, starting the car and reversing.

Prem pounded the trunk just as Mo drove off.

Mo broke the silence at a stop light a few blocks away. "Where should I take you?"

She couldn't bear the thought of Marcus seeing the dusty, gray trailer compound. Plus, if Prem beat them there, it might be unsafe for him. So she directed them to Janna's.

Janna's house was dark when they pulled up.

"You live here?" Marcus asked.

"No, a teacher I know."
"You gonna be okay?"
She nodded.
"Why'd he say, 'Your father'?" Marcus asked. Hurt, confusion, and mistrust clouded his tone. "I thought he was your father."
"Stepfather," she said, her throat raspy with the lie. "I'm sorry. For what he said."
Her real father and Raj had used that word against people they worked with in Guyana, and against Ravi's first girlfriend, the mother of his illegitimate child. Neena never really understood the word, but she'd once swallowed its bitter message. In Guyana, she'd avoided the Black kids at her school, and she was even a little afraid of the girls. But in America, watching *The Cosby Show* and *The Jeffersons*, she thought the rules were different. After all, Mr. Michael's associate was Black.
"It's not your fault," Marcus said.
Everything felt like her fault.
"Call me, okay?"
She shook her head, no, without consulting her heart. Her eyes filled with tears. She'd been so stupid, thinking Marcus could save her. He was just a boy, and she'd wreck his world with hers. She loved him, and maybe he loved the part of her he knew. But there was so much he didn't know—her real name, her age, her status, her father. Shaking her head felt like the first honest thing she'd done in a long time. "I can't."
"Hey, hey. We'll work it out."
She kept shaking her head.
"Marcus, just let her go," Mo said. "Mom's probably waiting up, and I'm dying for this night to be done. Take it from me, brother, that shit is not worth it. That racist crap, that's nothing anybody can work out. Not you, not me, not her. It was nice to meet you, Neena, but I need to get my brother home."
The words were a slap she deserved.

24

Plaid

David answered the door in checkered pajama bottoms and a blue cotton robe, clothes Neena had washed and folded numerous times. He ran his hands through tousled hair and squinted. "Neena?"

She'd expected Janna, not her husband. She didn't know what to say to this man. "Mr. Parker. Hi."

He looked beyond her, perhaps for a car, and she was glad she'd convinced the boys to leave as soon as the door opened. Would David have called them that word, too?

"Are you alone?" he asked. "Come in. Let me get Janna."

David left her in the entry and climbed the stairs, and she leaned against the wall. She removed her heels and pressed her sore toes into the impossibly soft carpet. The alcohol high had waned, but she wobbled, nonetheless. She wanted to dive into the carpet and close her eyes, soak up the candy-sweet smell of the house. But time had made the house feel foreign. She hadn't been there since Valentine's Day.

"Honey! Are you okay?" Janna rushed down the stairs in a silky pink robe, looking disheveled and frightened.

Neena shook her head. Guilt and shame washed over her. She'd done this. She'd made everybody's life a mess.

"What happened?" Janna asked, pulling her into a hug.

Her face hit Janna's shoulder, and tears streamed. She couldn't control the deluge. She breathed in Janna's warm, soapy smell and succumbed to the wave of emotion. She'd planned to say she attended a friend's party, that her father was angry she went, that she needed a place to stay until he cooled down. But words wouldn't come out.

"Oh, sweetheart. Did Prem hurt you?" Janna pronounced his name correctly, and the invocation of the beast interrupted Neena's meltdown.

She took a deep shuddering breath and nodded. It wasn't an outright lie to say Prem hurt her even if she knew Janna meant something else.

Janna held her shoulders and looked into her eyes, but Neena couldn't meet them. She stared at the floor, tears dripping.

"Do I need to call the police? Take you to the hospital?"

Neena looked up sharply. "No! Please, no."

"Did Prem hurt Lila?"

Neena shook her head, although she had no idea what Prem might have done to Lila. Her tears fell faster.

"I need to call CPS," Janna said. "This is unacceptable."

"No, Janna, please. They'll deport us," she whispered, wiping her face.

"Oh, honey," Janna said, tucking Neena back into her shoulder. "Let's get you to bed. We'll deal with this in the morning."

Neena's head throbbed as she made the bed and tucked the mattress into the sofa the next morning. It felt like a magic act, transforming the impromptu bedroom back into David's office. She had dusted and vacuumed that office numerous times, but she'd learned the plaid sofa's secret only the night before. She replaced the cushions and picked up her folded dress, stuffing it into the duffel Janna had handed her, full of hand-me-down clothes. Standing in a pair of shorts and a T-shirt, she surveyed the room to make sure she'd removed every trace of herself.

"Stay as long as you need," Janna had said the previous night. "David hardly uses this room."

But that was untrue. When Neena cleaned the office, coffee stains, crumbs, and papers in the trash bin told her David used it often. She'd be an intrusion. She had no choice but to go back and take her punishment. Or move in permanently with Yvonne if that was an option.

She found Janna drinking coffee at the breakfast table. Beyond the large sliding door, faint orange streaks washed across a slate-colored sky.

"You're up early," Janna said.

"I wanted to leave before the girls got up. So it's not weird."

Janna cocked her head. "Oh, honey, they'd be excited to see you."

Neena shook her head.

"Have some breakfast at least."

Neena shook her head again. She was desperate not to face David and the girls that morning. She lacked the energy to fake a smile.

"Sweetie, we have to talk. It's my obligation to inform CPS if your father is abusing you."

"Please, Janna. They'll deport us. We don't have papers. It will only get worse."

Janna pressed her fingers to her forehead. "I spoke with a lawyer friend from church. She's looking into options."

Lawyer friend. Options. The hairs on Neena's arms shot up. "He probably calmed down. He just yells, really. And, anyway, I can stay at Yvonne's, my neighbor."

Janna stood, walked to her, and stared into her eyes. "Neena, tell me the truth. Does he hit you? Or . . . anything else?"

"It's just yelling," Neena said, without breaking eye contact. She'd gotten good at lying.

"And you *want* to go home?"

"Yes." *Home.*

Janna sighed and pulled her into a hug. "Okay, give me a sec. I'll call and let them know I'm bringing you."

This was absolutely the worst idea. "Please, can't you just drop me off?" If Prem knew she'd stayed with Janna, things might escalate. Could she still end up with Mr. Michael?

"No, no. This is the right thing, sweetie," Janna said, walking toward the office. "Wow, all cleaned up already. You're just amazing. Why don't you grab something to eat from the pantry while I call." She closed the door.

Neena stood in the hallway, her temples throbbing with panic. She couldn't tell what was being said from Janna's muffled words.

A few minutes later, Janna exited the room with extended arms. "Honey, let's sit."

They sat on the plaid sofa, Janna holding her hands.

"He was upset," Janna said.

Neena studied the clash of their skin—Janna's pink against her brown, both against the sofa's yellow plaid. She thought of the compatible plaid her fingers had created with Marcus's.

"He made some accusations and used some colorful language I will not repeat. He was surprised you were with me. He thought you'd gone to . . . um . . . a boy's house?"

She thought of the boy and his house, of that boy's soft lips on hers, of *that word.*

"He says he doesn't want you to come back," Janna said.

"I'll stay with Yvonne until he calms down."

"Oh, honey, he doesn't sound like he'll calm down. He didn't even want you to retrieve your belongings. I had to threaten CPS."

Neena looked up in alarm.

"I know he's your dad and you want to go home, but why don't you stay with us a while? You'll be safe here, and the girls would be thrilled. I worry you're unsafe anywhere near your father. I cannot let you stay there."

Cannot let you stay there. Was that a threat?

The sky felt too blue and the sun too bright when they reached the farm. At the flower stand, Yvonne had arranged buckets of colorful gerberas and white daisies into a rainbow-colored American flag. The garishness nauseated her.

"I'll get the gate," she said, hopping out of the car and reaching for Yvonne, who ran over. They hugged, and Neena's heel pressed into the pebbled ground. She'd borrowed a pair of Leslie's flip-flops to avoid having to wear her heels, and they were too small.

"Lo siento," Yvonne said, her lips touching Neena's ears. "It was Papi. He thought someone stole the car, and he yelled for Oscar. Jefecito heard, then one thing to the next, and everybody flipped when Javi said we might be at the club. You okay?"

Neena nodded as Yvonne pulled back to assess her.

Estelle had walked over, too, and she shoved Yvonne aside to give Neena a hug. "Gracias a Dios! I was so sick, worried for my poor Neena. So sorry."

Neena tried not to sink her head into Estelle's soft shoulders, fearing it would trigger fresh tears. A car pulled up, and children jumped out and ran toward the flower stand.

"Don't worry about your papi," Estelle said, pulling out of the hug. "You stay with us. It's her fault, anyway." She thumped Yvonne and turned toward the stand.

"She'll stay with me," Janna said, exiting the car. "I think it's safer, for now. I'm Janna."

Estelle stopped and looked back. "Okay. Yes, good. She needs safer." She sounded hurt.

"Just for now," Janna said, almost apologetically. "While Prem calms down. We have room."

"You have room for me?" Yvonne asked, laughing.

Estelle hit Yvonne's shoulder again and said to Neena, "Call us, chiquita. Your papi was mad, so maybe your friend Janna is right. Safer there. For now, sí?"

"Sí. Gracias, Estelle. I'll just get my stuff."

Estelle smiled and returned to the stand.

Yvonne hugged Neena and pressed her lips close to whisper. "Did you call him?"

Neena shook her head, suddenly worried Yvonne would call Marcus on her behalf. "No. Please. Don't call, okay? Promise?"

"Yeah. I won't." Another car pulled up to the stand and Yvonne gave her a final squeeze. "Call me tonight, okay?" she said, going to deal with the customers.

Neena slid open the gate. She retrieved her backpack and the few pieces of clothing she'd kept at Yvonne's, then returned to Janna's sedan. As the car crunched toward the trailer, her body tightened, bracing itself for Prem. But she was greeted by her brown suitcase, on its side, its contents spilled out.

Janna gasped.

All of her possessions had been tossed from the trailer.

Clothes covered the ground. The Christmas paper she'd saved had been ripped and flung about. The knockoff Barbie lay naked, missing a leg. Her makeup mirror was smashed, and the small makeup case Janna had gifted her sat cracked, its powders broken, lip colors gouged out. Only her dried Valentine carnations remained intact, unearthed from their hiding spot in a drawer and placed atop a sheet of paper that read, "SLUT DON'T COME BACK," in lipstick.

She couldn't breathe, couldn't swallow. She clutched her neck.
"We should go," Janna said, putting an arm around her. "It's like he's begging me to report him."

Report him. Deport her. Deport them all. Perhaps that was the answer. She could walk back through the garden gate of her Guyanese house. Her family might take a minute to recognize her, but Roshi would fling herself into her arms and the little ones would hug her legs. There would be the joy of eating her mother's metem and carrying Indy on her hip. But then what?

Prem would hunt her down for revenge and any money she still owed. Lila, too. And who would be punished? Her siblings? Plus, there would be no more school, libraries, or novels. No more driving. No more dressing up and dancing at clubs with abandon. And she may never get kissed again the way Marcus kissed her. She'd be resigned to resurrecting sweet, obedient Sunny, forever apologizing for wasting their money and letting them down.

Neena couldn't return. Her life had been knocked off-kilter, yet again. But moving backward wasn't a possibility.

She nudged a piece of broken glass aside with Leslie's flip-flop and knelt to pick up a shirt. She folded it and placed it on her lap.

"Honey, we'll get you new things," Janna said.

But Neena continued folding until she had a pile. She found the doll's leg and tried to pop it back on, but the joint was too loose.

Janna tiptoed around the glass to help. They filled the brown suitcase with anything salvageable. Neena threw the ruined things into the dumpster and returned with a broom and dustpan from the laundry shed.

"Let them clean it. You didn't do this," Janna said.

But she shook her head no. She wanted to erase as much of herself from this place as she could. She wanted Lila to walk up and know Neena owed her nothing.

MAYA

ATLANTA, GEORGIA

I DROP INTO THE OFFICE chair and stare at Dwayne's text. **You're Sunny, aren't you?** He knows. Of course he knows. He's not an idiot.

I bury my head in the crayon-scented backpack in my lap feeling woozy, as if I've come to a sudden standstill after a long run.

Then I reply: **Yes.**

For the first time in forever, I crave a drink. I rest my head on the desk and a tic I'd silenced years ago returns. *Dear Roshi—*

It jerks me up. I push back in the chair to suppress it, and the chair's wheels catch on something. Camden's toy car, the one Nico lost or hid. A black car, with a button on its base to turn on lights. The brake lights glow red and I remember KITT, the car from *Knight Rider*. *Dear Roshi*. This time I don't stop myself. *Did you ever see that show again? Did you know I lied to you that day? Have you ever driven a car?*

Tears fall as I try to picture the woman who'd written the letter. I see a child's face, a child's smile.

Roshi, a whole lifetime sits between us. Who are you? I don't know who I am anymore. Everything's out of control.

A voice in my head says, control what you can. This, just as Dwayne texts: **Be there in an hour.**

It's as if she's spoken to me.

I take a deep breath. Dwayne might have upended my timeline, but the plan hasn't changed.

I type the website I'd memorized from her letter into the computer's search bar, R&RBakeryandGoods.com. Such a simple thing, but it feels so heavy, breaking this wall I'd sheltered behind for years.

I came close to googling her as the world joined Facebook, as Dwayne and my friends asked why I wasn't on yet. But I feared the slippery slope—contacting her only to reveal myself to the man who could dismantle my life and separate me from my sons. It was easier to leave well enough alone, to not create more secrets I'd have to keep from Dwayne. So, I dug in my heels and proclaimed social media untrustworthy and a waste of time. I kept my image offline, even declining to provide a picture for my employer's website. On our cooking blog, photos are limited to my hands.

My pinky finger hovers over the enter key. What if she's already gone? Or what if the chasm between us is too large? What if the person she remains in my head clashes with reality? What if I don't even recognize her?

Fuck. Just do it.

It takes two clicks to reach the storefront where she smiles at me, that placid smile that never changed. My breath catches. Ma flashes in her face. And me—I'm there, too! A reflection that has nothing to do with a mole.

At this half reunion, my throat tightens with joy and an unexpected pang of jealousy.

In the website's banner picture, she's with family, standing in front of a shop that's built into the bottom-house of a concrete

Guyanese home. She's not a fourteen-year-old, eyes still clouded with helplessness. She's a confident middle-aged woman, shorter than I'd have guessed, and rounder. She wears glasses, and her graying hair is pulled back in a bun. I wonder how old this picture is, if she still has hair, or if cancer has taken its toll.

A man, who I assume to be her husband, drapes an arm over her shoulder; two young adults stand behind them, and two younger children, one about Cam's age and one a little older, stand in front. My nieces and nephews, I'm certain. The kids' resemblance to my own children is uncanny, and I wonder if I'd have known they were family had we passed on the street. I realize how unfair I've been to my boys, keeping these cousins from them.

Behind the family, blue accordion shutters are open to reveal baked goods in the shop. Salara rolls sit stacked in a glass case, their red pinwheels facing out. My birthday dessert. I've never made it for my own kids, but Roshi must make it regularly.

A memory pulls me to our bottom-house, our mother kneading the dough while Baby, Roshi, and I grate coconut for the filling. We each got to put one drop of red coloring in the coconut-cinnamon mixture before Ma spread the dough, filled it, and rolled it up. I can see her hands sealing the loaf with an egg wash, and tears come again. *Ma pass last year.* My anger has dissipated. Ma probably couldn't read or write well; she never had the power to save me.

A link on the website takes me to a sister store, located in Queens. It's run by Roshi's older daughter, the one who likely hunted me down. That store features one-of-a-kind furniture, and a blurb indicates that Roshi's husband, Ronald, hand-makes the pieces. Pictures on that site show family members at both stores, in New York and in Guyana. In their travels, had they ever stopped at the Atlanta airport, mere miles from my house?

A group shot shows a large gathering near a table laden with goods from the bakery. Everyone's dressed up, as if for a wedding. Studying the faces, I realize Roshi and her family are amid my other siblings, all grown up with families of their own. Raj, Ravi, and Mo, grayer and older. Ma's there, too, hardly recognizable behind an enormous pair of sunglasses and a defeated half smile. My father stands at the edge of the group, smaller than I remember, unsmiling and limp-armed, as if forced to join. I'm the only one missing.

I click away from the photo before it can undo me and land on a picture of Roshi and her daughters laughing. They're in a backyard. Laundry hangs on a line, a mango tree sags with fruit, and chickens peck the ground. It's so ordinary, so very Guyanese, and I can't help but feel Roshi won a race I never knew was afoot. She has cancer, yes, but she thrived despite the odds stacked against her, never having to pretend she was anyone other than herself.

I want to stay on Roshi's site, but Dwayne will be home in forty minutes and I still have so much to do. It's not enough to talk about Roshi, my immigration, and the cancer. I'll need to talk about that last day in Miami. The man pursuing me. It's the only way Dwayne will understand.

What if he doesn't understand, my mind whispers. What if my secrets are too much to accept? I flash back to the picture of him with just the boys, the one of them having fun without me. I don't have to die to lose them. I could lose them with the truth.

My chest thumps and sweat prickles my pores as I google *him*. The energy of fearing him and keeping him buried all these years has created a festering sore inside, and it smarts. Typing his name feels like a callout. Over the years, I've tried never to think of him, as if he could home in on any energy I emit. If he'd found me, he wouldn't have left me alone, and now I might be offering myself up. But, after so long, can he prove my identity is false? Would anyone believe him, a man with a record? I'm certain he can't prove what I did that night.

I don't find him in the prison database, and I'm not surprised. He might have been imprisoned in Guyana, not Miami. Or just deported. But then an image search brings up his unforgettable face. My heart sinks. I click the link, feeling as if I'm summoning him. The website is for a community magazine in Canada, and he's featured as a local gas station owner. They paint him as a good guy with a family, someone who imports and exports Guyanese goods. I feel nauseated. Hardworking, they call him. A valuable member of the community. He's made himself someone believable, someone who still holds power.

I google: *can you get deported for false papers after decades?*

The answer is yes.

My hands tremble as I close the computer. Dwayne will be here in fifteen minutes. I can't fall apart. I have to go through the backpack and figure out how to explain myself to him. I have to get him to forgive me because the alternative would kill me. A pain pierces my chest as I imagine losing him and the boys.

The bag's stiff metal zipper moves with reluctance to reveal a folded stack of clothes, much of it from Janna and Yvonne. Janna, who's probably worried about me over these years, who I channel as I plan my yearly Halloween party. And Yvonne, another sister I've wronged. *Chica! Lo siento.*

Thinking of them, my mind tries to construct alternate universes where we could have stayed close. Was it possible to live in a world where the person Yvonne and Janna knew jibed with the person Dwayne knows? Jibed with the girl Roshi knew?

No. I couldn't have looked at Yvonne again without thinking about that night. I wouldn't have been able to build a life on my own terms.

Tucked beside the clothes is a wad of documents, including my citizenship certificate, the last thing I shoved in the bag. The document lists a previous alias, Neena Das, but it was granted to me as Maya Augustina. The certificate features a photo of me staring hard at the camera, looking bold. But I was terrified. I'd sworn multiple times, once with my hand over my heart, that I was telling the truth.

The presiding judge had asked the group being sworn in to state our birth countries. I muttered, "Guyana," and a man nearby said, "Us, too." He was with his wife and two teenaged kids, and they hailed from Berbice. They hugged in celebration after getting their papers, and I was intrigued by them, the first Guyanese people I'd seen since leaving Miami for Jacksonville. But when the mother beelined for me after the ceremony and asked "where exactly" I was from, I panicked. I shook my head and said I had to go. She'd recoiled from my rudeness, but I couldn't risk being recognized and having everything I'd worked for erased in an instant. Guyana was an everybody-knows-everybody country, and who knew who she knew.

I had recently completed my dental hygiene internship, and Jacksonville had begun to feel small. Teachers and classmates often ate at the restaurant where I'd worked, and I routinely saw familiar faces at the grocery store. I didn't want to run into the friendly Guyanese family who knew my alias and where I was from. So, I packed up and drove to Atlanta, where I started my career and disappeared in the bustle.

That was five years before meeting Dwayne.

I imagine showing him the certificate and explaining my name change.

The day I became Maya was the day I left Miami. I drove until I ran out of gas, trying to think of a last name to launch my fresh start. My gas gauge hit zero in St. Augustine, and it felt like a sign. Marcus Augustin was the name of a boy I loved, and in that city, I realized he shared initials with Maya Angelou, the author I'd chosen as a namesake. That's how I became Maya Augustina.

Every form I signed reminded me the penalty for perjury was imprisonment. But I had no choice. I became Maya to save my life.

An electric hum makes me jump. It's the garage door opening below. Dwayne's five minutes early.

I peer out the window as his car enters the driveway. His eyes meet mine, and the hurt in them is unmistakable. I want to look away, but I don't.

He pulls in, and I watch dogwood petals whirl through the air as the wind picks up. I think of that snow globe, stolen so many years ago, shattered on the floor. Of pink makeup powder littering the ground. I've picked up the broken pieces of my life so many times before. This time, I'm doing the shattering, and the fallout is out of my control.

PART FOUR

NEENA–CINDY

1986–1987

MIAMI, FLORIDA

25

Highlights

Slipping into life at the Parkers' was like being thrown into a play without a script, reminiscent of her initial days in America.

That first evening, Neena mirrored the family's motions when she sat at the dinner table, placing a napkin on her lap. She hadn't expected them to eat so formally, for everything to be laid so beautifully on the table. The girls placed utensils on lacy placemats as she filled the water glasses. Meanwhile, Janna displayed food in flowered dishes, as if this were a nightly ritual. It made Neena realize how little she knew the family despite having spent hours in their home.

"Leslie, your turn to say grace," David said, and everyone clasped their hands. Neena followed suit.

Leslie muttered an indecipherable string of words that ended with "Christ our Lord, Amen."

Neena coughed to swallow a giggle, prompted by these unexpectedly reverent words from Leslie's mouth.

"Tonight, we must add extra thanks for being blessed by Neena," Janna added, and Neena's face twitch-smiled at the word *blessed*.

"Okay, time for highlights," Janna said, picking up the platter of baked spaghetti and offering a spoonful to her. It looked like a mass of bloodied worms. Janna continued speaking as she served the girls. "I'll go first. I loved having Neena here today, helping her settle in."

Settle in. Janna had pulled out the couch, made the bed, and placed Neena's items into the closet. But Neena felt decidedly unsettled.

David passed a bowl to her, and she placed chopped lettuce and croutons next to the spaghetti to match his plate before handing the bowl to Janna.

Nicole jumped up in her seat and leaned over the table. "Neena helped me with my puzzle. And I'm almost done."

"In your seat, Nic," David said.

Nicole sat back down and picked up her napkin, which had slipped to the floor. Janna twirled spaghetti with a fork and spoon.

The spoon-fork method looked complicated, and Neena feared attempting it, feared failing something that was clearly mundane in this family. She took a piece of buttered garlic bread from a basket and placed it on the remaining white space of her plate.

"I have two highlights," David said. "Welcoming Neena, and the Argentina game. That Maradona is some player."

Pressure filled Neena's head as the family's eyes rested on her. It was her turn. A highlight from the day. Her trashed room. *Slut, don't come back.* A de-limbed doll in her jam-packed suitcase.

"Um, this," she said almost inaudibly, feeling numb.

The adults smiled and nodded.

She tried to load the dishwasher after dinner, but David took a glass from her hand, saying, "Nope. This is my thing."

"He's right," Janna confirmed, laughing. "I make dinner, and he does the dishes. It makes him feel useful."

David chuckled. "Yes, I love filling the dishwasher."

Neena's face twitched as she watched a man do kitchen work. How would she fit into this family?

That night, hearing footsteps, she imagined David prowling outside her door. She wanted to hide in the closet, tuck herself into her suitcase. The footsteps moved about the house before returning upstairs. Neena lay awake listening to creaks and groans, her mind drifting from Marcus, to Yvonne, to the trailer, to Guyana. The air conditioner's hum was nearly silent, unlike at the trailers. There, window units droned to form a rhythm with all the snoring. Neena hadn't realized how much she'd relied on the noise to fall asleep. She was imagining sneaking out of the window, walking under the dark sky toward the farm, and tucking herself in beside Yvonne, when she finally fell into a fitful sleep.

Lucid dreams of Marcus and Prem woke her while it was still dark. It took a long moment to remember where she was.

She transformed her bed back into a sofa, thinking of Annette, her haughty friend in Guyana who'd flaunted her American things. Would Annette be jealous of her living in an undeniably American house with undeniably American people? She was lucky to be there, she knew, but she didn't feel enviable sitting on the sofa, staring at dark blinds, waiting for the yellow glow of sunrise.

Lila was likely in the fields cutting flowers, and here she was doing nothing. She imagined Lila saying, "She ran off with a boy," to explain her absence to Jefe or anyone who asked. Would Prem tell her father that? He'd have to reach out to Mr. Michael for her address, and she couldn't imagine that. He hated that man.

Her head hurt. She'd have to explain this turn of events to her family herself. But after being silent so long, what would she say?

At seven, the girls pattered downstairs, and shortly after, shrill cartoon voices chirped from the TV. David and Janna sang, "Good morning," a bit later, as clinking silverware and closing cupboard doors filled the kitchen with noise. Neena knew she should join them, but she couldn't move. She didn't belong there.

Janna knocked, and she jumped to open the door.

"Morning, did you sleep okay?" Janna asked.

"Yes, thank you," she said, reluctantly following Janna into the kitchen for breakfast.

She accompanied the Parkers to church that day, dressed in a white blouse and a flowered skirt. She sat crammed between Nicole and Leslie in the sedan's back seat, as the whole family sang along to a song on the radio that she didn't know. One about a man doing something in the name of love.

At the beige stucco church, Janna introduced her to friends saying, "This is Neena. She's from Guyana. She's staying with us a while. Yes, a little like an au pair."

Neena smiled, shook hands, and nodded at comments about Jim Jones before sliding into a pew next to Janna and David. The girls had found their friends and run off to something called Sunday School. Janna handed her a Bible, full of remarkably thin and soft pages, and Neena felt like a shell of a person, an empty thing waiting to be filled.

The choir brought goosebumps to her skin, and the preacher started a sermon of difficult-to-follow English. She thought of her family, likely singing warbly Hindi bhajans and listening to prayers they didn't understand either. The ground swayed as she pictured them sitting cross-legged and making offerings around a dancing fire, while she sat stiffly in a pew.

A few days later, Janna asked for Neena's help labeling and packing Leslie's clothes for camp, where she was to stay for two weeks.

As Neena folded clothes, Janna retrieved a box of stationery from Leslie's desk. "I'm going to tuck a few stamped envelopes in her bag. Otherwise, we won't hear from her the entire time. Last year, she never wrote. But she was only gone a week."

Neena imagined her family saying, "She not write us all year." She cleared her throat. "Um, Janna. Could I maybe have a card to write to my grandmother. In Guyana?"

"Of course, Neena. Of course." Janna looked at her with surprise, then hastily handed her a small stack of stationery and some stamps. "Here you go. I should have thought to ask. I mean, that's who raised you, right?"

Neena nodded.

"My friend, the lawyer, she mentioned some legislation in the pipeline. If it works out and you get legal status, you can visit her again. Won't that be nice?"

Neena's eyes watered. *Visit her again.*

"Oh, honey. I bet you miss her. Especially now."

"Yes." Though she and Janna were talking about different people, Neena didn't feel like she was lying.

26

Ocean

As Neena stared at the blank paper, light-hearted mental letters to Roshi came to her.

Dear Roshi, I live with white people now. They eat raw leaves every night. They call it salad. It could use some pepper sauce.

Hollow words. Certainly not enough to meet her family's heavy expectations.

She imagined the letter-carrier riding his bike up their muddy road, handing the letter to her mother at the garden gate. Even if it were addressed to Roshi, Shali wouldn't hand the letter to her sister. Nothing received at their house was ever private. Shali might save it until her father and the boys got home. They'd read it aloud after dinner, and everyone would conjure her in their minds. *Sunny.* She'd stand like a jumbie come to life and speak. What could she possibly say after such a long silence, after she'd turned into someone unexpected, after her world turned upside down? She certainly couldn't address Roshi with jokes. Roshi might not even hear the letter being read, even if she had gotten hearing aids.

But silly mental letters were all that came to her as she adjusted to life with the Parkers.

Dear Roshi, little white girls squawk like setting fowls every morning, pecking rainbow marshmallows from each other's bowls and arguing over which cartoons to watch. They play with ugly dolls called Cabbage Patch Kids. (Imagine a ball of roti dough with two eyes!)

Dear Roshi, American houses are easy to keep clean if you walk behind the children with a broom and duster, and if you fold their laundry while they watch I Dream of Jeannie. *I'm not here to wait on them hand and foot, their mother says, but what else is there to do?*

Dear Roshi, white girls are more pink than white. They burn and peel if they sit in the sun too long and need special lotion to protect them. Sometimes their hair, soft as a baby chick, gets tangled worse than a ball of thread. It can take an hour to untangle.

Dear Roshi, American cooking is like magic. You layer stuff from cans, boxes, or jars into a Crock-pot, and later, the whole thing is done. Some days, you don't cook at all. You order pepperoni pizza over the phone, and it shows up at the door. It's like a big sada roti covered with tomato choka, cheese, and bits of black pudding. That sounds weird, but it tastes like a party in your mouth—sweet, salty, sour, and just . . . I wish I could send you some.

Dear Roshi, American girls prefer to dance in special classes instead of at home. Nicole wears a pink leotard to ballet class, and she did a dance on stage that we all sat and watched. Leslie takes gymnastics, where she dances, too. Once, "Wake Me Up Before You Go-Go" came on the radio (it's such a good song!), and I said, "Let's dance." Nicole jumped about like a lunatic even though she takes proper classes, and Leslie called me a weirdo. Nobody dances at home like us.

A GIRL WITHIN A GIRL WITHIN A GIRL

Dear Roshi, white girls pay to go to camp where they fish, boat, sleep in the dark, slap mosquitoes, and use outside bathrooms. They write home about it, complaining, but it sounds like Guyana.

Dear Roshi, American dads wear ties and carry briefcases and do work called management. They tickle their kids and carry them piggyback upstairs to bed. They read stories to them, sometimes even making up funny ones from their head.

Even in these imagined letters, she couldn't bring herself to tell the whole truth. That she felt jealous of Mr. Parker's affection for his girls, while harboring an irrational fear of him. That she sensed a growing resentment from Leslie, who said her black moles looked like a connect-the-dot picture and called the curry she made gross. That despite missing Yvonne and the structure of farm life, she feared going back. That she made herself as useful and unintrusive as possible so that the Parkers wouldn't tire of her. That anytime she glimpsed a gold car, or even a white truck, she panicked because she expected Prem and Lila to show up at any moment to haul her back.

But a couple weeks after she moved in, Janna paid her, and she wrote a mental letter that felt truthful.

Dear Roshi, I have eighty dollars right now. Eighty whole American dollars! For two week's work. I hid it in my suitcase, but I keep checking it because I worry I counted wrong. To have that much money to my name is something else. It's for cooking, cleaning, and taking care of the girls. Can you believe that? I never expected money. Cleaning felt like the least I could do to stay here. I don't know what to do with it. Janna says I should save it for college, that it's my way out. Lila and Prem would probably say I owe it to them, but when

I do the math, knowing how much I worked this past year, I don't think I owe anything. I might sneak some home in a letter. Ma and Daddy can use it for the bushland. To think, in just a couple of months, I can pay back what they paid to send me. Isn't that crazy?

She pictured her parents receiving the money and rejoicing, uttering her name with reverence, bowing at her prayer flag. For the first time since wanting to write home, she finally had something truthful to say to make them proud.

But when she sat, pen in hand, words still wouldn't come. The truth began and ended with *Dear Ma, I have money for you*. She didn't know how to explain her living situation with the Parkers without indicting herself, or how to hint at the abuse she'd suffered without going into details. Even her words about the Parkers felt untrue. They turned white people into an exotic species of gentle pink-skinned, yellow-haired pizza eaters who handed out money. A lie.

She still hadn't written a word when the Parkers packed the car to gather Leslie from camp and continue on a long-planned trip to the beach. Janna had insisted that Neena join them. She even handed her a swimsuit to pack.

They retrieved Leslie from a campground a couple hours outside of Miami, set in a green glade, nothing like Guyana. During the rest of the drive, Leslie gabbed about all the games she'd played with her roommates. The sun was well past its apex when David drove through a quaint, sleepy town. He parked behind a small row of ornate stilt houses, the first such Guyanese-styled homes Neena had ever seen in America. But what Neena couldn't make sense of was the massive sheet of blue the homes faced.

"The ocean," Janna said, seeing her stunned expression.

She'd read about the ocean and seen blue on maps, but she had not known to expect magic. Looking out at the distant horizon, she grew unbalanced. It felt as if they'd reached the edge of the world.

The air tasted mildly of fish, and the roar grew steadily louder as she approached the water, crossing a shell-encrusted beach.

The girls ran in and out, chasing small waves, and Neena caught their joy.

She walked until the water was shin deep. The undertow buried her feet as if the ocean had set a claw into her. This was no backyard pool, but she felt compelled to walk farther. She wanted to feel water all around, to look out and see only blue.

At about waist deep, her shorts and underwear soaked, a wave crashed against her. The undercurrent toppled her, and she scrambled in the salty, turbid water to find her footing. She coughed and gagged as she emerged from the brief burial, her eyes and sinuses stinging.

But she remained there, facing the oncoming waves. *Dear Roshi, imagine looking out, seeing nothing but blue, the world disappearing. That's the ocean.*

She thought of Marcus, too, whom she still hadn't called. *Dear Marcus. I'm a rough, splintered thing. But I wasn't always that way. Standing in the ocean, I'm smooth again.*

Reality sat suspended as she built sandcastles, tossed Frisbees, and learned to play badminton and volleyball. She hunted for sand dollars, roasted marshmallows over a bonfire, and spent an entire afternoon reading, feeling like a child again. The ocean air worked like liquor, dulling her worries about her precarious future.

On the beach house's balcony, she finally found the words to say to her family.

Dear Ma, Daddy, and everyone,

I can't believe it's been over a year. In some ways, it feels longer. Never shorter!

I'm currently living with the Parker family. I met them through Lila, and I help to take care of their house and two girls, Nicole and Leslie. They love swimming in the backyard pool and doing cartwheels between the fake flamingos decorating the front yard. Right now, I'm at the beach with them, at a vacation house. You would not believe such a place exists. From the verandah, you can stare at the ocean and feel like you're flying, seeing so much blue.

This past year, I met a lot of people—white, beige, and black—who were wonderful to me. I paid off Mr. Michael by working at the farm. It was backbreaking work, even if the place is full of beautiful daisy and sunflower fields. I also cleaned houses with Lila and cooked all the dinners. All while still attending school! All my debts are paid, so I'm saving money to send home. Maybe you can buy that bushland after all. I'm enclosing twenty dollars. If it arrives safely, I will send more.

I am sorry this letter is overdue. For so long, I wanted to write to say I'm doing good. I can only say that now that I'm out of Prem and Lila's house. They weren't good to me.

I'm not sure how long I'll live with the Parkers, but please write back to me here.

With love,
Sunny.

Her eyes lingered on *they weren't good to me,* the closest she could come to revealing the abuse.

Back in Miami, a few weeks before the start of high school, Janna behaved as if Neena could stay for good. She grew comfortable on the pull-out couch and learned to sleep in past sunrise. She read books from the family's shelves, watched cartoons with the girls, and fell into the house's rhythm.

Yvonne came over after she was allowed to drive again. They blasted the radio and played pool volleyball with the girls, and Neena allowed herself to imagine the absurd possibility of a life like Nicole and Leslie's, with space to breathe and laugh.

In Neena's office bedroom, Yvonne said, "It's real nice here, but Jefecito might want you back home." She handed her an envelope. "He said to give it to you when I see you."

Yvonne bounced on the sofa, waiting for her to open it, but she tossed it in her closet, trying not to look shaken.

That night, she pulled a folded, stained sheet of paper from the envelope. She recognized it as a log sheet from the farm.

This is what you owe. Food, bed, and money paid to Michael. That lady can't hide you forever. So watch your back.

The numbers scribbled on the log sheet lines added up to three thousand, five hundred dollars. She felt as if an ocean had gobbled her whole.

27

Own Kind

Although the high school was within walking distance, Janna offered to drop her off the first day, and she was grateful. She feared Prem might be lying in wait. Her butterflies quelled as she strode the maze of locker-lined hallways and fluorescent-lit classrooms, comfortably similar to the junior high's. The school was larger, and a myriad of brown and Black kids filled its halls; some even sounded Caribbean. But their laughter and jokes, even that first day, hinted at deep-rooted ties. Neena avoided their curious eyes and sought refuge in the library. She befriended the librarian, Mrs. Mulligan, hoping to make the book-lined shelves her personal sanctuary.

As she walked home, Prem's phantom nipped at her heels. Every time a car drove past, her heart sped up. She varied her routine daily, zigzagging through neighborhood blocks and noting spots of refuge in clumps of palmettos, overgrown oaks, even a well-trafficked corner convenience store.

School had been in session for a month when Janna offered to mediate a talk with her family. Perhaps seeing the panic on her face, Janna said, "But if you're not ready, honey, that's okay. We love having you. It's just I thought I saw Prem drive by, and I wondered if he was ready to talk."

She shook her head vehemently, unable to speak.

A week later, Janna walked into her office-bedroom with a letter. "I think your grandmother wrote," she said, "But it's addressed to Sunny?"

The air grew sludgy as she took in the colorful Guyanese stamps and Raj's block print in the return address, "From the Kissoon Family." What had Janna thought of that? Did it even look like a grandmother's handwriting?

"My nickname," she said, pushing aside her homework.

Janna retreated to the kitchen to stir the chili Neena had helped start. Neena closed the door, pushing out the overwhelming scent of spiced beans that had filled the room. She pressed her nose to the letter. Its faint damp odor opened a portal back home.

Dear Sunny,

We received your letter and the money, and we are all very happy to hear from you. Ma can finally sleep sound knowing you are safe as the letter is very long overdue. We been trying to locate Michael because the address he gave us is wrong. A letter we wrote for your birthday and another one at Christmastime came back saying "no such addressee." Daddy went by the Leguan house to see the old lady and verify the address, but she was never home. We send another letter at Phagwa, and that one return, too. It seem as if Michael disappeared. So we feel great relief hearing from you because Daddy was planning on visiting the old lady again and waiting till she got home. We feel good to know you are seeing wonderful new things, like flamingos and beaches. Your schooling must be good because you sound hoity-toity. Laugh.

Your letter find everyone here healthy, but things poor with work. It's all about Burnham politics these days. Some places only hire and advance negroes, or pay coolies less, so we feel eager to join you in America to make good money. You got us dreaming about a house with a swimming pool, not flood and caca in the backyard. Laugh. In seriousness, you would not believe the flooding we got last month. It killed half of Ma's garden.

Some good news. Roshi and Pappo been going to a deaf program in town, and they talk with their hands now. The new hearing aids work good, so they hear when we call for them, too. But they mostly talk to each other with hands and leave everyone out of the conversation. Guess we tasting our own medicine. Laugh.

Pappo want to see pictures of the house you clean and American cars, and Indy want a picture of you. She say she can't remember you. Laugh. But we all think a picture would be nice if you can get one since you must look different now. Except for that mole. Laugh.

Roshi and Baby been selling peera and sugar cakes at the roadside (no more salara or buns since flour got scarce), and they been making good small change. Jeeve been winning school races, and they say he could try out for the national team. What if he win and end up on TV and race against Jamaica? That would be something.

As for Ravi, he and Mala expecting any day. Ravi move in with Mala family last year. No big wedding, just a small pooja. Mo carrying on being Mo, making people mad and getting himself in trouble. He say you must really look like Arthur pickney now, since your skin probably turn white. Big laugh.

We look forward to more letters and any money you can send. Everything dear these days with inflation. Daddy say

to send money with Michael once we get in touch with him. He say you can't trust the post office, but the $20US you sent came. So decide if you want to try again.
    Your loving family.

As with the first letter, everyone had signed their names at the bottom.

Roshi had added: *You rich! I want come America and get rich, too. Very happy I hear from you. Miss you. Your loving sister, Roshini.*

Below that, there was another scribbled postscript.

    Sunny, this your father writing. I get troubling news from Prem and Lila. They send a letter saying they catch you gallivanting with niggas at night and walking around half-dressed. They say you run off to live with some white people who steering you the wrong way, and they say you still owe them money. Sunny, you better not be shaming us there in America. Remember, only your own kind will take care of you. Go back to Prem and Lila. They the ones who know the paperwork to get you legal and apply for us. Them and Michael. When we come, we need they help, and we don't expect to arrive to debt and shame.

Neena had devoured the first part of the letter, relieved that they'd worried about her, chuckling every time Raj told her to laugh, and cherishing Roshi's small note. But the weight of her father's words buckled her knees and she fell to the floor.

    She'd prayed Prem wouldn't contact her father. She'd stupidly hoped his and Lila's hatred of Mr. Michael would deter them from getting her address. Now, she looked like a liar, painting herself as a live-in maid in her letter. It twisted her gut to hear her father had sided so easily with Prem, without giving her a chance.

She folded the bottom of the letter to hide the postscript and reread Raj's words. She tried to imagine Roshi saying, "Wow, you rich," with her hands. She tried to picture the roadside stand piled with Baby's sugar cakes. She tried to see Jeeve flying like a kite down the track, and Indy, hands on hips, demanding a picture of her big sister. But her father's words cut through.

Did her father want her to be abused? Could he force her back to Prem's? Or worse, to Mr. Michael, to be married for papers?

She gritted her teeth. She would never go back to Prem and Lila's. She wouldn't pay them another dime. She'd paid in blood and sweat. And she would never marry a stranger. Ever.

She buried the letter in her suitcase.

At dinner during highlights, she said, "My grandmother wrote today. She's doing great. She opened a shop to sell desserts," and when Janna "oohed," a pit formed in Neena's stomach.

Neena eyed the amber liquid David poured over ice after dinner—whiskey, kept at a wet bar in the den. The glittering liquor bottles caught her eye every time she dusted the bar's glass doors, but they'd felt distinctly off-limits. Plus, she had too much to lose.

Still. On the fold-out sofa bed, as her father's toxic words thundered in her head, she craved a dulling sip of liquor. Deo was trying to tunnel inside her to revive Sunny. Stupid mousy Sunny who wouldn't dare defy him, who'd sacrificed herself to please him, who once thought she was special, a favorite. Railing against that version of herself, Neena tiptoed down the hall, eased open the cabinet, and took a long burning swig from a bottle. Her heart hammered and a mélange of emotions coursed through her: remorse and guilt, fear that she was rotten and no better than her father, and an intoxicating hit of courage.

Dear Roshi, do you still do everything everyone says? I can't do that anymore. Is something wrong with me? Am I wicked?

The liquor muffled her father's words but amplified hers. Who was she? What was she if not her family's savior? The tie between her and them, once as solid as rope, was now a fractured disappearing contrail. She felt a desperate need to run, to leave her stuffy room.

The window sash whispered as she let herself out. She dropped onto the grass with bare feet, and its cold touch reminded her she was alive. But as she wound through the dark streets, she felt utterly adrift.

Dear Roshi, I've become a jumbie. Homeless. Haunting things.

She passed a house with two men on the porch. They turned to her, and impossibly, they became her father and Prem. She gasped audibly at this trick of her mind, and they laughed as she quickened her steps. It wasn't until she found herself in front of Marcus's house that the tears came. She hid behind a bush and cried herself dry. Voices and a dog's bark finally brought her back, and she saw she'd become a crazy person.

Dear Roshi, they should call me Mad Buck.

She glanced at Marcus's darkened house, willing him to come outside to save her, half expecting him to appear. She hadn't called him because she didn't know how to tell him the truth. That was the wrong choice, like so many of her other choices. Ditching her sister. Stealing. Drinking and sneaking out. Why couldn't she do anything right?

Back in her room, she scolded herself for leaving. She was lucky Janna hadn't caught her. Janna had saved her from the dark, gnarled path her father wanted to shove her back onto. Where would she be without Janna? She was lucky. Blessed. She should tread lightly, be the sweet perfect girl Janna believed her to be. Then, she stood a chance.

But as she lay on the pull-out bed, the future loomed like a deep void.

28

Cake

She struggled to banish Prem and her father from her mind that week and to focus on school, her supposed "way out." The Parkers were her real way out, and she didn't want to mess up. But sometimes everything inside her roiled, and she found herself in front of the liquor cabinet, craving a drink, struggling to control herself.

The day of her fake birthday, Janna asked, "Would you like a little pool party?"

"You don't have to do that," Neena said.

"I want to. Please. Invite Yvonne. Maybe some friends from school?"

She thought of Marcus. She ached from missing him, and the fantasy of him saving her had never fully left her mind.

That evening, she snuck a swig of liquor and dialed Marcus's number before her courage failed. It'd been months since their terrible date.

"Neena, hey, how are you?" he stammered when he answered.

"Hey." Her greeting came out hoarse, and she cleared her throat. "I'm good. I, um, live at Janna's now. She, um, well, today's my birthday—"

"Today? Happy birthday! What are you, fifteen?"

"Um, yeah." Her throat tightened with the lie. Janna was celebrating her seventeenth birthday, but she was still just thirteen. Her fourteenth birthday wasn't for another month.

"We're both Libras. I'll be sixteen in a few weeks."

She nodded as if he could see her. She wanted to ask if he liked his new school, if he was happy, if he missed her as much as she missed him, but a lump filled her throat.

"So, um, you'll be getting your driver's permit soon, then," he said after a beat of silence.

"Maybe. I'm in driver's ed."

"That's cool. Me too. How's school?"

"Good. It has a library."

He laughed, and the sound softened her.

"How's yours?" she asked.

"Great. I'm going out for the basketball team, so I'm pretty busy. Between that and band."

"I'm sorry I didn't call sooner. It was just . . ."

"No, I get it. It was a lot."

"Yeah. It was a lot." A few seconds of silence passed before she said, "So, I was thinking. If you want, maybe you can come over this weekend, Saturday? Janna's having a thing. For my birthday. Nothing big. Just Yvonne. And Janna's girls. They have a pool."

There was a silence, and he said, "I, uh, have homecoming."

Homecoming. A dance. Her own high school advertised a similar dance, and kids talked about going with each other. Was he going with someone?

Tears welled. "Oh, yeah, I get it. I just thought . . ."

"But I can stop by for a minute."

The backyard party was the first get-together ever held in her honor. She helped Janna hang streamers and balloons as David grilled burgers. Yvonne brought Estelle, who'd made Neena's favorite tamales. This felt like plenty, especially as the festive air pushed her worries to the recesses of her mind. But knowing Marcus was coming made her positively effervescent.

He arrived while she was playing Twister with Yvonne and the girls. She wanted to launch herself at him, but she held her pose, feeling that electricity between them. Her loose T-shirt revealed her new bikini top, a gift from Yvonne, and she was acutely aware of his eyes on her, eyes that told her he still believed she was pretty. "Caribbean Queen" played on the radio, and she thought this could be their song. If she ever told him the truth. If he saved her.

He was dressed somewhat formally, in black slacks and a black button-down, and he held a wrapped gift. His eyes barely left hers, even as David handed him a cup of punch.

Yvonne made a move, and Neena purposefully landed on top of Nicole, ending the game. Laughing, Neena ran over to him, arms reaching out, but Marcus held the gift out between them. He leaned over and pecked her coldly on the cheek.

"Wanna play Twister?" she asked.

"Sorry, I can't stay," he said, "Mo's waiting in the car. I just wanted to say hey, and happy birthday, you know." He handed her the gift.

"Can you stay for some food? Or at least a piece of cake?" Janna asked, coming over with a burger on a plate.

He smiled and shook his head apologetically at the burger. "Maybe cake? The homecoming game starts soon, and I'm in the band."

"Gosh, what a busy day for you," Janna said. "Yes, let me get the cake ready."

"You can open it now, if you want," he said of the gift Neena now held.

"Oh, thanks." She unwrapped a copy of *I Know Why the Caged Bird Sings* and a journal inscribed, "For all your thoughts, Marcus." She noted the absence of "love" before his signature.

"My mom says it's good. I haven't read it, but I thought you might like it."

"Thanks. Your mom's books are always good." The words sounded transactional, undercutting the gratitude she felt, and she didn't know how to fix it. *Mo's waiting in the car.*

Janna brought out the cake, covered in lit candles, and everyone sang "Happy Birthday."

Her eyes watered at the overwhelming attention. She blew out the little fires and said, "This smoke," as she wiped her eyes.

Janna gathered the group for a picture. The girls sat on either side of Neena. Marcus stood behind her, his hand on her shoulder, grazing her bare skin. Janna, Yvonne, and Estelle filled in around them.

"Say 'cheese,'" David said, snapping the photo. Neena decided she'd ask Janna for a copy to send to her family. *Your own kind*, her father had said. She'd show him what her own kind looked like.

As she cleaned up the backyard with Janna after the party, Neena couldn't stop thinking of Marcus. Something inside her surged—she had to see him again. She told Janna that Marcus had invited her to his homecoming dance; he didn't have a date and had been hoping to ask her all along; Yvonne could drive her since Marcus had to go directly after the band performed. In her room, she called Yvonne, who'd returned home, and whispered a corresponding lie. Her hands trembled. She wasn't sure why her brain had concocted such a crazy scheme, why her mouth uttered such crazy words, why a crazy beast overtook her sometimes.

As soon as the Parkers disappeared into their rooms after dinner, Neena hurriedly poured small, hard-to-notice portions of David's whiskey, tequila, rum, and vodka into an old jam jar. She hid the concoction in a backpack purse she'd found on a recent trip to Goodwill with Yvonne, and she slipped on a satiny red dress she'd found there, too.

"Well, don't you look beautiful," Janna said. "I need to start shopping at Goodwill." She posed Neena by a wall and insisted on snapping pictures from every angle. "Should I expect you home by midnight?"

"Yes, but I can come in with the key, if you don't want to stay up," she said.

Yvonne showed up and played along, but once they got in the car, she asked, "When did Marcus ask you?"

"I'm just going to show up," Neena said.

"You crazy? Don't you need a ticket or something?"

She hadn't thought of that. She'd thought it was a school party you attended by choice. She'd imagined walking in, magnetizing Marcus toward her with her red dress.

Yvonne went on. "My school made you buy tickets. And they weren't cheap. But who knows. You look good. Maybe they'll just let you in."

"I hope so," Neena said.

They drove in silence a bit before Yvonne said, "Hey, I didn't tell you before 'cause I didn't want to jinx it. But I applied for this job at the mall, and they called back. I start Monday!"

"Yve, that's great," Neena said. "You're getting off the farm!"

"We're all getting off. Papi found a house to rent. Three bedrooms!"

"We got to celebrate! Here." Neena pulled out the jam jar and unscrewed it.

Yvonne took a sip and sputtered. "Puta, you trying to poison me? What's this shit?"

Neena laughed and took a sip. Acrid liquid burned her gullet. "It's bad, but it'll work. I stole it from David's liquor cabinet."

"You shouldn't risk that," Yvonne said, and Neena nodded, chastised.

When they pulled into the school's parking lot, Yvonne whistled. The lot was abuzz with cars and kids, dressed to the nines. Red cloth lined the ground leading to the front doors, where dazzling couples were taking pictures.

"This is fancy. You just gonna walk in? By yourself?" She retrieved a pack of cigarettes from her bag and passed one to Neena.

"I don't know." Neena lit the cigarette.

They smoked and watched processions of kids until Mo's car pulled up to the curb.

Neena clutched the dashboard. This was the car Prem had smacked, the car that drove her to Janna's, the car that brought Marcus to her earlier that day.

Marcus exited the back seat wearing white pants, a blue shirt, and an orange tie, looking more beautiful than she'd ever imagined he could. He reached in a hand, and a pretty girl emerged wearing a puffy dress, flounced with blue and white tulle, belted with an orange satin ribbon to match Marcus' tie. An orange flower sat on her wrist. Marcus threw an arm around her waist, and Neena's throat clotted. She dropped her head. She couldn't bear to watch.

"Maybe it's a cousin or something," Yvonne said. "I mean, he came to your party."

She was grateful for Yvonne's kindness, but she shook her head no. Deep down she knew he no longer loved her, if he ever really had. He'd come to say goodbye. That's probably why her brain cooked up this crazy scheme.

"We should go," Yvonne said, starting the car.

"No." She needed to endure this.

Mo took pictures of the matching pair on the red cloth, and she thought of her father's words, *your own kind*. Marcus' brown-skinned date matched him in more ways than clothes and race. She matched him with a lightness of being.

Two girls in fancy dresses that looked like tiered cakes ran up to Marcus's date, and the trio hugged. Neena imagined them squealing, complimenting each other's dresses, and laughing at inside jokes, years old. They were clearly popular girls. Marcus's new girlfriend looked like someone with a home and a family she didn't need to lie about. Someone who'd only ever been called one name her whole life, never *whore*. Someone whose father would never call Marcus *that word*.

Marcus disappeared with his friends through the double doors, and Yvonne said, "Fucking cheating scumbag."

No. He wasn't a scumbag, and he wasn't cheating. He was exactly where he should be, better off without her. She took a gulp of the noxious alcohol and said, "Let's go dancing."

Riding an alcohol and nicotine wave, Neena disappeared into the music at the club. For a few moments, she forgot Marcus. She forgot her father. She forgot Prem and Lila. And she forgot her precarious situation on Janna's couch. She felt free.

In the bathroom, she found a driver's license on the ground. A brunette smiled up from it. Cindy Tipton. Quick math told her Cindy was nineteen. As her hands tucked the card into her purse, Neena felt a pang of guilt. Stealing had cost her so much not so long ago. The Barbie hairbrush. The water globe. That mug. She should leave this thing alone. But in some ways, it felt like a gift from the universe.

She'd never look like Cindy Tipton, but if Cindy Tipton looked like her, Neena might feel free forever.

29

Pretty Little Bomb

At church on Sunday the following week, the preacher preached about a man named Job, and guilt ate at Neena. She thought of Cindy's doctored ID and the cigarettes she bought with it, both hidden in an old playing card box inside her purse.

Earlier that week, her heart hammering, she'd used a craft blade from David's desk to slice around Cindy's picture, feeling as if she were watching someone else's hands. She hadn't expected this to work, but the photo slipped out easily, leaving a blank space. She was committing a crime, she knew; she should throw away the card, she knew; but she couldn't bring herself to stop.

Janna had handed her a stack of prints in duplicate from the "homecoming" photo shoot, and one of the photos presented a perfect headshot. Her face was the perfect size, placed at the perfect angle, in front of a white wall. A gift from the universe, like the ID. She glued it in.

She double laminated the ID using the library's laminator while prepping library card envelopes for Mrs. Mulligan, feeling guiltier than she'd ever felt. And on her way home from school, she asked for a pack of cigarettes at the convenience store. The cashier barely glanced at the ID before handing her the pack.

Now she wondered if God had tested her. She was borne from a family of cheats, who'd cheated together to get her where she was. Maybe God wanted to see if she could overcome that. She'd failed.

Roshi, are you wicked, too?

As the preacher spoke, Neena vowed to do better. She would cure the flaws embedded inside her. She wouldn't use the ID. She wouldn't drink or smoke or sneak out again. She wouldn't betray the librarian's trust. She would turn the other cheek. She'd send money to her family and honor them because maybe her father was a test sent by God, too. She would study and do well and figure out how to make things right for everyone. By the end of the sermon, she decided she could salvage her own rotten soul.

She stayed on track until a week before her real birthday in October, when she received another letter from her father.

Dear Sunny,

Your birthday coming up, and everybody send wishes for a prosperous year.

I writing you because we finally get in touch with Michael. He say the letters we write before bounce back because the farm people know you as Neena Das, not Sunny Kissoon. That is troubling news, and he will sort it out. I give Michael your new address, and he plan to visit next time he in Miami. He find a boy for you, and he say you can marry when you turn sixteen but only if you start writing the boy now. Then the court will believe the story, and you can apply for us sooner. But he need a down payment.

He plan to pick up any money you have this month. Don't send money in the mail. A bunch of blackman run the post office here, and money disappear from envelope all the time.

Michael say you might owe money to Prem and Lila like they say. Sunny, make sure that debt pay off. We can't arrive with that debt on our head.

And I hope you learn some sense and stop going around with that blackie. Think about how we raise you. Don't bring your family shame.

I expect you to send word with Michael soon.
    Your ever-loving father,
    Deo

A deep rage ignited within. She tossed and turned on the sofa-bed, mentally penning angry responses, unable to sleep. At two in the morning, she crept from bed and stole a swig of liquor, hoping it'd knock her out. At three thirty, she pulled out a flowery greeting card from a set Janna had gifted her, and she found a copy of the group photo from the party.

She wrote, "My new friends," on the back and taped a hundred-dollar bill there. Under the money, she wrote, "500 – 120 = 380 owed." She considered paying the entire sum, to be done with her father. She'd saved over five hundred dollars since living with Janna, and Janna had exchanged her smaller bills for large ones to make it easier to save.

But Neena wasn't stupid. Theft likely occurred at the post office whether Black, Chinese, or Indian men worked there, and lumpy cards were probably suspicious. She hoped the single bill would make it through to prove her point. She glued the perimeter of the photo inside the greeting card's cover to hide the money. Then she wrote:

My dear ever-loving father,
    You raised me to tell the truth, so here's the whole truth.

The only thief I know is Michael. Everything Michael says is a LIE! He probably lied about finding a boy. Even if he didn't, all he wants to do is enslave me. I don't want anything to do with him and I'm not marrying anyone for papers! You should never have given him my address. If he shows up, I will call the police.

He blackmailed Lila. She paid to keep from getting deported. But Lila and Prem aren't saints. They treated me like GARBAGE. Worse than garbage. They used and abused me, and now they say I owe $3500US. But I'm not paying a dime. I paid plenty in blood.

I live with people who actually care about me now, who pay me for the work I do. Where do you think I got money to send to you? It's from the people who aren't my own kind! I don't know if I should thank God or a jumbie for where I am, but I know who I don't need to thank—Michael, Prem, Lila, or YOU! If it were up to you, I'd be a slave to Lila and Prem, and now to Michael! They think they can buy me for a few hundred dollars, but I am no one's property, and I AM NOT YOUR SLAVE. I am not marrying a stranger just because you say so.

I am enclosing $100 to start paying off the money you paid to send me here, but I'm not sending anything with Michael. After that, I am done with you!

The daughter you sold,
Sunny

Her hands shook as she addressed and stamped the purple envelope, decorated with pansies. A pretty little bomb. She put the card in the mailbox before leaving for school at seven, and her whole body trembled as she glanced back at the red flag, pointing up like a middle finger.

That afternoon, the red flag was down, the letter was gone, and Neena regretted the words flying through the air toward her unsuspecting family. Was there a way back after her tirade? *Dear Roshi, I'm sorry.* She should have written a separate sweet note to Roshi and the rest of her family. Was it too late? Anxiety tore at her gut, and she craved a sip of numbing liquor. She told herself she was being tested, that she was risking too much. But after dinner, as Janna and David chatted in the kitchen, she found herself sneaking a swig, unable to stop, hating herself for it.

Something's wrong with me, she thought as she sat in her closet, licking a fingerful of peanut butter to mask the odor. Then, *Roshi, you'd love this stuff.* Tears pricked her eyes as she thought of Roshi never getting to try peanut butter. Peanut butter was her favorite American food, and for her birthday, Nicole had gifted her three versions—creamy, chunky, and grape-swirled. Neena loved the gift and hoped she could send some to Roshi. Except now she'd lost her again. A loss that felt more permanent.

An emptiness yawned inside her. Loss was all she knew. She'd lost her childhood, her innocence, and Marcus. And she'd lost her whole family, twice—first when she left Guyana, and now with this letter. She buried her head in her pillow and sobbed, trying to push away the pain.

Knowing that Michael could turn up at Janna's door and looking over her shoulder for Prem, her anxiety grew to a fever pitch that week. She smoked the pack of cigarettes she'd hidden and used the fake ID to buy more, the butterflies in her gut a welcome distraction.

She smoked before school, near the convenience store, and again before coming home. Mouthwash, peanut butter, and perfume covered the odor, and she washed her clothes often.

On Halloween night, the night she turned fourteen, she snuck a sip of Janna's wine before joining the girls for trick-or-treating. Janna had gotten them all pastel sweats and plastic masks to look like Care Bears, and Neena was the green one. She posed for a picture and walked with the girls to a few houses. She felt silly standing there with her pillowcase, begging for candy, so she returned to help Janna at the front door.

Plopping candy into kids' sacks, Janna said, "This is one of my favorite things to do," and Neena couldn't understand why. It felt like such a waste—giving mountains of candy to kids who already had everything. *Dear Roshi, Halloween is weird.*

She wished she could admit it was her real birthday. Was her family celebrating her, splurging to make salara—a treat she hadn't tasted since her twelfth birthday? As her bitter words sailed toward them? She felt sick.

She told Janna she had homework, retreated to her room, and called Yvonne. She desperately wanted to get lost on a dance floor.

"I'm so tired, chica," Yvonne said. "I just took the girls trick-or-treating, and I got work tomorrow. And the move Sunday."

The girls. Work. The move. Jealousy constricted her body. Neena hadn't met these *girls*, but they were all Yvonne talked about lately. After landing her job at the mall, Yvonne had started dating Al, a father with two daughters and the owner of a watch kiosk near the clothing store where she worked. Yvonne had become instantly obsessed with his preschool-aged kids. And now that Yvonne was moving into a new rental house, Neena was certain she'd see her even less. Was she losing Yvonne, too?

She helped Janna clean up, wishing for an opportunity to sneak a drink. But it never arrived. David and Janna retreated to the den to watch a movie after the girls went to bed, and she lay on her bed consumed by cravings. They felt physical. Like if she didn't get something in her system, she'd explode.

She grabbed her purse, pulled the green sweats over the boxers and tank top she slept in, and jumped out the window. Lights flickered from the den. She ducked under the window as she made her way to the wooden side gate, which she eased open. She clicked it behind her and scampered across the yard.

That first cigarette drag, a block away, instantly softened her shoulders. After two cigarettes, a feeling of soft cotton wool cocooned her. Wanting to make the feeling last, she found herself in front of the convenience store, craving a drink, hoping the clerk wouldn't ID her.

Dear Roshi, I don't know who I am.

As she reached for the door, two guys in Halloween costumes exited with a plastic bag. One wore a purple wig and a half-buttoned shirt under a beige trench coat. The other wore a bomber jacket with a cowboy hat.

Without a thought, she flashed a smile. "Hey. Can you do me a favor?"

The wigged boy eyed her up and down. "What kind of favor?"

She rummaged in her purse for some money. "Buy me a small bottle of vodka? It's like three bucks. You can keep the change." She held out a five. "I'm Cindy."

The boy's wig tilted, and his eyes landed on her mole. "Hey, aren't you that chick in my history class? That quiet chick, up front."

"I don't know." She slid her gaze to his pale hairless chest and hoped her face didn't betray the recognition that stabbed her. Lenny. A troublemaker, forever exchanging words with the teacher, horsing around and missing class. There was a rumor he sold drugs. Or did drugs. He'd once winked and made a kissy face at her.

"Yeah, it's you," he said. "I'm Lenny. You go by Cindy?"

She started to back away, but the boy in the cowboy hat said, "We're going to a Halloween party around the corner. They got plenty of booze. Free."

"A party? Like with dancing?"

Lenny draped an arm around her shoulder. "Yeah, and I want the first dance, dollface."

"I don't have a costume," she said as he guided her to his car.

Lenny laughed a high-pitched Woody Woodpecker laugh that startled her as he opened the passenger door. "Nobody cares."

Neena climbed into the back seat and Lenny revved out of the parking spot. A part of her wanted to scream, "I change my mind. Let me out." But exhilaration had replaced her pain, and her father and Prem had left her thoughts. She stayed there, teetering at the edge of a cliff.

30

Off Rails

As Lenny drove, she fashioned her hair into two side ponytails with hair-ties from her purse and drew three enormous freckles on each cheek with black eyeliner. She applied heavy mascara and red lipstick, then pulled off her too-hot sweats, revealing boxers. A few trick-or-treaters had worn similar makeup with pajamas to mimic a rag doll. Now she was costumed.

Lenny pulled up to a house buzzing with music. Neena sometimes passed this house while walking to school, but it had been transformed. People roamed the lawn, decorated to look like a graveyard, and orange fairy lights outlined the door. Parked cars crowded the street.

Guiding her inside, Lenny rested a hand on her hip, claiming her. He high-fived and chest-bumped people, introducing her as Cindy. In the crowded kitchen, he poured her a drink, and Neena soon found herself dancing close to him in the living room, lost in the haze she'd craved. He fondled her bottom, and she let him.

During George Michael's "Careless Whisper," he kissed her. It was too wet and scratchy, and she didn't feel any of the feelings Marcus gave her, but she didn't stop him.

A few drinks and dances later, he led her down a hall.

"Where we going?"

"I have a gift," he said, pulling her into a quiet room.

"I just wanna dance." The echoey room started to spin.

"Trust me, you'll dance." He tugged her toward the en-suite bathroom. A line of white powder appeared on the counter, and he snorted it through a short straw. It happened so fast and the room smelled so sweet, she wondered if he was snorting baby powder.

"It's good blow," he said, snuffling, pressing his nostrils and offering her the straw.

She laughed and held it up, realizing the straw was a rolled-up dollar bill, unsure of what to do with it.

He mimed the motion and she obeyed.

The powder hit the back of her throat, and her head shot up in reaction to the tingle, the metallic bitterness, the sting. Then, the high hit her. "Feels like my birthday," she giggled.

"I know, right?" Lenny said, sniffing more.

They returned to the bedroom, and he threw her onto the bed. Panic tainted the edge of her high, and her body tightened. *One thing.* If she resisted, would he take away this feeling? She lay back, grateful she was already flying.

She drifted into the buzz, barely registering his touches and kisses. She wanted to be gone when the pain came. But pain never came. He moved against her, igniting an ephemeral bit of pleasure before he was suddenly still.

They kissed and did another line of powder. She danced on the bed, and he messed around with her body some more, and she didn't care because she was afloat in a perfect world.

When they returned to the living room, the crowd had thinned, and musky smoke thickened the air. A few kids sat on a couch, sharing an enormous bong, and Lenny joined them, pulling Neena onto his lap. She danced and twirled her fingers, hearing calypso rhythms deep in the music. Somebody handed her the pipe, and she inhaled earthy smoke. The burn made her cough, and she laughed, leaning against Lenny and closing her eyes to swim in the high.

She was dimly aware of being moved, of curling herself around a pillow and rolling about on the floor, watching the colors behind her eyelids. A door slammed, and she startled up. People sat in stupors or lay draped over furniture, but Lenny was nowhere in sight.

She wobbled home as the sky lightened. Only when she approached Janna's house did she realize her sweats were in Lenny's car. As was her purse, with the peanut butter and mints she needed to mask all the smells. It held her fake ID and some money, too. Would he steal it?

The chemicals in her system made her clumsy. She latched the side gate too loudly and opened the window too jerkily. She took off her shoes and tossed them inside before hoisting herself up and tumbling onto the carpeted floor. She stood, slid the window shut, and gasped.

Janna was sitting on her bed.

Her heart rammed against her chest, and her brain tried to sharpen itself.

"Where have you been?" Janna asked, her voice calm.

"Um, a party." The words came out slurred.

Janna's silhouetted head nodded slowly. "With Yvonne?"

"No. Um, some friends."

"You should have asked. I was worried."

"Oh." Her head felt thick.

"You've been drinking."

"No." She swayed where she stood.

"I can smell it, Neena, among other things." Janna sighed. "I'm not really sure what to do here. We—David and I, *we're* not really sure what to do. We're not your parents, but this . . ." Janna gestured to her.

"I'm sorry."

"David says liquor has been disappearing. Have you been stealing it?"

"No . . . Igotitattheparty." God, why were her words running together?

Janna sighed again. "David thinks I acted too rashly, separating you from your family. I worry he's right. You were drinking that night, too. I'm not saying Prem didn't overreact, but maybe I did, too. I didn't know you had a drinking problem, Neena."

Neena shook her head. She didn't have a drinking problem. Janna hadn't overreacted.

"Children need their family. As much as we care for you, we could never replace your parents. This was meant to be temporary."

Neena shook her head again. *Your parents, temporary.* She'd screwed everything up.

"This isn't working."

Neena dropped to her knees. "Please."

"Neena, you must understand. I'm violating all kinds of policies here. I should have called CPS. That was the proper move. The school still thinks you live with your parents."

Tears streamed down her face. She'd squandered God's good will. Unlike good and righteous Job, she was fucking it all up. What was wrong with her?

"And now with this drinking and sneaking out, I don't know what to do, Neena. We have our girls to think about. They look up to you. This is not the example we want for them."

Neena saw herself through Janna's eyes. She was a wicked, feral thing.

"Maybe you can return to your grandmother."

Her grandmother? Guyana? Did Janna want to deport her? Neena scooted forward on her knees and pressed her palms together. "No, please, Janna. I'm so sorry."

Janna gripped her forehead. "It's not meant to be a punishment, Neena. Your grandmother raised you. I thought you might be happiest there, safe from your father."

Safe from your father. Sobs wracked her. "I'll be better," Neena said through gulps. "You were so nice, taking me in. I mess up everything. I'm sorry. Please, Janna."

Janna sighed and knelt to hug her. "Oh, darling. Go to bed. I'll talk to David. We'll figure something out."

When the doorbell woke her up, it felt like only moments since she'd tumbled into a restless sleep. Her head throbbed. She was sticky and in need of a hot shower. She smelled smoky and sweaty, and her boxers were twisted around her body. Remembering what she'd done in them, she wanted to vomit.

She heard Janna answer the door, and then Mr. Michael's voice. She shot up from bed, looking around for proper clothes.

"I don't understand," Janna said. "Prem sent you *here* to get money from Neena?"

Fuck.

"Oh, no. She name not Neena. And not Prem send me," Mr. Michael said, "Sunny real father, in Guyana. He the one send me." Mr. Michael was clearly exaggerating his patois to unnerve Janna. He laughed and added, "Sunny might still owe Prem and Lila. That's a whole different matter."

Neena pulled on a loose T-shirt but had no time to look for pants. She shot out of the office into the foyer. "Mr. Michael. What are you doing here?"

"Oh, ho!" Mr. Michael lifted his sunglasses to eye her up and down. "Look how big you get. You clothes not fit." He laughed.

She tugged at her shorts.

"You know this man?" Janna asked.

"Course Sunny know me," Mr. Michael said. "Me the one bring this girl to America. She grow big, but Sunny know me good good. Me and she daddy went to school. Me know she whole family in Guyana."

"Janna, please excuse me," Neena said, striding to the front door. She ignored Janna's confusion as she pulled the door closed behind her.

Barefoot, she stormed the white truck as Mr. Michael's lecherous friend stared from behind the wheel. She'd been warned, but she still couldn't believe her father had sicced this man on her. And that Mr. Michael tried to out her to Janna.

"This a nice house you living in, Sunny," Mr. Michael said, sauntering down the path, hands in pockets. His chest puffed from his white shirt, unbuttoned one button too far.

"You need to fucking leave," Neena hissed, shocked at her own words. The ground didn't feel solid, the sun felt too bright, and dizzying drugs still coursed through her body. She crossed her arms to keep from swaying.

"Listen to this girl playing with fire, cursing her elder out like that. I come all this way to do your daddy a favor, and this the respect you show me? After all me do for you?"

"All you did was steal people's money."

"Oh, ho!" Mr. Michael pulled his hands out of his pockets, and Neena steeled herself for a slap. He glanced at the door. "That the lie you believe? And that the thanks I get for bringing you? For finding somebody to marry you? And what, you didn't steal money yourself? Lila and Prem tell me you leave them high and dry."

"That's bull. They kicked me out. And, anyway, I worked off every dime I owed when they enslaved me. But you got your money, so how's that your business."

Mr. Michael laughed and crossed his arms. "You turn into one hot pepper, but if you not careful, you guh burn yourself." He picked at a pockmark. "Look, me not got all day. Your daddy send me to collect money, and I make this trip out of the kindness of me heart. The only reason me not pick you up and shake the money out your pocket is 'cause I know that white lady's standing inside watching me. But your daddy not guh be happy when me show up empty-handed. He still owe my fee for finding that boy, whether you marry or not."

Of course, Mr. Michael was charging her father fees for phantom tasks. Neena fumed. "Tell my *daddy* I'm not paying shit. And I'm not marrying anybody, 'cause I'm not his slave."

"Slave?" Mr. Michael said. "You call this slavery? This high life? You sure turn into one ungrateful bitch, begging for deportation papers."

Maybe it was the chemicals still in her system or the feeling that she had nothing left to lose, but she clapped her hands together and laughed. "I'd like to see you try. Deport me and see what happens when I tell the white lady you kidnapped me and brought me here when I was just twelve. Narine Jagroop—you still using that passport? You already admitted it yourself—saying you brought me here, telling her my real name, talking about my family, demanding money. She's seen you, and her best friend is a lawyer."

Mr. Michael's face fell.

"Try it." She glared at him, spat on the ground, and returned to the house, her whole body shaking.

Inside the house, Janna stood beyond the foyer, arms crossed, clearly angry at being dismissed. The girls huddled at the top of the stairs, and Neena hoped they hadn't heard much. Through the obscured front door glass, she saw the white truck drive off. Her bluff had worked.

"To your rooms, girls," Janna said before addressing Neena. "Let's talk in the office."

That Janna called the space "the office" felt telling.

"Who was that?" Janna asked after closing the door.

"Mr. Michael. I'm not sure if Michael's his first or last name. He's the smuggler who flew me here. Like he said." Neena sat on the edge of the unmade bed, her heart galloping. Had she really told Mr. Michael off?

"He kept calling you Sunny, said you're not Neena? That your father isn't Prem. I'm reeling from all that. What is going on, Neena?"

If she told Janna the truth, she'd be returned to Guyana. She was certain. Mr. Michael wouldn't deport her, Janna would, because Janna would want her with her rightful family. But she could not return to her father. She would not.

"Sunny's my nickname," she said. "I mentioned that before. And this whole thing . . . well . . . it's weird. But in Guyana, there's this other man. He lived near us, near my nani, my grandmother. My mother might have slept with him, I don't know. He could be my *real* father. Prem used to beat her up and say shit like that."

"Neena!" Janna looked at the door as if the girls were there, hearing the swear word.

"Sorry. But it's true. Anyway, that man loaned money to my grandmother or something. And she told him I'd pay it back because I sent her cash when I wrote. I shouldn't have because he's friends with Mr. Michael, and now he's sending him to shake me down."

It was such an insane, convoluted story.

Janna shook her head. "Why didn't you come to me?"

"I never expected this. I told her I'd send money little by little. I didn't expect . . ."

Janna rubbed her forehead with her hands. "Your own grandmother. And I thought . . ."

"Yeah." Neena looked down, knowing Janna felt bad about her

suggestion the previous night. And she felt bad for making Janna feel guilty, for spinning such absurd lies. She wished she could start over, redo everything.

"That man, the smuggler," Janna began, "Is he dangerous? Should I worry about your safety? Our safety? The girls?"

"Oh, gosh no, Janna." Neena sat up and looked Janna in the eyes. "He wouldn't come near you or the girls. Never. You're white."

"What?"

"I mean, American. I should have said . . . Look, he brings people here illegally, and he makes a lot of money. He wouldn't risk you calling the cops on him."

Janna tilted her head and spoke slowly. "Are you asking me to do that, Neena?"

"No!" Neena shook her head vehemently. Her brain hurt. "I don't have papers, Janna. He can deport me. And Lila—I mean, my mom. And . . . dad. It'd be bad." What would happen if she were returned after renouncing her family? Where would she live? She wanted to disappear.

"David will be livid. First last night, and now this."

"I'm sorry. I'm a mess. I'll leave this weekend. Don and Estelle have a new house. They'll let me stay."

"Neena, I just—"

"It's better this way. I stayed too long. You were so nice to take me in. It was only supposed to be temporary, right?" She brushed away a tear. Relief, fear, and self-hate swirled inside her. "And if I keep working for you, I won't have to mooch off them. I can pay rent."

Janna sighed and rubbed her forehead, and Neena wondered if she was being fired from cleaning, too.

"I can still clean, right?" Neena asked. "I always tried to do a good job."

"You did an amazing job, Neena. It's just, we never felt good about a child cleaning our place. When it was a summer thing with your mom, that was different. But—"

"Please, Janna." Her savings wouldn't last long if she paid rent, and she couldn't imagine asking to live with the Hernandezes for free.

"I'll talk to David. Maybe once a week. Saturdays, so it doesn't affect school."

"Thank you."

"You need to prioritize school, Neena. You're smart. School can get you places. I don't want you going off the rails. You were doing so well."

She *had* been doing well. Until the letters. Until last night. What the hell was wrong with her, and why was she craving a cigarette? She needed to do better. She needed to fix herself.

"There's no rush to grow up, Neena. I know you're dealing with a lot of grown-up things, but you're just a kid, honey. Don't forget that. It's okay to just focus on school and being a kid."

Neena forced a tight smile and nodded. A kid? She'd stopped being a kid so long ago. Even if she wanted, she could never be a kid again. She'd crossed a chasm too large.

31

Plan B

Wood-paneled walls enveloped her at the Hernandezes' new rental home. The old house was brown inside and out. Coffee-colored carpet, stained and threadbare, covered the floors. Dark cabinets dominated the kitchen. Even the air smelled brown and stale, though Estelle had opened the windows and bleached everything.

Neena's bags were packed, but she hadn't yet worked up the nerve to ask about moving in. She felt unmoored as she helped organize Yvonne's new bedroom that Sunday, folding and rearranging clothes Yvonne crammed haphazardly into drawers. Yvonne set up the sewing machine and yammered on about Al's newer, nicer two-bedroom condo.

"Yve, can I move in with you?" Neena blurted out, interrupting her. She threw herself across Yvonne's bed to hide her embarrassment.

"What? And leave Janna's palace? Chica, you're crazy."

Neena buried her face, which had sprung a leak.

"What happened? They kicking you out?"

Neena nodded though she couldn't bring herself to admit the truth. She still felt filthy. She sat up and brushed away tears. "It's . . . I took some liquor . . . and David knows." She'd crept around the Parker house the previous day, avoiding David, who seemed to avoid her, too.

"Crap, Neena. I told you not to do that."

Tears fell hard at this reprimand. "I don't know what's wrong with me."

"Shit, I knew you'd get caught."

Neena nodded. "I can pay rent. To your parents. I'll still work at Janna's."

"Papi's strict now, you know. They hide the liquor, and they barely trust me. You can't get caught here."

Her heart sank. Even Yvonne didn't trust her.

"But, yeah, of course you can move in. And if you pay rent, it'll help when I move out."

Neena sat up. "Move out?"

Yvonne motioned wildly at the closed bedroom door and whispered, "Shh. Al asked me to live with him, no charge. I'm thinking about it."

She'd never even met this Al, and here Yvonne—her best friend, her hermana—was talking about living with the guy after only a month of dating?

"Papi will be pissed, you know, 'cause we're not married. But this house is a dump, no offense. It needs so much work. You should see Al's place. It's almost like Janna's. And, I mean, I like him. It's nice to be with a guy and, you know, stay at his house." Yvonne giggled.

Neena nodded. The world was a nebulous, changing thing. Nothing stayed still for long. Everyone left. Even Yvonne would one day leave her without a second glance. Her insides grew numb.

"Al has the girls two days a week and some weekends. And I like helping with them."

Neena nodded again, growing hollower.

"This is good for me," Yvonne said. "And look, you'll get your own room."

Neena smiled. Her own room was overrated.

Yvonne opened the door and shouted, "Mami, can Neena move in? She can pay rent."

Estelle hugged her in the dark kitchen and said, "It's too much, chiquita," after Neena suggested contributing fifty a month. But Neena insisted. Without them, she'd be homeless, or worse, forced to return to Prem and Lila. They were saving her, and she was done taking charity. She'd already squandered too much charity.

They welcomed her like family, but Neena felt like an intruder as she shoved her bags under Yvonne's bed. Drifting as she had, she'd become utterly misshapen, a flimsy thing that didn't quite fit anywhere.

Monday, Neena waited for Lenny outside the history classroom.

"Cindy," he exclaimed, approaching with open arms. He looked scruffy in baggy jeans and a loose T-shirt. A patchy beard covered his chin.

"Hey," she said, trying to swallow her shame. People looked at her sidelong as though they knew what she'd done with him, as though she were marked.

He pulled her close and kissed her mouth, his whiskers grazing her skin, and she pushed him away.

He laughed his shrill, stupid laugh and asked, "What can I do you for?"

She looked down at his clunky high-top sneakers. "I need my stuff. I left it in your car."

"I'll hook you up after school," he said, as if he were selling her something. A kid walking by chuckled.

When she got to his car, he was inside, smoking. He offered her the joint, but she shook her head. They were on school property, and she was determined to stick to her plan: retrieve her purse and fix herself. She'd already lost too much, and she couldn't get caught up with him. She wasn't even attracted to him.

"Where's my stuff?" she asked, sitting low in the front seat, not wanting to be seen.

"At my house," he said, starting the car.

She reached for the door handle. "I gotta get home. Just bring it tomorrow."

"Relax, dollface. I can take you home." He revved out of the parking spot, throwing her against the seat.

She stared ahead and tried to look as though her heart wasn't racing.

"You live near here, right?" he asked. "I've seen you walking to school."

She didn't respond. Had he been watching her?

"But I never saw you out partying before this weekend."

She shrugged and flushed. "I don't usually . . ."

He laughed his stupid laugh and touched her knee. "You should. It was fun."

She pushed his hand aside and said, "Look, Lenny. I'm not looking for a relationship or anything." She felt badass uttering this line, heard in a movie.

"Who said anything about a relationship? I'm just having fun, dollface. You like fun, don't you? You seemed to, the other night."

She stared out the window.

"You're kind of a nerd, aren't you? You planning on graduating?"

She shrugged, thinking of Marcus calling her a nerd.

"Then what? College or something?"

She shrugged again.

He was eighteen, he confessed, and he was taking their history class for the second time. He needed a D to graduate. "Maybe you can tutor me," he said, laughing.

She kept staring out the window.

"But if I don't graduate, I'll just expand my business. That's plan B."

She turned to him, wondering what he meant.

Perhaps seeing her question, he released the wheel with the hand that wasn't holding the joint, pressed a nostril, and sniffed twice, winking.

She snapped her head back to the window.

"My cousin Joey supplies me, you know, and I supply the school. It's small-time right now, but it got me this sweet ride. I mean, I had to fix it up, but it's nice, right?"

Neena glanced at the dashboard as if assessing the car, but she was only thinking about getting out.

His house turned out to be mere blocks from Yvonne's new place, and Neena told herself she wouldn't let him drive her there. She didn't want him knowing where she lived. She didn't want to enter his house either, but he marched ahead of her, saying, "Close the door so the cats don't get out," before disappearing inside.

The dim interior reeked of cat litter and stale smoke. A TV played in a corner, and in front of it, a woman sat in a recliner. Two cats sat in her lap while others milled about the living room.

Neena went down the dark hallway where Lenny had disappeared and peered into the only open door. Clothes covered the floor and unmade bed. A bowl with dried pasta sauce and a dirty fork sat amid food wrappings and clutter near the bed. Lenny swiveled around in his desk chair, holding her sweats and purse on his lap. On the desk behind him, in the only clutter-free space, sat two white lines of cocaine. "Come and get it," he said.

She stood paralyzed a moment before shaking her head.

"I don't get you," he said swiveling the chair side to side. "One minute, you're like super freak, all over me. And then, you're a cold fish." He swiveled around, snorted a line, and turned back, snuffling. "Damn, that's good. I'm trying a new batch. Sure you don't want any?"

Her throat felt hollow. Yes, a part of her wanted some. The part that remembered what it felt like to fly and feel nothing but sky. But she couldn't. Not there. Not in that house. Not after everything. She shook her head again.

"Suit yourself." He spun around, gripping her purse. His smile told her she'd failed a test.

Her legs moved toward him, and she heard herself say, "Look, I just can't, all right? I got kicked out of where I was staying because of the other night. I'm at this new place, and I don't want to screw it up, you know. Just give me my stuff."

He stopped spinning and stared at her. "You a foster kid or something?"

Foster kid? "Something like that," she said, holding out a hand for her things, training her eyes away from the powder.

He held up the purse and winked. "All right. I got you. But if you ever need anything, you know where to find good old Lenny."

She took her things, willing her hand not to shake. *Leave this house. Leave now. Run.*

A block away, she checked for the ID, cigarettes, and money—all there—and she found a note in her purse with Lenny's name and number, wrapped around a joint. Smiling, she told herself she'd make the joint her test. She wouldn't smoke it, and every day she ignored it would mark a victory.

Javier was mowing the lawn when she got home, and Don and Oscar were painting the interior walls, transforming the dingy brown living room into a creamy yellow space. The owners had discounted their rent for the work.

"Wow," Neena said. "Looks brand-new. Smells good, too."

"I made enchiladas," Estelle called from the kitchen.

Neena hugged her in gratitude. "Gracias," she said, feeling hopeful. In Estelle's arms, she was safe from Prem, Mr. Michael, and her father, and she didn't want to screw it up.

At school, she evaded Lenny, but he found her anyway. Twice, he visited her in the library, bringing her food from Taco Bell, asking her to tutor him in exchange for blow.

He entered their history class calling, "Yo, Cindy, my girl. What's up," always making a show of kissing her cheek. Soon, other kids were calling her Cindy, even though the teacher called her Neena. Boys occasionally shouted, "Super Freak," behind her back, and Lenny's stupid laugh always followed the taunt. He made it impossible to forget her failures.

Janna picked her up on Saturday mornings to clean, and there, too, she had to face what she'd squandered—the pristine office, the plush carpet, the full bookshelves, the pool. She felt shame every time she dusted the liquor cabinet, which was now locked.

"I think I saw that white truck the other day," Janna said one Saturday, soon after she'd moved. "And I swear your dad was inside with that Michael fellow."

Her insides numbed, and she tried not to react. Mr. Michael was calling her bluff and making nice with Prem. Perhaps he would get her deported after all.

Walking to and from school, she continued to watch her back and change her route. But late November, on her way home from school, a car revved behind her, and her heart dropped.

"I see you still walking the streets."

Prem.

He pulled up alongside her, grazing the curb with his tire. Leaning across the passenger side, he said, "Where's my money?"

She ran.

He drove to match her pace, shouting. "I hear you pay Don rent. I wonder, how can that be when you still owe me money?"

She turned around abruptly, running toward a group of kids who'd come into view.

"I want my money, you hear?" he yelled before peeling off.

The house was empty when she got there, and she felt unsafe. She locked herself in the bathroom and huddled on the bathmat, unable to cry. Every cell in her body vibrated with the shock of seeing him after so many months. She didn't realize how protected she'd been at Janna's. Don and his boys, being undocumented, didn't hold the same sway. Now, Prem would hound her. Even if she gave him all the money she'd saved, he wouldn't leave her alone.

That night, she came close to smoking the joint. But, holding it, she thought of Lenny, and she realized he could help her.

She sought him out after school the next day and asked for a ride home. Lenny pretended to faint from delight, then laughed his ridiculous laugh. "I knew you always wanted me, Cindy baby."

"Cindy's not my real name," she said getting into his car, sinking low in the seat.

"You'll always be Cindy to me, dollface."

She lit a cigarette and he said, "Want something stronger?"

"No."

"I keep thinking about that night. You and me. It was fun. We should do it again."

"You're no good for me. And I'm only using you for your car."

He shrieked with laughter. "You shoot from the hip. I like that."

"Anyway, you're only interested cause I'm saying no."

He laughed again, and she smiled. Were they friends?

"There's a party later in case you change your mind." He pulled up in front of the Hernandezes' just as Yvonne was getting home from work.

"Who're you?" she asked, walking toward his car.

"Uh, this is Lenny," Neena said, getting out.

"Hola, Lenny." Yvonne leaned in the passenger window. "Nice car."

"Thanks. Tell your friend only good guys drive cars like this."

"Goodbye, Lenny. Thanks for the ride," Neena called as she walked toward the house.

When he drove off, Yvonne said, "He seems nice."

For a second, Neena wanted to confess everything—Lenny's role in why she'd been kicked out of Janna's and the truth of Prem. That he wasn't her father, that he believed she owed him thousands, that he had . . .

She shrugged and said, "He's nice enough."

Yvonne's boyfriend, Al, came by with his girls for dinner that evening. He was taking Yvonne on a trip for the long Thanksgiving weekend, and Don insisted they meet him first. Neena was shocked to discover he was a blond man. She thought Yvonne liked brown guys, like her. As they ate, Al kept touching Yvonne, and his matching hazel-eyed twins clung to her as if she were their mother.

Neena could barely look at them. How was it that Yvonne had two perfect ready-made families to choose from, while she had none?

After Yvonne left, she lay in bed, feeling the emptiness of her life.

For weeks, she'd suppressed the urge to drink, but it bludgeoned her now. She crawled under the bed, next to her suitcase, craving something, anything, everything.

Roshi, the world is a storm of heartaches, one after another. I can't handle it.

She found the joint and lit it by the open window. Smoke filled the hollow inside her, and she berated herself. *Roshi, maybe I don't deserve a family.*

The long weekend loomed ahead like another test, and she knew she'd fail it, too. The Hernandezes would work extra hours for holiday pay, and Janna was out of town, so she didn't need Neena to clean. Neena would be alone with her messed-up mind in an empty house, fearing Prem or Mr. Michael at every sound.

She knew now that she'd go with Lenny to the party he'd invited her to. She'd become Cindy and play his girlfriend in exchange for a sniff of white powder. It was the only way to outrun the shadows that chased her.

32

Procedure

After the Thanksgiving trip, Yvonne all but moved in with Al, and Neena struggled to regain sobriety. Mornings, she painted her face and told herself today was the day she'd clean up. She remained steadfast through school. But the gnawing always returned when she sat in Lenny's car. She feared Prem's prowling shadow. She feared Yvonne's empty room. She feared her father's voice, shouting "traitor, traitor, traitor." So she let Lenny take her to his filthy house, where he plied her with vodka and cocaine.

Dear Roshi, why am I so weak?

At home, she focused on walking a straight line from the front door to the bedroom, and if Estelle asked where she'd been, she'd say, "My boyfriend's," inwardly cringing at the thought of Lenny being her boyfriend. Friday nights, she controlled her use to wake up sober for Janna the following morning. Then, she'd wreck herself the rest of the weekend.

The Saturday before Christmas, Janna handed her a letter when she got in the car. "I think your grandmother wrote."

Neena's heart flipped seeing *Caimraj Kissoon* in the return address. Did Janna still think this was her grandmother's name?

"I have a favor to ask," Janna added. "Leslie got her period this week, and I want to take her out for a special lunch. Do you mind watching Nicole today?"

Neena nodded, but her insides drained at the mention of *period*. How long had it been since she'd gotten hers? Over a month? It had been a while.

At Janna's, she kept the unopened letter in her pocket and the implication of a missed period at bay as she vacuumed and dusted. She forced both things from her mind as she erected a gingerbread house with Nicole and accepted gifts from Janna. She felt thoughtless for not having bought anything in return. She entered the Hernandezes' home knowing she'd have nothing to give them but bad news.

In Yvonne's room, she clutched the unopened letter and huddled in bed, numb. Visions swirled in her head. Crack babies. Lila bleeding herself out, saying, "You know what this means." Mrs. Fredrickson, the librarian, saying, "You're a young lady now." Her father shouting, "We hope you not shaming us."

She punched her flat stomach, wanting to expunge the monstrous thing growing inside. She punched hard, but nothing happened.

She needed a drink, a hit, something. *Dear Roshi . . .*

Hoping for a positive message from Roshi, she opened the envelope.

Dear Sunny,

You wrote to speak the truth, so I will write the truth from our end. Your last letter create a lot of hardship here, especially with you saying you feel like a slave and claiming Daddy sold you, with you refusing to marry for papers.

Daddy is ready to cut off ties, saying you are shameful and ungrateful. He forbid me to write back, so no one know about this letter. I just want you to know you have driven your father to the bottle. I bet you can imagine the fights. We are all grateful for the $100US you send, but truth be told, Daddy already piss half. If you send more, he might piss it away for spite.

Michael turn up with stories about how you curse him out on the road, wearing nothing but a panty in broad daylight. Michael suspect you are whoring around for money, and Daddy believe this since it go with what Prem and Lila claim.

Ma and the rest of us don't want believe that nonsense. But the picture you send show you among pure strangers, even a blackie, and we can plainly see your red brassiere. So we don't know what to believe. It pain Ma not knowing where you will be tomorrow. We want you to do good and be safe. And we hope to reunite.

Please write back. Let us know you're doing okay. But wait to send money. Maybe try in a couple months, after Daddy cool down.

I want to leave off with good news. Ravi and Mala welcomed a baby girl. They name her Amelia, and she is pretty like her name. Believe it or not, they already expecting again. Laugh. So, call yourself Aunty Sunny.

    Your loving brother,
    Raj

A smaller note on folded paper inside the envelope read:

Dear Sunny,

I miss you. I go to school and learn good, especially to talk with hands. I worry about you, my little sister, and hope you okay.

Ma and Daddy mad about your letter, but I don't feel mad. I just feel sad missing you and glad you meet nice *people and think you look pretty. Writing is hard for me, but I work a lot at this one and Raj say he will send it. Hope you okay.*

> *Your ever-loving sister,*
> *Roshini*

Below the words, Roshi had drawn a hand with two fingers bent into the palm. It was labeled: "sign for I love you."

Neena bawled into her pillow. She folded the papers and tucked them deep in her suitcase. Then she walked the few blocks to Lenny's house. No one answered, but the door was unlocked, so she let herself in. In Lenny's room, she pushed aside dirty laundry and video game clutter to unearth a half bottle of vodka. She climbed into the unmade bed, taking long burning swigs.

Dear Roshi, I am not okay. Can you tell? She'd sometimes fantasized that some otherworldly force, God or a jumbie, magically transmitted her thoughts to Roshi. Now she wondered if Roshi had, in fact, sensed her distress, prompting her to write *hope you okay* twice.

She'd drunk herself into a stupor by the time Lenny showed up with a blurry handful of friends.

A crimson-haired girl sat on the bed and stroked Neena's head. "Where'd you find this one, Lenny? She don't look too hot." Her accented voice felt like a warm hug.

"That's Cindy," Lenny said. "She's a *freak*, if you know what I mean. And she could dance circles around you bitches."

Voices laughed, and the girl drawled, "Honey, you good?"

This small kindness brought tears to Neena's eyes, and the girl said, "Aww, Lenny, she's crying."

"Give her this."

A pill landed on her lips, and someone brushed it away.

"Jesus, Leonard. You want to kill her? Let her sleep it off."

Someone turned on music, and the group smoked and laughed as Neena slipped in and out of sleep.

At some point, someone slid under the sheets with her, and Lenny said, "Fuck, take the sheets off so we can see."

Someone else slid in, and she feared it was Lenny. Would he screw her in front of everyone? She sat up and slurred, "I'm pregnant, dammit, I'm pregnant."

"Oh, shh, Cindy darling," the girl with the sweet voice cooed, "that's nothing we can't take care of."

In early January, Neena copied facts from Cindy Tipton's ID onto forms at an antiseptic-scented clinic before lying back on a paper-covered gurney for the procedure. *Procedure*—a blessedly sterile word for an awful thing she did not want to think about.

Charlotte, the redhead who'd called her darling, had scribbled the clinic's name on a scrap of paper along with her phone number. Neena, too embarrassed to call the girl, looked up the clinic in the yellow pages and took a bus there the week prior. She'd peed in a cup and let a nurse peer inside her to confirm that, yes, she was pregnant. Every part of that visit had shamed her—the paperwork, the table with its stirrups, the posters about diseases, and the bag of condoms they'd handed her after.

Knowing she couldn't handle this *procedure* sober, she'd snorted a line before changing into the paper gown. Now, she was blissfully numb. She felt a twinge of pain handing over a third of her savings afterward, but on the bus ride home, the whole thing seemed like a dream.

She was determined to return to a life of quiet nerdiness. To pull herself together for Roshi's sake. To write back and say she was okay and mean it. But the next week at school, she was unable to sit with herself. Everyone knew what she'd done, she was certain.

There were looks, whispers, laughs. Even Mrs. Mulligan seemed to sneer. And the air vibrated with a supernatural presence as if the baby's jumbie hovered nearby. She'd never be okay again.

Lenny beckoned, and while her brain screamed no, she moved toward him, needing the safety of his car. She loathed him, but she feared Prem and Mr. Michael more, jumping at the sight of every white or gold vehicle. Lenny's joints and lines of powder pushed everything away. But every time she used, she imagined Roshi shaking her head, and her shame grew. Which made her crave more.

She spent most school days blitzed in Lenny's car, numb at parks and beaches, or strung out at random houses. She spent nights dancing in clubs or comatose in his bed. Several times, she woke up in strange rooms full of strangers, unable to recall whole days. Disgusted with herself, she plunged into darkness again. She stopped going to school, hid from the Hernandezes, and told Janna she had too much homework to keep cleaning.

By mid-March, she'd burned through her savings. Embarrassed that she could no longer pay rent, she secreted her bags from the Hernandezes' while they worked. She barely slept there anyway, practically living with Lenny, where at the very least Prem couldn't find her. She left a note for Estelle saying, "Thanks for everything. Moving in with a friend. Now Javier gets his own room." She drew a smiley face and thought of Raj writing *laugh*, knowing no one would laugh. Certainly not Yvonne. They'd seen each other only twice since Christmas, and both times, Yvonne had chattered on about Al and her promotion at work. They lived on separate planets.

Two weeks after Neena stowed her suitcases and duffels under Lenny's bed, she missed her period again.

On Lenny's grimy bathroom floor, she stared at blue lines on a test strip. She'd made him use condoms or the pull-out method when she was lucid, but there were those blackout nights. She vomited bile, imagining the deformed growth inside her and the procedure she'd endured not that long ago. How had she allowed this to happen again? Who was she? *Dear Roshi . . .*

"I'm pregnant," she told Lenny when he eventually came home.

"Again?"

"I need money to get rid of it."

"Fuck? How much is it? It's tight this month."

"Well, I need it. Unless you want a crack baby."

He laughed. "It's your crack baby, not mine. Maybe you should have it. It could be your little pet."

An image of a baby roaming the house like one of the cats came to her. Then the baby morphed into a creature on Lenny's mother's lap, looking strangely like her sister Indy. Acid burned her throat.

She stood and pushed a finger into Lenny's chest. "You did this, so you better fucking pay. And forget touching me as long as this thing's in here." She slapped her stomach.

Lenny laughed. "Girl, I can have another junkie ho in a minute. And I don't owe you shit. How'd you even know it's mine?"

"Fuck you," she said, reeling from his words.

"And when the fuck did all your crap end up here? I never said you could move in."

He picked up two of her bags and marched to the front door.

"Don't touch my stuff," she yelled, following him.

He flung them into the yard, but by the time she retrieved them, he was at the door with the rest of her things.

Neena sat on the concrete stoop amid the detritus of her life, feeling the depth of her fall.

Dear Roshi, how did I get here?

Shame burned her. The Hernandezes would take her back, she knew, but she couldn't bear them seeing her so ruined. She reached into her backpack and pulled out the paper with Charlotte's number, a weak lifeline.

She and Charlotte weren't friends, exactly. But Charlotte had been kind the few times she stopped by for weed, and they'd gone dancing a couple times. Charlotte got paid to dance at a strip club and had once suggested Neena work there. She dialed the number from the living room, staring at Lenny's mother, whose gaze never left the television, a tabby on her lap.

MAYA

ATLANTA, GEORGIA

The floor rumbles as the garage door closes below me. I hear Dwayne exit his car and walk into the mudroom. I should go to him, say hello, say something, ask if the market has stabilized, at the very least. But I'm a coward, afraid of looking him in the eye, unsure of where to start.

What was my plan? My mind reels.

Dwayne, the thing is . . .

Dwayne, here's the truth . . .

Dwayne, I never meant to lie . . .

I was born Sunny. Sunita. Sunita Kissoon. But that doesn't mean the Maya you know isn't real. I'm not a lie.

A battered blossom is wedged in the windowpane, petals broken and bent. Dwayne, that flower is me, I think, and the ridiculous thought calms me.

I empty the backpack on the desk and retrieve my old purse as footfalls vibrate the stairs. I feel him in the doorway behind me as my fingers find a small stack of ripped paper, next to that crinkly old bag of peanuts. I turn to him with the shreds in my hands. It takes me a moment to raise my eyes to his, and I'm pained by the anguish I see there. The confusion.

I want to wrap my arms around him and bury my head in his chest. He must read these thoughts because when I step forward, he shakes his head slightly and steps back.

Though I deserve it, this rejection stings. Touch is our language. We've been like magnets our entire relationship, never not touching. A panic rises inside me as if I've already lost him.

I sit down on the carpet, my eyes locked on his, and he sits where he is, too. I see Roshi's letter in his hands; he must have grabbed it from the kitchen counter where I'd left it.

I reassemble the bits of paper I'm holding like a puzzle. My birth certificate. I haven't touched it since the night I stowed the pieces. I push the assemblage toward him.

He studies it, and I clear my constricted throat before speaking. "That's why I'm obsessed with Halloween. It's my real birthday."

The confusion in his face doubles. "Why didn't you just tell me?"

I look down. "I . . . I wanted to. But . . . it got so hard, and it's complicated. I was afraid you'd leave, and I . . . I'd already lost so much family . . ."

"You have to spell it out for me, Maya. Or should I say Sunny?" He waves Roshi's letter. "Who is Roshini? What's this about your father? Were you ever a foster kid? Was that a lie, too?"

I nod.

His face grows incredulous. "I feel like I'm in the twilight zone here. What's true?"

A hot tear slides down my cheek. "Me, I'm still true."

"I don't know what to believe." His voice is devastatingly calm.

Failing and feeling desperate, I say, "I might have cancer. I might have the gene." My eyes water, and I picture a lump spontaneously erupting inside me, punishment for using these words to avoid saying everything else.

He closes his eyes and sighs. "I know. And I'm sorry. And it scares the hell out of me. But my brain can't go there right now. Not yet. Not until I understand who you are."

This is fair. This was the plan. I stand to retrieve the clothes and documents from the desk.

Dwayne drops Roshi's letter next to the birth certificate as I lay out items. The lacy white dress, yellowed and tousled, still smelling of mosquito-coil smoke. The flowered frock I wore to the airport, unchanged after all these years. The black mesh overlay, that flimsy armor I'd wielded as Neena. Leslie's butterfly T-shirt. A green skirt. My fake IDs. Neena's birth certificate. Naturalization, name change, and citizenship papers. And an envelope crammed with letters spewing vile words that will stab Dwayne when he reads them, that still stab me.

I pick up the dress made from a curtain and begin the story I've never told anyone before. "I wore this the last time anyone called me Sunny. I was twelve, and my father believed I was his ticket to America. He believed . . . he believed so many false things. And I paid the price." Words pour out after this.

When I get to the rape and my ripped-up certificate, Dwayne reaches for my hands and says, "Come here." But it's me who refuses his touch, shaking my head, needing the distance between us to finish.

I tell him about fighting back, about Yvonne and Marcus, about Mr. Michael's threat of marriage, about getting kicked out, and about restarting at Janna's, where Prem hounded me. But I choke up when I get to my father's letters, the letters I now see were my unspooling.

"He really screwed me up," I say as I spread the letters out. Shivers shoot up my arms as his hateful words come back verbatim. "I was just a kid. I'd lost Marcus. When my father wrote, spitting so much poison, the ground disappeared. I felt like I lost my family for the second time. I spiraled out of control. And then . . . I got pregnant."

Dwayne looks up sharply. "Did you . . . ?"

I squeeze my eyes shut and nod tightly. "It's hard to relive those days, even now."

Dwayne picks up the letters, and I say, "I never wanted you to feel his hate. I can't bear for the kids to feel any of it."

After reading them, he speaks quietly. "He sounds like a piece of work, and I know you went through hell. But I'm a Black man, Maya. Hate like his is my daily fare. You know that. Sure, it's complicated 'cause he's your dad, but I still don't get why you didn't tell me. I'm your husband. This is shit we could have handled together. I thought we were best friends."

My eyes smart anew. "We are. I'm sorry."

"There was that family," he says, his eyes searching for a memory. "At the park. When the kids were little. The dad with the kites. I know you remember."

I do, but I'm surprised he does. It was so long ago, and such a brief encounter. The family blasted soca music and flew kites, and our kids started to play with their kids, who were the same age. Dwayne struck up a conversation with the father who said he'd made the kites, who said he could show Dwayne how, whose lilting accent, laughter, and kindness brought my brothers to mind, especially Jeeve. Desperate to leave, I escaped to buy ice cream. I returned with the treats and insisted on getting in line for the Easter Bunny to lure the boys away from the family.

"You acted so weird. So skittish. So unlike you," he says. "I looked up Guyana later because I'd never heard of it. I'd assumed the family was Indian, like I'd once assumed about you. That's why I remember. For a second, I wondered if the people who'd abandoned you could have been from Guyana. But you said you hadn't heard of it either."

I drop my head in regret, tears brimming.

"You had chances, Maya. Would you have told me if your sister, your *deaf* sister, hadn't written? If she didn't have cancer and if there wasn't a gene. Would you have lied to me about *all* of this forever?"

His words are a whip, and tears drip down my cheeks. But I'm done being dishonest. "I don't know."

Hurt crumples his face.

I rush on. "But not because of you. It's me. I . . . I chose you, and the boys, and our life. With you, I got to be . . . the best version of *me*. I didn't have to be that girl who . . . who those things happened to . . . who did things." The truth of these words hits me as I speak them and I swipe tears from my face. "With you, I felt whole. I thought I'd outrun them, you know, Sunny and Neena with all their baggage and shame. So, yes, I might have kept running. But she . . . they caught up to me. And I'm glad. Because I wasn't whole. I'm only starting to feel whole now, now that you know."

"But you, *they*, didn't do anything wrong. Don't you see that?"

I meet his eyes and shake my head.

A rolled-up green plaid skirt sits in the lineup of things. I unfurl it, releasing a hint of perfume and dregs of buried memories. It's time to talk about that last day. What I did. *Him*.

"I told you I *danced* in Miami, before I moved to Jacksonville for school."

"Yes. For a few months after your so-called foster care. When you supposedly got all your tats. And got dry."

I ignore the sarcasm. "It was more than a few months, but yes, I got dry then and got my tattoos. I'd wanted to start over, do my own thing, and dancing gave me that. But I knew I couldn't dance forever, and without papers or a diploma, jobs are limited. So, when I got a chance to get my papers, I took it."

I lay out Neena's birth certificate and the naturalization and citizenship papers with her name and my face. "The thing is, technically, they're not *my* papers. So, technically, I'm still undocumented. This is why I never wanted to apply for a passport, why

I told you I didn't have a birth certificate. I couldn't even look at it, and I didn't want to explain this name. I could still get deported if someone outs me. Maybe even jailed for fraud."

Dwayne chuffs a breath as he swallows this. "Shit. I get how that's hard to admit, but I would never have outed you, Maya. Don't you know that?"

"It wasn't you I was scared of."

"Who then?"

I purse my lips.

Dwyane stares, and I want to backpedal, to not have to say what I'm about to say. In less than an hour, I've become a stranger to him. How will he see me when he knows the full truth? What will I lose?

I plow ahead. "He'd turn me in if he finds me. Because I sent him to jail."

Dwayne shakes his head disbelievingly. "Who? What happened?"

"It was . . . that day I left Miami, it was . . . I ran because . . ."

"Spit it out, Maya."

His face fills my head, but I'm unable to utter his name. I whisper, "I killed someone."

PART FIVE

SYNTHIA

1987–1988
HIALEAH, FLORIDA

33

Glitter

"You all right, darling?" Charlotte asked in her Southern drawl. She turned her face side to side to assess herself in a bulb-lined mirror, missing half its bulbs.

Neena gripped the chipped Formica counter and stared at this girl who'd saved her. Hair, the vermillion of fall leaves. Eyes, the emerald of peacock feathers. Unreal colors Neena had only ever seen in pictures on a wall calendar. Charlotte applied mascara, opening and closing her lips fishlike with each stroke, looking like a creature from a calendar herself.

"You look like you're gonna hurl," Charlotte said, putting away the mascara wand.

Neena nodded. Was she really about to strip naked? She, who once felt naked in shorts? She wasn't Charlotte, so beautiful and bold. "I can't do it sober," she said. "I need a bump."

Charlotte faced her. "Hon, you're so close. You don't want to go back there."

No, she did not want to go back there. She'd been free of alcohol, pills, and powders for two weeks. And, at Charlotte's place, she'd been free of Prem's phantom. It was too much to throw away.

Charlotte and her roommate, Kimmy, owed Neena nothing, yet they offered her their couch until she could pull herself together, saying they'd been down on their luck before, that they were paying it forward. She'd spent five nights shivering and vomiting from withdrawal on the couch, and they assured her a couple weeks' wages at the club would pay for *the procedure*. This amateur night was her audition. She couldn't afford to choke.

"Here," Charlotte said, pushing a pack of cigarettes and a lighter toward her. "You'll be fine. You don't have to win to get hired. Just get through it. Fake it till you make it, right?"

Neena felt a wave of gratitude. She lit a cigarette, savoring the burning tobacco scent as she took a deep drag. The rush of nicotine calmed her. In the mirror, her reflection blew smoke from shiny red lips. *Dear Roshi, would you still recognize me?*

Kimmy, who worked as a beautician, spent the day perming then dying Neena's hair a deep maroon. And Charlotte had dressed her up in a minute green plaid skirt, a white button-down, fake eyeglasses, and six-inch platform shoes. The clothes hung loose on her frame, which had grown skeletal the past months. She looked like a kid playing dress-up, and she feared she'd get laughed off stage. She nudged open the shirt to reveal the lacy push-up bra underneath and wondered if Marcus would even recognize her.

"Synthia," the house mom called, checking a clipboard. "You're up."

Hours earlier, Neena had handed this leathery blond woman named Vicky her fake driver's license. On the woman's form, she'd written *Synthia* on the line for stage name, *schoolgirl* for costume, and *Eddie Money—"Take Me Home Tonight"* for song, Charlotte's suggestion. Then, she'd watched a few professionals and other amateurs take the stage, desensitizing herself to naked bodies. But she was still dreading her turn.

"Breathe, darling," Charlotte coached. "Go slow, or you'll look all spaz. Remember, their eyes follow your hands. And they want a tease, so tease them."

Neena finished the cigarette and approached the house mom, who stood by a curtained door atop a short flight of stairs. Dressed and made up as she was, Vicky didn't look like any mom Neena had ever met.

"Couple minutes," Vicky said, erasing the name above *Synthia* on a large dry-erase board. "Through there when the DJ calls your name." She motioned to a side door with her chin.

Her *name*. Neena had picked the stage name because it felt like an iteration of the one on her fake ID, Cindy. But seeing *Synthia* on the board, she realized it was more an iteration of her real name, Sunita. She shivered. Was it a sign? Perhaps as Synthia, she could start over. Really start over.

Standing behind the curtain, thumping with music, her body tensed. She couldn't blow this chance as she'd done every other one. Everything depended on this.

The DJ said, "Gentlemen, get your wallets out to welcome the naughtiest little nerd you'll ever meet. Our next amateur tonight is Synthia!"

"Let's see what you got," Vicky said, nudging her forward.

"Break a leg, honey," Charlotte called from the back.

The song started, and Neena walked through the door, numb with anxiety. *Fake it till you make it.*

Wolf whistles and blinding stage lights greeted her. She wobbled in the platform heels before strutting down the catwalk, snaking her body to the beat, trying to look confident. She felt herself moving too fast, *all spaz*, as Charlotte had warned.

Neena focused on the song's bass line and danced against its beat to slow down. She bit the tip of her index finger and played with her hair to start the tease as she'd seen other girls do. In the dimness beyond the stage, someone breathed out cigarette smoke, and it swirled with mesmerizing asynchrony, calming her. I should move like that smoke, she thought.

Pressing her back against the pole, she danced her arms upward in slow Bollywood style. The move reminded her of Jeeve, and she smiled.

As she gyrated into a squat, someone shouted, "Yeah, show it to me, baby," and her smile disappeared.

But she steeled herself and opened and closed her thighs to flash glimpses of her lacy underwear, mimicking moves she'd studied earlier. Men whistled, and one man, who looked eerily like Prem, winked. A small panic flashed inside her, but she told herself that he wasn't Prem. And he couldn't touch her.

Gripping the pole with one hand, she spun her back to the main audience and lowered her torso, dancing her bottom up until she could see through her legs—another borrowed move. She stared at upside-down faces, then danced herself upright, miming a slow hump against the pole. Yvonne would hoot with laughter, she thought, and she allowed her smile to return.

"Take it off," voices shouted.

This was inevitable. It was the reason she was there. She couldn't put it off any longer. As she teased a shoulder from her shirt, her mind left her body. It returned to Annette's living room so long ago, to her curiosity about the Barbie doll and the naughty surprise of the slick peach-colored plastic under the doll's tiny clothes. To Janna's full-length mirror the first time she saw her whole naked body. That startling reflection. That was what these men wanted, the titillating shock of bare skin.

She thought this as she dropped her shirt and eased her underwear down. Faces glowed around the catwalk and men waved money, hollering to see her breasts, begging for her to drop the skirt. She was barely clad amid a roomful of leering men, but she suddenly felt an inexplicable surge of power. There was something intoxicating about the unbreachable barrier between their desire and her body.

Charlotte's advice returned to her: *They want a tease, so tease them.* She glided her fingers along her inner thigh. She skimmed her crotch, dragged her hand up her torso, and stroked her bra. She released her breasts from the cups one at a time, before unclasping. Then she dropped her skirt to reveal her bare body. The audience roared, and dollar bills rained. And she felt as if she were flying.

The DJ shouted, "Synthia, gentlemen," and she wanted to be the badass they applauded.

34

Begin Again

She stepped into new skin to become Synthia—a name she chose, an identity she created, a life that was all hers, blessedly unconnected to her past. In this new skin, she felt rootless, born from nothing, free.

With a daily half pack of cigarettes, she kept drug cravings at bay and grew more lucid. The following weeks, she took every available shift and played up her youth to sell dances. She learned that biting her lips and averting her eyes like an innocent earned big tips. Everyone had a schtick, and virginity became hers.

Two weeks in, as she counted out money for the *procedure*, she bled. It felt like a gift from the universe, a sign she was on the right track. She had feared a second procedure, the power of another derailing jumbie. But she'd been spared the guilt and left with money for rent. She cried tears of relief as her body expunged the past, as the future became imaginable.

The next day, she explored the neighborhood to collect flyers for rentals and subleases, and she reveled in the vibrancy of urban living. The girls' condo complex stood a block south of a small park with swings and a basketball court. The opposite direction led to a grocery store and the salon where Kimmy worked. A mile west took her to a highway, across which sat a walled residential neighborhood with houses resembling Janna's. The strip club was a quarter mile east, walkable past an eclectic assortment of bars, restaurants, and shops.

She browsed a store that sold trinkets and clothes Yvonne would have loved, resisting the temptation to pocket things. She bought a pastry and a café con leche from a Cuban bakery, and she picked up groceries to cook dinner. She wanted to live like this forever.

To thank the girls and give everyone a break from the boxed meals that filled the freezer, she cooked a curry.

"Fuck, honey. If you can cook like this, we might just keep you around," Charlotte said.

"You should be so lucky," she joked, but she prayed Charlotte meant it.

The previous week, it dawned on her that the girls were a couple. They shared one of the condo's two bedrooms and crammed the second with stuff acquired over their three-year relationship. Clutter spilled out into the living spaces so that the Queen Anne sofa Synthia slept on butted up against a china cabinet full of knickknacks. Armchairs and small tables lined the walls and were covered in boxes, many filled with books.

"You know," Synthia said, "I'm good at organizing. I'm happy to clean while I'm here. To thank you."

Charlotte laughed and eyed Kimmy playfully. "You mean you don't like living in a thrift shop?"

Kimmy's overly freckled face pinked. "I probably need to go through some of it." She had the translucent skin and light eyes of a white person, but her hair and some facial features read Black. When Synthia met her, she thought of her brother Ravi's unwanted child and a word she hadn't considered in forever—Dougla, the slur hurled at biracial people in Guyana. She thought, also, of Marcus. Would their kids have turned out as striking as Kimmy?

"How about start with the books?" Charlotte said. "Maybe donate the ones you finished."

"Can I sort through them first?" Synthia blurted, feeling her skin go hot. She'd been dying to go through the books partly because she coveted Kimmy's after-work routine. Kimmy changed into a swimsuit as soon as she got home, and she read by the condo's leaf-littered pool, where she swam laps. But Synthia had been worried about overstepping boundaries, keenly aware that the girls were her last lifeline. Now with her body unburdened, she relaxed.

"Good lord," Kimmy said, "you don't need permission for that." She swiped thick curls from her face, flashing her tattoo—a string of words that encircled her wrist.

"What's your tattoo say?" Synthia asked.

Kimmy twisted her wrist as she read, "'We take to the breeze . . . we go as we please.' It's from *Charlotte's Web*. I did it after Charlotte and I got together."

"I got her name on my ring finger." Charlotte slipped off a wide ring to display her ink.

"Vicky used to be anti-tattoo," Kimmy said. "So we put them where we could hide them with jewelry."

The pair laughed and locked eyes, and Synthia felt like an intruder. She knew Kimmy was twenty-seven, that Charlotte was twenty-three, that the pair met at the club before Kimmy threw out her back and changed jobs. Synthia was curious about their full story, but having no desire to share hers, she didn't pry.

The following afternoons, she went through boxes and cabinets, unpacking collectibles and organizing books, making piles to read. She vacuumed and dusted and turned the living room into a livable space. She stocked the kitchen with staples—rice, flour, lentils, and spices—and she cooked chilis and casseroles in a Crock-pot she found in the back of a cupboard.

The pair offered her the spare room for two hundred dollars a month if she helped them clear it. And she rejoiced.

Together, they emptied the room and unearthed a chaise Synthia decided to use for a bed. They positioned it in the center, adjacent to a bureau to house her clothes and toiletries. Then they lined the walls with bookshelves and cabinets, filling them with books and Kimmy's thrift store finds.

"Have you read all these?" Synthia asked Kimmy, as she rummaged through a box of books.

"No, I wish. But this is one of my favorites." Kimmy held out *The Fountainhead.* "Take it. You'll like it. It changed my life. Made me realize no one was gonna look out for me but me."

Charlotte, who was pinning a map of the United States on the wall, said, "Ahem! What am I, chopped liver?"

Kimmy laughed. "Present company excluded, of course."

Synthia took the book, eager to read it although she'd long learned that lesson.

Later, with the door closed, she danced on the chaise and pinched herself. Then she studied the map, running her finger along roads that led away from Prem into the wide world.

She read *The Fountainhead* and swallowed Ayn Rand's message of self-determination whole. At the club, she wielded her new confidence, even if men tested her daily.

Most of the clients were generous and respectful. But the low tippers and hagglers reminded her she was a commodity, and a few of them made her feel worthless. Unsmiling rich guys who called her "the exotic one" or summoned her with their index fingers. Others who pinched her bottom, as if that were tip enough. Once, a sneering man held up a ten-dollar bill and said, "It's yours if you suck my balls." She'd plucked the money out of his hands, tucked it in his pants, and said, "I'm good." She told herself she chose to be there. She had the power, and she'd show them.

She briefly doubted this mantra when Lenny showed up.

He tried to palm her a packet of coke, saying, "You know you want it. I'll give more for a fuck out back. For old time's sake?"

"Fuck off. I'm worth more than your other junkie hoes," she'd said. But after, she hid in a toilet stall, shaking with shame, trying to convince herself this was true.

Then a man summoned her, testing her still harder.

She'd just danced a set to Madonna's "Like a Virgin," wearing white lace. Afterward, the DJ insinuated she was a bona fide virgin, as usual, and she batted her eyes shyly.

"You got a request for a private," Vicky announced when she returned to the locker room.

She'd been avoiding the secret back rooms. Girls made hundreds there, but she was wary of acts that earned such large tips, of crossing a line she couldn't uncross, of being that close to the men.

"I'm good," she said. "I'll stick with the floor."

"Sorry, honey. It's Jerry," Vicky said, raising an eyebrow. "We try to keep him happy."

A lump formed in her throat. Jerry was a regular who commanded a VIP booth. Girls fawned over him, and it was rumored he was a detective.

A dancer nearby said, "Ooh, Jerry found a new pet. Do it, girl. He's a big tipper, and you won't look twelve forever. That's what he likes."

"Quit running your mouth, Eileen," Vicky shouted, before turning back to Synthia. "Room three, ten-minute set."

Synthia had no choice.

The ten-by-five room had a thick, curtained door. A bouncer guarded it along with five other rooms. Inside, a chair faced a low stage. Jerry sat with his legs stretched out, tie loosened, sport coat draped over the chair's back.

"Well, hello," he said as she entered. He smiled widely through a trim beard.

She couldn't meet his eyes. She popped a two-song tape into the wall stereo and pressed the start button, hoping the ten minutes would go by quickly.

Jerry placed two twenties on the stage. She smiled despite herself. It was a big tip for just ten minutes. Plus, she'd get half of the thirty-dollar room fee.

He smiled as she danced to the first song, and just as she relaxed, he beckoned her.

She hesitated.

"I don't bite," he said.

I'm in charge, she thought, as she danced toward him.

He stood and stroked her legs. She flinched but kept dancing.

"Can I get a taste of the virgin?" Before she could respond, he'd gripped her bottom and pressed his face into her crotch. She froze, and the world blurred.

We try to keep him happy. A scream might get her fired. Or worse, deported.

He pushed her thong aside with his nose and said, "You like that, don't you?"

She made an mmm sound as his scratchy beard abraded her skin, wondering if she could get a disease that way, the one they'd been talking about on the news, the one she feared Lenny already gave her. His teeth nipped her, his tongue probed, and he moved a hand in his pants.

At long last, the song ended. She fled the room feeling sick, worried he'd take more next time.

Eileen said, "Big tipper, right?"

She nodded and smiled tightly.

"I was one of his girls," Eileen said, stretching on the floor, "before I got old and my leg got all jacked up. I swear, as soon as I pass this goddamn GED, I'm out of here."

She studied Eileen, a brunette about Charlotte's age. Would Synthia still be dancing at twenty-three, like them? No, she decided. There was a future outside the strip club for her, and she'd find it. She lit a cigarette and smoked it down to the filter, resetting herself.

    The following day, she got *Begin Again* inked like an anklet on her right leg, the words repeating three times in a closed circle. With every prick of the needle, she chanted this mantra. She couldn't avoid the Jerrys and Lennys of the world. The Mr. Michaels and the Prems. But she didn't have to let them topple her. She could brush them aside, brush herself off, and begin again every time they tried. She'd done it before, and she'd keep doing it as long as she needed to.

35

A Little Birthday

She lived four months in this frozen reality. Then, one afternoon, Kimmy knocked on her door, waking her. "You have a phone call."

Dazed, she picked up the receiver. She'd never received a call there before.

"Puta! Feliz cumpleaños," Yvonne said, as if it hadn't been almost half a year since they'd talked. "Cómo estás?"

Was it her birthday? In a moment of confusion, she couldn't recall her age. According to her fake ID, she was twenty, but Yvonne believed she was turning eighteen. She was three years younger than that, though. So, fifteen? Or almost fifteen? It felt absurd.

"Uh, hey," she said, rubbing sleep from her eyes. "My birthday's not for weeks."

"Ay, I knew it was September. Couldn't remember the day," Yvonne said.

"How'd you find me?" she asked, her words regrettably cold.

Yvonne sounded unfazed. "From Lenny. Ran into him at the gas station."

Lenny. Of course.

"So, you go by Cindy now?" Yvonne said. "Or, what did Lenny say, Synthia?"

Her stomach sank. Did Yvonne know about the dancing?

"He said you live with his friend. You good? I was worried sick when you left."

A twinge of guilt shot through her. Leaving felt like a lifetime ago. "I'm good. I was . . . I should have called. Sorry."

"Sí, no. I wish you called. But I get it. I was by Al's, and you were mad, right? I get it."

She shook her head no. She couldn't have Yvonne blaming herself. "It wasn't you, Yve. Really. I was . . . I don't know. Lenny wasn't good for me, and I . . . You know what, it doesn't matter. I'm good now. I got a job and a car! I just bought it from a neighbor."

"A car? I wanna see it," Yvonne said. "Oscar can look at it, too. He works at this mechanic shop now. Even has a novia. Says he left the farm 'cause I left first."

"That's great. How's everyone else? Javi? And Estelle and Don?"

"Worried. Worried sick. Mami says come tonight. She's making tamales. We could do a little birthday, early."

"I don't know." Anxiety rippled through her. She was scared of dipping her toes into any version of her past. "I've got—"

"Ay, chica, you can't say no to Mami. She's right here. She wants to see you."

"Neena, ven esta noche," Estelle shouted into the phone.

Tears sprang to her eyes. She didn't deserve such kindness, not after the way she'd left. But while she felt bad about hurting them, they could hurt her, too. They might disapprove of her new life. Or alert Prem of her location. She couldn't have that.

"Janna called last month, you know, to see if we heard from you."

She nodded again and wiped her eyes. "I'll call Janna. I will. But Yve, I gotta tell you, my job . . . it's . . ."

"Yeah, Lenny told me."

She whispered, "Don't say anything, okay. Especially to—"

"Ay, you must think I'm stupid."

Synthia laughed. "Sorry. Just, you know . . ."

"So, tamales? Tonight?"

A week earlier, she'd purchased a small blue hatchback from Georgia, a retiree who frequented the condo's pool. It had belonged to Georgia's late husband, and it was just sitting around, rusting, the woman said. She hoped to sell it to good people like Synthia or Kimmy, people the old man would have liked. The car was seven years old with only fifty thousand miles, so it was definitely not rusty, and Georgia only wanted three hundred dollars for it. Though she knew little about cars, Synthia knew this was a very good deal.

Title in hand, she drove to the beach, squealing, unable to contain her joy. She laid back on the hood, staring at the seagulls swirling above, feeling freer than she'd ever felt.

But as she drove from the city skyline toward the Hernandezes, angst bloomed inside her. She felt the fingers of her old life. The more familiar the roads grew, the more her body rebelled, as if just nearing that life meant it could reach out to seize her. She started to shiver and breathe hard, and she had to pull off the road to calm down.

She forced herself forward, not wanting to disappoint Estelle again, telling herself this was no different than performing at the club. When she danced, she became what the customer wanted, then she went home to be herself. She would become what Yvonne's family wanted; after, she'd return to the life she chose, unharmed. But in her old neighborhood, she felt Prem at every intersection.

In Yvonne's driveway, she checked her face in the visor. Her makeup was light—just a touch of lipstick and eyeliner—and she'd pulled her hair into a ponytail. But the blond streaks in her permed burgundy hair were impossible to hide. They marked her as someone changed, someone edgier, someone they might reject.

"Neena," Yvonne squealed, opening the front door. "You're like if Madonna and Whitney had a baby! I love it."

Synthia's body softened. Yvonne always knew just what to say.

The rest of the family marveled at the car, and Oscar confirmed it was a good deal.

Estelle held her at arm's length. "You look good, niñita. Pero, flaca. You been eating?"

Synthia smiled. "Nothing as good as your food." They walked inside, where the buttery smell of homemade tamales welcomed her. As did the TV, playing a Spanish soap opera.

"So, what's the new job?" Don asked.

"Waiting tables," she said, blurting out words she'd rehearsed. "With this girl, Charlotte. Her house is near the restaurant. I can walk if I want."

"Bueno, bueno," Don said.

"Sorry I didn't call," she said. "Sorry." As the words came out, her anxiety eased. This was another thing that had knotted her gut. This necessary apology. Was it enough?

"Está bien, Neena," Estelle said, hugging her. "You are safe. Todo está bueno. Let's eat!"

Food covered the kitchen counter. Meat and cheese tamales, salad, homemade salsa, cilantro rice, pinto beans, and dulce de leche. Synthia even appreciated the clutter on the dining table and stack of paper plates. She'd worried they'd make a big deal about her being there and try to make dinner formal, as Janna would have.

"I missed this," she said, piling her plate with food, realizing just how much she'd missed them all.

As the others fixed their plates, they updated her on the farm and their jobs. She sat with Yvonne and Estelle at the table, while the guys sat in front of the TV.

"How's Al?" Synthia asked, surprised Yvonne hadn't mentioned him yet.

"Pendejo," Yvonne said.

"What happened? I thought you liked him."

"I did. But maybe I liked the girls more." Yvonne laughed. "I miss those niñas."

"That sucks, Yve. I'm sorry."

"It's fine. I mean, it's stupid. He mentioned marriage, and I said, I don't have papers, that Mami and Papi overstayed visas, and he went loco, said I lied. I never lied. It never came up. He was like, are you with me for a green card? And I was like, adiós. I don't need that shit. I was getting tired of him anyway. It was like I was married, and I'm too young for that."

"You don't need no gringo for papers," Don called from the living room. "Reagan passed a law. It's good for us who are here. Jefe told me to get a lawyer and apply. Lila and Jefecito should apply too, get you some papers, Neena. You're young and, in this country, you're nothing sin papeles. It's like jail."

Neena smiled tightly. Her head swirled with this life-changing news — not needing marriage for papers. She thought of the lawyer friend Janna often mentioned, and her face burned thinking of asking Janna for help after disappearing as she had. She didn't want to need Janna, just like she didn't want to need a man for legitimacy. But Don was right. Without papers, she was nothing, and the club might jail her forever.

36

Yellow Kite

It took a week to work up the courage to call Janna. She waited until the girls were out of the house. Then, sitting on the kitchen floor, she dialed, feeling sick. She was going against every directive from her new bible, *The Fountainhead*, which preached that a good life is one created by oneself, without help. But that kind of freedom belonged only to those with power. Without papers, she had none, no matter what she told herself.

When Janna answered, Synthia froze, and Janna had to repeat hello.

"Um, Janna, hi. It's, it's Neena," she said, finding her voice.

"Neena, oh my gosh, it's so good to hear from you. How are you, sweetheart?"

She filled her voice with cheer and said, "Great, actually. I'm doing real good. I have a job, and I'm staying with this girl I work with. She's real nice."

"I'm so glad to hear it. I was so worried after you disappeared."

"I'm gonna get my GED," she blurted though it wasn't true. She'd looked into the test at the library after Eileen mentioned it and learned she needed a Social Security number to sign up.

"That makes me so happy, honey. I'm glad to hear that. Where do you work?"

"Um, a restaurant."

"That's great. Which one?"

"This Cuban place. Habana Cafe," she said, surprised at how easily her brain formulated this specific answer. She'd walked past the restaurant and glanced at the menu on the door, but she'd never gone inside. Worried Janna might try to visit her there, she added, "I work in the back mostly. In the kitchen. You know how I like to cook."

Janna laughed. "Well, it sounds perfect. You are a great cook."

She cleared her throat and offered the apology Janna deserved. "I'm sorry I never called. I should have. After everything you did."

"Well, all that matters is that you're doing okay, sweetheart. I was worried, you know, that I'd been too hard on you. That, if you were still with us—"

"Oh, gosh no, Janna. It had nothing to do with you. Or the Hernandezes. You and everyone, you've been so great. I just . . . I just needed a fresh start."

There was silence, and she imagined Janna nodding.

"I appreciate everything you did for me, Janna. Really. And I hate to ask for more, especially after . . . disappearing. But I have a favor to ask."

"Sure, sweetie. Do you need money?"

"No, no." It stung to hear Janna assume she'd called for money. "It's not that. I just, you said something about a lawyer once?"

"Yes, of course. I just spoke with Margo last week. So, you heard about the new law?"

"The Hernandezes told me about it. Do you know how it works? Would the lawyer, um, Margo, be able to help me get my papers?"

"Well, I don't know a lot," Janna said, "but I did discuss your situation with her, and she said, you being a minor, that your parents needed to apply for you. They'd also need paperwork to show they've been working here these past couple years. But they'd have to do it soon. You turn eighteen in, what, two weeks? And I know you're estranged."

Synthia's gut sank. "Um, couldn't I just say I worked for you?"

"I asked about that, honey. Margo says that's tricky since you were a minor, and I paid you in cash. Plus, she'd still need your birth certificate and work papers from your folks."

Synthia dropped her head onto her knees.

Janna went on. "I know it's not what you want to hear, but I think you should give your parents a call. As far as I understand, this law is meant to stop illegal immigration, so from now on, it'll be difficult to get work without documents. But they're offering amnesty to those who are already here. So, getting your folks on board, and soon, is really important for you."

A sick feeling took over her body. She'd be stuck without papers, praying for a man to save her. She thought of Marcus, whom she'd long stopped fantasizing about, of Al and Yvonne's breakup. Would anyone love her enough to overlook the baggage she carried?

"Do you think Margo can help the Hernandezes?" Synthia might not be able to help herself, but perhaps she could help Yvonne.

"Certainly. I'll call Estelle and set that up. And I'll discuss your situation more with Margo. I really want this to work for you, Neena."

She nodded and said, "Thanks Janna. I really appreciate that."

"Oh, and honey, before I forget, your grandmother wrote. Twice. I wrote to the return address notifying her you'd moved. I would have given her the Hernandezes' address, but I didn't want that Michael fellow showing up there. I hope that's okay. Give me your address, and I'll forward the letters."

She feared revealing her location. A part of her wanted to tell Janna to toss the letters, which were probably full of poison anyway. But the part that ached for Roshi reluctantly recited the address. She added, "Please don't tell anyone where I live."

She hung up the phone and stared at it. It was the same beige color as the one at the trailer, the one Prem had used to smack Lila, the one Lila had once picked up to try to save her. Lila wasn't perfect, but there were moments they'd felt like a team. Synthia wondered if it could happen again. The clock said four-forty-four, and it felt lucky. At this time, Lila could be at home. She made a wish and dialed.

"Hello?" Lila answered brusquely.

Synthia's heart pounded, not believing she'd actually dialed, grateful Prem hadn't answered. "Um, Lila. It's . . . it's Sunny."

There was silence.

Fearing Lila might hang up, Synthia rushed on. "I, um, I was calling because I talked to, um, Janna. And Don and Estelle. And, um, I was wondering if you were going to apply for amnesty? Under the new law?"

The silence stretched out. A part of her imagined Prem somehow listening and figuring out her location. But Prem wouldn't be quiet this long, and no one could track her from just a phone call. She went on, "Janna says we don't have a lot of time to apply. But she knows a lawyer who could help. I've been working, so I can pay the fee for us, to pay you back."

She squeezed her eyes, cringing at having to beg. Then she took another leap. "We can even do it without Prem if . . . if he, you know, doesn't trust the government."

She heard a click. Then the phone honked the disconnect tone. She returned the receiver to its cradle feeling a complicated relief. At least she'd tried.

Three days later, Kimmy handed her a manila envelope, asking, "Is this for you?" It was addressed to Neena. Inside was a note from Janna (*so great to hear from you*) and Raj's letters.

A GIRL WITHIN A GIRL WITHIN A GIRL

Dear Sunny,

I hope this letter finds you in good health. We have not heard word in some time, probably because things left off so negative. I am writing to update you, and I'm sorry, but I must start with bad news.

Jeeve got a massive case of gastro. It took him from running and winning races, to sleeping in bed. Been two weeks now. He says something is eating him from inside, and maybe that's true. He lost a lot of weight. Ravi and I pay for the clinic, but the medicine did not help.

Also, the house is getting empty. Roshi left, and on bad terms. Roshi started teaching at the deaf nursery school, and we were all very happy. But Pappo catch her kissing a teacher, a deaf black man. Of course, Daddy got in a rage, saying you influence her. He forbid Roshi to teach, so Roshi ran off. Daddy pulled Pappo from the school, and all we know is the boy's family took Roshi in. They live far, in an area none of us feel safe visiting, so it has been months since anyone seen Roshi. We suspect they got married.

I, too, am leaving. On better terms, but not the best. I am marrying, and you will never guess who—your old school friend, Navi! Her father works for the ministry, and he got me a job there. I expected Daddy to be happy for me, but he said I am disgraceful for marrying a sixteen-year-old girl when I'm twenty-one. As if he didn't marry Ma when she was seventeen. I told him he's just jealous Navi's family can help us, and the man raised his fist at me. So, I hit him back. He needs to learn he can't control us anymore. Ravi should have beat him years ago. Anyway, both Ma and Daddy stop talking to me, saying I think I'm better than them. Truth be told, how can I not feel shame? With Daddy back on the bottle hard, wasting money, and Ma now expecting a baby! Yes, more news! And I am not sure if that bit is good or bad.

The baby will be younger than Ravi's kids—can you believe that? Mala is due with number two anytime. Ma says she will tie her tubes after this, and Mala will tie hers, too, because they only want two. I will have Navi do the same after we have two.

Now, just good news. Ravi joined Mala's brother fixing houses, and they moved into their own house. Mo got a good job chauffeuring for the bus company. So, they are on their way up. Pappo is back at the local school, and apparently, he is the best at maths. Either the hearing aids work real good or he takes after you. Laugh. Baby still sells sugar cake and peera, and Indy helps now. Indy is excited to be flower girl in the wedding, even if Ma and Daddy will miss it.

Both me and Navi wish you could attend. Navi said to tell you Annette moved to New York last year, so all her best friends left. How far is New York? Maybe you can visit.

Now, the best news for last. Navi's father has a tourist visa for later this year. Plus, his sister put in for their family years ago, and papers might come through soon. As Navi's husband, I can move with them. Can you believe that? Wouldn't it be funny if I get citizenship before you? That is how this crazy world works. Laugh. But Navi's father said after we move, it would take five years for citizenship, and another five to ten to bring everyone over. At that rate, it could take fifteen, twenty years for the family to reunite. Michael never mentioned that!

When Navi's father comes, he can stop over in Miami to look in on you, and you can send money with him if you want. That way, daddy can't piss it away, and Jeeve can use it for better medicine. Pray for your brother, please. We hope to hear from you soon.

    Your ever-loving brother,
    Raj

Roshi was gone. With a Black boy. Ostracized from the family. Why hadn't Synthia written back when she had the chance? If only to say she was safe, to ease Roshi's worry. *Roshi, where are you? Are you okay? Is he good to you? Will I ever see you again?*

The letter contained so much, but that bit of information shook her. She'd always imagined her family in that gray box of a house, living exactly as she'd left them, Roshi especially. But everything had splintered. Her mother pregnant, Raj on the outs, Jeeve sick, and Roshi gone.

Was it all because of her? *You influence her.*

Tears ran down her face, and she brushed them away. Kimmy and Charlotte sat watching TV on the other side of the door. She didn't have the luxury of falling apart.

She reread the part about Raj arriving soon. Legally! The new foot in the door. Had she lived her hell for nothing? And he was marrying Navi, a girl who'd treated her like excrement? Of course, Navi pretended they were best friends now. She imagined Navi's father discovering her naked at the club, relaying lurid details, confirming she was a whore. That girl would scorn her again in a heartbeat.

She balled up the letter, ready to fling it out the window. But she gripped it in a fist.

In twenty years, she'd be thirty-five and Roshi would be thirty-seven. Ancient. Her new sibling would be older than she was in that moment. Her brain hurt doing the math.

Her body quivered uncontrollably. She needed to pull herself together. She opened the second letter, hoping it contained good news.

Dear Sunny,

We received a letter from a lady named Janna calling you Neena. She says you left her house, and she doesn't know where you live now. Of course, all this bothers us, that you're still going by that name, too. As we don't know where you live, Navi's father can't visit when he comes. Sunny, we are worried you are not safe. And, you know how I hate to repeat anything Daddy says, but now I wonder if he's right. Maybe you can only trust your own kind.

Anyway Sunny, I'm sending this letter to Janna's address because I don't know where else to send it. I'm sending a copy to Lila and Prem's address, too, because it brings important and terrible news.

Sunny, it is with great sadness I have to inform you our brother Jeeve has passed. We are all shocked and grieving, not sure how this happened. His diarrhea didn't get better, then he got a bad fever, and when we took him to hospital, they say his blood got poisoned. It happened two weeks after my wedding, and in honesty, he looked so good there, we thought he was improving.

The funeral is in a couple of days, and I know this letter will arrive a week or two after that. Even if I could get word to you in time, I know you can't come. We are to fly white kites at the conservancy and scatter his ashes after the service. I will fly one yellow kite for you because it was your favorite color. Maybe that will bring you some peace because I know how this news will hurt you.

  Your loving brother,
  Raj

A primal sound escaped her body. *Jeeve has passed.*
Charlotte called, "Hon, you okay?"
She couldn't answer. Jeeve was gone. It made no sense. He was the most vibrant of them, the one with inconsumable energy, the one who talked and laughed the loudest.

She buried her face into her pillow and sobbed, clutching the letter to her chest.

As her sobbing subsided, she registered Charlotte and Kimmy's hands patting her back.

"Someone died" was all she could say through hot tears. Her world, which she'd so tenuously put back together, was shattering all over again.

37

Papeles

The lawyer's office wasn't as grand as she imagined. It was in a nondescript strip mall along Highway 1, between a donut shop and a hair salon. Janna's sedan was parked between Lila's small gold car and Yvonne's beater. She pulled up nearby.

She'd spent the previous week sleeping on her chaise, not working, and she'd still be there if not for Janna's insistent messages. "Your mother wants to meet." "It's important." "Neena, if you don't call, I'm coming to get you."

Not wanting Janna to show up at her door, she called back. Janna explained that Lila had shown up at her house that morning with bruises and the paperwork ready to file for amnesty. Without Prem. Janna had called Margo and arranged for Lila to piggyback on the Hernandezes' appointment. All Synthia had to do was show up.

Through the office's glass walls, she saw Lila, Don, and Estelle sitting in leather armchairs at a desk. Lila looked more birdlike than ever, hunched and skeletal. Janna stood behind an empty chair. And the Hernandez siblings sat on a long bench, their backs pressed against the glass.

She pasted a smile on her face as she approached and pushed the heavy door open.

Everyone turned except Lila, who looked down and clutched her purse, her cheek and eyes marred with bruises.

"Aww, Neena, look at you." Janna reached for her and touched her hair. "What a great color."

Synthia hugged the entire Hernandez family next, who stood to welcome her. Only Lila remained sitting, poisoning the air with her forward stare.

The lawyer reached an arm over her desk. "I'm Margo. Everybody's told me so much about you. It's lovely to meet you, Neena." She spoke with a surprising accent—Eastern European? In her flowered dress and hair-clipped blond hair, she looked like a librarian, challenging the TV notion of a slick lawyer that Synthia had expected.

Synthia sat, angled away from Lila, and Margo spoke about the new law, something called IRCA. She told them amnesty applications were being approved quickly, that their applications might breeze through. "Being an immigrant," she added, "I know you are afraid of the government. But don't worry. If you have the paperwork, this will be easy."

She processed the Hernandezes' papers first—documentation of farmwork, overstayed visas, birth certificates, and ID cards. She photocopied and stapled things, pointing to lines, instructing them to sign here and there. Then she snapped photos of them in front of a white wall, and she gave them receipts for the cash they handed her. Synthia watched numbly.

"This law was tailor-made for you," Margo said, finishing up with them. "Your paperwork and timelines are perfect."

At that comment, Don flashed a giant smile and Lila gripped her bag harder.

Before they left, the Hernandez family hugged Synthia and thanked everyone. Then she was alone with Janna and Lila.

Lila's hands shook as she passed over an expired passport and proof of farmwork to begin their application. Synthia was surprised to learn Lila had used work and tourist visas legally for years, coming and going from Guyana, even bringing young Neena once for vacation in 1978. That trip made Synthia eligible for amnesty since no stamp indicated Neena ever returned to Guyana.

"If your mother hadn't brought you," Margo said, "it'd be different paperwork. She'd have to apply for a family reunification visa after being granted amnesty, and that's been taking five to seven years for adult children. They might even start to take longer after this wave of amnesty. You're lucky we can do it like this, and that you are still seventeen. You cut it close. If you came in after your birthday next week, the paperwork would be harder."

Synthia felt nauseated. She was beholden to Lila, sliding in on her coattails when the woman had participated in her abuse. She told herself it was the least Lila owed her, and that she was helping Lila, too, by giving her a chance to escape Prem.

A heavier worry also weighed her down. By officially taking Neena's name, she'd be divorcing her real family. But hadn't they divorced her first? They'd severed her from Roshi, and Jeeve. And now, they had Raj. They didn't need her anymore.

Still, the weight of the lie sat in her chest as she watched Lila sign the documents. Then it was her turn. Margo asked for the correct spelling of her name—*N-e-e-n-a D-a-s*—and gave her a document to sign. She initialed lines, swearing it was the truth. Synthia kept expecting Lila to object, but she never did.

When the lawyer went over the fees, Synthia fumbled in her purse and pulled out rubber-banded wads of singles, feeling her body heat up.

Outside the office, Janna held her and Lila side by side. With wet eyes, Janna said, "You can come out of the shadows now, to protect yourself from that man."

Synthia glanced at Lila, whose dark-rimmed eyes met hers. In that moment, she wondered if she'd always misunderstood Lila. Was the hate she read simply fear or guilt? Lila had been powerless to protect her from Prem because she couldn't protect herself. Perhaps that helplessness manifested as rage. Perhaps it made her leave the real Neena behind in Guyana in the first place. Synthia's insides fluttered as if a long-dormant jumbie had just woken inside her, and she exhaled her resentment. She smiled and opened herself to the possibility of kindness.

    Lila's eyes softened, as if acknowledging this. She reached into her purse and produced a letter, torn open. The twin to the letter Raj had sent. Synthia's eyes watered as she took it, and Lila reached an arm around her. As the woman's bony body pressed against hers, she realized it was the first time they'd touched.

38

Ambush

On some level, Synthia never expected the papers to go through. She expected an official somewhere to figure out she couldn't possibly be Neena. She expected Prem, Mr. Michael, or her father to discover the secret plan and stop everything. Sometimes she imagined the jumbies intervening—Neena's, the lost baby's, even Jeeve's. So, when Margo called on a Wednesday afternoon a few months later, saying, "Good news. Everything's in," Synthia almost didn't believe it.

She'd been sitting cross-legged in front of the full-length mirror behind the front door, wearing only a bra and underwear with a fan trained on her. The girls were out, and the condo's air conditioner was broken. She'd applied liquid green eyeliner to one eye, and she raised that eyebrow in surprise at this news. She twisted the phone's extra-long cord and stared back at her reflection. She looked ghoulish.

"Did you hear me, Neena?" Margo asked.

"Uh. Yeah. It's great." Synthia stood and turned off the rattling fan, then muted the music videos playing on the TV.

"It *is* great," Margo continued. "Congratulations! I need you to sign a few things, pick up your green card, all that good stuff. And I'd like to go over the next steps. Can you swing by tomorrow morning, at nine?"

"Who else is coming?" If there was a rude undertone to Synthia's question, she didn't care. She hoped to avoid Lila and Janna, even the Hernandezes.

She hadn't seen Lila since their meeting, and she had no desire to hug the knobby woman again.

Janna, she saw at Christmas, three months earlier. They went to church, and as the family ate, Janna suggested she make more of an effort with Lila, who'd started cleaning for her again. "Family's important, Neena," she'd said. Napkin on lap, clinking the flowered plate with her fork, Synthia told her she preferred to choose her own family. Janna's eyes filled with disappointment, and Nicole and Leslie stared at Synthia as if she were from another planet. Only an alien could defy their mother. Synthia had left before they opened gifts, even though she wanted to see the girls' reaction to the necklaces she bought for them. She was grateful for Janna, but she couldn't handle sitting under her microscope.

She'd spent New Year's with the Hernandezes, where she'd also delivered gifts of thanks. But she hadn't seen Yvonne since. Yvonne had gotten busy as a manager at her store and had thrown herself into a new relationship with a man named Peter.

"No one else is coming," Margo said. "Don and Estelle came by already, and so did your mother. She left your birth certificate for you. And I haven't called Janna. I thought you might want to tell her the good news yourself."

"Thank you. I'll be there at nine."

"Great. And Neena, congrats again."

A mixture of joy, angst, and apathy brewed inside her. The news changed everything and nothing.

Sure, she could finally fill out the GED application sitting in her room, but she'd go to work and dance tonight. And again tomorrow night. She'd make dinner for her roommates, who never pried into her past, and she'd read by the pool with Kimmy. She'd sleep surrounded by books, safe inside a life she'd created.

The fantasy life sold to her by community college brochures felt no closer. She could no easier imagine herself striding across leafy campuses and sitting next to smiling students in dental hygiene classes. Though the dream was alluring—working for a respectable dental practice after just a few years of classes, making decent money—it felt surreal and unreachable.

She resumed applying makeup, her head ringing with the quiet of the condo.

Her eyes shimmered with green and gold eyeliner, and she obscured her under-eye mole with a series of stars. She was legally, inextricably linked to her dead doppelgänger now. But she doubted that they'd still resemble each other, even if the girl had lived. She doubted, too, that she still resembled anyone in her biological family, who had no idea she'd just cut herself off from them.

It'd been almost a year since she'd had a drink, but she suddenly craved one. Of all days, didn't she deserve one today?

She retrieved the bottle of tequila Charlotte hid in a cabinet above the fridge. She poured a shot over ice and rattled the glass to mix. Her mouth filled with saliva at the heady smell.

Back at the mirror, she stared at herself holding the glass. Being unclothed was her norm these days, but she hardly ever examined her bare body. Narrow hips, average waist, and medium chest—the body belonged to both a girl and a woman, a child playing at adulthood. Black moles dotted her skin. The large tear-shaped one amid a small constellation on her face. Two on her ribs, a few across her arms, one on her left shoulder. Others the mirror couldn't reflect. Men deemed her attractive, she knew, but as she stared, her reflection morphed into something grotesque. She put the drink down and pressed herself nose to nose with the ugly, made-up poser. A blood-curdling scream sprang from her throat.

Something had unhinged inside her. She screamed again.

A strange energy rippled through her. She was at a crossroads. Her reflection picked up the drink, toasted her, and brought the glass to her lips. It felt like miming, as if the reflection mocked her. Then Roshi flickered in her face, and she felt Roshi right there.

Roshi, have you ever stared at your naked self? Screamed like a crazy person? Drank tequila? Just when everything is going right? I'm the one they should call pagli.

She smiled, and it felt as if Roshi were smiling back. Undoubtedly, Roshi would have laughed at her. Then she felt Roshi shake her head. *Don't drink it.* Roshi wanted her to be free, and she was so close. Why would she ruin everything she'd worked so hard to get? She ran to the kitchen and poured the drink down the sink.

At six the following morning, after her shift, she drove straight to a coffee shop about a block away from Margo's office, worried that she'd sleep through their nine o'clock meeting if she went home first. Her ears buzzed, and every color seemed overly bright as she sat down at a small table and opened Maya Angelou's *I Know Why the Caged Bird Sings*, the book Marcus had gifted her. She'd been too pained to read it before, but Kimmy said it was one of her favorites, and enough time had passed. The first pages felt incomprehensible. She blamed this on the caffeine and nicotine coursing through her, barely staving off her exhaustion. She read and reread until a dawning recognition stabbed her.

In so many ways, she was Maya, the main character, trapped in the wrong body, the wrong place, peeing her pants as others laughed. She, too, lived by the novel's opening lines: "What you looking at me for? I didn't come to stay."

She raced through the first third of the novel, to the point where the unthinkable happens. Tears filled her eyes and acid rose in her throat. She shut the book and looked around the coffee shop, fearing people could see through the pages to that word. *Rape.* But nobody looked her way. The clock on the wall said her meeting would begin in five minutes. She wiped her eyes, smearing her mascara, before tucking the book deep into her purse like contraband, and hurrying to Margo's office.

Her hand was already on the door pull when she saw two bodies across from Margo's desk. Prem and Lila. Prem stared at her, and the world blurred.

The little gold car was parked right in front—how had she missed that?

She wanted to run away, but Margo jumped up to greet her.

"Neena, hello," Margo said, wide-eyed at the door. "Guess who showed up."

Synthia stepped into the office and drifted from her body. The door hissed close on its pneumatic hinges.

A wide sneering smile stretched across Prem's face, and Lila, bruised again, stared into her lap.

"Oh-ho. Look who's here," Prem said, leaning back in his chair and stretching his legs out against Margo's desk. "The newest American citizen. All decked out, too."

Synthia was in sweats and sneakers, certainly not decked out. But she hadn't removed her glittery makeup.

"Not a citizen, Mr. Das," Margo said, a forced smile on her face, her eyes on Synthia. "A legal resident. It's quite different. Just the first step."

"I can come back." Synthia turned to go, but somehow, Prem's fingers were around her forearm. She gasped. Vile memories of his hands flooded her, morphing with images from the story she'd just read. She stumbled back, shaking, as he continued to grip her.

"Where you going?" he sneered. His sour breath bathed her.

Beneath that, there was an overwhelming smell of fertilizer and pesticides she'd never noticed before.

She tugged to pull away, but he held on.

"Mr. Das," Margo said, wedging an arm in the space between them. "Please unhand your daughter."

"Unhand my daughter. Ha, ha. You hear that, Lila? Unhand. *My*. Daughter." He made a show of dropping Synthia's trembling arm.

"Neena, perhaps you *should* come back later," Margo said.

The tremble worked its way from Synthia's arm through her whole body. She turned to go, but Prem barred the door with his body.

"No," Prem said. "The whole family here. That's the way things should be. And I want this girl to look me in the face and say, 'Thank you.' She got me to thank for where she is. She wouldn't be no American citizen, or legal American resident or whatever, if not for me."

"Sir, she is a resident because of your wife, not you."

"Is that so?" Prem looked over at Lila, still staring into her lap. "My wife did this? You saying my wife got herself legal, got this girl here legal, did all this behind my back? My wife got everybody here legal but me?"

"As I mentioned, it is not too late for you. But the deadline is approaching."

Synthia felt faint.

Prem stroked her arm and said, "Hear that, Husk? I'll be legal just like you and your mother, here. And then, I'll come after you for all that money you owe me."

She stumbled away at this light touch, reaching for a wall to keep steady.

Margo moved in front of her as if to guard her. "Sir, please do not threaten my client. You should know if authorities apprehend you for a crime, such as, say, domestic abuse, while you are still undocumented, you could face extradition and permanent barring from this country. Amnesty would be off the table."

Prem stepped toward Margo. "You threatening me with your fancy talk, lady?"

Margo leaned in. "Actually, it feels like *you* are threatening *me*. Just as you threatened your daughter. I am under no obligation to serve you. Please leave."

Lila looked up now, and Prem's head swiveled to survey both women. "I see. Some kind of ambush going on here."

"No ambush. You entered my office without an appointment. The only person who has an appointment today is Neena, and I'd like to meet with her now."

"You kicking me out?" Prem said, leering and bringing his face closer to Margo.

Margo crossed her arms. "Yes."

He stared at her.

"If you do not leave right now, I will call the authorities."

Prem spat on the carpet in front of Margo's foot. "Get up, Lila. Let's go. I told you this bitch would get me deported." As he bristled past them, he hissed, "Watch your back," his eyes maniacal. He pulled Lila outside and tried to slam the heavy glass door. But the hinges only released a forced sigh.

After the gold car peeled off, Margo touched Synthia. She flinched before allowing the woman to hug her.

"I am sorry," Margo said. "I didn't know how to warn you."

Tears stung her eyes as she leaned into Margo, still shaking, still smelling him, still feeling that touch. "He'll come after me." Every time she gained even a little control of her life, he returned to shake it.

"No, he will not," Margo said. "You are a legal resident. If you feel threatened, you can call the police. Lila has the bruises to prove abuse, so they may very well detain him."

"Lila will deny it," Synthia said, but a light flickered on inside her.

Margo sighed. "That can make it harder. Your other option is distance, just as you have been doing. And a name change provides the most distance. At your age, without a credit history, it is just a few forms at the Social Security office. I can always help."

Synthia cocked her head at this unexpected suggestion. *What you looking at me for? I didn't come to stay.* She always knew she'd change her name again, that she wouldn't actually go by Neena. But she hadn't expected Margo to sanction this.

"For now," Margo said, pivoting the conversation, "let's get you set up." She returned to her desk and retrieved some forms from a file drawer. "Here is the paperwork for the DMV. You have been driving without a license?"

Synthia nodded, thinking of Cindy Tipton's ID, looking over her shoulder at the door.

"You're lucky you never got pulled over. Fill this out and get to the DMV today. It is important. The second thing is a bank account. I assume everything you have is cash?"

Synthia nodded again. Wads of rubber-banded money sat under her car's back seat and in the spare-tire well. If Prem had known the little blue hatchback he'd passed was hers and contained so much money, he'd have certainly broken in and taken everything.

"I understand the fear of banks. I'm an immigrant, too. But, trust me, the bank is safe. You will build credit and pay for things with checks. No one can steal your money there. See that building?" She pointed across the parking lot. "It is a national bank, offices everywhere. I send my clients there." She glanced at her watch. "I have some time. I can help you open an account now if you want."

As Synthia filled a bag with her cash, she glanced around for Prem, fearing he was still near, waiting to pounce. But an hour later, she held a slim checkbook with a balance slip for six hundred dollars. It had felt strange to hand over so much of her hard-earned money for a receipt. But she knew it was a giant leap toward freedom.

"So, the DMV next?" Margo said, hugging her to end the visit.

Synthia didn't want to let Margo down, this woman who'd just gone out of her way to hand her the gift of legitimacy. But as she nodded, she knew she'd put off the DMV. A plan had gripped her mind, one that would hand Prem exactly what he deserved and keep him from ever upending her life again. And she couldn't rest until she set it in motion.

39

Vice

She drove to Lenny's house. As she approached the front door, she was overcome with the sensation of being out of her body.

"Well, if it isn't Synthia," Lenny said, enunciating the name like a DJ welcoming a dancer on stage. "I knew you'd come back. Nobody compares, am I right?"

She smiled blandly and entered. A year had passed, and nothing had changed. Lenny's mother, still parked in her recliner, glanced at her without a word, and the air reeked of cat piss. Synthia floated down the hall behind Lenny to his room as if watching herself from afar.

A girl lay asleep under the wrinkled bed covers, matted brown hair clumped on the pillow, her face only half visible.

"Who's that?" Synthia asked.

"Last night's fuck," Lenny said.

She shook her head and pulled money from her purse, a hundred singles. "Can you hook me up? Ten dimes, weed and blow."

"Woah, all for you?" Lenny asked. "I'd be happy to supply your girlfriends, you know. Give you a cut and everything."

"Just having a little party. For my birthday."

"Do I get an invite?" Lenny asked.

She chuckled. "Girls only. Some dancers I know."

"Fuck. Now, I really want to come. When's this shindig?"

She rolled her eyes.

He rummaged through his closet and brought out a duffel. "We can start the party now," he said, waving a small bag of powder. "Birthday gift. On me."

A small craving tickled and passed. She'd been that girl in the bed once. She would never return there. "Nah, man. Time and place. I don't party in the middle of the day anymore."

He laughed and filled a paper sack with baggies of cocaine and marijuana. He held up a larger bag full of white capsules and raised his eyebrows. "Sleepers?" he asked.

"Pass." With Lenny, she'd taken small doses of roofies to sleep. She didn't want him thinking she'd use them on her friends.

"I'll toss some in. For old time's sake."

She shrugged. "Whatever."

He tried to kiss her lips when he handed her the bag, and she shoved him off.

"Oh, don't be like that," he said, "I'm hooking you up here."

"Yeah, and I paid you."

She drove to Yvonne's next, the brown paper bag like a bomb in the glove box. What the hell was she doing?

She sat in the driveway, watching hot air ripple above her car's hood. The world pulsed as if showing her its heartbeat, and she felt a little high. She needed sleep, but sleep would evade her as long as she sensed Prem's phantom hovering over her shoulder, felt his unsettling touch, smelled his disgusting smell. She got out of the car and rang the doorbell.

Yvonne answered, a blush brush in hand. "Hola, Neena. Qué

pasa?" she said, erasing the months of distance between them with a smile and a hug. "I got work in an hour."

"Just picked up my papers," Synthia said. "Thought I'd swing by."

Like at Lenny's, she floated half out of her body as she followed Yvonne to her room. She sat on the bed as Yvonne applied makeup, showing off a shimmery new lipstick. Finally, she blurted, "Prem ambushed me at Margo's. With Lila . . . my mom. He found out we got papers without him. Now he wants to get legal, but he just can't. I have to get him deported."

Yvonne balked. "Your dad? But you never see him anymore."

"He threatened me," she said. "He'll come after me once he's legal. I know it."

"Why?"

Synthia shook her head like a mad woman. "You don't know, Yve. He won't leave me alone. He thinks I owe him money. And he . . . he did things." She whispered the last word.

Yvonne turned and stared, forehead lines deepening. "What things?"

"He would . . . he would . . . he used to . . . come in my room." She whispered the last words and dropped her face into Yvonne's pillow, wetting it with tears.

Yvonne's arms encircled her back. "Aye, Neena, I knew it. Did he . . . ?"

She nodded vigorously, hoping Yvonne wouldn't say the word. She couldn't bear to hear that word.

"I wondered, you know, when you slept by us."

Synthia pulled herself together and sat up. "He can't stay, Yve. He can't get legal. He'll hunt me down. And he fucking beats Lila up all the time. He can't stay." She was in a tunnel with only one way out, and she needed Yvonne's help.

She laid out her basic plan—plant drugs in Prem's car, lure him to the club, start a fight, and have Jerry-the-detective find the drugs and book him. "I was going to sneak over tonight and hide the bag under the seat. They don't usually lock the car, and they never look under the seats. Maybe you can visit tomorrow and hang out at the stand with Estelle? Like at seven, when he stocks? Mention the club, say you're going to visit me Saturday night, that I work then. That's when Jerry comes." The holes in her plan glared as she spoke.

"You think that'll work?" Yvonne asked, voice heavy with doubt.

"I have to do something. He can't get legal. He'll have all the power. You should have seen how he looked, like he wanted to kill me. And Lila, she won't do shit."

"But, this Jerry, this cop? You sure he'll help?"

She nodded and smiled tightly, not wanting to admit Jerry was the most fragile part of her plan.

"Okay. But don't put that stuff in the car yet," Yvonne said. "If they catch you or find it, you're screwed. Do it after he gets to the club."

"I can't just go outside when I'm at work. And he might lock the car."

"I'll do it. Oscar used this thing when I got locked out of my car. It goes in the window and pulls up the latch. It's easy. I can do it for you."

"You'd do that?"

"Hell yeah. We're hermanas, remember? And that bastard deserves it."

Synthia canceled her Thursday evening shift and waited for Jerry in the club's parking lot. As the minutes ticked closer to eleven, she questioned her brazen, farfetched plan. She hadn't slept in over twenty-four hours, and exhaustion hit her like a drug. Was she doing the right thing? Her head swayed.

She forced her mind on a single thought: Jerry wants me.

Jerry had continued to request her, calling her his special pet, even as he pursued other girls. All because she denied him sex.

The first time he'd unbuttoned his pants, she scooted away and said, "Uh, no. I'm a virgin, Jerry." She'd batted her eyes and bit her lips to stay in character.

"I'm no monster, pet," he'd said. "I just want you to touch it. Have you ever touched one?"

She'd shaken her head no, and he placed an additional twenty on the stage, sighing with pleasure at her answer. Then he pulled her hand to his pants, the conversation over.

Near Christmas, he placed a hundred-dollar bill on the stage and winked. "A little gift. But I've been a good boy. Don't I deserve something, too?"

She'd said, "Get another girl," not bothering to soften her words.

"I don't want other girls. I just want your pretty little mouth there. Just this once."

Even as she shook her head and repeated no, he pulled her close and forced her head to his crotch. She pushed him away and stormed out, refusing his money. But he laughed and kept requesting her, enjoying the game.

"Don't know what it is about you, but I'll take what I get," he'd said the last time he summoned her. She'd only let him touch her bare feet, a fetish of his.

Now, she banked on his words.

Jerry emerged from the club's back door at eleven fifteen. He usually left the club near eleven, likely for a wife at home. As he strode toward a minivan, Synthia wondered if he had kids. But he walked past the van to a black sports car, which he opened with a chirp.

She shot out of her car and called, "Jerry."

He danced his shoulders side to side and said, "Well, well, well. Jello!" He'd definitely had more than a few drinks. "Missed you tonight, pet."

She swung her hips as she approached. His eyes roved her black mini dress and leopard-print platforms.

"Nice ride," she said. "Can I check it out?"

He raised an eyebrow and scanned the empty lot. "I don't normally do things this way, sweetheart."

"Aw, I thought you missed me."

"Or do you miss me?" He opened the passenger door and placed a hand on her bottom to guide her inside.

A shiver shot through her. She hadn't planned this part well enough, and suddenly, she was afraid she'd just offered herself up for free. If she were trapped in a car with Jerry, he could violate her, and then refuse to help. And she'd lose her only bargaining chip. She needed his commitment first. She crossed her legs outside the car to keep him from shutting the door and said, "Can I ask you something?"

"What's up?" He rested his arms on the door and leaned toward her. His smell, a mixture of cologne and booze, filled the space between them.

"You're a cop, right?"

"Where'd you hear that?" He sounded sober now, and she feared the rumors were false.

"Everyone knows you take down drug dealers." She chuckled to feign confidence.

"What are you getting at, pet?" His tone turned defensive. "This is a legal establishment, and I haven't done anything wrong."

Did he think she was threatening him? "No, I just . . . it's my father. I need a favor, and I thought . . ."

"You thought what?"

Had she already failed? "He raped me." The words landed between them. She stared at a circle of murky green lamplight on the asphalt wondering how such a loaded word could fall from her mouth so flatly. A word she never planned to say.

Jerry cleared his throat. "Your father?"

Synthia nodded.

"Raped you?"

She noted Jerry's equally unemotional utterance of the word.

"I'm sorry to hear that," he said, "but what do you want from me?"

She looked up. She hadn't expected him to be so dismissive. "I thought, I don't know, you being a cop, you could help. I just, I don't know. I . . . I just turned eighteen, and he—"

"Jesus." He stood and ran a hand through his hair. Then he spoke coldly. "That's not really my department, darling. And, anyway, you'll need to prove it. You should go to the hospital, get a rape kit."

She shook her head. Whatever a rape kit was, it wasn't part of the plan. "No. Not like that. He's illegal, my father. And he smokes weed. I thought, I don't know, that you could deport him. For the drugs."

"He's illegal? Are you illegal?" Jerry's face lit up with promise.

"No, I have papers."

"I don't know, honey. I don't work immigration."

"Please, Jerry. I'll do anything," she whispered, sliding her gaze to his shirt. She felt sick offering herself up so pathetically, but she repeated, "I'll do anything."

"Stand up."

"What?"

"Stand up."

Her body tightened as she stood. He slipped one hand down her dress and his other hand up her skirt. She stood rigid, the dress twisting like a tourniquet at her waist.

He sighed and released her, and she shuddered in relief.

"Checking for wires," he said. "Look, don't go around telling people you work underage. You can get this place shut down."

He was scared, she realized, as if she held power against him. But she didn't know how to play cards like those.

"I'm sorry," she said. She was in over her head. It was a stupid plan, made under the delirium of exhaustion. She'd contact Yvonne and call it off, just move and hide and change her name like Margo suggested. What had she been thinking?

"It's fine. Just don't mention my work again, you understand?"

She nodded, chastened.

"I don't do business outside the club. I keep things legit."

"I know. I'm sorry." She turned to go, but he put a hand on her shoulder.

"So, what?" he asked. "You want me to bring him in for questioning, find out he has no papers, call immigration? I can't bring him in for no reason. You know that, right?"

"I—"

"It can get complicated, sweetheart," he continued. "And they may let him go. Especially if I can't prove he's done something. We can only guarantee extradition if he's committed a crime."

Her eyes watered again. A crime. What was a crime? She was surrounded by criminals walking free. She, herself, was a criminal walking free. She blinked and looked down at his shoes, shiny and expensive-looking. He dressed like a *Miami Vice* detective, and she imagined him in a shiny expensive-looking building, sitting at a shiny expensive-looking desk, handling proper crimes.

"I don't know how it works," she said. "He does drugs, and he hurt me. And he won't leave me alone. I thought, maybe you could help."

Jerry assessed her coldly. "You can get him here?"

She nodded. "Saturday."

"I can't make any promises."

40

Criminal

When Prem strutted into the club Saturday night, Synthia ducked out of sight and her heart dropped. Mr. Michael and Mr. Michael's wiry peon walked in beside him, the men slapping each other's backs like pubescent boys. When had they become friends?

She rushed into the locker room to find Yvonne practicing moves and laughing with a couple dancers.

"This is so much fun," Yvonne said. "If Papi wouldn't kill me, I would so work here."

"He's here," Synthia hissed, taking a stool in a corner.

Yvonne joined her. "Bien. Vamos."

"No." She dropped her forehead on the counter. "He's with people. Michael and that sleazebag friend. They probably drove the truck. It's not going to work."

"The white truck?" Yvonne asked.

"Yeah."

"Give me the stuff. I'll do it now," Yvonne said.

Synthia shook her head. "No. Jerry won't arrest three guys, and what if he arrests the wrong one? Let's just go."

"But he's a fucking cabrón. He has to pay. Think about what he fucking did to you. And Lila."

Synthia squeezed her eyes shut. She did not want to think of what he'd done to her or to Lila. Seeing him had made her sick, but it also exposed the foolishness of her plan, a plan that involved her somehow planting a dime bag on him, then baiting him to assault her, prompting Jerry to intervene. She couldn't imagine facing him, much less touching him. Or Mr. Michael.

"I have gloves and everything," Yvonne whined. "All that for nothing?"

Synthia smiled despite herself. Yvonne acted as if they were in a movie. She'd stolen Oscar's tool and transferred the drugs to a Friendly Flowers plastic bag. And she'd gotten gloves to avoid leaving fingerprints.

A different plan formed in Synthia's mind as she considered Lila, likely asleep at home with a new round of bruises. Lila, who, despite her flaws, had helped Synthia get her papers. But the papers would mean little with Prem hounding her, trying to ruin her. And with Mr. Michael now on his side, she'd remain as imprisoned as ever. Rage resurged inside her.

From her daily use locker, she retrieved Yvonne's oversized purse, which held the collapsible tool, gloves, and drugs. "Give me a sec," she said, heading to a toilet stall. Hands shaking, she retrieved the roofie pills. She crushed the contents of the plastic baggie with her shoe and tucked the packet inside her leotard bottom.

When she returned, she said, "Okay. Do it." She handed the purse to Yvonne and dropped her car keys inside. "Then meet me at the back door. I'll be out soon."

Yvonne squealed with excitement.

Yvonne exited the club, training her face away from Prem and the others, who were watching a striptease on the main stage. Synthia hid in a shadow behind the bar.

Prem hooted and hollered from the edge of his seat, while Mr. Michael and his friend reclined back, occasionally looking around, their eyelids heavy with alcohol. Her skin crawled at the sight of them.

She retrieved a twenty-dollar bill from her bra and placed it on the work counter. "Three doubles, Rob. I'll pour them."

Rob, the bartender, took the money and returned to his list of orders.

Synthia tried to catch Jerry's eyes, but he never looked her way. She grabbed three glasses and filled them with ice cubes and tequila. She turned her back to the main counter and retrieved the baggie. If her new plan were to work, she needed them visibly wrecked, especially Prem. How much did she need and how many pills had been in the bag? She didn't have time to think. She sprinkled powder into the glasses, dropping an extra-large clump into one. Her heart hammered as she stirred the drinks and forced herself not to look around to see if anyone had seen her. She marked the extra-strong glass with two lime wedges for Prem, and she dumped the empty baggie into the trash, wrapped in wet paper towels she'd used to wipe her hands.

Her body lit afire and sweat beaded her skin. *Criminal.*

She feared she'd turn around to find Rob staring in disbelief, but his eyes were on a buxom dancer who mesmerized everyone with her acrobatic pole moves.

Charlotte was working across the room, and Synthia beckoned her.

"You don't look right, darling," Charlotte said.

"I'm not," she said. "You mind doing me a solid? Take these to those guys. Tell them it's on the house." She indicated the two-lime drink. "The double is for the gray shirt, the one who looks like my father."

"Family?"

"Family I'd rather not see."

Charlotte nodded.

Synthia hugged Charlotte tightly as she reached for the drinks. "What's that for?"

"Nothing," Synthia said, releasing her. "Just thanks. That's all."

Charlotte raised her eyebrows and took the drinks, and Synthia receded into the dim alcove beyond the bar to watch, wondering if Jerry would even help her. Jerry wasn't in his VIP spot, and she feared he'd left.

"Let me guess," a voice said in her ear, making her jump. Jerry. "That brown-skinned man who looks like he's never been out of his house before?"

An inexplicable twinge of embarrassment shot through her, as if Jerry had insulted a brother or friend, not a man she despised.

"Yeah," she muttered. "Gray shirt. With those other two."

"All illegals?"

She shrugged.

"What's the plan?"

"Too drunk to drive."

"Nice and simple," Jerry said, and walked away.

Charlotte served the drinks, and Prem scanned the club.

Synthia dropped out of sight, conscious of her leotard's plunging neckline and her sheer fur-lined robe. She trembled, as if his lecherous eyes had touched her.

From the alcove where she stood, one door led to the locker room and another to the club's back exit. She was tempted to run outside dressed as she was, but she nodded to the bouncer who guarded the doors and walked into the locker room. She threw on the jeans and T-shirt she'd worn to the club and grabbed her purse.

"Where you going?" Vicky said. "You haven't covered house yet."

"I don't feel good. I can't work."

"You signed in, so you owe house," Vicky said.

She handed Vicky the thirty-dollar house fee, a small price for freedom. And she left without a backward glance.

Yvonne was waiting outside in the car.

She climbed into the passenger seat and asked, "Did you do it?"

"Hell yeah. You?"

Synthia nodded and shrugged.

Yvonne whooped. "Puta, we got to celebrate. Let's go dancing."

41

Maya

She awoke to the phone ringing. The answering machine picked up, and Janna's voice said, "Neena, please call me. It's important."

She was drifting back to sleep when the events of the previous night returned to her. Her eyes shot open. Janna had to be calling about Prem.

After leaving the club, Synthia tried not to consider the what ifs. She and Yvonne danced till four, and she'd relished the simple joy of a packed dance floor, no audience in sight. She'd chain-smoked strong menthols to suppress her cravings for the alcohol Yvonne kept offering and to push away thoughts of Prem. But smoking an entire pack made her vomit after she got home.

Now, she sat up with a sour mouth and a tight chest. Had Jerry arrested and detained Prem? Had Prem gotten in a car wreck and killed someone? So much could have gone wrong, and the macabre possibilities weighed on her. She hadn't been thinking. It was as if she'd been in a psychotic fog.

Next to the chaise, Yvonne lay tangled in a sheet. Synthia tiptoed over her friend and out of the room. She eyed Charlotte and

Kimmy's closed door, then crept to the balcony with the phone, closing the door on the cord. It was past seven, but the sky was a mottled gray.

She was about to dial Janna's number when the phone rang. Expecting Janna, she answered. "Hello?"

Someone breathed a shuddering breath as if finishing a cry.

"Janna?" Synthia asked.

The person let out a deep exhale and cleared her throat. "It's me."

Lila? Fuck. "Uh, hey."

"Janna gave me your number."

Fucking Janna.

"She didn't want to. But then . . ."

Of course. Prem had to have been detained, and Janna wanted Lila to break this news.

"It was you, wasn't it?" Lila said in a husky voice.

"What?"

"I know you did it."

Her face constricted and her throat thickened, but Synthia managed to say, "I don't know what you're talking about."

Lila began to cry, and Synthia sighed. She'd done the woman a favor. Lila should be thanking her, not sobbing. Did she want Prem to beat her senseless the rest of her life?

"He's dead," Lila finally said.

"What?"

"He's dead." This time her words were so flat Synthia wondered if Lila meant it as a euphemism, like "he's dead" because deportation ruined his life.

"Who?"

Lila huffed. "Prem. Who else? He found out where you worked, and the next thing I know, he's dead."

Dead? Prem? The world dimmed, and she went numb. It was the drug. She'd given him too much. She'd known this as that extra clump fell into his drink. But she didn't think it'd kill him. Would the police test his blood and trace it back to her? Or worse, to Yvonne?

Lila spoke tonelessly. "They arrested him. Him, Michael, and that, that, *associate*. And they found drugs. In the truck."

"What happened?"

"He was drunk. So drunk he fought the police. They hit him, and he fell and hit his head. He passed out in the jail cell, and in the morning, he was dead."

Synthia felt both sick and overcome with relief. She'd wanted him out of her life, and she'd gotten that. Had part of her hoped to kill him?

"You can deny it, but I know it was you," Lila said, calm now. "Who else could it be? How else could drugs end up in Michael's truck? At your workplace."

"I don't know what you're talking about," she heard herself say, wondering if anyone saw her spike the drinks, hoping the trash bag was long gone, fearing Charlotte might speak up.

Lila chuckled. "Fine, but you got Michael, too. Two birds, one stone, like they say. They found a bunch of fake passports in his glove box. They're detaining him."

Synthia tried to process this.

"I got a call from jail this morning saying they had a Mahindra Prasad on the line for me. Turns out, that's Michael's real name. Mahindra Prasad. He got on the phone and started threatening me. Saying he knows it's me who set him up. Me and you. Saying he's gonna turn us in, make us pay, tell the government you're not Neena, that we lied."

A shiver ran through her. She'd gotten rid of Prem, but she'd incited Mr. Michael in the process. Maybe his associate, too.

"Look, you and me, we . . . Well, things don't always go like you want. But you should know he will hound you. You can bet he'll bad-talk you to your family, poison them with lies, try to find you through them. They're the only ones who can prove you're not Neena."

Synthia rubbed her forehead, throbbing with pressure. She pictured Mr. Michael contacting her father, telling him she was a murderer, a drug user, an ungrateful snitch, a whore who got naked for money. Her father would believe she was a traitor and a whore, but a murderer?

"I'm done with him," Lila said. "I'm leaving, going someplace he can't find me. You should do that, too."

What you looking at me for? I didn't come to stay. Leaving was always part of the plan.

After a stretch of silence, Lila said, "It was hard for me, you know, when you showed up, after Neena died. That day I said I would send you back, I almost drove to the airport and left you there. But I'm glad I didn't."

Tears smarted Synthia's eyes. Was this an apology?

"Prem left me for dead last night. I could barely walk. I waited by the door with a bat. I wanted to kill him, even if it meant jail. You . . . You . . ." Lila hiccupped back a cry and sputtered, "He . . . I . . ."

Synthia filled in the words. *You saved me. I should have saved you. He was a monster. I'm sorry.*

Lila calmed down a little. "You were more like Neena than you know," she said.

In the bedroom, Yvonne snored lightly, last night's clothes strewn about. But three suitcases and a few duffels sat in a corner, already packed with most of Synthia's belongings. The ratty brown suitcase loomed among them, emanating pain. Stuffed with outgrown hand-me-downs, it had traveled so far with her. But its journey would end there. It didn't belong in her fresh start.

Careful to minimize noise, she unzipped it and retrieved her old purse, that packet of peanuts still crinkling inside. She found the white church dress, smelling faintly of smoke and chemicals, and placed it on her lap. She added the dress made from a curtain, one of Lila's button-downs, the mesh top Yvonne had sewn, and Leslie's butterfly T-shirt. She folded the one-legged Barbie and Marcus's blank journal (his notes and her family's letters inside) into the clothes. Then she added Charlotte's green plaid skirt and the Angelou book. She tucked all this into the colorful backpack still smelling of crayons. A summation of herself.

Staring at it, she felt hollow. Not Sunny. Not Neena. Not even Synthia, really.

This was always the plan, she reminded herself, to carve out a life that wasn't defined by her past. *What you looking at me for? I didn't come to stay.*

The moment Margo had suggested a name change, she knew she'd become Maya. She'd escape north to a city where no smell, taste, or vision could trigger a latent memory. With her papers, she'd reinvent herself. She'd get a simple job as a waitress or store clerk and work her way through school, keeping her head down, erasing her past and forging a future she chose. When she felt secure, she'd contact Yvonne and explain everything. She'd find Roshi, too.

But her plan had already derailed. Prem dead. Mr. Michael in jail, with a vendetta against her. *It was you, wasn't it?* She saw herself disappearing into crowds, hiding in libraries, looking over her shoulder. Would she ever feel secure? Would her family assume her guilt because she ran? Would they believe her?

Her head hurt, and she almost broke down. It was too much. But the tattoo on her ankle caught her eye. *Begin Again.* She gathered last night's tainted clothes and threw them into the brown suitcase. She zipped it up and crept from the apartment. She walked it down to the dumpster and tossed it amid greasy pizza boxes, half-eaten fast food, and garbage bags. And she walked away.

Back in the apartment, she tucked a note into the bureau that contained her dance clothes. "C & K: You gave me room to begin again. Thanks for saving my life." It felt woefully inadequate.

She tried not to look at Yvonne, snoring under the chaise, as she grabbed her remaining bags and left the room. She'd return to write a note, she told herself.

She'd folded down the car's back seats and was rearranging things for best fit when a bang startled her.

"What the fuck?" Yvonne said, banging on the car window again, looking disheveled. "What's all this shit? You're hightailing? No adios? I wake up on a fucking strange floor, and all your shit's gone."

"I was coming back."

"The hell you were."

Her sinuses burned at this accusation, and tears formed. Maybe Yvonne was right. Maybe she would have stolen away. Maybe she was worried Yvonne would have stopped her, and maybe she didn't want Yvonne any more involved than she'd been. Maybe she hadn't wanted to utter the words *he's dead, it was me*. Or maybe she just didn't know how to say goodbye, never having had a proper one before.

She leapt out of the car and hugged Yvonne. "We're hermanas, remember?"

MAYA

ATLANTA, GEORGIA

Dwayne looks at me as if I'm a stranger.
And I am.

Raw, skinless, and ugly. A three-headed monster. The opposite of everything I've ever shown him. In our lifetime together, this is our most intimate moment. Me, so bare. Him, freshly wounded.

"I'm sorry," I say, feeling the inadequacy of my words.

He shakes his head and brushes his face dry. "It's . . . I'm . . ." He takes a deep breath. "For me, Maya, the sky just caved in."

I drop my face into my hands. *Please, please, don't leave me*, I want to beg, but I can't give voice to the possibility. I'm a liar. A person capable of killing someone and hiding it. A person who hid an entire family until it threatened her health. A person who denied her own deaf sister. I would leave me.

I look up and he's staring past me. We're still on the floor, mere feet apart. But the space between us gapes. I want him to hold me and tell me I'm not a psychopath. Say it will work out. Say I will not lose everything. But he won't even touch me with his eyes.

"That man deserved to die," he says to the wall. "If he hadn't,

I'd have wanted to kill him myself. But it's a lot, Maya. After *all* these years. To know you kept all of this from me . . . I'm feeling pretty fucking flattened."

I nod and try to meet his eyes through my tears.

"I . . ." he starts again, still not looking at me. "I need some space, some time." He stands abruptly and turns to the door. "I'll call Vernon. Try to contact your sister. Find out about the cancer." The door closes behind him with a click.

The sound is worse than a slam. It shatters me. I crumple into a ball amid the relics of my past and sob into the white dress. This is the reckoning I've always feared. All these years, I'd spun myself into the perfect wife and mom, dreading a misstep, worried that Dwayne couldn't love the ugly truth of me. Was I right? Was his love conditional?

Panic ballons inside me, and I take little breaths to quell it. Remembering Dwayne's directives, *contact your sister, find out about the cancer*, I sober up. There's still the very real risk of cancer and the very real task of reaching out to Roshi.

At the computer, I hear his car leave and feel a fresh stab. Will this be our new normal, not touching, driving off without goodbyes? I feel like I've lost him. Even if he returns to me, will things ever be the same?

Our buttoned-up world has ripped right open. But there's still one final seam to unravel.

I pull up Roshi's website and draft an email to her.

Dear Roshi,

It's Sunny. Thank you for looking for me. I'm glad you found me, but I'm devastated about the cancer. It's shocking news. Same with the news about Ma. As soon as I get a passport, I will come to see you. If you want, we can video chat before.

My husband's cousin is a cancer doctor, and he can look

at your medical paperwork if you send it. He can also tell me about the gene.

I hope you're feeling well and hope to hear from you soon.
With love,
Sunny

It takes me an hour to write these words and hit send. Mere minutes after, I receive a response.

Sunny?!?
OMG. I almost die with shock at your email. Just today, I write my kids about you.

I will send paperwork soon. Please tell me what your doctor say.

Sunny, I feel so much shock right now, I can't tell you! I am so happy to find you my sister. So happy. Please come visit me soon.
Love,
Roshi

Joy fills me, briefly eclipsing my grief over Dwayne's anger. I read and reread the email, imagining Roshi doing the same in front of her computer screen, wherever she is.

Minutes later, I receive a second email.

Sunny,
Wow, still can't believe you real.

Here is my doctor paperwork, what I send my daughter today. I had chemo medicine yesterday. I feel so sick, vomiting, near dead. Only good feeling is hearing from you.

I hope the cancer don't kill me before I see you again.
Love,
Roshi

Worry replaces my joy as I print out her labs and doctor's notes. Seeing her married name, Roshini Williams, printed so officially on the documents suddenly makes her and the cancer so real. I burst into tears and clutch the papers as if clutching her.

Interrupting this breakdown, Dwayne texts: **I will pick up the boys and take them to my mom's for dinner. They'll skip activities. Vernon stopping by to see you soon.**

My gut knots at his formal tone. I feel unmoored, as I'd felt so often as a child, every time I was cut loose and forced to begin again. I can't begin again.

I want to text back, *please don't tell anyone yet, please forgive me, and I can't talk to Vernon without you.* But I've lost the right to push back. I picture him conferring with his parents, Denise, and Vernon, the group deciding to eject me from the family. Can I face them at the party this weekend? Will I be uninvited? Who am I without them, this family I chose?

Roshi sends another email, trying to set up a video conference. I shut off the computer. I need to be in a more stable place.

The kitchen is a void without the boys. They should be here, eating snacks and starting homework, making noise. I picture them at my mother-in-law's, overhearing Dwayne, glimpsing sign language, becoming poisoned against me. An old deep craving grips me, and I consider running to the store for a pack of cigarettes.

But I pace the stairs and wait, rehearsing what I'll say to Vernon. I need to stick to the facts: sister, breast cancer, gene. I worry that Vernon, who's only ever known my foster family lie, will want more of an explanation. What will I say?

The garage door rumbles unexpectedly, and I halt midstride. Dwayne's car.

He walks into the kitchen and meets my eyes with his bloodshot ones before looking down. I can smell the cigarette smoke from where I stand, and my cravings spark again. We gave up smoking together over a decade ago when I got pregnant with Cam. Has he also taken a drink, breaking his thirty-plus years of sobriety?

He sits with his head in his hands at the counter, and I want to run to him, ask if he's okay, beg his forgiveness. But I blurt, "Did you tell them?" My voice betrays selfish panic, my fear that he's turned Denise and his mom against me. Even the kids.

He shakes his head. "Couldn't bear for them to feel what I'm feeling."

I grip the banister with relief. I can't bear for them to feel what he's feeling either. For them to look at me with heartbreak.

I take tentative steps toward him, and pat Roshi's documents, sitting on the counter near him. "My sister. She sent her labs. For Vernon."

He looks up and reaches for the papers, clearly just as grateful as me to talk about anything other than my deceit and his broken heart.

He reads, or pretends to read, and I sit in agony. In my head, I scream, *I'm sorry, don't leave me,* and I clasp my hands to keep from reaching for him. When Vernon knocks on the door, I'm relieved.

Vernon enters seeming to already know the facts—sister, breast cancer, gene. He knows my mother died of cancer, too. He congratulates me on finding my family and ignores the tension in the air.

After reviewing Roshi's papers, he says, "She's responding well."

"She's not dying?" I ask, incredulous.

"Not according to these labs and scans. It looks like her doctors are doing all the right things. She's got a good shot at remission, a really good shot."

I sigh and half laugh at Roshi's melodrama. "So, she doesn't need your trials?"

"She'd have to fail standard therapy to qualify, and that's always a possibility. It's an aggressive type. But they caught the lump early. She's lucky."

"What about the gene?" I ask.

"We'll need to get you checked out. And, if you have it, the boys, too, down the road."

"The boys, too?" Dwayne echoes. "But it's breast cancer."

Vernon's face goes soft. "It can put them at risk for other cancers. But we'll check Maya first. She might not have it. Our genetic counselor can set it up tomorrow."

"What if she tests positive?" Dwayne asks.

"We'll cross that bridge when, and if, we get there," Vernon says. "There are options depending on what we find. But the results won't return for a few weeks."

Dwayne looks at me for the first time. "That's a long time to wait."

After Vernon leaves, Dwayne says, "I texted Todd." Todd, his cousin-in-law, a corporate lawyer who once worked at the DA's office. "He can talk to us tonight."

"Tonight? Now?"

"Yes, I need some answers. We need some answers, Maya, sooner rather than later."

Please don't leave me. "What'd you tell him?" I whisper.

"Just that we need urgent legal advice. Call's in twenty minutes." he says, retreating into the room he sometimes uses as a home office and shutting the door. Alone again, I wipe tears from my eyes and return to pacing the stairs.

The office door opens when it's time for the call. Dwayne starts a video conference, and Todd's face fills the phone screen. "Hey, man, what's up? What's going on with Maya?"

Dwayne turns the phone to me.

After awkward niceties, I relay an amended version of my story. My illegal entry, the abuse, multiple homes, amnesty,

Prem's death, and Mr. Michael's threat. It's easier to tell this time around, and to his credit, Todd keeps a straight face, never interrupting. Neither does Dwayne, though I feel him staring as if double-checking my story.

"I was a kid," I say, after I finish. "And I thought I could erase my past, you know. That that was the only way to be free." I chuff a laugh and turn to Dwayne. "All these years, I thought I was free, the real me. But I wasn't. This mess, this is the real me."

His eyes bore into mine.

"Should I turn myself in?" I ask Todd even as I continue to look at Dwayne. I have a sudden wish to come fully clean.

Todd chuckles. "Let's not do anything drastic, okay? The laws are pretty strict and there's no leniency for turning yourself in. You'd be deported and blacklisted from the country for five to ten years."

"What?" Dwayne pushes back his seat and stands next to me, his face now in the screen that Todd sees. "But she was twelve when she came. And she was trafficked and abused. We're married. We have kids."

"This is not my area of expertise, but I'm almost certain she'd have to go back. We could petition for reduced time, but that wouldn't be guaranteed."

"Zero leniency," Dwayne says, shock on his face. "She's worked and paid taxes her whole life. We've got kids! What about DACA?"

"Sorry, man," Todd says, looking genuinely sorry. "DACA's a mess. And the statute of limitations for trafficking and abuse have long passed. There's no statute of limitations on illegal entry, though."

"So that man *can* get her deported?" Dwayne asks.

"If he has proof. He can always send a tip, but ICE gets false tips daily. I doubt they'd pursue Maya on a tip. Like you say, she's a tax-paying, law-abiding citizen. But death and birth certificates, that might get someone's attention." To me, Todd adds, "Does he have those?"

I shake my head. "I don't think so. I think he lives in Canada now. Runs a gas station."

"Spell his name," Todd says, and I spell out *Mahindra Prasad*. For the first time, it doesn't feel like an invocation.

Todd taps computer keys. "Yes, he could be in Canada." He taps again. "But maybe that's because he's been barred from the US. Look at this." He turns his phone to an online document. "There's a Mahindra Prasad on the no-entry list. If it's our guy, he was probably arrested and detained a second time. I can submit a form for details if you want."

I shake my head. "Could he find out?"

"No. But we might get a photo to verify it's him." Todd's face returns to the screen. "Look, off the record, and this conversation has been entirely off the record and in strict confidence by the way, it would be difficult to prove you are anyone other than Maya. As far as I can see, changing your identity harmed no one. So, to me, you're Maya, and *Sunny* was your childhood nickname. Just stay off the guy's radar, like you've been doing. If anything comes up, I'll go to bat for you."

Dwayne and I stare at him.

"We cool, man?" Todd asks, and Dwayne says, "Yeah."

It feels like they're agreeing to be my secret keepers.

When the call with Todd ends, Dwayne dials his mother, standing a foot behind me. He tells her that my biological family found me, that it turns out I have a deaf sister, and he asks her to keep the kids overnight.

Hanging up, he says, "That's all they need to know."

I turn to him, tears of relief pouring down my face. He pulls my body close, and I clutch him.

Kissing my wet face all over, he says, "Sunny, Neena, Synthia, Maya, my love. I got you."

MAYA

TWO MONTHS LATER
ABOVE GUYANA

The plane descends in a crisp blue sky. Below, matted forests sharpen to reveal rivers, jigsawing the land into islands. Deep memories stir. The smell of decaying leaves. The mineral taste of black water. Spongy soil underfoot. I prickle with sweat as if I'm in that humid underbrush, twelve again, running through the fields.

Dwayne's touch brings me back to reality. His hand loosens my clenched fist and entwines our fingers into a brown lace. He brings my hand to his lips and kisses it. "It'll be great."

I lean into him. The gift of his love and forgiveness.

He was with me when I video conferenced with Roshi, months earlier. Her round face had filled the screen as if peering into the camera. Then she bugged her eyes out and shook her hand with the sign language for *wow*. She mouthed and signed, "You look fancy. Like rich lady. So tall. But too skinny. Magga."

With these words, she shattered the decades-old ice between us.

I laughed and moved my fingers to retort, "You got short and fat. But I think you're richer than me. Two stores?"

Her eyes popped again, this time at my adept sign language, and she laughed heartily. Her overloud childhood croak came through, and her fourteen-year-old face flashed from behind the adult one.

"How are you?" I signed. "Still feel you're dying?" I meant it as a half joke, as I'd already emailed her about Vernon's optimism, and she'd acknowledged her doctors said the same.

But she nodded earnestly and signed, "A lot. When me see my bald head, yes." She leaned her patchy scalp into the camera. "The chemo medicine make me vomit. I hope you don't get it."

"Me too," I signed. "In few weeks—I find out about gene."

She mimed biting her nails. Then she pivoted the conversation. "How you learn sign so good?"

I revealed Camden's deafness, and she held one hand to her mouth and signed, "Sorry," with the other.

"Doesn't slow him down," I assured her. "Just like you. Deaf community great here, with my husband's family." I panned the phone to Dwayne, who was watching from the side. He signed hello and she grew shy, signing hello back.

Together, Dwayne and I showed her our life through pictures on the wall. She made me slow down to explain our Halloween costumes, identify vacation spots, and name the friends and family in social photos.

"Beautiful life. Beautiful family," she signed. "And hot husband!"

We all laughed.

Then she signed, "So crazy. You and me, with matching Dougla family."

I was reluctant to use the slur, to even think it in describing my family. But she finger-spelled the word with ease, reclaiming it.

Then she grew solemn. "Been so long. Why?"

I shook my head. "Don't know. Complicated. Michael wanted deport me, and I thought you all would believe him, tell him where I live. Daddy, especially."

She shook her head and signed, "Daddy a fool. Only he believe that nonsense. You kill Prem? Put drugs on people?" She screwed up her face and sucked her teeth.

Guilt surged through me, and I felt Dwayne's eyes.

"Me not hear Michael name long time," she signed. "Last me hear, he in Canada?"

I nodded to confirm. "I don't think he can hurt me anymore. But don't tell anyone my new name, okay? Especially Daddy."

"I won't tell. But don't fret Daddy."

"How you forgive him?"

She waved her hand as if swatting a fly. "Can't let him vex me. Me visit when Ma got sick. By then, he changed. Me bring Ronnie and the kids, he not say anything bad."

"I'm surprised he didn't move to New York. Raj didn't sponsor him?"

She laughed. "Yes. He went for a year, with Ma. To Queens, where Raj lives. My older daughter and son live there, too. But Daddy and Ma hate it. They say it's work, work, work; everything expensive; Raj bossing them." Roshi laughed again and scrunched her nose. "They're right. Too busy. Loud. And people rude. No fun. Ronnie and me prefer Guyana, too."

A young girl jumped in front of the camera and spoke, with words and sign language. "I don't prefer Guyana. I'm going to New York this year."

Roshi introduced her as twelve-year-old Angie, her youngest child.

Angie said, "I'm going to live with my brother. Ma promised, for school."

I couldn't help but think, book-talk with a lovely cadence.

Roshi shook her head and signed, "Not sure. It's better for school, but we afraid to send. She only twelve."

I nodded. "Like me when I left."

Roshi dabbed her eyes then and signed, "Yes, yes," while Dwayne hugged me.

Now, as the plane lowers and the ground accelerates toward us, Dwayne hugs me again. I sink my head into his chest with deep gratitude. The week prior, my lab results returned, and I learned I did not carry the gene. Roshi, too, is doing well, having successfully completed her therapy. My gut is all jitters anticipating seeing her again.

Our boys are in their seats, heads bent over devices. They're eager to meet their cousins, some of whom they've already befriended through online chats and video game sessions. Even Cam is excited because, although Roshi's kids can hear, they speak fluent sign language, and Angie shares his passion for LEGO.

I've brought her a LEGO set, but I've also brought her a vintage Barbie doll and Barbie lunch box filled with apples. She's likely outgrown dolls and probably even has access to American fruit, but I couldn't help myself. My bag is crammed with all kinds of gifts for the rest of the family. They'll all be there, this family I've denied for so long.

My childhood home awaits, along with my father. Roshi and Dwayne will accompany me to visit him, but he'll have to earn the privilege of meeting my boys. Everyone will meet Ravi and Pappo, though, who still live nearby with families, running their own businesses. I've emailed Mo in Barbados, Baby in Trinidad, and Indy in New Jersey, and we're planning a reunion next year. Raj, who's still married to Navi, has not responded. Neither has Soma, the sibling I have never met. If they harbor resentments or need more time to adjust to my sudden appearance, I don't blame them.

I press my face to the window. The forests have given way to orange-red mines, proof of the country's burgeoning industries. Sandy roads fade from red to yellow to white. Rooftops come into view, belonging to houses that border a canal. Under the sun, they sparkle like a string of fairy lights.

A long curl of smoke winds up from a patch of green below, and I hunt the land. When I see two bodies on a dirt road, my right hand raises automatically. The plane moves too fast to keep them in sight, but I wave and wave.

ACKNOWLEDGMENTS

We novelists create in the dark, sculpting from thin air. When we emerge from our caves, holding up imperfectly stacked words, we seek adoration. But we need candor. I'm grateful to my early readers who balanced their unflinching honesty with encouragement.

Mark Spenser, my first reader: your speedy, positive responses propelled me to the finish line. Dan Logan, Maria Rolan, Jas Snow, and Nadya, my alpha readers: your collective insight helped overhaul a faulty early draft; I'm grateful to Noel Fudge, whose novel swap group brought us together on scribophile.com. Joshua Loveday, Beth RL, Cassandra Wright, Oliver Konsmo, Amy Gee, Carman Webb, and Pamela Sullivan: thank you for your insightful feedback on critiquematch.com. Sarah McKenna, Laura Johnston, Judy Hock, Margaret Kohn, Anu Krishnaswamy, Erin Anadkat, and Nigar Kavlicoglu, my beta readers: you each revealed a different weak spot, helping me shape the novel into what it is today. Liliana Cattoni, thank you for finding my Spanish errors. Shabana Sharif and Alica Ramkirpal-Senhouse, thanks for your feedback on my Guyanese creole. Sarah Bedingfield, my agent: thank you for loving this story while it was still imperfect; your editorial insights truly elevated it. Coralie Hunter: your razor-sharp scalpel helped me chisel the "final" draft into something I'm incredibly proud to release into the world. Seems a novel cannot be crafted alone in a cave. It takes a village, after all.

ACKNOWLEDGMENTS

I'm deeply grateful to Zibby Books, Zibby Owens in particular, for making me feel like a rock star from day one. It's a dream to be championed by a publishing house and to work in such a positive and transparent environment. Birthing a book is not easy, but the whole Zibby team, full of amazing book-birthing doulas, made it seamless and fun. Thank you, everyone.

Heartfelt thanks to my parents, Rharna and Satyavati, who gave all they could so that I could be all I could. Mom, thank you for answering my unending questions at the drop of a hat. Rookmin Balram and Ramesh Samsundar, thanks for sharing your memories. Deep thanks, also, to the big fat Guyanese family who nurtured me, including my younger sister, Vanessa, and my deaf older sister, Amanda, without whom I wouldn't be who I am today. To my husband and kids—Suresh, Tej, and Kesh—thanks for believing in me, even when you had no idea what I was doing, holed up in my cave. This story, a small something sculpted from nothing, is for all of you.

ABOUT THE AUTHOR

NANDA REDDY is a Guyanese American writer and former elementary school teacher. She immigrated to the United States with her family when she was nine years old. She loves visiting off-the-grid places, hiking, and painting with watercolors. She currently resides in Reno, Nevada, with her husband and two sons. *A Girl Within a Girl Within a Girl* is her first novel.

@nandareddyauthor
www.nandareddy.com